Voices of the South

AUGUSTA
PLAYED

AUGUSTA PLAYED

A NOVEL BY

Kelly Cherry

LOUISIANA STATE UNIVERSITY PRESS

Baton Rouge

A portion of this book appeared in *Decade*,
December 1978.

The author wishes to thank the Virginia
Center for the Creative Arts for a period of
residency during which this novel was com-
pleted.

Copyright © 1979 by Kelly Cherry
Originally published by Houghton Mifflin Company
LSU Press edition published 1998 by arrangement with the author
All rights reserved
Manufactured in the United States of America
07 06 05 04 03 02 01 00 99 98   5 4 3 2 1

Library of Congress Cataloging-in-Publication Data
Cherry, Kelly.
    Augusta played : a novel / by Kelly Cherry.
        p.   cm. — (Voices of the South)
    ISBN 0-8071-2279-3 (paper)
    1. New York (N.Y.)—Fiction. I. Title. II. Series.
    PS3553. H357A94   1998
    813' .54—dc21   97-49987
                                                              CIP

The paper in this book meets the guidelines for permanence and durability of the
Committee on Production Guidelines for Book Longevity of the Council on Library
Resources. ∞

'They soon were wedded, and the nymph appear'd
By all her promised excellence endear'd:
Her words were kind, were cautious, and were few,
And she was proud—of what her husband knew.
  'Weeks pass'd away, some five or six, before,
Bless'd in the present, Finch could think of more:
A month was next upon a journey spent,
When to the Lakes the fond companions went;
Then the gay town received them, and, at last,
Home to their mansion, man and wife, they pass'd.
  'And now in quiet way they came to live
On what their fortune, love, and hopes would give:
The honied moon had naught but silver rays,
And shone benignly on their early days;
The second moon a light less vivid shed,
And now the silver rays were tinged with lead.
They now began to look beyond the Hall,
And think what friends would make a morning-call;
Their former appetites return'd, and now
Both could their wishes and their tastes avow;
'Twas now no longer "just what you approve,"
But, "let the wild fowl be to-day, my love."
In fact the senses, drawn aside by force
Of a strong passion, sought their usual course.
  'Now to her music would the wife repair,
To which he listen'd once with eager air;
When there was so much harmony within,
That any note was sure its way to win;
But now the sweet melodious tones were sent
From the struck chords, and none cared where they went.
Full well we know that many a favourite air,
That charms a party, fails to charm a pair;

And as Augusta play'd she look'd around,
To see if one was dying at the sound:
But all were gone — a husband, wrapt in gloom,
Stalk'd careless, listless, up and down the room.'

—George Crabbe
(from "THE PRECEPTOR HUSBAND")

CONTENTS

Part One

GOLD

I

Norman Gold, hearing the clicking of her high-heeled shoes on the pavement behind him, began to sweat. He slowed his own walk. Click. Unmistakably hers. When she turned off onto West End Avenue, Norman congratulated himself on his detective work, which was not bad for a *luftmensch* with his head in the clouds. He knew where she lived.

So, a little knowledge is a dangerous thing! They say.

Sunlight crackled on the dried-out grass between sidewalk and river. Tufts of greenery grew where the cement had given way to time and weather. Fresh tar glittered in the middle of the road up ahead, like the stripe on the back of a garter snake.

2

It was 1966, and Augusta, in the season of her name, was gorgeous. She knew it, too, and didn't in the least mind, though her own beauty wasn't the most important thing in her life. She had dark honey-blond hair, parted in the center, which rose and fell in two wide wings over the temples, giving her a look simultaneously cheerful and angelic. She looked too healthy to be entirely ethereal. Someone had once told her she looked like Tuesday Weld by Vermeer, luminous, innocent, but adult-eyed. Her eyes were rather wide-spaced, rather long and rather hazel, though on occasion exactly the same color as her hair. She had a creamy complexion, a high forehead, a straight, narrow, small nose, and one feature less than classical: her upper lip was unbowed, and this little note of assertive sexiness, which was what men always noticed first about her face, was the fault she fretted over. She tried drawing a dip in her lip with a red outlining pencil, but the pink flesh still showed through close up, and eventually she decided she would live with her mouth the way it was. She couldn't wear lipstick when she played the flute, anyway.

That was what she was generally doing—playing the flute.

At twenty-two—twenty-three come October—Gus was an extremely promising young flutist, potentially, her teachers said, a great one. She had been touched with a certain power, the capacity not so much to charm as to awaken, to make sound as visible to her listeners as light. Her talent was in some measure merely the specific, instrumental reflection of her spirit-at-large, since everywhere she went, she seemed to shed a kind of happy light, an inspiriting, lively-making illusion worked by her hair and skin and the forward mouth and having nothing to do with how she might actually feel at any given moment except that, being who she was, she was usually surrounded by people who were animated and made happier by her presence, and, not being one of those who cling to misery as a mark of individuality, she found it difficult ever to remain gloomy for long in such good company. This life-enhancing dimension had been apparent in her music even at the beginning, when many of the notes were still wrong.

Gus had begun late, but that is not necessarily a bad thing

to do with the flute. At twenty-two, most virtuoso performers are getting on, but a great flutist may yet be born.

First, Gus took a music degree in Greensboro. (North Carolina was her home state.) Her parents wanted her to have "something to fall back on," a phrase that always gave her a silly, teetering sensation. Now she was at Juilliard, studying with Julie Baker—for her lessons, she went to his home—and she had already had a couple of summers in Siena with Gazzelloni. She hoped someday to study with Zöller in Germany. She had, in fact, begun to make a specialty of contemporary music. A considerable percentage of it was being written for the flute, where the older repertoire was limited, and not many flutists understood modern notation or were as quick as she was at sight-reading it. Of course, the audiences were correspondingly small. The composer Walter Piston had said, "When the computer gives a concert, which sooner or later it will, you can be sure that only other computers are going to go hear it."

Gus let herself into her apartment on the third floor, tossed her flute case onto the couch-bed, and flew to the window, just in time to catch one transient glimpse of Norman's blue-shirted back as he made a turn to the right at the corner. She had never yet managed a good look at his face, but the back said everything. He always had on olive chinos, that faded workshirt, and boots. Boots, in August! There was only one deduction she could draw—he must want to appear taller than he was. The trouble, she noticed, was his legs; they were too short for his torso. He looked as though he'd stunted his growth sneaking smokes in the neighborhood sandlot. She'd bet anything he saw himself as Peter Falk.

And he had been listening to her. She knew it. He had done it before—here, there. Around. Other girls could feel men's eyes on them, but she was a musician, and she knew when a man was listening to her heels click-clicking on the sidewalk. Sometimes he was in front of her, and sometimes he was in back. He had to be doing something at Columbia. He looked too old to be a student, too intense to be a teacher . . . He was writing a dissertation, maybe. The streets of this neighborhood were pocked with Peter Falk types who were writing dissertations. They ate lunch in the West End Bar and caught all the foreign flicks at the Thalia. Half of them had gone to Erasmus High in Brooklyn. Yes, but this one was different. He was the kind of man who made demands. He had singled her out and she felt his curiosity was profoundly possessive; he wasn't simply interested, he was riveted, absorbing her like a book, and this made her feel absorbing.

It also made her neck ache, she thought, pulling her head back into the room. The sun had been in her eyes, and now she blinked, adjusting to the room's dimness, and was wiping the windowsill soot from her hands when the telephone rang. She picked it up.

"It's me," the caller said.

"Me" meant Richard. He always thought "It's me" was sufficient identification, as if "me" couldn't possibly be anyone else.

"Is it you?" she asked, joking. "Is it really you?"

"Come on, Gussie," he said, mournfully. "Don't do that to me."

"Do what?"

"You know."

"Well, why did you call if it wasn't because it's a beautiful day for having your leg pulled" — she dropped her voice, mock-huskily — "the way only your Gussie can pull it?" Her voice became normal again. "Where are you calling from?"

"I'm at the recording studio. I called to say I love you, Gussie."

Now, Augusta didn't know what men meant by love, but on the whole she thought it was polite not to argue when they said they loved her. She liked Richard. She was even very fond of Richard. But she didn't think she loved him. Perhaps it was because he was married, but she couldn't very well ask him to get a divorce simply so she could find out whether she would fall in love with him if she felt free to. Besides, she had a suspicion he might fall out of love with her if he weren't married. He liked being able to say, as he was saying right now, "I miss you" — though he was only a subway ride away. She had met him when he came to North Carolina for a semester as a visiting artist-in-residence — Richard was a conductor — but in New York, ironically, they got to see each other only about one-fourth as often. That was sad, because part of what Gus liked about him was his looks. He was tall and dark, and all his reactions were extravagant, but delayed, coming after the fact by about thirty seconds, so that she never fully trusted them, though she knew this was the essence of his personality, not some special machinery for dealing with her.

"Richard," she said now, turning thoughtful, "do you believe in marriage?" She waited thirty seconds, then added, "Naturally, I'm talking about marriage in general."

"Do I believe in— Why don't you ask me if I believe in God? I might be able to answer that."

"I wasn't thinking of spending my life with God."

"I think about it, about spending my afterlife with him, that is. Not anytime soon, you understand, I'm not even forty yet you know" — he said it as if to absolve himself of something, responsibility perhaps — "but in a general sort of way, someday. It's in the cards. My father had a heart attack at fifty-two."

"I didn't mean to make you so morbid," Gus said.

"Marriage bears certain similarities to death."

"Thanks a lot! That's not very helpful."

"You weren't thinking of getting married?" There was an edge of panic to his voice. It was barely discernible, but it was there, a thin line.

"I wasn't thinking of dying, either."

"That's good," he said. "I was counting on seeing you this weekend."

"You were?"

"Uh-oh," he said. "That obviously means I shouldn't."

"No, it doesn't mean that especially. But I'll be out Saturday night." She was going to hear the Philadelphia, with the unbeatable Murray Panitz playing flute.

"I'll call first and let you know," he said. "Cheerio!"

Cheerio? Richard was Passaic-born and Massachusetts-schooled, and he had never been to England except on tour, during which he saw only the same dispiriting views of hotel lobbies that he knew from a dozen other countries. There were landscapes, cityscapes, and now, in the latter half of the twentieth century, hotelscapes. His ringing, determinedly undisturbed sign-off reverberated in the room after Gus had hung up.

The receiver was sticky when she put it back on the hook, and she realized she'd been sweating. She didn't do that often; usually, her palms stayed cool and dry as climbing ivy in a sheltering lee. A good thing, too, for a flutist. Then why was she sweating now? It was hot in the apartment, but not that hot.

She tapped on Tweetie's cage and he began to swing and sing. She filled his water bowl. He was a sparkling bright yellow, as if somebody had taken a chunk of sunshine, like a twist of clay, and molded it into a tiny mop of flying feathers with a heart that would just about bust if he couldn't sing it out at least half the day. His full name was Tweetie-Pie, and he was certainly a genius among canaries, irrepressible, bold, and a trifle vain. Gus frequently let him perch on her finger while she spoke to him in baby talk, but only if no one else was around.

The room itself was unremarkable, a typical efficiency apartment. There was a single bed which doubled as a couch, a table and chairs, a floor lamp and a favorite table lamp, a music stand, Tweetie's cage, and light white curtains that billowed on breezy days but currently hung as still as if they were painted strips of wood framing the view in the window.

But speaking of pictures — that was the one unusual feature of the room. There were pictures everywhere, pen-and-ink sketches or watercolors, largely green. Gus's father was an illustrator for books on natural history; he did all kinds of animals, birds, butterflies, flowers, grasses, trees. When Gus was little, he had made her a leaf series, each drawing mounted under glass and properly labeled. Gus had hung these on the white-painted walls. The table was white and the chairs were white and the curtains, as stated, were white, and the cotton bedspread on the couch-bed was white, and most of the pictures on the wall were green, but on the wall at the foot of the bed she had tacked postcards of composers.

She put Rampal playing a Telemann Fantasy on the record player, and then she stripped to her slip and stuck a pencil behind her ear and plumped the pillow behind her back as she sat down on the bed to read. Briefly, she glanced at the postcards on the wall facing her. Beethoven, Bach. Verdi, debonair in top hat and white silk scarf. Now there was a man.

3

RICHARD HAD NOT MOVED from the telephone after hanging it up. His hands were shaking, but he didn't bother to disguise the fact. Richard was one of those people who do not so much meet life head on or sidle into it shrewdly or sidestep it gingerly as *bump* into it. It seldom occurred to him to look where he was going. His work made so many inroads into his emotional center that if he stopped to evaluate this experience or that, he would never get anything done. His strategy therefore was simple: quick passes at a bottle of Scotch to propel him through the day, a dreamlike attachment to the surface of the world as it presented itself to him, and a tendency, while gazing into other people's eyes, to fall into deep reveries which he himself could not later recount. But for all the half-despairing, half-delighted stillness of his soul, he was physically fidgety, constantly flinging his long arms outward as if eager to embrace anyone or anything in his path. The one thing that destroyed him, from time to time, was separation: he could not bear to be parted from anyone he *had* embraced. For the rest of it, he was merely chronically but appealingly nervous. The only time he ever really calmed down was on a stage in the middle of a performance. Then, when he might legitimately be expected to be keyed up, something at the very core of his being unwound and played itself right on out, sweet as anything, like fishing for marlin off the coast of Florida.

4

Norman Gold's father was a silent partner in a small munitions firm and a judge with a chance to step up to the Supreme Court if the right man won in the next election. When Norman was growing up, his father had been district attorney. During the war, his father was shipping arms to Palestine secretly, laying the groundwork for the new state. None of this had left much room for Norman. His father blew cigar smoke in his face, trying to be friendly.

When Norman started school, he faced another problem,

an albino bully known as Snowball. Norman could have gone to his father for help, even though his father was an exalted wheeler-dealer who lived in a cloud of smoke and laid down the law like Moses, if only he hadn't been D.A., but because he was, Norman couldn't approach him without appearing even more cowardly than he felt. So every day for the first six years of his education Norman, instead of "going" home, "escaped" from school. He started thinking about his breakaway long before the afternoon bell rang. He was tough and power-packed but short for his age, with eyes like SOS signals, gleaming, tight, dark curls the texture of electrical wire, and the feeling, dating even from the time before Snowball, that he had been set down in a hostile environment for the purpose of proving that he could outwit it.

Every day, when the afternoon bell rang, Norman gritted his teeth—he had read this phrase in a book and was under the impression that doing it would help him get to the end of the block faster—and ran. Snowball was nowhere in sight, but this was because Snowball was behind the fence. The fence began halfway down the block and ended abruptly 50 yards later. Fronting on the sidewalk, it enclosed nothing—nothing but a sandlot—but hid everything. Every year, the lot very nearly washed away in the spring rains, and the slush of Snowball's steps was audible out on the sidewalk . . . a soft, repulsive squishing. As he ran, Norman imagined that he felt a horrible kind of tickle in his heart, the tip of terror poking at him like a switchblade. At the end of the block, the candy store was an oasis, unless it was a mirage—and that it wasn't a mirage was something Norman had to establish over again each time Snowball's mild eyes, tinted with so delicate a touch by the creative hand, fixed on him through the slatted fence and then, for a split second of grace, closed.

One night six years later, when he was twelve, watching a movie about Tchaikovsky on television, Norman had begun to scream and hadn't stopped, and after that he didn't have to go to school anymore. Instead, he rode the subway four times a week to the King's County Clinic for sessions with one Dr. Morris. The sessions weren't until late in the afternoon, and until four or so Norman stayed in bed, a navy robe awkwardly bunched around his legs, expounding on psychoanalysis or the nature of tragedy or Spitfires to the gang who dropped in after school. Occasionally he got out of bed to sit at the card table with his tutor. Mitzi would fry a steak for him, with a side dish of buttered spaghetti. Norman said he would have Mitzi fry two steaks instead of one, but the tutor was always too nervous to eat. Unhinged, no doubt, by the huge house with the hand-carved molding and the kid in it who gave audiences rather than took lessons.

Norman ate again at dinner time. For several years, it seemed to Norman that three meals a day was a starvation diet. He was a skinny kid and he became a skinny adolescent but there was a sturdiness of bone and strength of sinew that suggested he might fill out in middle age, thicken, grow round and burly like his father in old age. For now, he could eat everything in sight and still look like a street orphan.

As soon as he was through, he excused himself from the table so he and his blood-brother Philip Fleischman could make the first showing at Loew's, which they pronounced "Loewie's." If he had a heavy date, one of his dad's yes-men would chauffeur him in the D.A. car, but usually he took the bus with Phil. There was no longer any need to run from Snowball. For one thing, Norman and Phil, together, were a team to reckon with, having mingled their blood in a ritual with peculiar validity, according to a formula which Phil swore had been handed down among the men in his family for generations, by a homesick Sioux Indian who had decided to retrace his route over the Bering Strait back to Pinsk. Norman did not entirely believe this story, but he was not prepared to disregard it, either; stranger things were true, and if there were Jews in Wales, why not Indians in Pinsk?

For another thing, Snowball had entered adolescence along with the rest of them, and what had once been the source of his machismo was now being transformed into a permanent embarrassment. They used to see Snowball on the bus, a three-ring notebook on his lap to hide his hard-on. "Hey, lessee whatcha reading," Phil would say, pretending to grab for the notebook. Snowball looked as though he'd turn to water, evaporate, disappear into thinnest air, leaving only a faint, unpleasant trace of moisture behind him on the seat.

Four years of this, and Norman took the Regents for an equivalency diploma, which wasn't the same as graduating from Erasmus High with Phil but was good enough. On a hot August day ten years before the one on which he found out where the girl with the flute case lived, he had registered at Brooklyn College. He stood in a long line and in front of him and behind him he could see dozens of others who looked just like him, thin and greedy as unweaned pups. The last line led outdoors. He raised his hand to mop the sweat from his face. Light was breaking on his head, like a comber.

5

Now Norman was doing his doctorate at Columbia in Cultural Musicology, a newly defined academic field that boiled down to historical social analysis from the vantage point of music. It is possible that Norman was the only cultural musicologist in the country, the area *per se* being definitely an intellectual frontier, formally speaking, although certainly there had been forerunners, musicologists of the old school and music historians who here and there blundered unsystematically into the insights Norman was attempting to organize single-handedly into an arrestingly original world view with real conceptual muscle, capable of yielding fresh and if necessary lethally incisive slants on immediate problems. For example, what precisely had been the repercussions, if any, of the Wagner-Nietzsche dialogue? What statements might be made about Soviet society on the basis of its effect on Shostakovich's symphonies? Did contemporary music instrumentalized from cards shuffled and selected at random incorporate a philosophy of chance as a controlled element, or was it more properly viewed as an outgrowth of the jazz riff? Why did a girl with legs like hers carry a flute?

Norman's questions frequently veered into sexual ones. The separation of mind from body which commentators on modern society sometimes name as a root cause of dissatisfaction was not one of Norman's difficulties. He had once managed to make it with a psych major from Barnard between classes, barely beating the clock by the skin of her *vagina dentata.* The classics library was a handy place; hardly anyone ever used it.

But Norman didn't just think about sex; he thought *with* sex. It was one of his tools for dissecting culture. Between Brooklyn and Columbia had come the New York Institute. They didn't normally accept non-Ph.D.'s, but Dr. Morris, neatly folding his handkerchief into diminishing squares, explained that that august body on occasion did indeed clasp to its bosom exceptional students in allied fields providing they willingly signed a document stating that they would not title themselves analysts or engage in a practice upon completing the course, especially if they were championed by himself. So Norman let himself be championed. What appealed to him about psychoanalysis was the feeling of being in control, of knowing more about other people than they knew about themselves, of being one up on his own subconscious.

At first he went through periods of making Freudian slips, of recycling in his dreams at night the complexes he was examining during the day, and even of inadvertently punning bilingually in French or Yiddish. These awkward stretches eventually wore off, and, dead seriously, he settled down to thinking about the sexual implications of the late quartets. The Oedipal relation of Beethoven to Mozart and Mozart to Haydn. The latent content manifest in Leonore's sartorial transformation . . . Norman considered that these questions were at the nucleus of the nature of human culture and he expected them to relinquish important conclusions in time, but he saw no reason not to use them in the meantime to score now and again. Certain types of broads went apeshit, as he explained it to Phil, for this kind of talk, and furthermore, one thing he did not like to do, he admitted it (again to Phil), was live alone.

He had moved in with the painter D. D. Jones, at her request. Dee Dee did a half-dozen nude studies of him and one mixed media portrait (for hair, she sewed clumps of black thread to the canvas, a task that took weeks), and cooked like a dream. When she got her one-man show, scouring for materials and hanging paintings kept her too busy to cook. Norman said good-bye to Dee Dee, moved in with Bunny Van Den Nieuwenhutzen, and enrolled at Columbia. He had flirted with City University of New York, but at the time eighty percent of the students at CUNY were children of survivors of the Holocaust, and Norman was not. It made him uneasy—he couldn't say why exactly. It was as if a particular history had been programmed into his genes, and yet his own development exhibited none of the coded consequences. He was a mutant. While seven-year-olds in Europe were being packed into boxcars and shipped off to the camps, he had been taxiing to F. A. O. Schwarz with Mitzi, to spend his sixty-dollar-a-month allowance. And no matter how often he and Morris went over this ground, he was still afraid of the dark. Finally Bunny Van Den Nieuwenhutzen couldn't stand it any longer. "Listen, Norman," she said, "I don't want you to take this personally. It's not like I'm trying to reform you, or anything. Listen, who am I to try to reform another human being, for heaven's sake? I know you're just a weak ordinary slob like the rest of us and can't help it, because after all, when you look—I mean really look—at the human condition, which is what my French teacher used to call it only in French, who the hell isn't? To err is human, I always say. So the way I figure it, reforming you is out of the question. I would not presume. But, Norman, I am telling you, I can't *stand* it any longer. Let there be light, okay, but not all the time, it is like living with an optical jackhammer, if you know what I mean."

He did.

"It's nothing personal, you understand," she said again, packing his bag.

"Farewell," he said. "Good-bye, *vale, au revoir,* so long," he said, kissing her plump neck ardently and with some relief.

And that is how he happened to be living alone, in spite of his not liking to, when he began to notice the girl with the flute and the good legs who trekked daily back and forth between Juilliard and the place where she lived.

The day he returned to his apartment after discovering where she lived, he went through the papers to find out what was playing that Saturday night. You do not get to be a cultural musicologist without acquiring a working knowledge of the habits of musicians and music students. Music students went to concerts, either with tickets or passes, or as ushers. But suppose, he thought at once, suppose she stayed home? Maybe she lived with someone. All the class in those good *shiksa* bones, she was the type to shack up with someone who was mildly dissolute and mildly successful, someone about fifteen years older than she was. He had made an informal survey of her kind. You almost had to, out of self-defense; some of these Gentile chicks would eat a man alive—they were seismic at the psychological center, convulsive; they opened up like the San Andreas Fault and then they swallowed up whatever or whoever fell in.

But this one looked different. The matter of the temperature, for instance. The others he had observed, no matter how glacial their makeup or their manners, betrayed their hunger in blood-warm glances, passion pounding at the back of the eyeball, contained and desperate. This one was cool, very cool. Even in a literal sense, she was cool. Even in this heat, when other girls' hair stuck to their foreheads and their makeup turned orange and they had moons of wetness on their tee shirts under their arms, and their hands felt sticky, like the roof of a car parked under a gum tree, she walked down the street with her chin high, clicking in her high-heeled shoes, her hair bouncing like a commercial, looking as if she smelled of talcum powder. She looked as if nobody had any claims on her—she didn't owe anybody anything, she was free and clear of all obligations, and the more he thought about it, the more convinced he became that she didn't live with anyone. Saturday evening, he stationed himself across the street from her building.

She came down at seven, and walked into his life.

6

It was stuffy in the store. The clerk was a Gypsy. He wore a gold hoop in one ear, and his eyes and mouth seemed to have been pasted onto his face. He slid up and down the length of the counter on one side and Norman and Augusta moved up and down the other looking at rings and things. Norman whispered to Gus that he felt like a toy magnetic

Scottie, and then they both fancied they caused the clerk to move left or right, or that his movements determined theirs. Gus got the giggles; she tried to hide it, but she could feel her face breaking out in smiles like a rash. Then Norman wished she'd hurry up and choose so they could get the hell out, it was too close in the store, and the clerk was too deferential, deference dripped from him like perspiration. Eventually Gus chose a cultured pearl. Norman slipped it onto her finger later, during lunch in the deli, the spot of beauty slamming the eye down toward the nail, which had been chewed to the quick. A flutist should not bite her nails: Norman said this to her. She looked up. "I don't bite all of them," she said, taken aback. "Just this one."

And that made it all right?

"Of course," she said. "I call it containing tension. What would you call it?"

Instead of answering, Norman ordered Hungarian goulash and a root beer. Gus was too excited to eat. She had met Norman two weeks and three days ago ("I can tell you how to get to Carnegie Hall," he had said, coming up to her on the street. "Practice, practice! Well," he had gone on, not stopping for an answer, "what else could I say that would let you know I know what you're all about and am not just some nut from nowhere?"), and now she was engaged to him. She had not had time to decide what she thought about this. She felt slightly out of breath, as if she had been running although she hadn't, and her face was always just a little bit flushed these days, her eyes opened a little wider than usual, as if she were on the verge of an adventure. That was how she felt—adventurous, exhilarated, overflowing with capability and a little frightened at the same time.

The delicatessen wasn't kosher; it was run by a mesomorphic Berliner with a ruminative turn of mind. The Berliner wore a large tablecloth tucked into his belt, and used it as a napkin when serving hot dishes, as a towel to dry his hands, and, if he thought he was unobserved, as a handkerchief. The broad tip of his nose was bristly. His eyes were small but candid; when he spoke about his wife, they became expressive. His wife, the Berliner told them, was responsible for the mural, five feet high and winding around all four walls of the establishment, which depicted in somewhat sketchy fashion a winter scene of unspecific locale, including reindeer and a profusion of holly berries, anachronistic in late summer. The low ceiling to the landscape lent it a comic-strip character, although it was evidently meant to be taken seriously. The Berliner certainly took it seriously. He explained to Norman and Augusta that his wife had studied in Munich. Studied what? Gus wondered. To avoid having to praise the painting, Gus asked the Berliner if he and his wife missed Deutschland, and how they came to be on the Upper West Side, instead of in Yorktown, for example.

But Gus supposed that from one point of view, an omniscient point of view, all places would be equally peculiar. It was like that spurious mathematical case for creation: since the odds against the existence of this particular world were astronomically high—to be precise, infinite—the theory of probability, so this argument went, favored a belief in the existence of God. But the odds were exactly the same with respect to any instance of the particular, and it wasn't the theory of probability which favored a belief in the existence of God; it was just people, who had always been on the side of religion, with or without the theory of probability.

Nevertheless, whatever the odds against it might be, here she was, herself, at a table with a groom-to-be named Norman Gold in a deserted restaurant with wooden floor (the delicatessen was too new to have caught on yet with the students in the neighborhood), and so completely mesmerized by the moment that it was as though nothing had existed before or would follow. She wheeled the ring around her finger. In her reverie, from seeming miles away, like a man on a mountain top hallooing into the heavens, the Berliner could be heard saying, in answer to her question about whether he missed Germany, "Does a man miss his mother? His father? His wife, if she's away?"

"I don't know," Gus said—then blushed. She didn't know what prompted her to answer rhetorical questions. She glanced at Norman, to see if he had been disturbed by her mistake.

Norman had stopped eating and was looking at the Berliner. The man's nose, he thought, looked like a live entity separate from the rest of his face. It had something of the character of a hedgehog. "It's interesting," Norman said, "that you think of your mother first."

"And isn't it a pity more people do not."

"But your childhood can't have been very, uh—"

"Often there was not enough to eat, this is true."

Norman looked down again, reflecting on the goulash on his plate. Suddenly he was angry. He didn't want to be—he had just got engaged, for Christ's sake, and coming into this cool darkness from the gaudy sunshine, the blue skies overblown and expansive like Anna Magnani in last night's movie, he had felt fine. Really fine. Now he emptied his eyes of emotion and looked again at the Berliner, impassively, thinking, You liar, you pig. The man reeked of self-satisfaction, and nobody achieved that in middle age who hadn't been born to it. Norman felt the muscles on the right side of his neck contract; his shoulders knotted. There was a film of soap on the spoon he hadn't used. Shifting his gaze, he shivered at the prospect of snow. There were images in that landscape which the Berliner's wife had failed to paint; they were there, hidden, waiting to be ferreted out, like the objects in one of those drawings for children. If he searched hard enough, he could make out hovels half-buried under mud and icicle, men on horses, men in tanks, the mangy cur licking its wounds beneath a fallen log, flash of bone jutting through the torn skin. Sometimes Norman dreamed this same scene. There was no excuse for it, no cause contiguous enough to serve as explanation, and yet the scene existed as a part of his brain's terrain, he had a map imprinted on his cerebrum, he knew every crevice in the snow-laden fields, every turning of the town, knew Levke, knew Sammele the beadle, the rabbi, and hot-eyed Rebecca. He also knew better than to take any of it seriously, the woman's mural or the mural in his mind. To the man, he said: "You were there during—"

The man wiped his hands on the tablecloth.

Gus lowered her eyes.

"You must have known," Norman said.

The man said, "We didn't know."

"How could you fail to know? You knew..."

"There were rumors, but there are always rumors. If not about Jews, then Communists. Your neighbor's wife, the skinny old man who never talks. Maybe he doesn't talk because his dentures fit not quite right and embarrass him."

"What in God's name do false teeth have to do with anything?"

"I know someone who has false teeth," Gus said, "and he's barely thirty. There are people in this country who just don't have even the money it takes to take care of their children's teeth."

"You see?" said the man.

"See! Do I see? You're fucking-A-right I see." What he saw was that some irreversibly Aryan line of reasoning homed in on him no matter where he turned. It approached him from the East; it came at him from his left, where Gus hung on his elbow. He could feel the tension in her fingers as she touched his sleeve, five little jabs of nervousness. Don't make a scene, she was saying; he could hear the words in her head.

The man reached over and tapped him on the back of his

hand, as if sounding it to find out where to drive the nail. "I tell you, our parents knew nothing at that time, and what does an adolescent ever know? Behind my ears, I was wet." But his eyes, Norman saw, had adopted a deeper hue, filling with the same sentimentality that the discussion of his absent wife had called up in him. It was as if somebody was pouring soft nougat centers into those chocolate-candy eyes. What can he be thinking of? Norman asked himself, confronting the novel notion that someone might remember the Holocaust with affection. What is he remembering?

"Near the end, when everybody was called up, including boys, I was a member of the *Hitlerjugend*, and to fly the aeroplane I learned speedily. When you are flying, you are feeling less as though you are holding yourself above the ground, and more as though someone is keeping you from falling. You are suspended on a string from heaven. It is superbly beautiful. The puppeteer is as close to you then as ever he will be, and you can almost make out his visage behind the curtain of sky."

Jerk the string and the bomb hatch opened; jerk on another string, and a dozen shower stalls were soaked in gas; again on another, and Norman, his head flopping uselessly on his body, jigged away a lifetime to tunes he heard but barely, or heard and didn't like. Long before the man across from him had handed him this mirror, this way of looking at himself, Norman had seen himself in search of freedom. Something tugged at him, and something yanked him this way and that. As he grew older, he began to be able to predict the steps in the dance and could make several educated guesses as to the identity of the person or persons who pulled the strings, but he couldn't control the movements of his arms and legs, hold his head up or sit a given number out. Once or twice he had thought (waking in the dead of night, clammy as a corpse shocked into resurrection) that there might prove, ultimately, to be no release in knowledge—and since such a statement ran counter to the basic tenet of his lifework, he dismissed it again at once, as just another expression of his own desperation, an extremity, as it were, with which he had become intimately acquainted during his psychoanalysis. He believed, and knew that he must believe, that if he kept looking, if he dug deep enough, a beam would show and he could come out on the other side, and look back, and make sense of the shadows and fetid air that threatened any night now to suffocate him in his sleep.

Gus shuddered. Unlike Norman, she saw herself, listening to the Berliner, turned loose, floating in deep space, disconnected from everything she loved. "That kind of experience, it seems to me," she said to the ex-pilot, "hinges on a terrific confidence in yourself." She blushed. "Or in God. Suppose he tires of holding the string?" She imagined he might have gotten bored with the whole show and walked away. "Or suppose he dozes off and lets your line get tangled up with some others? His hand could cramp." But she shouldn't be talking in parables. She didn't know Norman well enough yet to know how he might interpret them.

Norman was watching her lips, pink but enterprising even in repose, never really slack, the wayward upper lip full of determination and humor, the way both lips took on purpose and shape in the act of speech. And thinking about her mouth, he lost track of what she was saying. He slipped his hand casually under the table, letting it lie on her lap, not with intent to quicken but just to let her know that he was with her. Maybe, he thought, he had some intent to quicken.

The man said, "I crashed in a meadow but no one would have known it from my face. One would have known it from the aeroplane, which was thoroughly destroyed. I washed my face in a brook. The accident made me thirsty, so I drank also from the brook. Then I walked away, as if nothing had happened. Sometimes I think I imagined it, the descent and the—the sense of it. I will try to describe this sense. It was as if one hundred percent of the universe contracted to a cone, and I was being sucked down into it, to the very narrow tip where things begin."

Now, so far as being a pilot went, Norman rode the subway; he could hardly drive, much less fly. He had never been through anything spectacular. He had never been a soldier or a prisoner, or anything but a student, analysand, and, for a few weeks one summer, a seller of baby pictures door-to-door on Long Island. He had also briefly worked for a firm of financial consultants, dialing people in the Manhattan telephone directory and trying to talk them into setting up a free appointment, at which they would find out from someone else how little it could cost them to save money. For this reason, the exploits of other men nudged Norman discomfitingly, pushed him into the past, where he stopped on the street, stood listening for danger, heard Snowball, the albino with a hard-on, slip and curse behind the fence, and then ran like hell for home. About once a month Snowball and his cohorts caught him, plastered his face in mud, yanked his pants down, foulmouthed his father. While his father was the D.A., they had it in for "Norm the Gorm." But his father the D.A. never even noticed them; boys like that were mindless microscopic existents, his father said, interesting to a sociologist but of no ethical consequence. "I got bigger fish to fry," his father said. His father said this until full-scale gang warfare erupted in vicious earnestness in the late fifties, but by that time Sid Gold was busy being a judge. By that time Norman had come into his own, the Julien Sorel of Ocean Parkway with large, suffering, intense, heart-hurting eyes and a young man's utter lack of scrupulousness about using them.

Meanwhile, he had learned to walk with his head down, since to shoot glances at Snowball ranked, apparently, as an insult of injurious proportions. He steered clear of dead ends.

All this caution had delimited Norman's sense of himself;

he felt that he knew himself inside out, and he was ashamed not to be aware of vast unexplored emotional territories. Even if he could discover them, he doubted that he would be brave enough to penetrate very deeply, though perhaps he did himself a disservice here, for he *was* intellectually aggressive, a prober of tunnels, a ravisher of motive, and if mystery was a woman, shy and sultry as sunlight on a hot, cloudy day, when the wind hung over the sky like seven veils, then he was her best lover, the one who knew how to strip to essence.

Gus, knowing the pressure of Norman's arm on her lap, smiled. The Berliner said she was beautiful when she smiled. Norman said she was beautiful even when she didn't, but that she was more likable when she did. These comments contained messages, but for whom were they meant? If for her, why did both men speak about her and not to her? Warned, she took her hand from Norman's elbow, as if suddenly she doubted he would be as careful of her person as she would. Suppose she *were* a book, or a score. Men were lackadaisical about library due dates, the energy that went into any work a woman did, and most of all, sexual loyalties. "Did the war touch your wife too?" she asked, addressing the Berliner. She hadn't intended for her question to sound so obscene. She felt as though she'd bent over to pick up some idea that they'd left lying around on the wooden floor, like a peanut shell, only to learn that the back of her skirt had pulled up humiliatingly, exposing her most vulnerable parts.

The man said, "You want me to give you a yes. This would be the easy answer. But my wife is a free spirit; nothing touches her but art."

Norman laughed. "You read too much Nietzsche at the Gymnasium."

Gus was thinking about the wife that only art touched. Art seemed to her to have become a person. A man. A Mann man. Redheaded. She said, "Art's touch is cold." She didn't know why she said that. It wasn't what she believed.

Nobody answered her.

It became important to her to get a response, so she said, "It's like a crematorium that hasn't been used in twenty years, if you want to know the truth. Art's touch."

Still nobody said anything, but she wouldn't let it drop. "What I mean is," she said, "art is a kind of stony vault in which the ashes of our ancestors are housed. Even physicists' ashes. Even the ashes of dead dictators."

The Berliner capitulated. "Even that is to make of art a utility," he said, "like the water service or electric power. My wife says, there is an artist named Paul Jenkins, who has publicly consumed a canvas of pears, to illustrate that pears are for eating, not painting."

And at that, Gus and Norman glanced shyly at each other and fell in love all over again. They *were* on the same side after all! Augusta asked the Berliner, "What did they taste like?"—meaning the pears. And Norman said, "If you ask me, that's an extremely untrustworthy teleology."

The man seemed offended. "What do you mean?" he asked. "What teleology?"

"Look," Gus said, leaning over the table animatedly; her hair, grazing the table top, was so blond it hurt Norman's eyes. "Suppose a pear's most salient characteristic, the one that juts out from the others, is its shape. After all, I defy you to describe how a pear tastes; isn't it a bland taste, like gritty pudding? And consider the shape of the pear, how it *glows,* a mock light bulb. Maybe pears were meant for mock lamps. You'll say, What do I want with a mock lamp? But that's a whole different problem, to wit, our supply of mock lamps exceeds the demand for them!" Her eyes glittered, reflecting the incredible dark yellow of her hair, and on her finger the lustrous pearl gleamed, like a third, anomalous eye. Now when she turned toward Norman, he felt charged by her energy, and they left hand in hand, in good spirits, victorious.

7

Norman had to break the news to his father. He did not look forward to doing this. Well, part of him looked forward to it.

He took the subway to Brooklyn and went straight to the old man's office. The way he had it figured, it was wiser to tell his father personally in private; his mother would go along with anything. His mother's philosophy was, Never complain because it's all free anyway. "It" was life. His father's was, Nothing is free—they take it out of your hide every day and the best you can hope for is a decent return on your investment. This argument had been going on for the whole of Norman's time on earth, which now totaled twenty-eight years.

Waiting in the anteroom, Norman smoked a cigarette, taking exaggerated drags to keep his throat from locking. He cracked his knuckles. There was no window in the waiting room but otherwise it was posh: paisley pillows and rubber plants, plenty of walnut paneling. Jocelyn's IBM typewriter looked like the computer bank on *Star Trek*.

The luxury didn't hide the odor of hard work. The toil was there, even if it was neatly filed away in steel cabinets. In a way, Norman thought it was obscene of his father to go on working at his age; a man that old was a fool to lust after the law. By the time Jocelyn let him in, Norman was furious, but he could follow the line of his fury back to the Talmud, and he knew better than to blame his father for the sins of *his* fathers. For all those generations, law had been the truly beloved, embraced warmly like the Simchath Torah. Understanding inhibited him. Tolerantly, he said to his father,

"You're looking fit." It was like starting an avalanche by dislodging a single pebble. His father roared—or tried to.

"Why shouldn't I?" he demanded. "You think I'm not? I could take on a dozen wiseguys like you." He put an arm around Norman's shoulders, breaking away to feint and jab. "Sit. Did you eat already?"

"I'm not hungry."

"Jocelyn"—he was leaning into the intercom—"get lunch. How do I know what? Food. Get food." He turned to Norman. "Now tell me, what kind of a name is Jocelyn?"

For all the power behind his father's voice, it came out high—not feminine, but not so masculine, either. It was as if the old man's gender was fading away with age, like the color in his face. He could end up a pale, brown-specked, cigar-puffing, money-making bookworm. Not that he ever read anything but law. He had strong eyes and even now didn't need glasses. He peered into Norman's face, cheeping in that high, loud voice which always came as such an unpleasant surprise and made a listener feel rather as though he were pitching to a bunt. Norman backed away, using as an excuse the cigarette in his hand; his father shoved an ashtray across the desk at him and he put it out. Then he took a seat in a straight-backed chair and tried to get his bearings. His father sat down behind the desk, facing him. His father's head was bald and lumpy, with a neat white fringe encircling the bottom edge of the skull, like a slipped halo. With his squat, substantial pudge-body widening at the base, he looked like a cross between a cherub (belonging to the knowledgeable order of celestial beings) and a toad. On the right side of his head, alopecia had exposed a thick mole that ought to have been removed, if only as a precaution. But the old man's gaze was as sharp as Chopin's Thirteenth Prelude. Norman lit another cigarette, and his father said, "You smoke too much."

"I know, Pop."

"For a son, I have a chimney."

"I know, Pop."

"Hey, was the train on time? Did you stall? Did anyone get electrocuted on the third rail? Was there a mugging in Union Square?"

"I got here, didn't I?"

"Good," he said, "that's great. What an age. The wonders. Airplanes, rocket ships, miracle drugs, television by satellite—"

"Spare me."

"You don't eat right, Norman. You got no pep."

"No get-up-and-go."

They glanced at each other slyly, like vaudeville comedians checking out a rival act, and then they smiled, a kind of shorthand applause for each other. The old man laughed until he had to blow his nose to clear his sinuses. He had often explained to Norman that laughing was lousy for the sinuses.

"Pop—" Norman began.

"Come on, come on, I don't have all day. I'm an old man! I could die tomorrow!"

His father always overacted. Never knew when to quit. It was the thing about him that his mother had always been a little disgusted by, though she would never complain. "Look, Pop, this is serious," Norman said.

The old man folded his handkerchief back into his pocket and nodded.

"I'm getting married."

The old man was now acting serious. "It's time," he said, seriously. "You were the child of my old age." He looked grim, preparing to meet his maker. Inside, Norman knew, he was as excited as if the Messiah had just walked through the door. More. The Messiah wouldn't give him a grandson.

"Her name is Gus."

"Gus?" He looked bewildered.

"For Augusta."

"She's not a Jew?"

"No."

Norman watched his father's bewilderment deepen. It seemed to sink in through the nonplussed eyes and settle somewhere lower down, around the heart. "I see," his father said. But Norman knew that he didn't. He couldn't conceivably see because his eyes had gone dark. All the play had been banished from his father's features, exiled to some Siberia of the emotions for responses that had served their purpose and were no longer useful. What Norman saw across the desk now was his father's legal face, about as expressive as a municipal bond.

"You'll like her," Norman said, breathlessly. If only he could bring back the joker in his father— "She's a musician," he said. "That's almost like being Jewish."

"I'm sure she's likable."

"Well, naturally, I think so. I could be prejudiced." He knew he was grinning like a simpleton.

"How much does she want?"

"What?"

"You heard. How much?"

"How much what?"

"She's pregnant, isn't she? Or else just smart. They're all like that. It's not a big deal. But you wouldn't compound a mistake by marrying it."

"Gus is not a mistake."

"All right, an unfortunate choice. Of words. But you get what I'm saying, my drift?"

"And if I don't?" The ash on Norman's cigarette was as long as a caterpillar. It fell off before he reached the ashtray with it. His father looked at the floor mournfully. Norman stood up.

"You're the child of my old age, Norman."

"What the hell's that got to do with anything?"

"You should know."

"I should know! I should know better than to expect you might have learned something in your old age. Like, the whole world is not contaminated! Not everybody is a Nazi! Hitler is not some big honcho in Argentina and he is not going to deceive you in the guise of a Gentile daughter-in-law."

"Shame! Shame!"

"I'm leaving."

"Leave. What do I care? I could be dead the next time we see each other. Did I tell you about my blood pressure, the strain I'm under? What do you care about that?"

"Very funny, but this is my life you're making the butt of a joke. I don't appreciate that one bit."

The old man's face darkened as blood rushed to his cheeks. "Who's a ham?" he asked. "Not me."

As if summoned by the mention of food, at that moment Jocelyn appeared in the doorway, holding a brown paper lunch bag. She was wearing pink.

Norman said to his father, "I'll write a letter. Maybe if you won't *listen* to reason, you'll *read* it."

"You'll only upset your mother."

"Mother has nothing to do with this, don't use her as an excuse. You're behaving like an ass on your own initiative."

"Listen, Jocelyn, how a son talks to his father." He shook his head sadly.

"Corned beef on rye," Jocelyn said, holding out the paper bag.

Norman, possessed, snatched it out of her hands and threw it across the room. It landed against the wall behind his father with a soft plop.

"Now see what you've done," his father said. "And all because you let your head be turned."

"So," Norman said, "fast. Skip lunch. It won't kill you. And incidentally don't expect to see me again anytime soon, because you won't." But he was lighting another cigarette as he said this; it was his third in half an hour.

"A bad penny always turns up."

Jocelyn was picking lunch up off the floor. "Speaking of turning up," she said, hinting at significance.

"Oh no," the old man said.

Norman heard the hint in Jocelyn's voice and the gasp in his father's. He was silent for a minute, trying to think what it might mean. His father did not often gasp.

"She's waiting in the anteroom," Jocelyn said.

The old man thundered at Norman, but the words came out almost caressingly. Did his father know how he sounded, what a crazy effect he produced? It was a voice like a late summer sky, full of the threat of rain and streaked with sheet lightning—but the rain never broke, and the sweeping winds only roiled the dry air. It was a voice for a Jewish Lear, hurled into the sluggish, hoax-heavy, pollution-dark clouds that sat on the roofs of skyscrapers and tenements, blowing raspberries. The old man had got up and was standing under Norman—Norman was short but his father was shorter— shaking his fist and glowering. "You're excused," he said.

"Excused?"

"Yes, dammit, excused! Don't you know when to leave the table?"

"After the corned beef," he said. "Not before."

"Don't be smart. Smart I've got enough of to last me a lifetime. I don't need more from you. If you marry this person, you are herewith disinherited. I will make it official. I would make it religious, but that would ruin your mother. She would die of tears. I don't want your mother should drown. I got enough troubles, like I got enough of smart. You think I'm being funny, don't. I may express myself in your eyes peculiarly, but what it amounts to is about half a million smackeroos you won't see. Have I made myself clear?"

"Why do you care so much? It's not as if you've spent your life in a synagogue chanting prayers, for chrissake."

"I have a constituency. Also, I have values."

"Some values."

"You can think what you think, Norman, but a father's will is his labor of love. I earned every cent and how I leave it is my way of saying what I was working for. Remember this. After all, I could die today. This afternoon." "Oh, Sidney," a woman's voice wailed. "Not this afternoon! Just when I came all the way to Brooklyn to surprise you!" It originated from behind Norman. He wheeled around, the fateful cigarette in his raised hand. The hand struck a breast of mind-boggling proportions, and then Norman heard a faint sizzling sound, and there was a pause for collective astonishment, as they all gazed, united in fascination, at the fox fur catching flame on Birdie's bust.

8

ON TIMES SQUARE, Birdie Mickle was billed as Miss Chicken Delight. The neon said: SHE'S FINGERLICKIN' GOOD. It had taken her a long time to work her way up to neon, and every year on the way up was one year subtracted from how long she could hope to stay there, stripping with class being something you could do only so long as the body held up. Not that hers was in any immediate danger of collapse. She was, as the boys used to say, round and firm and fully packed, and that's not all: her chest was like a scaffold; a man could practically stand on it to get a better view of the scenery.

If Birdie's body was still good, she was convinced that this was at least partly because she kept her mind in shape. Birdie was no dope. She was a well-read woman, and why not? Should she let her life lead her, instead of her leading it? She read between numbers, and it wasn't to educate herself either, as she quickly informed any man who took a patronizing interest in the books in her apartment on Madison Avenue. She read because she liked to.

But Birdie's deep-down special interest, the ambition that lived in her heart like a secret lover, was interpretative dancing. At work, she was renowned for her rendition of "Baby, Pull My Wishbone, Please"—and what nobody even knew was that she had written it herself, words and all. She had talent, she didn't doubt that for an instant. The sad thing was, the business was tight. Sex in the sixties was free, so who needed the illusion of sex? You could walk down the street and see young girls half Birdie's age nearly as naked as she was by the end of her act, and in broad daylight no less. And as if that weren't enough, now the men were taking over. Male strippers were muscling in on the business. Birdie made her living by being just a little bit sinful, but if there wasn't anything sinful anymore, she would be flat broke, wouldn't she? Interpretative dancing had to wait while she made her way in the world. It had waited all these years, she guessed she could live without expressing her true self for a little while longer. But still, it is a terrible thing not to have an outlet for the terpsichorean passion that fires your limbs, for example.

As for the years she had waited— Birdie was forty, and the funny thing was—she knew it was funny because everyone else in the business lied—she didn't mind saying so. You had to lie to managers, certainly. Managers she told she was thirty-eight; but on the whole, forty was a fine age to admit to. It's not as if you get to be forty without earning it. Every bump and grind had cost her, but she wasn't sorry. Look what she had got for it: Sid Gold.

Birdie loved Sidney. She had met him when she was doing a cake job at a stag party on Atlantic Avenue. Some smartass had pricked the balloon on her behind with his swizzlestick, and everyone had laughed except Sid. And her. It stung like hell, that stupid rubber snapping against her bottom. It was like being goosed with a slingshot. She didn't mind pranks. She didn't mind kinks, most of them. But one thing she hated, and that was pain. From the big stuff to the kid stuff, S and M was for the birds and not for Birdie.

Sidney was very kind. He had a mushy heart and a cute fringe and a deep mind. Birdie gave him his own key to her place and he could drop in whenever he felt like it, though, being a gentleman, he usually telephoned first. This was as close to being married as Birdie cared to come, and she made sure that Sidney appreciated the honor she was bestowing on him. Of course, it wasn't all give and no take. There was no one Birdie liked having around more than Sidney. He was undoubtedly the most significant human being she had ever known, and the sweetest besides. Why, she supposed she would do just about anything for Sidney.

When he came to see her in the apartment on Madison, they turned the air conditioner on full and sat on the Empire sofa while she massaged his forehead. He said he couldn't get a real massage anymore. You went into one of these parlors and you were lucky to get out with your clothes on. You had to drink champagne in a sunken Roman bath or lie down in an all-red room that made your eyeballs ache, and what good was it to satisfy one pair when the other pair was popping out? Furthermore, he preferred Concord Grape. It showed you what the world was coming to, he said. Birdie blew on his fringe and told him the story of her life.

The apartment was in a high-rise with a doorman. It wasn't a penthouse but, as she pointed out to Sidney, she was on the way up. She had a dressing room adjoining her bedroom, so she could put on her face in private like a lady; the dressing table had a skirt and a three-way mirror. Basically, making up involved moisturizing the skin, pancake foundation, highlighter, translucent powder, blusher, eye makeup base, eye shadow (blue or purple, or both, and silver frost), two strips of false lashes on each eye, eyeliner, pencil, mascara, lipstick, lip outliner, and a stick-on beauty spot in the shape of a baby chick. (But on the Fourth of July and Washington's Birthday, as a patriotic person, she wore a beauty spot in the shape of a tiny flag.) Making up required about two hours each time she did it. In cocktail lounges, from a distance of ten feet, Birdie looked twenty. She liked being forty but she didn't like looking forty. Her hair color changed with her wigs. Lately, she was into platinum.

The rest of Birdie's apartment looked like a set from a Hollywood musical. This was because Birdie found the movies very helpful when it came to ideas for decorating. From movies she had learned the importance of plushness. She had plush carpeting, plush drapes, plush cushions, and in negligees she favored floor-length silk over the baby doll look, although she was barely five feet tall. She compensated with spike-heeled mules and hairdos-with-height. Sidney had showered her with gown-and-peignoir sets, and she was grateful. Sidney was a generous man. However, the fact that she accepted his presents did not necessarily mean anything. Not necessarily.

Because Birdie was not, repeat definitely not, and if you forgot it you could get your block knocked off by her purse, a whore. She had turned a trick now and then but she was not about to let anybody jump to conclusions. That was what a whore was, somebody who let other people jump to conclusions, and you didn't have to be a woman to be a whore, either. The world was full of respectable male whores, many of them politicians. Sid was an exception, and so, for that matter, was she. It was one of the things that they had in common. And like Sidney, Birdie always stated her arguments very clearly so there could be no misunderstanding. She liked having things out in the open. But if it made a man feel good to buy her a fox fur, she wasn't going to stand in his way. You start demurring and saying you can't and he shouldn't, and all you do is saddle the poor fellow with a lot of guilt which is not what anybody wants. Guilt a man can always get at home. A woman too, for that matter. Her father had laid just a whole lot of it, if you want to know the truth, on her, and look where it got her: forty years old and in love with Sidney Gold. She giggled. On the other hand, could guilt be all bad, if it led to this?

Sid, being deep, understood all this. If things broke for him, he might be sitting on the Supreme Court, but that didn't alter his inward self, and his inward self was a lot like hers. The hard shell and the slick surface were accreted, like hers. It was a kind of chitin, but they were piteous within, which was a quote from *Time* magazine. So Sid didn't laugh at her, and she didn't laugh at him, but they laughed with each other more than either of them had ever done with anybody else.

9

NORMAN WHIPPED the fox fur from Birdie's bosom and threw it to the floor. The Honorable Sidney Wallechinsky Gold watched his son stamping out the sparks. How much had he paid for that fur? It didn't matter—what did he care about money? Norman could think he was closefisted, let him. It wasn't that he loved money but that money was love. If Norman did not think that money was love, let him try living without it. The lack of it stunted your growth. Little children grew up warped in mind and body for the lack of it. As for himself, from being poor he had got rich, and to what end if not to shower his wealth on certain persons whom he loved dearly and wished to see thrive, like American Beauty rose bushes? And why should he pay to see weeds grow, would somebody please tell him that? God did not make the rain to fall everywhere in the world at the same time, indiscriminately.

Sidney Gold was liberal with the B'nai B'rith and the United Jewish Appeal, and he had staked Israel from the beginning. *Eretz Yisrael.* He had done his part to make *aliyah,* the return to the homeland, possible. He was goddamned if he'd support a *shiksa* in his old age. You could lose votes with a mixed marriage in your immediate family. True, he was not running for anything, but it was the same principle. People didn't like this sort of thing. It went deep. Hell, it went back to all those pogroms and camps and exiles and diasporas. Where was the point in surviving all those things *as Jews* if you were going to let yourself be assimilated into nonexistence? To the dead, it was disrespectful. Did they die relinquishing their unique souls so their grandsons could ridicule their beliefs? True, he was not himself a believer, but he could understand their feelings. And Esther's. What about Esther? She would be heartbroken already, her only son. And there was Rita, their daughter. Her husband would give her holy hell for this. Rita was married to an Orthodox Jew and lived in Far Rockaway, he was a good man, decent enough and God knows solid, like a Swiss bank he was solid, but hell, every time she took a piss she had to have a ritual bath. So it seemed.

10

Look, I'm really sorry," Norman was saying. "I didn't realize you were so—"

Birdie smiled magnanimously. "It's all right," she said, graciously. "It was just fox." Then she saw Sidney's brow beetling. "I mean," she said, "why it was special was only because Sidney gave—" But Sidney's brow, instead of smoothing, was creasing still further. It was capable of great creasing because with his scalp muscles he could pull the flesh forward from his bald pate. "Sidney," Birdie said, trailing off helplessly.

"This is my son the schmuck. Norman. He was just leaving."

"It's okay, I'm in no hurry. I should make amends."

Jocelyn was trying to squeeze past the trio. "Oh, I'm sorry," Birdie said, turning around and giving her a smile like the one she had flashed for Norman. It was her stage smile. She used it when she didn't know what the hell was expected of her, and at this particular juncture in history, so to speak, that was precisely the case. She could tell something had been going on here because she knew Sidney's aura very well. It was usually a comfortable nondescript brown, dried tobacco-leaf brown, but right now she could see clear as daylight, assuming it was a clear day, about a thousand pulsating yellow dots coursing around the contours of his spirit, and that spelled trouble to anybody who knew, as she certainly did, how to read it.

Norman was trying to brush the fox fur into shape, but singed hairs kept flaking off and drifting to the floor. "There must be something—" he said, holding the fur by its snout.

"Forget it," Sid said to Norman. "You have to keep that appointment."

"What appointment?"

"*That* appointment. You know. You said you had an appointment to keep. *Didn't you?*" Norman looked blankly at his father's winkings and eyebrow-liftings. "Good-bye," Sid said.

"Oh," Norman said, "*that* appointment. It doesn't matter. I can always make another appointment."

"That could create an adverse impression."

"On whom?"

"On the party with whom you have the appointment!"

"Oh," Norman said. "The party. I expect the party will understand. These things happen."

"Not very often, they don't," Jocelyn muttered, darting the rest of the way out of the room.

"Sidney—" Birdie began again.

"In a minute."

"I think the lady has a question," Norman said, grinning.

"No—" Birdie began yet again.

"The lady does not have a question," Sid said.

"I have an *observation* to make," Birdie said.

"Oh God," Sid groaned.

"I don't believe I've gotten your name," Norman said.

"Would you like my personal name or my professional name?"

"Her name is Birdie Mickle!" Sid said.

"My name is Birdie Mickle," Birdie said.

"Is that your personal name or your professional name?"

"Personal, definitely. My professional name is—"

But just then the telephone rang. Sid opened the door—they were still standing by the door, which Jocelyn had closed after her—and shouted: "No calls!"

"It's your wife," she said.

"I'll take it," he said, slamming the door again and sighing deeply, as if each breath were dredged up from the bottom of his soul, with an effort so enormous no one should know but if you happened to be a perceptive person you might just realize that lugging the world around on your shoulders was no fun. Weightily, he walked to his desk. "Hello, Esther," he said. "Yes, Esther. Yes. No, no. Yes, Esther. Fine, Esther." Then suddenly his tone changed. "She did? What about? What was her bearing? She was pleasant? That's good, that's very good. So? It would be better if she were unpleasant? Now listen. We could just pull it off. If her husband comes out for Amato, it could be just the support we need to put him in. Amato's word we already got. If Amato goes in, Leibowitz goes in, and if Leibowitz goes in, so do I. This is excellent news, Esther, excellent." His pale beige skin was suffused with a rising red glow. Birdie's face fell. She sat down in a chair, ignoring Norman. Norman asked her what was wrong but Birdie only shook her head. She could not possibly tell Norman that she had that minute realized for the first time that she was jealous of his father's wife.

For a second after he hung up, Sid Gold's mind was elsewhere.

Norman, mentally playing back his father's half of the conversation and realizing what was missing, said, bitterly, "You could have told her."

"Told her what?" Sid was genuinely confused.

"My news."

"Oh. Your news. I sincerely hope you will come to your senses and that she never has to be told."

"Told what?" Birdie asked.

"I'm getting married. As you might have gathered from my father's reception of this news, my fiancée is not a Jewess."

"What is she?" Birdie asked, wide-eyed.

Norman laughed. "That's good," he said to his father.

"She's right, you know. I could be engaged to a black girl. Or an Arab."

"Over my dead body."

"Is she an Arab?" Birdie asked.

"No," Norman said. "She's not pregnant either. Apparently, my father never heard of the Pill. Also love he never heard of."

"That's not true!" Birdie exclaimed. "Your father knows a lot about—"

"That's enough, Birdie," Sid said. "And as for you, who taught you to use such language in front of a lady?"

"What language? What on earth are you talking about? Love?"

Sidney looked—and felt—acutely uncomfortable.

"Holy Toledo," Norman said. "You don't want me to talk about the Pill. Is that it?"

Sid turned to Birdie, who was still seated. "You said you had an observation to make," he said, thinking it might be less exhausting to go back rather than forward so far as this particular discussion went.

"Oh yes," Birdie said, in a voice as clear and fresh as a mountain stream, which could be unnerving in Brooklyn. "It was just this. Not to worry about the fox fur, Norman, because Sidney can always buy me another." And she looked at them both ingenuously, not to say ingeniously, as if she had found the perfect solution to the most urgent problem of the entire afternoon. She batted her false lashes. She was aware of how she looked at them and of the effect it produced, but this did not mean that her expression was not an honest reflection of her real self. She *was,* she happily admitted, a dizzy dame. It's just that she was not a *dumb* dizzy dame. It was a subtle distinction, and not all men had minds that could grasp it.

Sid could see that his son was twitching with pleasure, galvanized. "Okay. You've had your laugh. Now go."

"I'm leaving," Norman said. He reached down and plucked Birdie's hand from her lap to shake it. "Nice meeting you, Miss Mickle," he said.

"Me too, I'm sure," she said.

"Half a million bucks," Sid said, just as Norman put his hand on the doorknob and turned it.

Norman opened the door. "I won't lose any sleep over it."

"You probably won't," Sid said, sadly. "But I will."

I I

Gus was in her apartment, waiting for Norman, when the telephone rang. It was Richard. "I have something I've been meaning to tell you," she said, twisting her long, wavy hair with her free hand, worried. "I'm getting married."

"Oh?" he asked, as if she'd said she was taking a trip, or changing schools. "Since when?"

She was confused. "Since when am I getting married, or when am I getting married?"

"Both."

She told him.

"Why didn't you tell me before?" Richard said. "Jesus Christ, I feel like a goddamn idiot, Gussie."

"I didn't know how."

"You apparently know how now!"

She was sitting cross-legged on the couch-bed, the white receiver at her ear, gazing dejectedly at Tweetie-Pie cleaning his feathers. (Tweetie was a bit of a dandy.)

She hadn't *wanted* to tell him before; she didn't want to

give him up—and more than that, she didn't want to have to tell him, as she was in effect doing, that she hadn't been faithful to him. "I thought, since you're married—"

"What's that got to do with it?"

"I'm not sure—"

"What's he do?"

"Who?"

"Oh, fuck. Your *fiancé*."

"You aren't being very nice about this."

"Oh, come on, Gussie, you sound like you just ate a persimmon. I feel like a fool, that's all. I'm going to miss you. I hope you'll be happy. Of *course* I hope you'll be happy."

"He's writing his dissertation in Cultural Musicology."

Richard broke out into laughter. "Whoop-de-do!" he cried. "What's that?"

"He's a kind of philosophical psychologist, not with rats, but he's not a shrink, either—" She knew she was being unfair to Norman, but she owed something to Richard too.

"I miss you," he said.

She wanted to say that she missed him—the words were already in her mouth, waiting for her to say them—but it wouldn't have been true. Occasionally, she missed his attentions, and remembered how dynamic he looked crossing campus with his tie loose, the desperation in his eyes that dissolved into light when he saw her coming toward him. "But you're married," she said again, still not knowing exactly what she meant to convey by that. It wasn't a point that had ever troubled her before.

"You don't have to tell *me* I'm married."

"Why don't you get a divorce?" The subject was safe, now; it had been taboo only so long as she had had an investment in it.

"Because Elaine loves me."

Gus chewed the ends of her hair.

"And you don't," he added, a little petulantly.

"Would you get a divorce if I said I did?"

"It's a hypothetical question now, isn't it?"

"I guess—"

"If I said I would, would you say you did?"

"I guess it wouldn't make any difference if I did, would it?"

"Not if you're going to get married anyway. To this whatever-he-is, some kind of culture vulture."

"Of course," she said, enjoying this new turn to the conversation immensely, "a person can be married and still have affairs. Take you, for instance."

"But you aren't me. There's no similarity." He was crooning in her ear, low and sweet, a slight abrasive edge to his voice stroking her eardrum like a wire brush sweeping softly over the snaredrum in an orchestra. "I know your type."

"What's my type?"

"You'll think you have to worship him, just because he's your husband. You'll think he's a reflection on your character, so he'll have to be perfect."

Gus laughed. She was meant to be a star, no question about it—hearing herself talked about by other people always intoxicated her. Her face shone and her eyes kindled. The phenomenon was delicate but definite. "You're being nasty again," she said, pleased.

"I'm owed, Gussie, owed, owed, owed."

"I don't see why—"

"Because I love you."

"That's not—"

"You owe me like I owe Elaine."

Secretly, Gus thought that Elaine did look like the type who was always collecting on old debts. Elaine had a complexion that must have glowed with a freshly scrubbed look, once, and now looked raw, and the doe's feet of her eyeliner ran into the crow's feet at the corners of her eyes. Altogether, she wore the righteous look of someone who's been prevailed upon to lend her heart against her better judgment. Gus used to see her in the grocery store on Tate Street in Greensboro, or at parties. Elaine stayed away from the school itself. "How is she?" Gus asked.

"Elaine is fine. I'm miserable."

"Why are you miserable?"

"Why shouldn't I be miserable? I spend half my waking hours trying to make everyone else happy."

It was true; an odd occupation for a man. "How is the new record coming along?" she asked. He was doing the Beethoven Eighth. You couldn't be too miserable, Gus thought, while you were recording the Beethoven Eighth. She said as much.

"You aren't giving up the flute, are you?" he asked, as if the possibility had just struck him. "Christ, that's unthinkable!"

"Don't be ridiculous," she said. But it was something that had been bothering her.

"I've been meaning to tell you," he said. "I'll get my manager to take you on whenever you're ready. You don't have to worry about that."

"That's nice of you, Richard."

"You didn't think I wouldn't come through, did you? I know what's expected of me—"

"Richard!"

"Don't sound so shocked, Gussie. Things always work this way. Almost always, anyhow. It's not so terrible. Life isn't so terrible. Even marriage isn't so terrible."

"I'm glad to hear Elaine is fine," she said, primly.

"Elaine is fine," he said. "Beethoven is fine. I'm fine. But I'll tell you what gets me down. The kids complain all the time. It's a case of nonstop wheedling. They fight a lot. Are you pregnant?"

"Of course not. Should I be?"

"If I were you," he said, "I would want to be."

"That's *your* problem. If you weren't so good-looking, I'd think you were queer."

"Flattery will get you nowhere," he said.

"Oh, gee, Richard, I really do like you—"

"I know," he said. He sounded very blue. "Everybody does."

Just then Gus heard Norman downstairs; he had his own keys now. The door downstairs banged, he took the steps two at a time. But now was not the moment to hang up on Richard. She *did* owe him something.

"That's not what I mean," she said, earnestly. "I care about you *more* than everybody else." The second door had not made a sound, and now Norman was staring at her from across the room.

"That's probably true," Richard said, heavy-hearted. "Nobody else cares even that much."

"Now you're being stupid. I'm not going to listen to this." It would have to be Elaine who did. She had Norman to think of.

"You're right," he said. "I'll call you later. Sometime. Someday. In ten years. Come disguised as a housewife and I'll meet you under the clock in the Biltmore Hotel."

She giggled in spite of herself, and put the receiver down in an expansive mood, but when she turned around again, Norman's face was white. Not his usual dark cloud-filled countenance-of-anger that she had seen before, but white. As white as the bedspread, the telephone, the curtains, the walls—all of which, she now noticed, had been dying into darkness for the past half-hour. In the dark room, Norman's face was spookily white.

12

THE ROOM had gotten dark while Gus was talking on the phone.

She switched on the closest lamp. It had a perfectly round white porcelain base with raised impressions of leaves. The shade was shaped like a Chinese coolie's hat. It was a lamp she remembered from childhood, the lamp she had colored by in the living room in Chapel Hill on rainy afternoons. Her parents had bought it shortly after they were married. Now Norman was standing next to it, his face above the central funnel of the volcano-shaped shade, and the bulb threw his features into eerie relief.

"Who were you talking to?" he asked.

"Nobody you know."

"That was obvious."

"He's an old friend," she said.

"No kidding. How old?"

"This is ridiculous." Then she remembered. "Did you see your father today?"

It took some of the tension out of his back and shoulders. Gus watched it go, thinking, Good riddance; Norman felt it go, sliding from his body like soap under a shower. He flung himself into a chair, sighed à la Sidney, and said, "Yes, I saw him." He had stepped on a wad of chewing gum, and he leaned over to pick it off with his thumbnail.

"Ugh," Gus said. "Here, use this." She handed him a sheet of newspaper from the pile she kept for lining Tweetie's cage.

"I don't think it's so goddamn ridiculous," he said, scraping, "when I walk into a room and overhear you telling someone you love him more than anyone else. You have to admit, under the circumstances, that that is not exactly a trivial statement."

"Oh, brother. You really beat all, Norman. I didn't say I loved him more than I love anyone else; I said I loved him more than anyone else does. If you had eavesdropped on the *entire* conversation, you would realize that."

"I think you're splitting hairs."

"I don't."

"Then just how much do you love me?"

"I love you," she said, laughing. "Why else would I be about to marry you? For your money?"

"That's what my father thinks," he snapped.

"Then your father's screwy. But I'm not surprised. Look at his son."

Norman was looking at Augusta. He adored her like this, high-spirited, quick. There was a lilt to her chin and nose in profile, like the Minuet in G. Her self-confidence ravished him. "It's just as well," he said, "that you don't care about the money. He disowned me."

"He what?"

"I warned you he's a prick."

"I didn't know anybody ever actually did that kind of thing anymore. It's rather feudal, isn't it?"

Norman shrugged. "Does it bother you?"

Gus found herself sitting down on the couch-bed. She hadn't said to herself, Now I will sit down; it was as if Norman's news had knocked her down. "It's not the money," she said, slowly. "It's what it means. If he's disowned you for marrying me, I guess I can assume that your family isn't going to welcome me with open arms."

"My mother will be different."

"It's a rotten way to start." She was suddenly shy. "It makes me feel funny," she said. "Ashamed, somehow. As if I'm not good enough."

"Don't do a number on yourself, Gus. It's just my old man. He's a rabid anti-Gentile."

"I hope you haven't inherited his prejudices."

"Would I marry you if I had?" he asked.

"I don't know," she said; "I don't know why you want to marry me."

"Because I need you to love me."

"But I do—"

"More than anyone else, and more than anyone else does—"

"I do!"

"More than your old friend—"

"Old friend?"

"—with the phone."

"His name is Richard."

Norman was running his thumbnail along the inside of her arm, where the veiny network that lay just under the skin, like the tracery of seaweed near a pond's surface, branched out into sudden complication, busy as a cloverleaf highway. He pressed his thumb into the tender crook of elbow.

"Hey, that hurts," Gus said. Norman pressed down harder, then released her.

"More than Richard," he said.

"More than Richard."

He had gripped her by both wrists and forced her under him. Her eyes smarted. "More than anyone else?"

"More than anyone else—"

He couldn't think of names; he needed names, but there were none to be had. It was as if he were watching himself from far off, from the back of a theater; he was on stage, acting a role that had been written for him by someone else—and he had forgotten his lines! Wildly, he asked, "More than your parents?"

Gus twisted her head away from his; his voice bored into

her brain through her ear like a pneumatic drill. It made her feel about as responsive as a slab of concrete.

"Answer me," Norman said.

He had to say it again: "Answer me."

"Yes," she whispered.

Then he rolled off her like a wave off a rock. He didn't know what to do now, and simply lay there, looking at the ceiling. He was sorrowful—but also amazed. He couldn't quite believe he was behaving like such a bastard.

Gus started to get up, but he pulled her back down.

"Now what," she said. She was wondering if she shouldn't just get out of this for good, right now. But Norman was looking at her with those lost-kid eyes, and she supposed she could understand why he had had to get her to say that. His father had kicked him out of the family because of her. She owed him something. Richard said she owed him, but she owed Norman.

"What are you thinking?" He kissed her bitten nail, touched his fingers to the scruff of her neck. "I'm sorry." And he was; he didn't mean to scare her. "I couldn't stop myself."

The light from the lamp was falling on her dark-honey hair, and he moved his hand up to touch it. She was sitting beside him, but he was still lying down, on his back. She was wearing a white blouse with a square collar, like a sailor's middy, and the light and the angle of his perspective made shadows under her breasts, so that the tops of them, through the cloth, seemed very white and full. He moved his hand to the top button. When he slipped his hand inside, her skin was hot. The classy coolness would melt in his mouth like an M&M.

"I don't know," Gus said. "I don't think—"

"Don't think," Norman said. "I thought, and look where it got me."

"Where's that?"

"Columbia," he said. She laughed, and he seized the chance to work her blouse out of her waistband. She sank onto his chest, her hair and blouse billowing over him like silk veils, white and gold in the bright night light.

13

Gus had a practice schedule and she kept to it rigorously. She practiced every morning from seven until eleven, except on the days when she had a lesson with Julie Baker; on lesson days, she knocked off at nine-thirty. Six afternoons a week she practiced again from two to four; once a week she swam in a friend's condominium pool or at the YWCA. Swimming was good for the lungs.

If she skipped a session, she felt disoriented. Playing the flute was the way she aligned herself spiritually, centering her soul in its happiest relation to the rest of the world.

Nevertheless, she knew that practice alone would not win for her the transcendently focal place she would like to occupy publicly. About this, Norman's hoary joke was wrong. A concert career took money.

When she telephoned her parents in Chapel Hill to tell them she had become engaged, this was the first thing they reminded her of. "You've explained it to me often enough," her mother, a keypunch operator, said. "You said you have to have money, or else you have to marry into the business. A conductor or an entrepreneur. Weren't you dating a conductor?"

"Not exactly," Gus said.

"You must have known how we would feel."

"But you knew it was a long shot. It was you and Dad who

wanted me to have the degree to fall back on. Now I'm falling back on it."

"No, you're not. You're just getting married. You haven't even *tried* yet, Augusta. All your life, you'll wonder—"

"I'm not giving up the flute, for heaven's sake!"

"Who will pay for the concert halls? Tell me that. Critics don't come to hear housewives. Who will pay for your first record?"

"Look, Mom. The odds were against me anyway. It's not just the money, it's the instrument. How many Rampals does the world need when there's only one Boulez Sonatina? The repertoire is limited, to say the least."

"But you knew that—" The disappointment in her mother's voice was rending Gus's heart; for a heart, she had an old sheet, and it was being ripped into rags. This was supposed to have been a *merry* telephone call.

"But I'm in love!" she said.

"Weren't we all? That doesn't mean you have to get married."

"Mother!"

"I'm sorry to shock you, but I don't see giving up your work and future for what? Children."

"Thanks a lot."

"You know what I mean. And that brings up another point," her mother added, crossly. "Are you pregnant?"

"No!" Gus said. "People keep asking me that," she said, sulkily. "You'd think two people never got married without one of them being pregnant."

"It's just that nobody expected you to get married. Not yet, Augusta. Do you know what your father and I paid to send you to Siena? What about Juilliard? Does this—this *Norman*—does he have any money?"

"No. Well, he did, but now his father won't give it to him."

"Did he do something to disgrace himself?"

"Apparently. He got engaged to me."

There was a prolonged wait, during which Gus could hear an ambulance screaming in the distance, a truck backfiring on West End Avenue, somebody calling to somebody else from the opposite side of the street, gears grinding at the stoplight, Tweetie splashing in his bath, her own breathing . . . but not a sound from her mother. Finally, in the Southern accent that always surprised Gus long-distance because in between telephone calls she forgot how it sounded, her mother said, "I guess you aren't planning on a big wedding."

"No."

"What would you like for a wedding present?"

"We'll let you know."

Another stretch, a silent space like a study hall. Gus said, "Will you tell Dad?"

Her father would be at work. This could mean in the field, in the lab, at the biology department at UNC–Chapel Hill, or in his studio at home. All her life, her parents had made a joke about how her father had a pencil attached to his hand permanently, like a sixth finger. Gus, hanging on, on the telephone, scanned the leaf sketches on the wall: holly, hawthorn, and mountain ash; laburnum, locust, Lombardy poplar, and willow; maple, sycamore, chestnut, elm, and oak; and the beautiful lime, with its leaf like a heart, its branches shady with waving valentines in the chlorophyll color of creation. There wasn't a trace of talent for music in Gus's family background, but her parents liked to say she got her manual dexterity from them.

"I'll tell him, but he's not going to be happy about this."

"So far, nobody is, except Norman and me."

There was a third interval then, while Gus waited for her mother to make up her mind how she felt. Gus's mother always thought to herself. She also laughed to herself, cried to herself, and in general kept herself to herself. From an early age, Gus had appreciated the fact that this made her mother easier to deal with than other mothers; by the time *her* mother came out with a statement or took a stand, it was a considered statement or stand, and a daughter knew exactly what the opposition, if there was opposition, was. There was none of the hysterical shifting around, none of the sniping from hastily grabbed positions, that her friends got involved in. On the other hand, it also meant that she had spent much of her life waiting while her mother reached a conclusion. Now her mother, in that softly resolute and faintly nasal drawl, a voice like a family heirloom from antebellum days, said, "You know we're always here for you to fall back on?" Like the degree.

And Gus said, "I know," because she did; she could base her answer of security on a lifetime of knowing that when her mother ultimately decided what she wanted to say, it was indeed what she wanted to say.

But after Gus had hung up, she couldn't bring herself to pick up the flute, she felt so emotionally tangled. It was two-thirty in the afternoon, and the weather had changed. It had been a summer so hot the city seemed to melt, things going liquid at their edges: the street at the far end of the block appeared to undulate like a black river, the skyscrapers looked molten, the sun looked as sticky as a lemon drop left on a dashboard, the sky bled into the gaps between buildings like an illustration into the margins of a page. Then the change had come. There had been a week of finely tuned rain, seven days of silky drizzle, and now the sky was blue again, but cold. The pigeons fluffed up their feathers to keep warm.

That night, Gus didn't see anyone. She sat at her table, next to a window which had been raised by a crack to let in the sharp, fresh air. The night sky was assertive, brilliant. Vega, that blue note Orpheus was wont to strum on his starry lyre, graced the northwest. The pearl on her finger danced in the light from the favorite lamp. Could she never look back, once married, on the future as it might have been?

Gus knew she had "something special" (she was afraid that to be more specific would be tempting the muse). Her tone was extraordinary. In 1961, when she was seventeen, she had had one summer in Maine at Kincaid's camp. It was the old master's last good summer; she had been the last of his protégés. When she had auditioned, he'd said simply, "I like what I hear, I like what I hear," in the steel-wool voice of someone who knew his preferences were all the aesthetic criteria anybody should need—and knew too that his listening time as well as his playing time was almost up. He had already had one stroke. When he died a few years later, he willed his platinum flute to his famous former student, the great Elaine Shaffer, but Gus had been the very last of his students, a seventeen-year-old with a tone straight out of heaven, a piquant upper lip, and an admirable ability to put away pounds of potatoes at the camp suppers without gaining a single ounce.

Then there were the summers in Siena with Gazzelloni. He was a different kind of teacher—arrogant, competitive, high-strung, but the world's leading flutist when it came to contemporary music. She learned Varese with him, Messiaen. (The latter he taught reluctantly; it wasn't new enough to interest him.) She learned Petrassi, Boulez, Berio, Nono. For a while, key-slapping—making a percussive noise by slapping the keys of the flute forcefully—was all the rage. She learned how to sight-read contemporary notation, how to improvise. In 1965, she graduated from college, having sneaked in a few lessons with Murray Panitz, the one whose sound seemed to her supreme—and having begun her first affair, with Richard. Now she was starting her second year at Juilliard, with Julie Baker, and should she do what she was doing, give it all up without a backward glance (because a backward glance would surely, like Orpheus's, be death)? A concert career, as Gus now said to herself again, does take money. It's an open secret: you need a backer. The world was not overrun with people wanting to spend their money on flutists. Pianists, yes; violinists, maybe. But not flutists. The world, of course, *was* overrun with musicians of all kinds who had everything they needed for a concert career except the money it took. She could switch to orchestra playing, but all these years had gone to learning the solo repertoire. Moreover, her tone had a rare, mellifluous quality, sweet as manna in the wilderness, blown on a wind out of Paradise into the desert, a tone mystic in its ability to fly straight to the hearer's heart. What a waste, to dilute it with an orchestra; and moreover again, she had her own ideas about what she wanted to do with the flute—it would kill her, having to subject herself to the rigidity of a stick.

She could wait for a more convenient marriage, as her mother wanted her to do. But who knew that it would come along? Men like Richard were always already married. Nor was there any guarantee that somewhere in the world existed a man who would not only marry her but finance a debut.

And besides, besides, besides—she reminded herself, slightly disconcerted to find that it had slipped her mind— she *was* in love. Richard was a beautiful dear friend and she loved having him call her, but he didn't do for her what Norman did. Norman took her breath away.

Took her breath away. The words seemed to wrap themselves around her throat like a scarf, strangling her. All at once, she felt cold, and jumped up to slam the window shut.

14

It was the season of second thoughts. Norman fretted over the lack of freedom in the world, as he saw it. He felt constrained and irritable, like a child in a playpen. He walked up Broadway to Columbia, hunched over in his unbelted Burberry trench coat, bucking the chill wind, and if he appeared to be carrying the weight of the world on his shoulders, it was because he was carrying the weight of the world on his shoulders. You see, if every proposition had to be either true or false, then the proposition "It is true that Norman Gold will marry Augusta" *had been* true or false, but *not* neither or both, long before they'd met each other; from eternity, in fact. And the proposition "It is true that Norman Gold will accomplish a revolution in intellectual thought" was already determined, came with its truth-value attached to it like a luggage tag. Or if truth or falsity only descended upon a proposition at a certain time, like the Shechinah, the Light of lights, on Mount Sinai when Moses received the Ten Commandments, or over the Shabbas feast on Friday at sunset, what happened to the conditional tense? "If Norman marries Gus, he will (will not) accomplish a revolution in intellectual thought" — was that true, false, both, or none of the above? The clear sky seemed hard as ice, as if a well-aimed pick might chip off cubes of cloud.

15

NORMAN AND AUGUSTA were married at City Hall on the last day of January, with Philip Fleischman, Norman's erstwhile blood-brother, and Phil's current girl, Dinky, acting as witnesses. Gus wore pale yellow wool, a navy coat, and bone-colored shoes and panty-hose, but the sleet turned the toes of her shoes black when the wedding party returned to the street.

"Right," Phil said, with a great air of taking charge, "who wants a drink?"

They went to Max's Kansas City, because Phil had a car and because he said Max's Kansas City was the place to go. Gus and Norman, as Upper West Siders, were both inclined to lose track of which was "the" place to go. Phil mocked himself for knowing the in-scene and blamed it on his profession, trendiness being an occupational hazard of counter-culture advertising, but the innocent glow in his round cheeks gave him away. For Phil, heaven was eating chick-peas in a crowded room with red walls screened by swirling smoke.

For Gus, heaven was being called "Mrs. Gold."

"Here's to Mrs. Norman Gold," Phil said, holding his glass high in the air. At that moment, the crowd standing next to their booth swung in their direction, an unpredicted surge of the human current, and connected with Phil's shoulder. The glass tipped, the drink spilled, and Dinky ended up with a lap full of liquor. During the confusion, Norman sprang his surprise on Gus: "Guess where we're spending the night," he said, whispering mysteriously into her ear. He named a hotel.

"You're crazy!"

"Bridal suite." His heart was full of love, overflowing like Phil's drink.

A suspicion entered Gus's mind. "Phil put you up to this, didn't he?"

"Phil," Dinky said disgustedly, "isn't capable of putting anybody up to anything. Or anything up to anybody."

"You don't even know what they're talking about," Phil said to Dinky. "Here, dry your own lap."

Norman said, "This conversation is getting entirely too gross for newlyweds. Gus and I are splitting."

"Where are we going?" Gus asked.

"You know."

"I don't," Dinky said.

"But I have to go home first. To pack."

"I packed for you," Norman said.

"The suitcase is in the car," Phil said.

Gus was not sure she liked this. She had thought she was getting married of her own free will, but it was beginning to feel as though she was being abducted.

Norman paid the check and they walked two by two back to the car. The wind was cutting a path down the street like a lawnmower made of air, whirring over the pavement. Dinky, a brunette model with exophthalmic eyes and a trick of wetting her lips with her tongue between words as if her speech might otherwise stall at her large, white teeth—it gave her a faintly oiled character, in keeping with the cosmetic and perfumery oils that surrounded her—said, "My skirt is going to freeze under my coat. Thanks to you, Philip. I'm going to get arthritis in my pelvis and be frigid for the rest of my life."

"If you ask me," Phil said, "you've got arthritis of the brain." He retrieved the suitcase from the trunk. "We could give you a lift," he said to Norman.

"No," Norman said, cutting him off quickly, hailing a cab. He wanted to be alone with Gus as soon as possible. Christ, she was his wife, and he hadn't yet had a second of peace in which to think what that might mean. It had to mean more than chickpeas in Max's Kansas City. All the way to the hotel, he was silent, thinking, his hand on Gus's bone-colored knee, a smile slung across his face in a wide loop like a lariat, smoke from his cigarette curling upward into his long lashes. Sleet coated the taxi's windshield, and with every sweep of the wipers, there was a thick whooshing sound that reached them in the back seat.

"Some weather," the driver said.

"Yeah," said Norman.

"You guys don't look like you're from out of town, if you know what I mean."

"We're not. And that's no guy," Norman said, jerking his thumb at Gus, "that's my wife."

"Hee, hee, hee," the driver laughed, drawing air inward with each long, harsh syllable. He never seemed to exhale. His back and shoulders, bent over the wheel, just kept rising, filling with heated air from the dashboard vents, the stink of gasoline and wet wool and cigarette smoke. Norman listened to the man's indrawn laughter and imagined the day when he would simply float through the roof of his cab, literally carried away by some joke.

Gus pulled at Norman's coat sleeve. She had been thinking too. The plan had been that they would return to her apartment, finish putting her stuff in boxes, spend the night, and in the morning, on the first of February, move her in to Norman's place. He lived on West Eighty-eighth, and like her, he had only one room, but his room was larger. She would have liked to keep her old room as a private studio, but they couldn't afford it, not with sources of income being cut off all around them. How could they pay for this? She tugged at his sleeve again, but he still didn't notice. In a fit of desperation, a kind of ontological claustrophobia, she said in a voice much too loud, "What about Tweetie-Pie?"

"Your wife has a lithp," the driver said. "Hee, hee, hee!"

"You," Gus said to the driver, "are an ass."

"Phil will bring him over in the morning," Norman said to Gus.

"I'm an aththt," the driver said. "Hee, hee, hee!"

That braying was still echoing in Norman's head after he and Gus—*his wife*—had been shown to their room and he had tipped the bellhop and shut the door and they had both thrown their coats on the settee in the first of the two rooms that composed their suite. He had managed to sign the register and stand upright without his knees buckling out from under him in the elevator, but he was sure the eyes of the hotel had been trained on him all the way. Now he and Gus were alone in a strange room and the quietness of it was overwhelming, appalling. Normally, being alone with Gus was an unself-conscious pleasure, but here, in this suite of rooms designed for Love with a capital L, every object in it invisibly labeled LOVE, Norman felt as if he'd been handed a sheet of instructions or a list of standards to be met. The settee shouted LOVE, the drapes shouted LOVE, the bed in the next room shouted LOVE, all in a disappearing ink visible only to the infra-red eyes of people in the know, the throbbing outlines of the letters pounding against his informed retinae.

"Take a look at this," Gus said, calling from the bedroom. "One of us, me I guess, is supposed to take a bath in this bathroom in here, and meanwhile"—she left the bedroom and walked back to the sitting room—"you take your bath in this bathroom in here. That way I'm in bed waiting for you when you come in, in your robe and pajamas."

"I don't have any pajamas."

"Well," she said, "then we'll have to forget the whole thing. Scrub the whole marriage. It just isn't going to work if you walk through that door in your jockey shorts. That is obviously not what the architect had in mind."

"Your feet must be soaking wet. Why don't you take your shoes off?"

"Okay." But when Gus had her shoes and panty-hose off, Norman put his hand on her cool calf, and ran his fingers up the inside of her leg, inching them under the elastic leg band of her bikini underpants.

"Take your dress off," Norman commanded.

They were standing by the window in the sitting room but the drapes were closed . . . heavy, figured drapes that made the room seem timeless—as if the room were airtight, sealed against the world and the corruption of change. A languid gold light, overrich as syrup, lay in thick, inert pools on the deep-pile carpet.

Gus reached both arms around her back to unzip her dress, and the action twisted her at an angle so exquisite in relation to Norman that she nearly fainted. Norman had to take his hand away to pull the dress over her head, and he brought her underpants down when he did. Then she shut her eyes as he drew the dress over her face and took her into his arms, dispensing with the bra, and when she opened them again, looking over his navy-suited shoulder in the direction of the door, she saw the bellhop.

She screamed.

The bellboy jumped. He would have put Nureyev to shame. He jumped so high, kicking his legs to turn around at the same time, that he could almost be said to be dancing. But he wasn't dancing. He was running, out of an instinct as old as the Lascaux Caves, an instinct for self-preservation that said it was not safe to look on another man's naked wife. It was evidently an instinct with as much urgency behind it in the twentieth century as in the Pleistocene period, and if Norman was anything to go by, it had retained its validity, because Norman turned around, saw the bellhop, and wanted to kill.

The bellhop had fled, a single, useless, courteous phrase

left lingering behind him in the room, the result of a kind of time-lag as if he were traveling faster than the speed of sound. It was, "Compliments of the management, sir," and it had been delivered with a magnum of champagne in an ice pail which the boy dropped clattering on the coffee table as he turned tail and ran. Norman took off after him.

The first leg of the race was a straight stretch of hotel carpeting from the room to the elevator; then there was a hallway-crossing, and the bellhop made a sharp swerve to the left. Norman caught hold of him in front of an open linen closet.

"You fucking popeyed bastard," he said (strictly metaphorically, as the boy, unlike Norman, had not even been thinking of fucking, and, unlike Dinky, was not at all exophthalmic, *and,* as Norman was to learn later, was definitely not illegitimate).

"You fucking popeyed bastard," Norman said again, with emphasis, unable to think of anything else—and kayoed him with a left uppercut to the jaw and a right to the stomach (Norman was lefthanded).

The boy fell backward into the closet, bringing down shelves of sheets, pillowcases, towels, washcloths, toilet paper, detergent, and a broom. Maids materialized from nowhere, blossoming in the doorways of rooms all along the hall, like primroses springing up after an April shower.

They were standing there, the primrose maids, dumbstruck, and the bellboy was lying there, among the linen, and Norman slowly began to realize what he had done. Without saying a word to anyone, carefully, like a silent film rewinding, he edged back in the direction he had come. When he was around the corner, he tore back to the room. Gus had locked the door.

"For God's sake, Gus," he shouted in a stage whisper, "let me in!"

Gus opened the door and he whisked into the room but

she latched the door again afterward. She was dressed in jeans and one of his shirts but her face was as white as dough and as ready to crumble as a matzo cracker. "What happened?" she asked.

"I hit him."

"You what?"

"What do you think I did? Asked him back to play gin rummy?"

"It's not funny."

"I'm not laughing."

Gus was. Hysterically. "Oh God," she said. "I'm sorry, Norman, but you should have seen the look on your face when you turned around and saw him."

Norman didn't at all like being laughed at, and, disgruntled, answered, "I was looking at the look on *his* face when he saw *you*."

This sobered her up. "The whole hotel will know," she said. "You were still *dressed*."

"What has that got to do with it?" he asked, puzzled.

"Well," she said, "well . . . I don't know how to explain it, but it has a lot to do with it. It's so . . . unequal, somehow."

"You're not in North Carolina," he said. "Nobody's going to be shocked. We were only doing what you're expected to do in hotels. You can guess what goes on in the other rooms."

"But they aren't bridal suites."

Norman was beginning to feel beleaguered, and he did not quite understand why this should be so, particularly on his wedding day. Holding himself in with the last of his patience, he took one more stab at getting through to Gus. She was *supposed* to be a fairly rational person; she was *supposed* to be straightforward, as girls went. How could the simple process of becoming a bride scramble a woman's brains beyond recognition?

"Gus," he said, "that is all the more reason they won't be

shocked to hear that you took your clothes off in this room."

"It's not the same thing," Gus said, wistfully. "For you to be dressed and me not is almost decadent. You can tell that by the layout of the bathrooms. We weren't *supposed* to start making love the minute we walked through the door."

Norman flung himself on the settee and tried to think. It seemed to him that lately he was thinking more and enjoying it less.

There, on the coffee table in front of him, was the champagne.

"I guess we could have a glass of champagne," he said. "If I can get the cork off." He was half afraid to try.

But the cork came off beautifully, and Norman managed to pour the champagne into the chilled glasses successfully, and that made him begin to feel better, and after a while he called room service and ordered Chateaubriand. Unfortunately, the radiator went on the blink, and the hotel had to send up a man to fix it because the room was growing cold, and he, the man, came up with the food. He talked all during dinner. He directed all of his observations, which were chiefly about the weather, the plumbing, hippies, and, for some reason, Howard Hughes, to Norman, man to man, dumping Gus conversationally, so that she felt like a dangling participle. She kept looking at him while he was talking—he seemed to think it was all right for a woman to look at him—trying to determine whether he had heard about their contretemps, but she couldn't decide yes or no. After he left, the radiator resumed its comfortable hissing, and the room grew warm again, as if someone had spread an invisible blanket over the settee and coffee table and chairs and carpet. She watched a late movie while Norman read the newspaper which the maintenance man had left behind, and when the screen said THE END, she went to the window and drew the heavy draperies wide open. It was snowing. The flakes were as large and soft as cotton balls. Illumined

by the street light, snow edging the sill looked like lace; falling against the traffic lights, it looked like colored sugar—
spun sugar, because it was spun in the sky by the winter wind
and spiraled downward in a vast and lovely confusion.

"I packed a nightgown for you," Norman said, behind her.

"I saw."

"It's getting late." He was proceeding cautiously, testing
gently, wishing he could read her mood in the way she stood.
Her hair was so close to his mouth that it seemed it might
leap to his tongue, like nylon to a metal comb. It was as if her
whole body was breathing, and he wanted to inhale every
inch of it. "Do you want me to meet you in bed, as planned
by the architect?"

She nodded, not yet quite ready to shatter her mood of
snow, but when they were both in the big bed in the other
room, she whispered, in the dark, "Norman, I'm scared."

He didn't answer at first, not knowing what she expected
of him. "I think," he said, "it's natural. At least, I hope it is,
because I am scared shitless. But I'm not sure you should tell
me that's how you feel if that's how you feel."

"Why on earth not, if that's how I feel?"

"Look at it, Gus." He lit a cigarette. "You're telling me
you're not sure I'm right for you. It may be a natural fear but
hearing you state it is not exactly reassuring to me. If you ask
me," he said, "it's a classic demonstration of displaced hostil-
ity."

"Nobody asked you. Would you mind putting out that
cigarette? The smoke isn't good for my lungs."

"You never told me that before, Gus."

"You never asked. I've worked very hard to develop my
diaphragm muscles."

Norman stubbed the cigarette out in the ashtray on his
side of the bed. He had to use the butt as a flashlight to locate the ashtray on the table, before he could stub it out.

"Anyway," Gus said, "you already got your own back by

telling me you're just as scared as I am. I don't know why we shouldn't be a little nervous. It's not every day that people vow to spend the rest of their lives together."

Norman felt as if his heart was a rose planted in the garden of his soul, and somebody was digging it up for transplant, every root torn from its rightful place. "Do you think you may have made a mistake?" he asked her, barely able to squeeze the question past his throat.

"That's not it!" What was it? A sense of missed possibility. She would have liked to marry the world; instead, she was cutting herself off from most of it. And she did mean "marry," not "sleep with." Or maybe "sleep with" *was* what she meant. How could she know, if she'd never found out? "Norman," she pleaded, thinking of the wide world to be seen, "let's go to Africa."

"Sure. First thing in the morning," he said.

"I'm serious. To see the hippopotami."

"And the rhinoceri."

"And the anthropophagi."

"Wildebeests."

"Elephants."

"Giraffes! Zebras! Gazelles!"

"The poisonous horned viper!"

"Come on, what do you know from horned vipers?"

"You see," Gus said, weeping, sitting up, and biting her knee, "you see how little you know about me? My father used to work in a zoo. When he was putting himself through school. He was an assistant."

"Take it easy," Norman said; "you're hysterical."

"I'm not, I'm not." She did know perfectly well what she was doing, but she couldn't stop herself; she wanted him to be just as alarmed as she was. When she caught the note of panic in his voice, she calmed down.

"Hey," he said, soothing her, "relax." He pulled her down beside him and stroked her forehead until she was still. It seemed to him that he held his future in his arms, and that it was going to require infinite attention and tenderness if it was to turn out the way he wanted. Deep exhaustion seized him.

So Gus pretended to fall asleep in Norman's arms, but he fell asleep first. The radiator stopped steaming. The room grew cold again; Augusta's nose on the outside of the blanket felt as cold to her own touch as a puppy's muzzle. She used to have a dog called Caesar. It seemed to her unbearably sad, that she once had a dog called Caesar and no longer did. She listened to Norman's breathing. There was always something urgent about it, his sleep-breath, something superintense, as if to breathe by night called for as much concentration as thinking by day. It seemed to Gus odd that she could never know her own night breathing as she knew Norman's, this rasp scrabbling through the netherside of day like a mole through mud: it was already imprinted in her brain along with the coded pattern of her own heartbeat. Time, slowed almost to a standstill, might be measurable only by some such corporeal signature. Then Gus thought of something else, and smiled to herself in the dark: Norman was sleeping with the light off.

16

THE PIECE OF PAPER was on the table in front of Norman. (The table was two feet wide and twenty feet long, a counter running two-thirds the length of the room; Phil had knocked it together one day when Norman was complaining about not being able to find a desk large enough. It was desk, dinner bench, shelf, telephone table.) Gus was at school, and the hum of the electric clock seemed to grow louder and louder in the dusty stillness of the enormous room. "What the hell," Norman said, as much to hear his own voice as for any other reason. Then he picked up the telephone at his elbow and dialed his father's office.

"I'll try," Jocelyn said, "but I don't think he'll take it."

"Tell him that the Mafia will be after his ass if he doesn't. It could be the end of a beautiful relationship between Amato and Leibowitz, and His Honor is going to find himself up a certain well-known creek without a paddle if that happens."

Sid was on the line before Norman had finished this speech, although he would not have said he was eavesdropping, exactly. Norman heard Jocelyn signing off. Did he detect a sense of relief? He wondered what Jocelyn did for a home life.

"What's this about the Mafia?" Sid shouted. "What the hell do you know from Leibowitz and Amato? Stick to musicology, Norman. You could offend your aesthetic sensibilities mixing in politics."

"I may have exaggerated. Actually, there's no immediate threat from the Mafia."

"I knew it. This is a trick. You're disowned, Norman. Didn't I tell you not to get in touch with me so long as you remain married to that—that *Gold-digger?*" There was a pause while Sid waited to see if Norman caught the pun. When Norman didn't laugh, Sid laughed for him. "Why the hell aren't you laughing?" he demanded, sinuses aching. "That was pretty good, wasn't it?"

"Yeah, Pop, terrific. But listen, I'm calling for a specific reason, and believe it or not, it's important to you."

"This I find difficult to believe."

"I'm being sued."

The electric clock began to hum again, and Tweetie, who

had been napping, woke up and pecked at his bird seed. Norman knocked a cigarette out of the pack against the edge of the table and lit it with one hand.

"Sued?"

"That's what I said."

"I *heard* what you said. What I want to know is why and by whom and what it has to do with me."

Norman cleared his throat. "I thought you might want to know those things. I say suit, but it isn't precisely a suit."

"How is it imprecisely a suit, I'd like to know?"

"It's more the threat of a suit, actually. And attendant publicity. When you get right down to it, it's the publicity that's the threat. From your standpoint, anyway. You see, there's this bellhop. His name is Mario—"

"A bellhop!"

"—well, and he's only fifteen. He didn't look so young to me, but there it is. I sort of slugged him. His mother objects. She says I could have ruined his looks and thereby his future. I don't even remember what he looked like."

"Where did you do this?"

He named the hotel.

"And what were you doing there, you should forgive me for asking?"

"Honeymooning."

"And you go around slugging bellhops on your honeymoon? What kind of a marriage is this?"

"I can't explain, it just happened."

"So, okay. This is not such a big deal, only weird. Where do I come in?"

"Like this. It's not justice Mario's mother wants, it's bread. Maybe that comes to the same thing, I don't know. I feel I had a perfect right to knock his goddamn block off, but her point is that if they take me to court, it won't matter whether they lose or I lose, because they will spread it all over the papers that the son of a Jewish judge who is hoping to sit on the Supreme Court is going around beating up Italian bellhops. She seems to be a very well informed woman, Mario's mother. And you know what it will do to the King's County machinery if Amato withdraws his support for Leibowitz. If Leibowitz even thinks that's a possibility, he'll dump you faster than if Bonanno already had a contract out on you."

"Don't tell me, I can surmise the rest. You're asking me for the money to keep you out of court."

"I'm not asking for it," Norman said, exasperated. "I'm giving you the chance to offer it if you don't want my name and yours in the news. It is still the same name even though you've disowned me. I'm only thinking about what this could do to you. Besides, I was under the impression you liked buying people off. As for me, I couldn't care less. It might even be a gas to go to court," he added, defiantly.

"*Please*, Norman, do not use that expression. Okay," Sid said. "It is clearly a case of being held by the short hairs. You want to come here tomorrow, I'll give you the money. I trust it's a one-time shot and that the asking price is not exorbitant."

"I'll be there at noon, Pop. This time, make mine salami."

17

Norman kept the matter of the "suit" to himself; there was no need for Gus to know about it. She was perfecting the Berio and the last thing she needed was to worry about money.

A new sense of his own capacity for being solicitous rose up in Norman; he felt as though he was expanding emotionally, stretching his feeling-muscles. There were nuances of emotion he had never realized in himself before. He worked on his dissertation in a state of heightened vitality. Every morning he kissed Gus good-bye, leaving her to practice in the big room. On days when she went up to Juilliard, she'd meet him at Columbia on her way back, and they would grab a bite to eat at the West End Bar. February was as cold as a chunk of ice; it melted into March. The wind clattered down Broadway like a truck. One day Norman met Mario and his mother in a pizza parlor at the Ninety-sixth Street intersection.

Mario's startling blue eyes were sullen and rebellious; he sat silently, every once in a while throwing his head back to shake the straight, dramatically dark hair out of his eyes. The rest of the time he cleaned his nails with a penknife, like a model hood, but the fingers were long and delicate, and his bone structure was refined, princely, almost spiritual, as if God, breathing life into his creatures, had happened to linger over this one with a long, loving, life-despairing sigh. His mother told him to sit up.

"This is all there is," Norman said to her, shoving the money at her in an unmarked envelope across the formica table top.

"I am not an avaricious person," she said. "I want only what's right for my son." She spoke in tones so low Norman had to lean across the table to catch them. Her face, under the soft-brimmed hat, was stunning, a large, handsome face with sad, let-down eyes, a mouth with a single fine crease on either side suggestive of a highly sensual cross between emotional deprivation and physical amplitude. Her figure, under the black cloth, was statuesque. She was wearing widow's weeds. Norman was not entirely sure what to say to a noble-looking, elegant widow in a hat in a pizza parlor who was blackmailing him. As he bent toward her dropped voice,

Norman felt dizzy. Her musky odor mingled with the smell of pepperoni and Parmesan. "I won't lead you on," she said, and for a moment, Norman felt disappointed. "I am not a blackmailer."

"That's good. There's no more where that came from." He said this loudly, all the more loudly because she spoke so softly, but still she didn't raise her voice.

She made a tsk-ing sound deep in her throat, a milky, female sound. "There *is* more," she said, with delicate emphasis. "There is always more. If there were not more, blackmailers—of whom I am not one—would go out of business. It is a law, an economic law." She looked at him, and Norman thought her glance managed to be simultaneously shrewd and sad, as if she were waiting for him to betray her. But as there was no earthly way he could do that, nor would he if he could, there was, to Norman's mind, something melodramatic in her manner, something of a pose struck purely for effect. He imagined this was attributable to his lack of information: if he knew the etiology of that tenderly accusing look, he might understand its appropriateness. In the condition of increased alertness that had settled on him since his marriage, Norman avidly desired to absorb the fullest amount of meaning from every experience circumstance vouchsafed to him. He listened intently. "An economic law," she repeated. "The basis of capitalism."

He couldn't help raising an eyebrow.

"You think a poor woman can't know about capitalism," she said, her eyes downcast, the hat tipped, her face in shadow. "Who has a better right to know? A poor woman, always at the mercy of men like Marx, Adam Smith, Keynes, Veblen, and John Kenneth Galbraith. I am a woman, a poor woman"—she had picked up the envelope containing two thousand dollars in notes of one hundred and was holding it in front of her chin like a Japanese fan—"I, a woman, will tell you something. After all, you have helped me; perhaps I should return the favor. *There is always more money where it comes from!*"

"Don't talk so loud, Mama," Mario said, embarrassed.

Her voice had risen alarmingly, and Norman hastily scanned the pizza parlor, but no one was looking at them. Mario's mother regained her da Vinci, grief-engraved pose. "My son is a man," she said, without any indication that she was aware of reaching a logical impasse. "So he does not understand economics. Where money exists in the first place, there is always more of it." It was a sort of steady-state theory of economics. "The ramifications of this law," she said, her fingers stroking the hollow of her snowy throat with a certain absent-minded seductiveness, "are astounding."

"Probably," said Norman, entranced, "but your theory has one flaw in it."

"Sit up, Mario. What do you mean, flaw?"

"I mean, even if there *were* more money where this comes from, I can't get my hands on it. So you might just as well lay off me."

"Is that a way to talk to a lady?" she asked, softly, the hint of aggrievedness strengthened. "I told you, I am not going to blackmail you. But I am giving you some motherly advice"—she threw him a nonmotherly look—"as if you were my own son Mario here, sit up, Mario. I am telling you, if you want more, you can get more. Now, you look to me as if possibly you're going to want more. How do I know? You're a young man, you have a young wife. You have a sensitive face, deep eyes. You are a thinker, a philosopher, an *artiste*. The machinations of big business are not for you. Neither are the working classes for you. Would you work from nine to five every day for somebody else, when your mind is on higher things? No. Your face tells me. So I say to you, as a mother would, Do unto yourself as you have just done unto me." She kissed the envelope. "Mario," she said, "don't pick your nails with the penknife."

"They're dirty, Mama."

"What I don't understand," Norman said, "is why *you're* doing this. Shouldn't you be at home?" He had a vision of her, wrapped in a black shawl and cleaning fish. "In the movies, it's the men who do this kind of thing."

"What kind of thing? I told you, I'm not blackmailing you, I'm earning the money for my son's education, that's all. Also I'm giving you a brief lesson in economics. Think of it as a trade. Besides, my late husband was a man of refinement and education. What makes you think all people of Italian heritage are members of the mob? You confuse us with Sicilians. My late husband, he couldn't stand cruelty. His heart was so tender that if he stepped on an ant by accident he hated himself for the rest of the day. A heart with Accent on it, a heart pounded with a mallet to make it tender. The mallet was Life, what else? He was like you, I would wager, smart but not too bright. And he worked too hard. He was a stockbroker. I met him at Harvard Business School; we were studying for our masters in business administration. He was a good man but, like my son Mario here, sit up, Mario, he was a man. Basically, he thought women should wear black shawls and clean fish, like his mother. The shawl could come from Lord and Taylor and the fish from Gristede's, it was the same thing. So I sat at home and read the theory behind the practice. Durkheim, Talcott Parsons, Max Weber. True economics is home economics. And I learned that my husband was a stockbroker with a Harvard degree but like all these men, he didn't really understand the first thing about money. He had a weakness for the horses."

"Mama!"

"Sit up, Mario. My son worshiped his father. This was reasonable, his father was a fine man, but what does it mean for the son in the end? Sadness, nothing but sadness. The heart took such a beating it gave out."

"Mrs. Solaroli—"

She patted Norman's hand, fleetingly, a pat so restrained it was as erotic as a caress. "Now my son shall go to a good school, with this"—snapping a crimson fingernail against the envelope—"and he will learn from professors to be a jerk about money like you. Or maybe he will become a Marxist. Would you like that, Mario?"

"No, Mama," Mario said, angrily.

"You see, he wants to be an actor. All the time, he's dreaming of Hollywood. Maybe this helps."

"Mrs. Solaroli," Norman said in a last-ditch, effortful push for *terra firma,* "I wasn't kidding. That's *it* for money from me."

Mrs. Solaroli stood up, her regally sad and hat-shadowed form towering over Norman. "Good-bye, Norman," she said, in that gently expiring voice, conveying dignity in the face of insurmountable tragedy, as if these were her last words on earth, "we will never meet again. I promise." She held out her hand and he took it; it rested in his for a single moment. "But maybe you will think about what I said, okay? Come, Mario. *Arrivederci.*"

As they left, Mario leaned down and whispered into Norman's ear. "Punk," he said, hissing, and looking at him violently with his beautiful blue eyes.

18

Each day, Norman expected to hear from Mario's mother, but she seemed to be well and truly gone. There were several snowfalls that winter. The snow lay in long-running ridges like ploughed rows with a black crust of soot on top. There was ice on the sidewalks in the morning and slush in the streets by noon. The chains of the garbage cans clanged against the railings, the tops of the garbage cans slipped and banged against the bottoms, and the tops of cardboard boxes flapped beside the stoops.

Gus felt lonely. This neighborhood wasn't at all like hers, only a few blocks farther north. The buildings here were secretive, blank-faced, closed in. There were no Puerto Ricans hanging around on the stoops to wave to you when you walked to the bus stop. There were two dwarves, in the apartment across the hall, but they kept to themselves.

In their own apartment, Gus and Norman had a double bed with a dark red and blue comforter, the infinite desk, a chest of drawers, bookshelves, a portable television on a stand, two phonographs (his and hers), Tweetie's cage, the favorite lamp, a windowseat under the center window in the tall set of three at the room's street end, a Persian rug Norman's mother had given him years ago when he first moved out of the house in Brooklyn, and a parquet floor. There was a bathroom the size of a closet, and a kitchen smaller than that; both apparently had once been closets. The tiles had peeled from the bathroom walls and schist crumbled into the tub and sink. The kitchen was swarming with cockroaches. Gus could keep them out of the stove—good thing, too, unless you liked fried cockroach—but they crawled over the boxes in the cabinet on the wall above the stove. After a while, she gave up learning to cook and the newlyweds lived off nonalcoholic eggnog, creamed herring, and hotdogs. So far as Gus could tell, Norman didn't seem to notice. Possibly it was what he was used to. Could he be used to fried cockroach as well?

During the day, when most of the tenants were at work, the landlord turned the heat off. Gus told Norman that she could barely manage to practice, her fingers were frozen. Norman told the landlord and the heat began to come up, a small blast at wide intervals. She played the flute in the big, attractive room, with the cockroaches in the kitchen at her back and her fingers tingling with the cold, and when she was through practicing there was nothing to do but wait for Norman to come home from Columbia. Some days she went to Juilliard and used a practice room there, but she couldn't live in a practice room—she had to let other students use it some of the time—and Eighty-eighth Street was too far to make the trip more than once in a day. Besides, she wasn't taking regular classes, and couldn't offer that as an excuse for being at the school all the time; and now that she was married, it seemed to her that the other students had no reason at all to be interested in her anymore. She very much liked to laugh and flirt, but now there was no one around to laugh or flirt with. She would put her flute away when she was through, switch on the television or play a record, and sit in the cold room looking at the cold sky or the cold white walls. The walls were not cheerful like the ones in her old apartment; they were starker, serious walls supporting a high ceiling, meaning business. Gus did not hang her leaves on them. The green seemed frivolous, carefree, out of place in this dark red and blue dissertation-writer's room. But Tweetie-Pie preened, swung, sang, and splashed as unstoppably here as in Gus's old place; and Gus herself, with her happy hair and willful lip, glowed like a candle in the jewel-toned room. Except when she was actively miserable, she smiled, whether she was aware of it or not; smiling was a long-time habit with her, and it persisted even in the change of circumstance.

But she was bored. Even playing the flute did not entirely take the edge off that—it was not as if she could look forward to playing it for real. Waiting for Norman to come home, she began to see how extensible time could be. Each day it stretched a little farther. The afternoons became longer and longer. Time was like a waistband that had lost its elasticity, and it sagged. If Norman came home at lunch, that made it worse: he sometimes came home at noon, horny as a toad, because, he said, he'd been thinking about her all morning when he was supposed to be thinking about the function of the oboe as a displaced phallus in the symphony. Suddenly it would occur to him that *his* oboe was displaced, and he'd rush home, swept by a large yearning for sexual shelter, to stick it where it belonged, but then he'd rush back to Columbia, and Gus was left in the empty apartment to make up the bed for the second time of the day. She decided she needed a job. He turned as black as his briefcase with anger when she told him.

"We could use the money," she said. All they had was his fellowship and some money she had saved from her allowance, which she no longer received.

"We have plenty of money." In fact, the fellowship barely covered his tuition and the rent, and now there were her lessons with Julie Baker, and food—although he wondered how food could cost so much, when it seemed to him that he never got any to eat—and bills for this and that, of which there seemed to be double now that he was married. He owed the telephone company three hundred dollars but they would never get him for that since he had installed a phone in Gus's name. So far as the telephone company was concerned, Norman Gold had vanished. They were getting by; how could Gus call him a failure like this? "You don't need to work," he said.

"But I'm lonely!"

"That is a hell of a thing to say to me," he said.

"I don't see why I can't say it. I'll get a job, and that will solve everything. It will kill two birds with one stone." She looked at Tweetie guiltily.

"I don't want you to work. You're supposed to play the flute."

"And why should I play the flute? For whom am I going to play it? Let's be rational," she said, "the way you're always telling me to be. Do I have a concert to give? No. Do I have a record to make? No. Maybe you would like to hire a hall for me so I can make a debut."

Norman didn't answer at first, and Gus told herself that she shouldn't have said that. She couldn't ask him to be somebody he wasn't—he was a theoretician, not a performer. What did he know about things like concert halls?

"Okay," he said, abruptly. "You get your program in shape. I'll pay for it."

"What are you talking about? We don't have the money for something like that. I don't mind, Norman! I really don't." She was frightened by the dark color of his face, the tension in his neck, the stoniness of his features. "I knew before we got married that I wasn't going to get to make a debut."

"I didn't marry you so you could give up your career."

"I don't want you to ask your father." She was looking at him closely, trying to determine if that was what he had in mind.

"I won't *ask* him," Norman said, not meeting her eyes.

"Are you thinking of getting a job?" It was the first time it had ever occurred to her that *Norman* might go to work. It had not yet occurred to him.

"Don't worry about it," he said.

She didn't. The fight was over, and Gus wasn't one for rehashing arguments. If Norman said she could give a debut recital, that was good enough for her. It was so simple! Why hadn't she ever asked him before? She would tell her mother—all she had ever had to do was *ask*. Norman wouldn't let her down!

Being married was not, after all, so very different from being engaged: Gus thought this with a buoyant sensation of relief, with a feeling of jettisoning darker, heavier freight. At night, in bed, she kissed Norman's reluctant mouth in the blue and white light from the stars and street lamps. It was cold in the room, but it was warm under the quilted comforter.

Norman capitulated, but not without reserve; he was surprised that she didn't seem to sense it, a certain tenseness in his back, a distance in his words, as if he were speaking a foreign language with great facility without having a clue as to what the words actually meant. He felt obscurely threatened. Then suddenly he felt painfully contrite, and, wanting to be friendly, leaned over her sleeping face, cooled her damp cheeks with the back of his hand and whispered. He wanted to ask her what went on in her mind during these silvery hours, but she was already as lost to his wakeful world as an antiworld.

In the morning, Gus woke up in a sunny mood. She took her flute out of its case first thing, and started to polish it. She had a silver flute made by Haynes, with a mouthpiece of gold and a low B key.

Norman made himself a cup of coffee and then wrote out the request for a renewal of his fellowship for the following year. He had been putting it off, but the deadline was tomorrow, and yesterday had shown him it was time to start thinking of the future. When he had finished, he dropped it onto Gus's lap. "Here," he said, "will you type this up now?"

She looked up.

"It's got to get in the mail today," he explained.

"I'm working," she said.

"It won't take a minute."

"Why don't you type it?"

He laughed. "I can't type."

"You mean you've been in school all your life and you never typed a term paper?"

"Will you type the letter?" he asked, getting sore.

"I suppose some chick typed your papers."

"That's right."

"I'm nobody's chick."

"Holy smoke, nobody said you were!"

"Besides, I'm working on my flute."

"It'll only take a minute."

"I'll type it when I finish this, okay?"

"No, not okay. It has to get in the mail this afternoon."
She didn't understand what he was trying to do to her. Didn't he just tell her the night before that she should get down to work? If she was going to be a professional, she had to practice like one. How could she do that and this at the same time? "You'll have to take care of it yourself."

"I explained to you that I didn't know how."

"Then go find yourself a chick with a typewriter," she said, carried away with her own cleverness, the sunlight sparkling on the polished gold of the mouthpiece, the promise of a debut, and Tweetie's cheerful good-morning.

"All right," Norman said, putting on his coat, "I will!" But after he'd got outside, cold air bringing him to his senses as if someone had waked him by pouring cold water on his face, he realized that he no longer knew any chicks. There was D. D. Jones, but she was such a hot-shot artist these days she wouldn't have time to type for him. He wondered what Bunny Van Den Nieuwenhutzen was doing.

When he went back up five minutes later, Gus was crumpled on the bed, crying. She sniffled, penitent and anxious. He patted her on the head like a puppy. He thought he didn't care about the letter anymore, that he cared only about making things right between his wife and himself, but when she typed the letter, he couldn't help feeling faintly satisfied; he became aware of a certain warmth in his groin, as if he'd scored.

19

ALL THIS TIME, Norman had had a sense of unfinished business, of something he had been meaning to do, only he couldn't remember what it was. It had something to do with Birdie Mickle, and something to do with Mario's mother. Now, under pressure of necessity, he made the connection. He had been meaning to find out Miss Mickle's professional name. He remembered this while he was shaving, and the thought excited him so much that he cut himself. He was not a good shaver at the best of times. His beard was heavy and, like his hair, wiry. He had to use a dog comb on his curls. If he used a regular comb, the teeth broke and all day long he rained plastic bits from his scalp.

He stuck a piece of toilet paper on the cut and joined Gus in the big room. She was pulling her panty-hose on. She fell back on the bed as she did this, and he rejoiced in the shape of her long legs, superimposed against the background of snow-filled window.

"I think I'll leave early today," he said.

"How come?"

"I'm broadening my horizons," he said, spontaneously. "I've been focusing too obsessively on the psychoanalysis of music. I think I should open up the field a bit, take a look at music as an index of cultural organization and disintegration. Of course, the composers are unconscious of these connections. They think they are writing the *Götterdämmerung*, for example, when they are really writing the swan song for the Third Reich. And that's another thing."

"What is?"

"Opera. Do you know what they listen to in Red China?"

"What?"

"Opera. An infallible sign of decadence in a nation. Of course, they say we're decadent, but that's only a matter of semantics. When did Rome fall?"

"I don't know."

"When the Italians began to listen to opera. Italy hasn't been a world power since Rossini. The nineteenth century was the last straw. It's the high notes that do it," he added, brimming with elation. "They scramble the brains."

"And you're going to make a dissertation out of this?"

"Poor Gus," he said, kissing her quickly and turning toward the door. "You thought you were taking up the flute out of free will but it was multiply determined that you should become a flutist. Penis envy generates its own necessities. If you examine the matter dispassionately," he said, only half-facetiously, "you will see that by playing the flute you are reflecting the situation of women in American society today. You are part of America in transition." He peeled the toilet paper from his chin. Just before she let go with her shoe, he picked up his books and slipped out the open door and shut it; he heard the shoe slam against the door and slide to the floor. He was grinning as he ran down the steps and hit the street. It was a bright, icy morning, and besides, a wife would have to get up pretty damn early to get the jump on him!

The next item on the agenda was a telephone. He headed for Low Library at Columbia and dialed his father's office. "I don't think he'll speak with you," Jocelyn said.

"That's okay," he said. "Actually, I just wanted a little information that I think you can give me. Do you know Miss Birdie Mickle's professional name?"

"Well," Jocelyn said, "I don't think—"

"It's perfectly all right," Norman said. "You see"—he lowered his voice conspiratorially—"Augusta and I thought Pop might come around to seeing things our way if we arranged a surprise meeting. I could ask Mother, but suppose this doesn't work? The old man might make a big scene, and it would only end with her being upset. Maybe you think we shouldn't try it at all," he plunged on, "but Augusta has her heart set on it. I hate to let her down. We haven't been married very long, you know, less than two months." He knew what his voice sounded like—it was a wonderful instrument. He could do with his voice what Gus could do with her flute: win the world. He played heart-beseeching, lightly laughing, boyishly sexy and ingratiating notes on it. Jocelyn said, "Well, if you're sure it's all right."

"I'm not sure, but I *think* so. I *hope* so." He laughed, engagingly modest. "It's worth a try, anyway, isn't it?"

"Yes, Norman, it certainly is," she said, to build his morale. "*I* can't see what's wrong with a son wanting to make it up with his father. Miss Mickle's professional name is Chicken Delight."

"Oh my God," he said, cracking up.

"What did you say? This connection's not very good."

"Nothing, Jocelyn. But I don't think she'll be listed in the Manhattan directory under that name, do you?" Immediately, he envisioned an ad in the yellow pages.

"Just a minute." She gave him the number. "She works at a place on Times Square. It's just called The Joint."

"Thanks a lot, Jocelyn. I always knew you were a decent person."

"I hope I haven't done the wrong thing," she said, plainly wanting her pay-off: reassurance. "Miss Mickle might not appreciate this."

"Oh, I think she will. She seemed like a well-intentioned woman to me. You both are. Women are terrific," Norman said, enthusiastically. "It's too bad that fathers aren't women."

"Don't tell your father I gave you her number."

"I won't tell a soul, Jocelyn. I'm going to call her as soon as I hang up now."

"Okay," she said. But after she hung up, Norman didn't ring the number he'd written on the inside of the cover of the Thayer biography of Beethoven. He sat in the booth for a few seconds, thinking, and then he buttoned and belted his Burberry trench coat, walked back out into the snow, and hailed a cab.

"Where to?" the driver said.

"Times Square. Do you know a place called The Joint?"

"Do I," said the driver. "Let me tell you, it's a real joint."

20

In other words," Sid said, "you're blackmailing me. I'm not surprised. I knew it would come to this. A one-shot deal, you said, but nobody ever quits with once already. This is a fact of human nature a former D.A. knows like he knows his own name. Myrtle it isn't. So," he said, again, "you're blackmailing me."

"I wouldn't say that."

"I would."

"It seems harsh."

"You're asking me to pay you to keep your mouth shut and you say *I'm* harsh? Oy, for a son I've got a regular little Talmudist. And do you call black white as well?"

"You're working yourself up into a real state of sweat for nothing, Pop. I'm not threatening you where it really hurts, am I? I could"—he reached past his father for the napkin dispenser; they were at a counter in a Chock Full O'Nuts—

"I could suggest that one person who might be especially interested to hear that you're getting nookie from a cookie on the side is Mother, but I would hate to involve her in this shit."

"You do and I'll kill you."

"Watch it, your chili is dripping." They were both eating hot dogs with runny chili. "That would be what? Filicide?"

"That would be a pleasure, that's what it would be."

"I don't see why you have to take it so hard," Norman said, shaking his head. "It's not as if I were doing anything contemptible. In fact, I think it is really a very existentially interesting situation. I have given this considerable thought. You disowned me, and now I have restructured the situation to give you the chance to buy me back. How many fathers get second chances in this world? You're a lucky man, Pop. Of course, if you don't think you're so lucky, I'll just drop in on Messrs. Amato and Leibowitz. Very likely I have a civic duty to do that anyway, and coming to you like this I am letting filial loyalty get in the way of my political conscience. It's not as if Birdie Mickle was an insignificant swinger, your average mere expense account item, a lady of the night or a fleshpot or whatever word your generation uses. She is *Miss Chicken Delight*. Her name is in neon. She has professional standing. Artistic ambitions. She could even be a feminist, what about that?"

"What about what?"

"Is she a feminist?"

"How the hell would I know?"

"No," Norman said, "I guess you wouldn't. However, that neon speaks volumes. The point is, if this became known, you'd be laughed off the bench. You wouldn't stand a chance at sitting on the big one."

"You are a snake in the grass, Norman. It occurs to me now that you probably did steal the diamonds."

"What diamonds? What are you talking about?"

"He doesn't remember," Sid said, addressing the hotdog in its paper boat in front of him. "Tell me, your precious Dr. Morris the same which to whom I paid a fucking fortune, he lets you repress the agony you caused your poor mother? Not to mention me, God forbid anyone should mention me."

"What's the matter, you can't take what you dish out?" They were sitting side by side, on stools, and Norman's face, thrust out over the half-eaten hotdog, was going black with blood. His bushy, brown-black curls gleamed under the fluorescent ceiling fixtures. The intense, ironic eyes were filled with heat; they looked as if they would be hot to the touch, like live coals. "Do you know what it really is I'm offering you, Pop? Redemption. The father redeems the son from service in the synagogue. Isn't that the way it goes?"

"How much is it going to cost me to keep you from sacrificing yourself to a nine-to-five job?"

"Fifty bucks a week. Salvation never came cheaper."

"So this is what happens when your son that you devoted your life to marries a *shiksa*."

"Devoted your life to! Christ. I mean, Christ, Pop. Christ Almighty, Pop. You hardly knew I was around! Your memory is playing tricks on you in your old age."

"My memory! What about yours? You're the one who doesn't even remember the diamonds!"

"I certainly never stole anything in my life, if that's what you mean, except for library books."

"What do you call this?"

"I already explained. Your difficulty with the situation is purely semantic. The underlying structure of it can work only to your own benefit. I'm talking about your spiritual benefit, though I grant you, that's never been one of your overriding concerns. What it is, is an interesting dialectic. Instead of being a materialist dialectic, it is far more comprehensive, operating in terms of the interaction between matter and spirit. Your spirit and my matter."

"You know a lot about my spirit."

"Not a lot. Enough. Enough to know that you'll pay to keep it untainted by adverse publicity. You already demonstrated that once."

"Would you really do it, Norman? Would you really try to bring your own father down publicly?"

"Who knows?" Norman said. "I might. You really disowned your own son."

"That's different."

"That depends," Norman said. "I don't think it's so different."

"Have it your way. So, once a week I mail you fifty dollars."

"Not mail. I don't want Gus—that's my wife, in case you've forgotten the name—I don't want her to know anything about this."

"Then how?"

"Just like this. A friendly father-and-son lunch. Or better yet, dinner. I could stand to eat a real meal. Gus hasn't learned to cook yet."

"All right, Norman. As I said, I didn't get where I am by being such a fool I don't know when somebody has me by the short hairs. There's just one thing I don't agree with you."

"What's that?"

"Miss Mickle is not laughable. I can see why you would say that. I can even see how other people, knowing only the outside of the situation, might think that. But Miss Mickle is the twin of my soul, and if she is ludicrous, so am I." He got down from his perch with dignity. "And the public, if I may remind you already, does not snicker at me the way my own son does." He paid the check, and then pulled two twenties and a ten from his wallet and laid them on the counter at Norman's place. Norman rammed the money into the back pocket of his green jeans without looking at it. For a moment he wavered, then he recovered his nonchalance.

"If she means so much to you," Norman said, "what does that make Mother? A casual lay?"

The Honorable Sid Gold picked up the leftover end of Norman's hotdog and shoved it into Norman's mouth, which Norman had carelessly left hanging open. Then he walked out of the diner, past rows of turned heads, feeling younger than he had in ages.

21

THE MARCH WIND flapped noisily at Sid's trouser cuffs and spat grit into his eyes. His head was splitting from his sinus trouble, and now his prostate, which for a while seemed to have decided to leave him alone, was acting up again. But his feelings were not all unpleasant — they were confused and erratic, but some of them were quite likable. He was particularly pleased to have an excuse to see his son, and glad the boy had not turned out to be some namby-pamby like so many of his friends' sons. The third generation had a tendency to be a little sissy. Art and analysis — the kids hardly stood a chance. At least Norman knew enough about the world to figure out how to put the screws on somebody, even if it had to be his father. He damn well didn't learn that at Columbia. No, Sid thought, proudly; he learned it from *me*.

With this mixture of feelings pressed against his chest like a poultice, Sid decided to skip work. Instead of returning to the office, he hailed a cab into the city and went to see Birdie. He felt like a truant, daring and excited, but it wouldn't do to show it: a judge who felt like a schoolboy, circa 1906! That was why he was crazy about Birdie—she felt the way he did inside and also, miracle of miracles, showed it on the outside. She was elated.

"Sid!" she said, kissing him full on the mouth, "I wasn't expecting this. I'll tell you frankly, Sidney, this is an honor. An honor from the Honorable Mr. Gold. Can I fix you a drink? Here, would you like Scotch?" Birdie was drinking Hawaiian Punch.

"I know I shouldn't drop in on you so sudden. How's by you, Birdie?" He sank onto the Empire sofa and took off his shoes. He liked the feel of the plush carpet on his stockinged feet. "It was an impulse, that's what caused me to come like this."

"Gee, Sidney, I think it's peachy. I mean, I really do. You think I'm being a cut-up, but I really do feel this is an honor, you just dropping in on me like this when I know you have all kinds of work at the office. That's why I gave you your own key. It's sort of like having a key to the city, isn't it? If you think of it that way, I'm your city. Now isn't that a lovely thought, Sidney?"

"I've had a rotten day, Birdie."

"No!"

"Like you wouldn't believe, Birdie. A man works all his life, he wants to be able to say he accomplished something. All I got to show for years of sweat and toil is grief. People think men my age, they get heart attacks but not broken hearts. They should only know. My heart is breaking, Birdie, breaking."

"Oh, Sidney, I cannot tell you how sorry I am to hear this!" She leaned over him from behind the sofa, handing him his drink and blowing softly on the white fringe of hair. The radio was playing semi-classical music. As Birdie frequently said, she heard all the rock she needed to hear at work; at home, she liked to listen to a more refined type of music, such as a person might do interpretative dancing to.

"You have a deeply sympathetic nature," Sid told her, kissing her hand as he took the drink from it.

"I was just working on my pasties before you showed up. I was making a new pair of feathers." She showed him her pullet nipples. "Do you like them?"

"They're some swell," he said. "I'll say. But listen, Birdie, will you excuse me a moment already? It's this damn prostate again."

She nodded, and he plodded silently in his stockinged feet into her bathroom with the cylinder shower and purple towels and *101 Jokes for the John.* Birdie sipped thoughtfully at her Hawaiian Punch. It must be murder being male, getting intimations of mortality every time your thing twinged. Sidney had had this trouble for quite a while now, but he refused to see a doctor. "For my sinuses," he had said, "I saw a doctor, and what good did it do?" Birdie had said it was not the same thing. "The difference," Sid had said, "is that the examination is not so nice, that's all. You know how they examine?" Birdie had nodded then too, not knowing. "Then," Sid had said, "they inform you that it's enlarged, which any dope knows without he sees a doctor. And what do they do for it? It still hurts when you pee. Only the doctor, he feels terrific, because he knows what you're going to owe him on the first of the month."

"I don't know, Sidney," Birdie said now, calling after him. "Maybe a doctor could help."

"This is nothing, you think my prostate is in pain, you should experience the deep distress of my heart. Talk about torment."

He left the door open, and she turned the radio off, waiting for the sound she loved to hear, his urine splashing into the blue water, but there was nothing. God, it was sad. She plopped another ice cube into his drink, and then, sitting on the sofa in the quiet room, she found herself reaching for his jacket hanging over the Louis Quatorze chair (a genuine copy). His address book was in the inside breast pocket. Hurriedly now, afraid that Sidney might give up and come back into the room without having taken his leak, she flipped through the pages. There it was—Norman, under G for Gold, the address on Eighty-eighth Street and the telephone number.

Why was she doing this? A woman's intuition, she said to herself, by way of an answer. Sidney did not call her the twin of his soul for nothing. It had to be Norman that was wringing Sidney's heart like a washrag; Birdie's own experience told her that no man breaks his heart over a daughter. Besides, she had met Norman in his father's office: she had known from right then that there was trouble between them.

She stored the information in her head—she was always a quick study—and slipped the little book back in the pocket just as Sidney shouted from the bathroom. "Aargh!" he shouted, "goddamn!"

"What is it? Oh, Sidney, what has happened?" She raced to the bathroom. He was standing in front of the john; the seat was up, and she heard the dainty trickle of a few drops, but that was all.

"Nothing happened. That's the trouble. It just burns like hell, Birdie."

She went around to his front, tucked him in and zipped him up. "I'm sorry, honeybunch, I really am. I know it's painful. I wish you would see a doctor." She led him back into the living room. He pulled her into his arms as he sat on the sofa again, and for an easy ten minutes they thought their own thoughts, curled together. Finally Birdie said, "I have to get dressed now, Sidney."

"I know. Sometimes I ask myself, Why do I want to sit on the Supreme Court? At my age, I should retire."

"It's all right with me if you want to retire, Sidney."

"I know. But I don't want to retire. I want to sit on the Supreme Court. I don't know why."

"It's natural to be ambitious, Sidney. I have always admired your ambition, as a matter of fact."

"You have?"

"Yes, I have. But if you want to retire, why, I can sympathize with that too. After all, you said it yourself—I have a sympathetic nature. Many is the night I have myself wished to retire, but in the morning I was always raring to go again. Ambition is a part of my nature too."

"I know. That's one of the things I admire in *you*," Sidney said, leaning over to put on his shoes. Birdie dropped to the floor and put them on him for him. Sidney pulled her up by the elbows. "In fact," he said, "there are quite a few things that I find admirable in you, Birdie. Listen." He was glaring at her; anyone could have seen where Norman got his intensity. "I want you to do me a favor, Birdie."

"Of course, Sidney."

"I don't want you to ever let anybody razz you, you understand?"

"About what, Sidney?"

"About anything. You just don't let anyone take you less than seriously, ever! You are not one hundred and one jokes, Birdie."

"But Sidney," she said, bewildered, "I never thought I was!"

22

In March, ten thousand kids staged a love-in in Central Park. That night, Gus and Norman had their own love-in, a flight into the relaxed world of harmonic voluptuousness. Then Norman introduced a new theme. They were lying in bed under the dark red and blue quilted comforter, an old movie showing on the television on the stand at the foot of it, and Gus was feeling quite gratified, when Norman went down on her. She had no idea what he was doing. His head, previously resting beside hers on the pillow, vanished, dropping out of sight as he slid down the bed in the direction of the TV set, those exuberant brown-black curls disappearing over her boobies and tickling her stomach. He dragged the comforter down with him as he went, leaving her top exposed to the cold air of the room. What was she supposed to do now? She didn't dare mention the comforter, because whatever he was doing obviously was so engrossing that he hadn't even noticed he'd pulled it off. But she felt like an idiot, wholly extraneous, lying there with goosebumps and not doing anything. In sex, as in the rest of life, she was used to contributing. Richard had told her she was exceptionally active in bed. She was not sure how many women there had been in Richard's sample, or how random a sample it was. And Richard might well say something that wasn't true simply to make her feel good. But in any case, there was passive and there was passive—what was going on now seemed to exclude her entirely, and this made her feel peculiarly self-conscious. Norman was too far down for her to reach him without sitting up, and she had the distinct impression that she was expected to stay in a supine position. There was nothing anywhere within kissing distance except air, cold air. She could hear the late movie but she couldn't see the screen, and trying to make the dialogue go with the cracks in the ceiling was a lost cause. It was *Invasion of the Body Snatchers,* and it seemed to have excited Norman terribly. "Norman—" she said. For an answer, he flicked his tongue where it said everything she needed to know.

That gave her a completely new outlook. She still felt embarrassingly useless, but all urge to complain about it left her. For years, she had been double-tonguing and triple-tonguing, but plainly Norman was the real performer in the family. She would tell him so!—later. She watched Norman's curls bobbing up and down between her legs, like a big bush gobbling a little bush, and was about to laugh when a low cry escaped from her throat instead, like a bird from a cage. Norman kissed her navel and sat up, obviously pleased with himself. She lay as still as a corpse, listening to that strange dove, her own sexual cooing, flap its wings in a far corner . . . until she realized that was no love dove, that was Tweetie, annoyed at being so rudely wakened.

"Are you all right?" Norman asked.

"Yes," she said, uncertainly, wondering why men always asked that. Perhaps they thought that orgasms were dangerous for women. Or it could be that she didn't respond the way women were supposed to. But how were women supposed to respond to this? Nobody had ever done it to her before. The only man who had had the opportunity, after all, was Richard, and he had never even informed her that it was a sexual option. She thought it was possible that Richard didn't know about it. He was older; maybe his generation didn't do this particular thing, whatever it was called. Look how long Norman had waited. "Norman," she said, "why did you do that?"

"Why!" Norman exclaimed, surprised. He had certainly never expected to have his motives called into question on this point. "Because I felt like it, that's why."

"But you never did it before."

"I never felt like it before." He got up and went to the icebox, bringing back to the bed a container of chocolate ice cream and a spoon. "You want some?"

"No thanks," she said. Then she said, believing she was complimenting him, "I wish you felt like it more often."

Norman spooned up the ice cream in silence, mechanically. If there was one thing he didn't want to discuss with his wife after going down on her, it was why he had gone down on her. Why couldn't women ever understand that a man's emotions weren't voluntary but responsive? "I can't help how I feel," he said, beginning to feel angry. For Christ's sake, his analysis had been an accomplished fact for years— it was over and done with, and some things he had talked about with Dr. Morris, he wasn't crazy to go over again with Gus. He much preferred talking about her.

She knew something was going wrong with the conversation and said, "That's not what I meant."

"What do you mean?"

"Nothing. I didn't mean anything."

She was hating herself for even having started the conversation. The television talk shows said young married couples should discuss sex candidly, but apparently that was only if the sex was bad. Here she was, trying to say it was good, and making things worse.

"You're getting ice cream on the sheets," Gus said.

"Fuck the sheets." Norman carried the now empty container back to the sink.

"I just meant it felt good," she said, calling after him. "That's all."

"Yeah," Norman said. He was looking at her from the kitchen, her creamy breasts and pink nipples and golden hair and saucy mouth and hazel eyes, and the well-tempered clavicle, and it hurt him profoundly to feel that all this musical grace and pleasure, this smile like light and this seriousness of intelligence and purpose devoted to the sensual joy of sound—that his wife, Gus, should be dishonest with him. If she wasn't content sexually, why hadn't she said so before? And if she was content sexually, why was she carrying on like this now? He knew why—it wasn't the sex she was criticizing, it was his work. She had as much as said so that morning. Why couldn't she admit at least to herself what she was really talking about?

Gus was wondering why Norman did something to her which she was presumably supposed to like and then got angry when she said she liked it. "Come on, Norman," she said, rising to the way he had said *yeah*, "don't try to bully me." She was proud of herself for thinking of the word "bully." It seemed to strike the right note between accusation and amusement.

"Women," Norman said, slapping his hand down on the top of the television set so that the picture jumped. He spoke his words lightly, as if joking, but to Gus his eyes seemed to be on fire. She could see the ceiling light reflected twice over in his pupils. "Women are the real body snatchers," he said. It occurred to Norman, as he said this, that he might just as well have said, "Men are the real body snatchers," but then he thought, with some exorcism of anxiety, that that would *not* be equally valid: men might violate, but they couldn't threaten to take back what they had given; they were only visitors to the void, not the void itself.

"If you're talking about what I think you're talking about," she said, "I already know all that stuff. Even the people who made that movie"—she pointed at the screen—"they probably know about it. Freud is old hat, Norman."

"I'm not talking about Freud, I'm talking about women the way they really look to men." He was using his seminar voice. "Now, you look reasonably human from most perspectives, but when my head is between your legs I can see just how sly you really are. You have devised a plan among you—or you do it out of innocent instinct—to incorporate our bodies in yours and take over the world. Metaphorically, of course."

"Why metaphorically? Why not really?"

"You asked me a question, I gave you an answer. If you want to be facetious, that's up to you. I'm talking psychoanalytically, of course, not sexually. Sexually I love women. Especially you. But psychoanalytically is another story."

"Did you ever tell this to Dr. Morris?"

"Tell it to him? He told it to me. I'm giving you a simplified version."

"Thanks. It's considerate of you not to strain my brain."

"Now you're getting huffy. I didn't say you were revolting, I only said women were, in a general psychoanalytic way. You yourself said it's something everyone knows. Why do you have to act so shocked?"

"I'm not shocked. I'm just shocked that you take all this so seriously."

"I'm not taking it seriously, you are."

"How can I not take it seriously? You just said you find me reprehensible."

"I *didn't* say that."

"You might as well have."

"Gus," he begged, "don't twist my meaning to suit your desire for vengeance. It's not my fault you're female. If you want to know what I think of you, I happen to think you're beautiful. I love you. Why do you think I married you?"

"It seems to me I asked you that once. Are you telling me now that the only reason you married me is for my looks?"

"I didn't say it was the *only* reason, I said it was *a* reason. Christ!"

"Christ yourself!"

"Now wait just a second. This is getting us nowhere."

"I think it's getting us just plenty of places. Don't try to calm me down. I don't need calming down. You calm me down, and then the next thing I know you'll be congratulating yourself for controlling your hysterical wife."

"You *are* hysterical."

"Maybe I have something to be hysterical about."

"I don't see that at all."

"How could you? You're not a woman."

"Thanks for telling me."

"Isn't that exactly what you want to be told?"

"Gus," he said, "don't try to be smart. It doesn't suit you."

"I know I can't ever expect to be as incisive as you are. My brain is too subject to feminine airinesses. You might think I was a dedicated flutist, but playing the flute is merely the way I pass the time when I'm not castrating my husband. Metaphorically. Well, at least I don't play the flute metaphorically. I suppose you told me to work up a program simply as a way of pacifying me."

"How did we get onto music?"

"There you go, trying to be logical again. You should know by now that women are incapable of logic."

"I never said that. Did I ever say that? Jesus God Christ Almighty, Gus, be logical for once!"

"I am recalling"—she held her fingers to the sides of her head and closed her eyes—"I am recalling that this very morning I had occasion to state, in a three-way conversation with your friend and blood-brother Philip Fleischman, that the kind of work you do, Cultural Musicology I believe you call it, is derivative. You construed what I said as an insult. I could tell it at the time. Whenever you're offended by something, your face turns dark. Anger is your first recourse, Norman. Where other people might cry or sulk or run away, your natural impulse is to reach for a gun, or it would be if you had a gun. I looked at you this morning when you were looking at Phil, but you weren't thinking about Phil, and even Phil knew it. You were thinking you would like to throttle me, because I said your work was derivative. All right. Now you've done it. Throttled me." She opened her eyes, her wide, honey-hazel, tilted, long-as-almond, sweetly questing eyes. Norman, looking at them, *could* have throttled her.

"If you think I gave you a truthful answer just in order to get back at you for this morning, that's ridiculous. You're the one who's evidently dissatisfied with the way things have been, not me."

"I never said I was dissatisfied!"

"Yes you did. Very subtly. I'll give you credit for that."

"I just wondered why you did something tonight that you never did before and why you never did it before. It's not as if I never did it to you!"

Dully, feeling frustrated, feeling somehow swindled, as if Gus had stolen a perfectly good evening and substituted something pyritic in its place, Norman tried to explain. "You have to admit," he said, "if you would just be dispassionate and think about it, that the female genitalia inescapably have an aura of mysteriousness. When you put your mouth on me, you know what you're blowing. It's visually loud and clear, so to speak. Women have these sticky recesses."

"You eat ice cream. You just finished off all there was in the icebox."

"I like the taste of ice cream."

She stopped. "I guess I get the picture."

"I don't think so," he said. "I think you're too wrapped up in yourself to get the overall picture. You're looking shocked and hurt again, but I'm not saying anything hurtful. I'm not even saying anything shocking. All it amounts to is that men and women have to approach each other with skepticism, but nobody said that was a tragedy. Except you. You're trying to make a tragedy out of it, and that's very Gentile of you. Listen," he said, laughing with anguish, doing his best to lift the doleful night out of its dark pond, "I'll tell you a tragedy." He lit a cigarette. He felt desolated. "Do you know how Webern died?"

"No."

"One night in Vienna during the occupation, Webern stepped out of his apartment and lit a cigarette, and an American soldier, seeing the light from the match, assumed he was a spy and shot him dead."

"That's *awful,*" Gus said.

"Yeah."

Gus shot Norman with her nailbitten finger, saying BANG, and Norman clutched his chest and fell back on the bed, lit cigarette pointing upward at the ceiling above his heart.

"What I don't understand," Gus said, leaning over and speaking carefully above Norman's closed eyes, "is what any of this has to do with you and me. Nobody says you have to feel about me the way Freud felt about Martha."

"It's descriptive law, not prescriptive. It's just the way things are." Norman opened his eyes and almost kissed her on the mouth but refrained.

"Then why does it *feel* prescriptive? I never felt this was the way things were until you told me they had to be this way."

"Can I help it if your education has been neglected? I warned you about those high notes, but you wouldn't listen." He rolled out from under her face, dragged deeply, and smiled. The smile didn't work, and he put it away, stubbing it out as he stubbed out the cigarette. It was late. Maybe that was the whole trouble. More and more, it seemed that the middle of the night was the only chance he and Gus really had to talk, and by then his mouth felt dry from too many cigarettes during the day and his brain was like a room full of stale smoke. He paced the Persian rug, naked. Gus got up, threw on his shirt, and drew the curtains across the windows at the far end. "You shouldn't stand in front of the windows like that," he said.

"Why not? I'm wearing a shirt."

"This is New York."

"I wish it was North Carolina."

"You wish we had never got married."

"That's not true, Norman."

"All right, I agree. It was low. But it wasn't as low as what you said about my work. Derivative!"

"I'm sorry if it sounded like a slam, it wasn't meant to be one. I was just stating a fact. My work is secondary too. It's not as if I were a composer."

"But you wish I were."

"Did I ever say that?"

"That *old friend* of yours. Richard. I suppose he's a composer?"

"Then you suppose wrongly. He's a conductor."

"But with original interpretations."

"I told you, I was only stating a fact. And I was trying to make Phil feel better. You may not have noticed this about your lifelong friend, but he happens to idolize you because you use your brain and he hates himself for having such a frivolous job. He likes it, but he doesn't think he should. How many models named Dinky can a self-respecting man date? So I was only pointing out that you and I are just as parasitic as he is. We all live off of other people's ideas, musical and so forth. It's a fact."

"Sure. And we both know, a fact is all you were stating."

"On the order of 'Roses are red'!"

"Some are," Norman said. "Not all. If you're going to state facts, you'd better get them right."

"All right, Norman, some roses are red. That's a fact. Did you ever hear me complain because some roses are red?"

"I've heard you complain because some aren't."

"Do you mean you think I don't respect you because you're not a red rose?"

"In effect."

"Well, that takes the cake."

"I don't know what you mean by *that.*"

"I mean—"

The telephone rang.

"Who would be calling at this hour?" Gus asked. "Phil?"

"Pick it up." She turned the television down.

"Hello?"

"Norman Gold?"

"Yes," he said, "this is Norman Gold. To whom do I have the pleasure of speaking at this ridiculous time of night when I happen to be having a fight with my wife?" He said this with his eyes locked to Augusta's.

"This is Birdie Mickle."

"Oh." He whipped away from Gus's gaze in a hurry.

"Do you know what you're doing to your father, Norman? You're breaking his heart. I just thought somebody should let you know."

"Uh," he said, looking again at Gus, "I can't talk now." He hung up hastily. Gus was still staring at him. Her eyes were narrowed.

23

TWEETIE WAS SLEEPING with his head tucked under his wing.

As Gus lay under the cover, wearing Norman's shirt while he watched the end of the movie, she was wondering if what they'd had could be called a love-out. Then the darkness swept over her, and she fell into a dreamless sleep. It seemed to her that she did not wake entirely, when morning came; she was not one hundred percent conscious. Some part of her spirit stayed sleeping, unwilling to rise and shine on Eighty-eighth Street.

There were days when her spirit, this part of it, tossed and turned, as if dreaming, but most of the time full consciousness belonged solely to her musical self; it was bright and lively, quicksilver, full of flash and cool lights. A certain still shadow, like the pattern of green leaves on a polished marble surface, began to overlay the musical part of her self, but no one found anything inappropriate in this; it was a natural development, a heightening, paradoxically, of brilliance. It had nothing to do with the part of her that was sleeping.

There was a routine now, a daily rhythm. They had quit fighting. To Norman, it seemed as if they had been jockeying for emotional space and now had reached an accommodation. The fact of his being married no longer interfered with his mental life so much. In fact, his favorite day of the week was the one which had formerly been his least favorite, Sunday. On Sunday mornings, they ate pancakes at a pancake house, bought the *Times* and returned to the apartment to loll on the big bed and read. They hung Tweetie's cage in front of the windows so he could enjoy the sunshine. As the weather began to turn warm, they went for long Sunday afternoon walks along Riverside Drive. Gus wore one of her white blouses and a red mini-jumper, and the wide wings of her wavy hair, wind-lifted above the temples, sparkled in the sun like the rippling, twinkling surface of the Hudson. Norman put his arm around her and felt rapturous, knowing that he had a place in the world and someone to share it with, knowing that she belonged to him and needed him.

Gus, too, felt that she was increasingly dependent on him, and though she tried now and then to pull back, there seemed little point in it. If she was half asleep, there was a reason for it. In that submissive, spiritually quiescent, inward-yawning, poppy-smotherous state, she drifted in and out of daily life, waking now and then to find herself in Norman's arms, and feeling for him that immensely deep half-fearful involvement one feels in a dream, bereft of any sense of self. She could look at him and feel her head spin—an attraction even more sexually powerful than she had experienced before their marriage. And the more Norman talked to her, explaining herself to herself, the more she needed to hear him talk—it was like a drug, replacement therapy for the attention she had sacrificed in marrying, and she depended on him for her fix. None of these terms was to be taken literally—Gus and Norman learned from television about Haight-Ashbury and psychedelic trips, and Phil Fleischman gave them the latest gloss on "Rock-a-bye, Baby," but all of this was merely fallout from the decade they happened to be living in. Norman and Augusta Gold, in their room on Eighty-eighth, watched the world on television but lived their own lives independent of the media—when they could.

There was, of course, the one area in her life where Gus remained totally alert: her music. She kept, as always, to her practice schedule; even more than always, she kept to it, working toward a debut in less than two years' time. Her constant playing drew out the two dwarves. They were extremely well-tailored dwarves. Their names were Tom and Cyril. Cyril was English. Tom was an actor, and they had met when he was studying drama in London. Cyril illustrated children's books. They were both shy and reclusive, but Tom had a way of charging at the world, and of taking charge; actually, it was only an extension of his stage personality. The real Tom was gentle, easily embarrassed, chronically anxious, and so easy to rag that no one dared to do it to him. Cyril explained all this to Gus one day when Tom was at an audition. Generally, Tom and Cyril were both at home, in the apartment across the hall, and one day they had followed the music down the hall, knocking timidly on the door to ask if they could come in to listen. So Gus practiced while Tom and Cyril sat at her feet, holding hands, on the floor or on the bed, and sometimes she went across to their apartment for lunch. Cyril made salmon salad sandwiches and lemonade. He vastly enjoyed doing this, and fussed over the linen napkins in their bamboo napkin rings. Their apartment had a finished look, a polished put-together and cared-for look, but Gus's and Norman's still kept its quality of impermanence. There was no money to buy furniture with. There was no point in fixing up the kitchen, which belonged to the cockroaches anyway, and if they had, there would still have been no way to erase the fact that this had previously been Norman's bachelor apartment. Gus wondered occasionally how many girls Norman had made love to in this room. All over New York, there were these islands of shelter, thousands, hundreds of thousands of living-holes, like waterholes, in which people lived and died and passed on their knowledge to the next generation, but Gus found it difficult to foresee spending years in this room of Norman's, although it glowed like garnet and sapphire. She missed her leaf pictures.

Norman took care of their finances, such as they were. After he told her not to worry about money, just work up a program, she did exactly that. She didn't know precisely where they got the money to live on, but his fellowship was substantial, and she knew that sometimes he simply didn't pay bills. She wondered also, from time to time, how much she owed the telephone company for the new phone he had had installed in her name—but it didn't matter as long as he paid it, and although she was from North Carolina and would never have considered reneging on bills a reasonable way to live, she had been in New York long enough to realize that if she objected, everyone for miles around (meaning Norman) would say she was sweet and accuse her of being conventional. Taking Con Ed and Ma Bell for a ride was justifiable self-defense. She did not entirely disagree, but she was afraid of getting caught. In a way, she admired Norman's temerity in these matters—it seemed to her a strictly masculine trait. Authority figures did not distress him.

She knew Norman's mother had helped them out with a hundred dollars. A letter had come, addressed to them both, when Norman was out, and Gus had opened it; there was a hundred-dollar bill inside, and a note saying it was to help them get started with. "I would send more," it said, "but I had to steal this from Sid's wallet. He's never let me have a checking account of my own. It's because my father was a rabbi. Sid has always felt it was his duty to see that nothing corrupted me, such as money. My feeling is that he owes you this for being such a stiffnecked old fool. Spend it in good health. *Shalom.*" The note was signed "Esther." Gus sat down at the long table and wrote a thank-you letter. The address in Brooklyn was printed on a stick-on label. She tried to make her letter casual, as if she had not been the cause of a total breach between father and son, father-in-law and husband, husband and son. She addressed the letter to "Mrs. Esther Gold" and left off the return address, in case Mr. Gold should see it. Then she mailed it.

She gave Norman the money and his mother's letter, but she didn't tell him that she had written to his mother. Gus wasn't supposed to exist for either of his parents. From time to time, Gus begged Norman to make it up with his father; now that she knew he wasn't going to get her debut money from him, she thought Norman should make every effort to repair the relationship. What if the old man died with this chasm unbridged? But Norman was adamant. He had said he wouldn't have anything to do with his father until his father acknowledged her as his wife.

"Don't you feel bad about never seeing your father?" Gus asked. "You said he was"—she looked around for a way to say this—"getting on."

Norman couldn't very well tell her that he was seeing his father once a week for dinner, the night he was ostensibly working late at Columbia, and that it was his father's money which was largely bankrolling them. So he said, "He's old enough to act like a human being. It's not my fault he's infantile."

"But suppose he died without your ever seeing him again?"

"That's what he wants," Norman said, chafing. "That's the whole point of disowning somebody. Now look, do you mind if we change the subject?"

When Esther wrote to thank Gus for her thank-you note, Gus answered in secret again. Before long, she and her mother-in-law were maintaining a regular correspondence, though they had never met. Neither of the husbands knew anything about it. Sid naturally was at his office or in chambers when the mail was delivered in Brooklyn, and Norman was usually at Columbia when it arrived on Eighty-eighth Street. Gus would put her flute down long enough to collect the mail from the box in the wall at the foot of the stairs, and then when she was ready to resume her practicing, Tom and Cyril, both late risers, would come across the hall to join her.

All this time, the one part of her spirit continued to sleep.

Norman gave her the money to make a down payment on Town Hall for her debut in 1968. It would cost a couple of thousand dollars, but Norman swore he would have the money.

(Norman's original intention had been to save the money he was receiving weekly, the weekly payments being both a chance for him to eat decently and an excuse for his father to see him, but the money dribbled away toward this and that; in the summer, for example, there was no fellowship money.

Norman wasn't worried; as Mario's mother had said, there would be more. It wasn't as if this was abstract knowledge; it had its analogue in his own experience. In his childhood, when he spent his sixty-dollar allowance at F. A. O. Schwarz's, he could always get another sixty dollars to tide him over until the next month. He had taken care of the down payment, and the rest could wait. The important thing was that Gus was booked.)

When Gus wasn't practicing or taking a lesson or swimming, she read Norman's books, many of which, she discovered, three or four or five years earlier had belonged to the library ... She did this even though there were times when she was tempted to sink onto the bed in front of the television at noon and let the rest of the day unfold unseen. There was not a whole lot of housecleaning she could do—the cockroaches held dominion in the kitchen and the bathroom was crumbling, and that left only the one room. It still seemed to her that marriage had left her with a great deal of time on her hands, even with a recital program to learn, but whenever she brought up the idea of her going to work, Norman hit the ceiling. She didn't dare push it any farther, for fear of offending his masculinity. His counter-suggestion was that she might start cooking, but she was not about to use that kitchen any more than necessary. Furthermore, something in this suggestion offended her—her what? Not her femininity, since to cook dinner for a husband was presumably feminine (even Cyril conceded that); but she had not got married in order to take up cooking. Then she thought again: maybe it *was* her femininity that was bruised. She would not have minded cooking if she had known how to, but her mother, the keypunch operator, had always refused to tolerate her mistakes in the kitchen. Her mother said that Gus had more important things to do, and certainly she meant it; but she also meant that *she* had more important things to do than teach Gus how to cook. The result was that

Gus, searching dutifully according to the Protestant ethic to fill every waking moment significantly, read not one but all of Norman's books, arriving finally at the Thayer biography of Beethoven.

24

ONE MORNING, while she was still in the middle of the Thayer biography of Beethoven, Gus came back to the room from downstairs with the mail, having been joined by Tom and Cyril along the way, just in time to slip the unopened letter from Norman's mother into the book before Norman himself raced up the stairs, shouting her name. "What are you doing here?" she asked, when he reached the top.

"Aren't you glad to see me?" He wiped the sweat from his face with his shirt sleeve.

"Of course!"

He laughed. "It's all right, Gus, you don't need to look so earnest. I believe you."

"Why shouldn't you believe me?"

Tom said, "Maybe we'd better leave."

"Yes, I think we should do," Cyril said.

"No," said Norman. "You just got here, I saw you. Stay."

"They came over to listen to me practice," Gus explained.

"Well, don't let me stop you. We'll all listen."

"Norman, I don't think—"

"How are you going to give a concert if you can't play to your own husband?" He was looking at her expressive lip, the high bare brow revealed by the scarf that pulled her thick hair back from her face, the polite, Gentile nose. He was proud of her; it satisfied him deeply to be able to refer to himself as her husband, especially in front of other people.

"Okay," she said, smiling, and picking up the flute. "Here goes—"

But as she put her lips to the gold mouthpiece and started to blow, she screamed instead, and jumped onto the chair.

"What is it?" Norman shouted, all of his defenses instantly mobilized. His first thought was, *Bellhop.*

"It's a mouse!" she screamed, pointing. "There! It went under the bed!"

Cyril, sitting on the bed, pulled his short legs up and screamed.

"You don't have to scream, Cyril," Tom said, sharply.

"She said it went under the bed! It's under me! I can feel the bed shaking!"

"The mouse isn't shaking the bed," Norman said, "you are."

"It's the same difference, isn't it?" Cyril asked, in a calmer voice. "There's a bloody mouse under here, and I'm not coming down from the bed until he's gone. Cor!"

"*Do* something!" Gus said to Norman.

"Are you going to stand on that chair for the rest of the afternoon?"

"If you don't do something, I am."

Tom said to Norman, "Have you got any ideas?"

"I could buy a mousetrap."

Tom shook his head. He had a broad, deeply grave face. It was easy to see why Cyril loved him. "The mouse is probably so frightened, it will never come out."

"Maybe," Norman said, grinning, "now is the time to build a *better* mousetrap. The world will beat a path to our door."

"You wouldn't think it was so funny if you had seen it," Gus retorted. "It moves so *fast.*" She turned around on her chair. "Look at Tweetie. He's upset too. He probably thinks where there's a mouse, there's a cat."

"I to't I taw a puddytat," Norman said.

"That's enough, Norman," Gus said uncomfortably; she frequently said the same thing to Tweetie-Pie when Norman wasn't around.

"You should have heard yourself," Norman said, looking up at her. "You said eek. E-e-k."

Gus began to giggle. "I know," she said, "it must be instinctive. I never thought I was the type to say eek."

"Eek!" Cyril screamed. "There it is!"

A small bundle of brown fur skittered across the Persian rug and parquet floor toward the kitchen and crawled under the icebox, cowering. It made high, squeaking sounds, like a piccolo.

"I have it," Norman said, snapping his fingers. "I just thought of the better mousetrap."

Cautiously, Gus got down from the chair. She was still holding her flute and now she took it apart and put it in the case, by touch—she had to keep her eyes on the trembling brown bit under the icebox. She didn't want it sneaking up on her. But it stayed crouched under there even while Norman went into the kitchen and pulled a pot down from the pegboard. Then Norman stamped his foot on the floor, and the mouse, terrified, ran back into the other room. Norman threw the pot at the mouse—and missed. "Shit," he said, as the pot flew off in one direction and the mouse in another.

"He's under the desk," Tom said.

Norman threw the pot again. This time it banged against the wall under the desk, and the mouse dashed across the room toward the chair Gus had been standing on. She leaped onto the bed. Cyril clung to her skirt.

"I'm going to catch that mother if it's the last thing I do," Norman said.

"Norman! It's only a little mouse."

"Don't tell me you're feeling sorry for it! If that's the case, why are you up there? Do you plan to spend the rest of your life standing on our bed with Cyril?" Norman had hit his head on the edge of the desk retrieving the pot.

The mouse had a long thin tail like a piece of cord and it was twitching wildly. Suddenly Tom kicked the chair aside and the mouse, not knowing which way to run, froze for an instant, and Norman, falling flat on his face as he dived, clapped the pot over it.

Nobody said anything.

"I've got him," Norman said.

Cyril asked the question that was on everyone's mind. "What are you going to do with him?"

"Gus," Norman said, authoritatively, "come here."

She did.

"Get a sheet of cardboard from one of the shirts in my drawer."

She did.

"Now slide it under the pot."

She did.

"Careful!"

"I'm being careful."

"Okay, now we've got him good."

"Now what?" Gus asked. "That still doesn't answer the question."

"Take the flippin' thing outside," Cyril suggested.

"That's no good," Tom said. "He'll come right back."

"Well, we can't just—" Norman started.

"What?" said Gus.

"Kill it. We can't just kill it."

"You'll have to," Tom said. "Unless you want to keep it. As a pet."

"Tweetie wouldn't like that," Gus said. Tweetie was already agitated, flapping dementedly against the bars of his cage.

"Oh God," Norman said. "How are we going to kill it?"

Tom looked worried, concentrating. "You can drown it."

"In the Hudson? How the hell am I going to carry it way the hell over there? Suppose it gnaws through the cardboard. Mice have teeth, you know. They are noted for their teeth."

"Be glad it's not a rat," Cyril said. "We had rats in Bristol. They came off the ships."

Gus shivered.

"You'll have to drown it in the—" Tom blushed.

"The loo," Cyril said.

Norman looked at Gus. "Do you know anything else I can do?"

She shrugged.

"Okay. It's being very still in there, do you think it's all right? Could it have suffocated?" He tapped on the cardboard to see if the mouse would respond. There was a sound of scurrying from the underside. "I hope you know how to swim," he said, talking to the mouse.

He carried the pot with the cardboard hat into the bathroom that wasn't much larger than a telephone booth, and Gus and the dwarves crowded in after him. Cyril whispered to Tom, loud enough for Gus to hear, "It's a jolly good thing we aren't any bigger than we are." Gus felt the color rising to her cheeks. There was an aura of manic exuberance about the whole business. They were all laughing at the absurdity of the situation, even Norman. Gus raised the seat, and Norman, turning the pot upside down, lowered it to the toilet. Swiftly he pulled the cardboard away and the mouse dropped into the bowl. "Swim, you bastard, swim!" he yelled, laughing. He flushed the john.

25

THE MOUSE SWAM as long as it could. It battled against the current in the bowl, but the flush made a whirlpool effect, and the mouse, scrabbling against the porcelain sides, squeaking hysterically, was sucked slowly under. The squeaks got higher and more hopeless-sounding. Its claws, trying to cling to the slick surface, were useless. The tiny, thin tail whipped frantically; it was never meant to function as a rudder. As if that tail was a cord being reeled in by some unseen giant hand extending from the sewer, the mouse went down the drain tailfirst, tugged by the undertow, staring helplessly up with bright, live eyes at the four faces leaning over the bowl. At the last, it stopped squeaking; only the whiskers, wetly drooping, quivered reflexively.

Afterward, no one knew what to say. They stood there listening to the water falling away through the apartment building's ancient plumbing system, wishing somehow the pipes would speak to them. New water filled up the bowl, and now there was no mouse in it. Gus raised her head and looked at Norman: there was horror on his face, though it was there only for an instant. It wasn't an expression that was natural to his temperament; it was unintegrated with his features, as if laid on with a spatula, a kind of stucco. Gus looked into his face, and it was as if she were seeing a funhouse reflection of her own. She ran out the room, tripping over Tom.

"Where are you going?" Norman said, coming after her.

"Out." She grabbed her book and her shoulderbag, but he caught her and held her by the shoulders.

"I came home to spend the afternoon with you," he said.

"I thought we could watch the war on television together."

"I'm sorry," she mumbled. "I've got to get out of here." She wrenched free and fled.

But where to? As a wife, she had fewer friends than she'd had when she was single. This was only partly attributable to men's interest in her being lessened by her sexual unavailability; it was also because she now had a "private life" and a "public life." Before, she'd just had a life. Now there were a great many things in her life that belonged only to Norman and herself, and this meant she had less to talk about with other people. There was a new circumspection in her bearing. When she wrote letters to old friends in North Carolina, Norman skimmed them, peering over her shoulder at the lettersheet in the typewriter, to make sure she had said nothing that he might mind other people knowing about. She didn't object to this because she was just as eager as he was that their marriage should be a success, and, as Norman said, if they did have any problems, presumably the people to solve them should be the people involved, not old friends in North Carolina.

The street was hot; the sun angled off the sidewalk like a billiard ball against the side cushion of a pool table and hit her full in the face. She loved the sensation of heat on her body, her shoulders under the cotton dress, like a massage. She began to relax. There was a phone booth up ahead, burning bright red in the summer sun, and on an impulse, she walked to it and dropped a dime in. She hardly realized whom she was dialing until she was halfway through the number. When he answered, she didn't know what to say.

"Richard?" she said. "It's me."

He didn't reply.

"Did you hear that? I seem to have adopted your old habit. I mean it's me, Gus. Augusta. Your Gussie."

His response was slow but welcoming. "Mrs. Gold," he said. It still gave her a thrill to hear herself called that.

"May I see you?"

"Now?"

"If you aren't busy."

"You can come here. Elaine is shopping. Elaine is almost always shopping, in case you never noticed. Is anything wrong?"

"No. Yes. I can't explain. It has to do with a mouse."

"You don't have to say another word. I understand everything. The mouse ran up the clock. Weren't we going to meet under a clock?"

"Don't go away, Richard," Gus said, flooded with an unexpected sense of elation. "I'll be there as soon as I can!" She ran for the subway. She knew the way because she had been to his apartment once before. When Elaine was shopping.

26

TELL ME," Richard said, seating her on the couch, putting her book and bag on the coffee table, "what is this about a mouse? You look beautiful, you know. Gussie, Gussie, it's been a very long time since you let old Richard see you. Does this character you married treat you well? I don't trust intellectuals, myself. They're murder when it comes to music. I suppose he's big on sixteenth-century *canzoni?*"

He was gazing at her romantically, his large, dreamy, dark eyes musing on her form; Gus was sure he didn't have the vaguest idea what he was saying—it was the automatic Richard, stalling while the Richard that lived inside the outer despairing handsome extravagant Richard carefully absorbed the fact that his Gussie was sitting on the couch in his apartment, half turned toward him.

"The truth is," she said, "it isn't really because of the mouse that I'm here. Richard, did I ever seem to you to be neurotic?"

"Neurotic? I don't know," he said, "I never thought about it. I guess you could be. I'm not sure I could tell if you were or weren't. What's neurotic?"

She blushed.

"I like the way you blush," he said. "In fact, I'd rather just watch you blush than know why you're blushing. You might stop it then. In any case, whatever's the matter, it can't be very serious or you'd be thinner. You always lose weight when you're distressed. Elaine always goes shopping, did I tell you?"

She sighed and leaned back against the couch. Richard was looking at her exposed throat. She meant him to. It was rather nice once again to be sitting next to someone whose attention was fixed on her so intently, but how could she talk to him about Norman without being unfair to him *and* Norman? Then he started to kiss her throat; she waited a few moments before she told him to stop and sat up. "I'm going to make a Town Hall debut," she said.

"You are? Terrific! When? Did you get in touch with my manager?"

"Yes," she said. "It'll be a year from December. Norman says we'll have the money by then. Baker is helping me with the program." She was talking rapidly—too rapidly, seeking to distract him. "I want to run the gamut from Bach to something so contemporary it doesn't exist yet. A première. There's a student at Juilliard, Dieter Schuyler. He's brilliant. He's writing a piece for me to close the program with."

"You'll be magnificent," Richard said, untying her scarf and stroking her hair. "I'll be there."

"I know I'll be terrified."

"The only time I'm not terrified is when I'm performing."

"Uh," she said, "I'm not sure how you mean that." She

moved to the end of the couch. It was a rich, cool living room, with zinnias in cut crystal vases and a record collection that spanned one wall from floor to ceiling. It was a living room that belonged in a magazine—not merely Upwardly Mobile but Arrived. Except for the well-stocked, well-used bar and the records, the family photographs over the bar and the fresh zinnias, there was little sign of human habitation. The living room wasn't intended for living. Real life was lived offstage, in the kitchen and the kids' room. But Gus appreciated the peace of this room, the lovely serene appointed stillness of it. Richard's profile was doubled in the floor-to-ceiling framed mirror on the wall at his end of the couch. From a certain perspective, his face was faintly owlish, with a beaked nose and large eyes and a pointed chin. "Richard," she blurted, "am I bad in bed?"

"Are you bed in bad?"

"Am I *bad* in *bed!*"

"Oh," he said, "no. At least I don't think so. I thought you were fabulous. But then"—he was thoughtful, trying to remember—"there aren't too many women I can compare you with. There's Elaine, of course."

"Of course."

"Well, it isn't really all that *of course*. I think Elaine would like to give it up altogether. She does her duty, of course. Did Norman say you were bad in bed?"

"No, he said I was rather good."

"Then what makes you think otherwise?"

"Do you cheat on Elaine much?"

"Gussie!" he said, gazing on her lugubriously.

"I mean with other girls besides me."

"I don't think so. No, I wouldn't say that I do. Sometimes, of course."

"You keep saying *of course* as though everything was perfectly clear, but Richard, I no longer know what to think about anything."

"Why is that?"

"For one thing, somebody keeps calling and hanging up."

"Well," he said, "that's only normal. That's standard for New York. Actually"—he reached for her hand—"I thought of doing that myself a few times. Just to hear your voice, you understand. But I didn't. It must be someone else who wants to hear your voice."

"Richard, I don't think these calls are for me!"

"You don't mean somebody wants to hear Norman's voice? Well," he exclaimed, indignant, "I can swear to you that I never telephoned and hung up in order to hear your husband's voice."

"I know," she said, sadly. "I wish it were you. I'd rather believe it was just you being crazy. I think Norman is seeing someone, and we haven't even been married for a decent interval yet. It ought to be like mourning. You shouldn't start cheating on your wife until you've been married at least a year, should you?"

"Is it only the phone calls that make you think this?"

"He works late. Once a week. He says he's at Columbia but I know he isn't because once I tried to call him there."

"He might have stepped out for a while. Gone to the West End Bar, or something."

"I don't think so. The guy in the office seemed very surprised that anyone would telephone. They were shut up tight."

"Well, he was there. This guy."

"But he wasn't supposed to be. He said he was a revolutionary. I think he was stealing files. He advised me to hang tough and keep the faith."

"And did you?"

"I said I would."

"It sounds like pretty good advice to me. I don't know that I have anything to add. Unless it's to suggest that you and I take up where we left off. It would give Norman something to think about besides musicology." He was leaning across the length of the couch, trying to blow in her ear, but she was too far away and he wound up blowing at her sleeve. She laughed.

"I think I better go," she said. "If Elaine walked in now, she'd think you lost your mind."

"She thinks that anyway. Who knows, she could be right. Elaine is very shrewd."

Gus had got up and was standing in front of the huge mirror, knotting the scarf at the nape of her neck. Her long, wavy hair tumbled out from under the triangle. "I need my bag," she said.

"Here it is." He looked at the book beside it. "Hey, Gussie, can I borrow this? I've always meant to read it."

"Sure," she said, "I suppose so." She turned to go. "I'm glad I saw you today," she said, softly.

"Me too. I miss you, Gussie." He tugged at a lock of hair.

"Stay in touch," she whispered, turning, and running.

He watched her go, down the stairs. She hated elevators.

He stepped back inside the apartment, sighed, poured himself a finger of Scotch, and sat soulfully down again on the couch. Elaine wouldn't be home until dinner time; even the kids wouldn't be home until three-thirty. He picked up the book Gussie had left; it was about Beethoven. He opened it. Once upon a time, it had been a library book. Her husband had written his name on the back of the front cover. There were other notes on the same page. He began reading them. It wasn't easy, because the handwriting slanted backwards and the words were jammed together; the notes crossed one another in different directions. Richard drank the Scotch and fixed himself another. After all, how often was a mere conductor privy to the innermost thoughts of a cultural musicologist? A certain sportive *joie de vivre* began to fill his being, as warming as the whiskey. Rossini as orally fixated, Beethoven's relationship with his nephew, cross-references to Goethe and da Vinci, church music, the Greek modes and the Apollonian and Dionysian split in Western culture—the notes were endless. Somewhere there was bound to be something about the phallic baton. Thank God a conductor only had to make music, not analyze its significance. Here, he thought, what's this? Birdie Mickle Miss Chicken Delight. There was a telephone number. What did Birdie Mickle Miss Chicken Delight have to do with Cultural Musicology? "I will pour myself a third Scotch and think about this," Richard said to himself, aloud, beginning to feel the effect of the whiskey. But instead of reaching for the decanter, he reached for the telephone.

27

SHE'S FINGERLICKIN' GOOD. Richard reflected on the sign at length. It was still light, but the neon flashed through the midsummer evening haze. Traffic lights blinked, and more lights were going on and off in the pinball gallery next door. It was the kind of New York night that presses people together, wraps them in a gauzy, good-natured sense of fellowship. A kid came up to Richard and walloped him in the back, near the left kidney. "Hey, mister," the kid said, before Richard had a chance to say anything, "it was an accident. Don't you believe me?"

"Why did you do that?" Richard asked, mournfully, but the kid had already drifted into the distance. The streets were packed with people. It was a warm, friendly night, the kind of night that promises excitement, and there was a mood of jubilation that seemed to snake through the crowd, striking here and then there. The war was over; it had lasted six days. Vietnam was momentarily forgotten.

Richard made up his mind and went into The Joint. The next show was at ten and by the time it started he was plastered. He stood at the bar. Finally Miss Chicken Delight came on, and before she went off again, she was looking, Richard thought, pretty plucked. What a bird. He caught her backstage.

"Mr. Hacking," she said, solemnly, "I told you, I do another show at twelve. I can't leave until after that."

"Come have a few drinks," he said, almost pleading. He was a great deal taller than she and every time he looked down at her he got dizzy. He had never seen a pair like these—not from this angle, anyway. "I have been looking forward to this meeting," he said. "Miss Mickle."

"What do you do, anyhow?"

"Do?"

"You didn't explain that on the telephone," she said, warily. "You do something, don't you? You're not one of these types who live on welfare, are you? I have never"—she drew herself up proudly, and the feathers on her nipples fluttered—"I have never resorted to welfare, although I have received unemployment compensation when it was an emergency. Sometimes things just go wrong."

"I'll bet," Richard said, dreamily, "that you could fly with those if you wanted to."

"With what? Oh, you mean these? No," she said, lifting her breasts and letting them drop again, "I'm afraid I can't make them flap. It's a question of pectoral muscles. I can twirl them, though. See?"

"Oh, yes," Richard said, "I see! But I'm not sure I see how it works. Will you do it again, please?"

"Sure. Here." She twirled her tits. "Actually," she said, "it's very simple. Any stripper worth her salt can do it."

"That's wonderful, Miss Mickle."

"Thank you," she said, leading him to a table, "but you didn't come here to see me twirl my tits."

Richard was pensive. "I think I did, Miss Mickle. I think that probably is why I came. Can you tell me what that is?" He was pointing at the purple chicken next to her mouth.

"My signature," she said.

"Oh," he said, "certainly."

"It helps to identify me. Professionally, I mean."

"I think it would be very difficult to confuse you with anyone else."

"You'd be surprised. This is a highly competitive business. But you never told me what you do, Mr. Hacking."

"Didn't I?" he said. "I told you I wanted to see you about a mutual friend."

"Norman Gold, you said."

"Yes. Well, he isn't really a friend of mine. In fact, I've never met him. But I'm a friend of his wife's."

"I don't understand what you want with me, Mr. Hacking. I have never even met Mrs. Gold. Not either of the Mrs. Golds," she added, feeling a surge of forlornness.

"Gussie doesn't know I'm here. I found your number in a book that she lent me which belongs to her husband."

"Norman."

"Yes. Although really it belongs to the library at Columbia. Gussie left it with me when she came to tell me that Norman was having an affair with you."

"Norman?"

"Yes. Although she didn't actually give me your name. She didn't say if she knew who it was, only that she thought Norman was having an affair with someone. But then I found your name in this book, and I figured why else would a musicologist have a stripper's private phone number? You see what I mean, Miss Mickle? So I decided to look you up and find out if you were going to continue this affair, because if you are, then I might be able to convince Gussie that she has a legitimate excuse for resuming her affair with me."

"But I'm not having an affair with Norman. I'm having one with his father. And he has prostate trouble," she added, sadly.

"I don't understand."

"You should. It's very common in men when they get older. It usually makes them horny, but Sidney sees it as a *memento mori,* if you follow me."

"I mean I don't understand what this means. You're supposed to be sleeping with Norman."

"No, I'm not. I'm supposed to be sleeping with Sidney, but he doesn't like for me to pester him."

"Then what do you do with Norman?"

"Nothing. I only met him once, and that was in his father's office. We have a beautiful friendship, but it's all on the telephone. Even that isn't all it should be, because I keep late hours. You'll appreciate that. Anyway, it all started because I tried to get him to stop blackmailing Sidney, but he said that if he agreed to that I would be depriving Sidney of his one chance to redeem his relationship with his son. Norman convinced me. After all, the father-son relationship is really special. Anyone who reads books knows that. Between fathers and daughters is a different story, I should know, but I guess more sons than daughters write books. Be that as it may, as a reader and a citizen I wouldn't want to come between any father and his son, much less Sidney and Norman. Why, Norman told me that if he didn't blackmail his father, they wouldn't ever get to see each other. It would be, like, kaput between them. This way, they see each other every week. Norman says he sees his father more now than he did when he was a kid. Sidney was D.A. then, you know."

"I didn't know."

"Now you do! I admire men of action, like Sidney. They're, you know, active. Mr. Hacking," she said, bending over to adjust the strap on her shoe and then looking up at him through her false eyelashes in a way he could only assume was entirely artful, "what *do* you do?"

"I'm not a man of action," he said, regretting this truth about himself more than he ever imagined he would.

"I don't believe that," she said, now straightening up and idly flicking one of her nipple feathers with a fingernail, "even for one little minute."

He gave in. "I'm a conductor."

"On a bus or on a train?"

Hell, she was going to think he was an idiot. "In an orchestra."

"A symphonic orchestra!"

He nodded, culpable.

"Oh," she said, "oh, oh." Richard couldn't believe his ears.

"You could go to Hollywood on the strength of that *oh*," he said.

"Oh, I'd much rather stay here and talk with you! I love intellectuals!"

"I thought you preferred men of action?"

"Action," she said. "I can take it or leave it. But thinking is something else. Men who think are really deep."

"Thank you," he said, "but I don't really think of myself as an intellectual. It's more Gussie's husband's thing."

"You're just modest," she said. "A conductor!"

"Do you like music?"

"I listen to the radio all the time. I have to listen to rock music here, but at home I listen to the semi-classical station. I read, too. And I do interpretative dancing. Interpretative dancing is just about the most important thing in my life, I expect."

"What's that?"

"You really don't know? Look, Mr. Hacking—"

"Richard."

"Richard," she said, smiling her scene-stealing smile at him. "Come to my place and I'll show you in person what interpretative dancing is."

"But your show—"

"It's okay. I'll tell the manager to put somebody else on. Jock can take my place. You pay the bill while I run get my raincoat. Oh—" she said.

"Yes?"

"I certainly am pleased to make your acquaintance, Richard!"

28

In the infinitely soft, velvet and satin, feather and fur apartment on Madison Avenue, with Désirée pillows, Richard sat on the Empire sofa while Birdie danced for him to Ravel's *Bolero*. He had always roundly detested this piece but, as he told her, she explored possibilities of meaning which he had never realized it contained. She was still wearing her meager feathers. "Birdie," Richard said—they were on a first-name basis now—"you have the sexiest . . . the sexiest . . ."

"What?" she asked, wiping the sweat off her brow as she dropped onto the sofa beside him.

He couldn't say boobs. He said knees.

"Thank you. I'm glad you think so. Knees are very important to a dancer. After all, they are an integral part of the leg, aren't they? Well, do you think I'm good?"

"I think you're *swell,* Birdie. Just swell."

"I mean, as a dancer?"

"Absolutely. You can take my word for it."

"As a professional musician?"

"Why not?"

"Will you advance my career?"

"Will I what?"

"You know. Give me a leg up. You're bound to have connections. Conductors are very sort of chic. Radical chic. I read about it. You move around in all the right circles, don't you?"

"I don't know," he said. "I guess so. Elaine does."

"Who is Elaine?"

"A relative."

"Richard," Birdie said, sucking her right middle finger, "I want to make a clean breast."

"Go right ahead, Birdie, by all means." He was ecstatic.

"It just so happens that you have met me at a very fateful point in my life. I have reached a crossroads. I need to take a giant leap forward. It's now or never. Will you help me?"

"I'd like to if I could, Birdie, but what are we talking about?"

"I know we've only met, but already I feel as if I've known you all my life. You don't have to pretend you don't know what we're talking about. I can look into your eyes and see that you read me like a pamphlet. In your heart of hearts, is this not true, Richard?" She had taken off his tie and had done it up around her own neck, and now she was undoing his shirt.

"Miss Mickle," he said, "I mean Birdie. I appreciate your interest"—he moved her hands away—"but you have to understand that I don't make trades like this. Good God, I'm much too worldly to make a promise like that simply in order to get a little—"

"What?"

She was looking at him with utter earnestness.

"You know."

"Oh," she said, "*that*. I was going to give you some of that anyway."

"What about Sidney?"

"He won't mind," she said, "because he won't know about it. Besides, Sidney likes for me to enjoy myself. But only," she warned, "if you take me seriously. As an artist."

"I do," he said, "I do, I do. And I'll tell you something else. I'm not really very worldly."

"I can't stand worldly men," Birdie said. "They're so . . . worldly."

"I couldn't have put it better myself." He flicked one of her feathers the way she had done in The Joint and watched it spin like a pinwheel.

"I can dance with my twat," she said, in the same clear, straightforward, chiming voice.

"Oh my God," he said, "I don't believe it, I don't believe it."

"I wouldn't say it if it wasn't true. Here, I have to take my wig off first. You help me."

"Anything, I'll do anything."

She turned around and started pulling bobby pins from her wig; when she finished, he was holding it. "Will you get me a big stage engagement?"

"Anything," he repeated, helplessly.

"Good," she said, taking the wig from his hands and walking out with it. She kept her wigs on polyethylene heads in her dressing room.

Richard started to ask her why she wore a platinum wig over her platinum hair, but then he thought better of it.

He watched her go—the buttocks shaking like a pair of maracas. He watched her come—the blind breasts staring at him (she had left the feathers with the wig, not wanting them to get crumpled). With his mouth on one of the pink eyes and his hand wandering toward the balletic twat, Richard suddenly registered something, a piece of information he had been processing in the back of his brain. "Did you tell me," he asked, "that Gussie's husband was blackmailing his own father?"

"Yes, but I explained, it's all for the best. Do you want to see me dance or not?"

"But I did."

"Not this way." Ravel was still playing in the background. "Get away." She pushed him off. "Now watch."

"Oh God, Miss Mickle," he said, "you really are an *artiste* of the highest caliber!"

29

Birdie admitted to herself that Richard was very handsome, but she had never allowed mere looks to sway her. Deep inside, no one was more beautiful than Sidney.

Poor Sidney. Birdie hated pain herself, and she knew it could be no fun for him, having to go all the time and then having it burn like that when he went. If she could have gone in his place, she would have, but there were some things you couldn't do for another person no matter how much you wanted to.

That was love, she said to herself, sighing, but it showed you that even love wasn't enough. Take Sidney. He loved her, and yet lately he didn't feel up to doing much about it, did he?

Sidney, Sidney. Sidney was the only man Birdie would ever have consented to marry. This was because with Sidney she felt exactly the same as she did by herself. No better, no worse, and no different. Other people might think this was a funny definition of love, but what did other people ever know about anything?

Birdie knew, for example, that some people would say her style was out of date, but so what? Most men lived their profoundest emotions in a psychic recess where time barely moved; time there inched along so slowly that clocks or calendars marking "real time" might be said to be to such felt time as Olympic hundred-yard-dashers are to joggers.

What Birdie knew was that she recovered for men an image of femininity lost since 1952 — but now by this emotional up-pulling restored — an image lodged deep in their consciousness somewhere between the first two-wheeler and a best-loved catcher's mitt, an image last seen at the Sadie Hawkins Sock Hop.

It was an image shinily shellacked like Birdie herself, with nostalgia, but Birdie herself never would long for the past or her youth. When Birdie was a little girl, even when she was older, she had had to hide in the closet from her father, because he would try to beat her up when he came home drunk. As she grew up, being clever, she learned another way of hiding, by taking her clothes off. The miracle about Sidney was that with him Birdie could keep her clothes on. However, sometimes she liked to take them off, and if Sidney wasn't interested, why not Richard? If Sidney knew, he would tell her to go ahead. Sidney would never stand in the way of her career.

As for Richard, she liked him a lot, anyway — he was a little dopey, in an egghead sort of way, but good-humored. On the other hand, she would never dream of marrying him. He naturally would not imagine that he might ask her, but men knew nothing about stuff like that. Men almost never knew in advance when they were going to ask a woman to marry them. Most men went into deep shock when they discovered what they had done. However, Richard need not worry about this. Birdie knew when a relative was a wife, and furthermore, she for one was not about to give up all her nights. A girl needed some time alone. Many nights, Birdie took off her makeup and wig and put on an original creation from Frederick's of Hollywood and went to bed by herself, slipping between the satin sheets. She made a little cave in the satin pillows for her head and slept on her right side. Obviously, she couldn't very well sleep on her stomach. She felt like a princess in a fairy tale, her soft cheek, defenselessly naked without its beauty spot, warm against the cool, floating satin.

30

Newark burned in July, and to Norman it seemed as though some kind of ash-cover lingered in the sky, a flake-fine silt falling on the television antennae and cables. He caught a whiff of something combustible in his own soul. Cooler weather brought some relief.

In October, he saw Phil Fleischman off on the march to the Pentagon. He would have liked to go himself, but he felt that his first duty was to his dissertation, which occupied him increasingly. He worked long hours in the library, taking notes, outlining, tracing his way through historical periods tentatively, backing off from dead ends, seeking new approaches, looking for the one way through that would appear, from the far end of the tunnel, inevitable, but which was uncoverable only by the most exhaustive, probing scholarship. Derivative! It still ate on him. What wasn't derivative, when you got down to it? The pieces were always the same. Certainly, there were minor modifications—extinct species, manmade elements—but the essentials stayed the same. The important thing was to put them together in a new way. God was, among other things no doubt, a toymaker, and he had designed the universe like an infinite jigsaw puzzle. Depending on how you fitted the pieces together, you came up with quantum mechanics, the social contract, or the *Grosse Fuge.* Norman was living in a state of high-pitched excitement, convinced that the work he was doing would eventually yield to his blandishments. He saw less and less of Gus, and he was not unaware that there was an element of self-protection in this. "Being entirely honest with oneself is a good exercise," Freud wrote, in a letter to Fliess. Norman agreed completely, but he couldn't do everything at once, and thinking about Gus would have to wait until later. In the meantime, it seemed to him that they got along about as well as young couples could be expected to. Sometimes in the evenings he watched her washing dishes, the jelly glasses and ashtrays and coffee cups and spoons, with the engagement ring parked on the top of the television because she wouldn't take a chance on a cockroach crawling over it on the drainboard, and the unconscious movements of her back and shoulders under the white blouse, the soft slap and swoosh of her hands in soapy water, the bright whiteness of skin at the back of the knee, her cascading golden honey-stream hair, the vulnerable girl-ness of an indented waist—these sights and sounds visited him with a great yearning. He felt that he loved her so much that it made him sad.

These gusts of feeling would sweep over him from time to time, leaving him lonely and on edge, and to defend himself against them, he felt it was necessary to establish a certain slight distance from Gus—nothing noticeable, nothing lamentable, but a bit of breathing- and elbow-room, a psychic space in which he could concentrate on his work. It pleased him that Gus was working hard herself, and it pleased him even more that in a way he was the cause, as he had promised to pay for her debut. Occasionally, a finger of anxiety would nudge him into wondering how he was going to persuade his father to come across with another two thousand, but this was not yet the most pressing of problems. Norman's philosophy was, What is the point in frittering away your best mental energies on the mundane when one's inner life offered such highs and lows as Maria Callas could only dream of?

Yes, and when he emerged from the library on winter evenings, the dark seemed to him to be celebratory. He felt festive. The Christmas decorations swooped across the street. Santa Claus chimed his bell next to a cardboard brick chimney. The air smelled sharp and wet, there were thick, punching-bag clouds poised to snow. Fragrances of smoked chestnut, popcorn, evergreen, peppermint, and motor oil invaded his lungs and made him heady. The blind man at the corner held out his cup and Norman dropped a Kennedy half-dollar into it, although he knew this particular blind man from years of passing him on his way back and forth from Morningside Heights, and the man was no blinder than he was. Who cared? It was the right time of year to be giving your money away. "Peace," the blind man said, with incomparable swagger. Norman answered with a restrained nod, oozing cool, but it was all for show: his heart was rising in his chest and felt so light it might just keep on ascending. Fuck being cool: he couldn't wait to get home.

Gus was out.

31

SHE HAD LEFT a note taped to the television screen: "Gone to look for a Christmas present for Tom and Cyril. Back soon."

Norman drank a quart of eggnog from the icebox and then switched on the news.

He had not noticed it before, but the room had gotten larger since his marriage. This was the opposite of what marriage was supposed to do. While he and Gus were still engaged, Kellogg, one of his professors, had warned him that the most important thing in marriage was a two-room apartment. (Kellogg was a tall, loose-jointed man with tufts of black hair extruding from his ears and nostrils, as if he had been rather carelessly stuffed with straw.) "If you live in an efficiency, your wife gets mad and locks herself in the bathroom, and you can't get in until she comes out. This can be pure agony, if you do what the typical American husband does in such a situation."

Norman had asked what that was.

Kellogg saluted him with his glass. "Drink," he said.

In the event, Gus was always afraid that the ghost of the drowned mouse would somehow rise one night through the sewers of New York, climb out of the john and claim its revenge. And Norman's favorite beverage, next to nonalcoholic eggnog, was root beer. So the apartment, when Gus was not in it, seemed to Norman to have swelled to unmanageable proportions; he didn't know what to do with himself in it. He was immensely relieved when the telephone rang. He turned the news down, carrying the phone from the desk. The long, ice-blue cord trailed behind him. "Gold here," he said.

"My name is Elaine Hacking. You don't know me," a woman said, "but I have something that belongs to you."

"Elaine Hacking," Norman said. "Hacking. Hacking. I don't think we've met."

"I've explained that you don't know me."

"I don't understand."

"You will," she said, "if I can meet you somewhere."

"Do I want to meet you?"

"If you want what's yours, you do."

"Why don't you come here?"

"I don't think that would be a very good idea."

"Why not?"

"Because, Mr. Gold," she said, "I must speak with you privately. It concerns your wife."

"But you said you had something that belongs to me, not my wife."

"I do. You see, Mr. Gold, I wish to make a trade."

"But I don't have anything that belongs to you."

"Your wife does, Mr. Gold."

32

WITH A HEART-CONSTRICTING SENSE of ill omen, Norman retrieved the crumpled note from the wastebasket, reread it— "Gone to look for a Christmas present for Tom and Cyril. Back soon"—and crumpled it again.

He met Elaine Hacking in a workingman's bar on Amsterdam Avenue, a gin mill. It was a place he hadn't been to since before he got married. In just that time, it had gone from bad to worse—it was almost empty. All over New York, Norman thought, there were these isolated pockets of ruin—existential potholes. One day the network would expand an inch too far: one hole would eat into a neighboring hole, and the entire city would collapse into a single giant cavity of poverty and despair.

"Okay," he said, when he was facing her in the only booth in the place, "what's this all about?" He lit a cigarette. He had paid for her vodka gimlet and he was beginning to be annoyed at all the mystery. There was a hole in the red leather seat and the stuffing was extruding—why did he keep thinking of Kellogg? was it because he was a cynic about marriage?—and every time he crossed his legs, the bench seemed to sigh.

"You want to know what this is all about, I'll tell you," she said. She reached into a large squashy leather bag, open at the top like a marsupial pouch, brought out a book and set it on the table in front of him. "It is about this."

"That's my book! I was looking for it just the other day."

"I said I had something that belonged to you."

"But how—"

"My husband's name is Richard."

"Richard." Oh Christ. Oh Christ oh Christ.

"I don't know if you knew that your wife and my husband were— What is the current term?"

"That was before I married Gus."

"Yes. Well, I found this book in my apartment one day when I returned home from shopping. As you will see"—she leaned across the table to turn pages—"there is a letter inside. Unopened. It's addressed to your wife."

"All right," Norman said, "my wife happened to lend a book to your husband. She forgot there was a letter inside it. That's no crime." But it was a crime, dammit, or ought to be. If Gus had some legitimate reason for seeing an old lover, because he was a conductor and could help her plan her program, say, why didn't she tell him about it? "The postmark on this letter is June! And it's never been opened? For Pete's sake, when did you find this book?"

"Last June, of course."

"Look, I may be dense, but why did you wait six months before you decided to return it?"

"For the reason you just gave. Maybe your wife just lent Richard the book and Richard forgot that he had it. He's never asked me about it. Richard," she added, testily, "is easily distracted. You must be too. This book's about three years overdue at the library."

"This letter is from my mother," Norman said, slowly. "I wonder why she would write to Gus."

"I'm sure I don't know. I didn't open it."

"So I see. What I don't see is why, if all you want to do now is return the book, you didn't just mail it to us."

"Because I thought you would want to be told that your wife and my husband have resumed their affair."

As she said this, Norman watched her nostrils flare. She had a red nose, and the skin over her cheekbones was tight and shiny. Her hair was drawn back over the temples, giving her face an exceptionally naked look—almost indecent. She must have been pretty once, when she was softer; even now, she was a type some men would admire—sharp-shinned, good on the tennis court, conscientious in bed, a standout among dinner hostesses, one of those women who are proud of their ability to save a man from himself. Such pride was nearly always justifiable, but Norman didn't like it, nevertheless. She looked as though she controlled her figure with low-calorie bread. She was still wearing her coat, and beyond the plain fact that she was taller than he was, he couldn't deduce for sure the shape of her body in its woolly pod. He tried to think of his wife sleeping with her husband. What could Gus find attractive in a man who had found this woman attractive? The more he thought about this, the angrier he became; rancor seemed to swell inside him, like an inner tube. At first, he was angry at the woman across the table—he was furious with her for being so sexually unappealing to him. If he had at least been moved to ball her, maybe he could have sympathized with Gus. He could have said to himself, Hell, marriage doesn't make people monogamous . . . What's to worry if you or your wife is getting a little on the side? It doesn't mean anything. It's just energy, and energy has only the significance its given context supplies. Screwing doesn't have to be *spiritual.* And justifying his own desires, he would render hers reasonable.

The trouble was, sitting across from this woman, he felt profoundly monogamous, and God damn it to hell, why didn't Gus feel the same way? Why had she married him if she didn't feel the same way?

For his money, his father said.

But his father had disowned him.

But Gus kept urging him to make it up with his father. Evidently, she had been pretty sure that his father would come around.

So now she had resigned herself to the idea that he wouldn't and figured she might as well crawl back into bed with her old lover. Whom she herself had said she cared about more than anybody else.

"What are you thinking?"

"Listen," he said, "are you sure of this? And you better be damn sure before you say yes, because if I find out you're wrong I'll tear you limb from limb." But even as he said this, he realized that it didn't make sense: he would give anything to discover she was wrong. It was the possibility that she was *right* that made him want to bash her over the head with her fucking purse.

"I'm sure. Why do you think I waited this long? To make sure. Richard lies to me. He's too nervous to lie well. He forgets he's said he's going to be at a recording session and when he comes home he says he had a board meeting. He is not very good at subterfuge, but he is persevering. This has been going on for six months and I have put up with it as long as I intend to."

"What do you propose to do?"

"I thought you might have some ideas about what ought to be done."

Norman finished off his drink. He smoked Kools, and his

mouth felt mentholated. "I'll see you to a subway stop," he said, instead of answering her. "This is not the best block to be walking around on at night." He put on his Burberry; it had a detachable lining that he used in the winter. He felt that he needn't have worn it tonight—his heart was on fire.

"Don't worry, I'll get a cab."

"It's up to you," he said, retrieving the book from the table. He held it in his hands. "It's a good book," he said, wistfully. "Your husband would have liked it."

33

EVERY DAY Norman thought about his wife cheating on him, and his heart clamored so loudly for revenge that instead of doing anything about it, he retreated inwardly—anything to get away from the noise, the emotional buzz in his brain. It was as if he had locked himself into an invisible bathroom. In this invisible bathroom, he conjured up wonderfully vivid scenes of sexual vengeance, Othellian in their pity-wrenching magnitude. For this reason, he said nothing. Every time he thought of confronting Gus or Richard Hacking, he envisioned himself strangling Gus to death, or at least punching her in the face, and if he could think of doing that to Gus, what might he actually do to the man she was making it with? Norman did not exactly despise himself for having these fantasies; he figured they were par for the course, psychoanalytically speaking; but he was terrified that he might accidentally-on-purpose act on one of these impulses, and, of course, the last thing he wanted to do was hurt Gus.

How could she look so—oh Jesus, it was a word that hit him with the force of revelation—pure? Because that was exactly how she looked, unpolluted, free from any corrupting admixture, influence or compromise, untouched by time. In short, unadulterated. The eyes were guileless, the mouth was frank, the nose as innocently abbreviated as the American sense of history. Yet she was sleeping with another man before they had reached even their first anniversary—and on top of that, she was writing to his mother, his own mother, behind his back. He kept the letter and the Beethoven book where they wouldn't be seen, under a pile of socks in the dresser; he couldn't very well return the letter to Gus without letting her know that he knew everything. It occurred to him that his inner life was like a book under a pile of rolled socks, size ten.

The way Norman had it doped out (Morris had helped) was that as a child he had felt unloved. Reconnoitering hostile positions, Norman concluded that there was some basis for this feeling. His father thought that the height of intimacy with someone was to blow smoke in his face. Norman was, as his father liked to say, the child of their old age, and his mother had clung to him like a last-minute reprieve from death, or, not to be so melodramatic, from mahjong. Receiving an allowance of sixty dollars a month, he could only conclude that his parents felt they owed him something; he was obviously worthy, he was existentially valuable, and yet he did not feel loved. Clearly, then, he was not at fault—they *ought* to have loved him. They even acted as though they knew they ought to love him. What Norman had discovered (with Morris's help) was that as he grew older he had, unconsciously, of course, directed a considerable amount of mental energy into the attempt to order the world in such a way that "ought" and "is" were equivalent terms. What ought to be, was; or, since he had to allow for the reality principle, *would be.* He was a compulsive optimist. He believed that cause and effect obtained in the moral realm, and to hell with Hume. "Ought" and "is" were not merely contiguous; the latter was necessarily entailed in the former. This had nothing to do with philosophy; it had to do with the way Norman's head whirled, veering like a *draydl,* whenever his life seemed to him to be out of control, either through accident or as a consequence of being in someone else's control. He desired passionately to be the architect of his own experience and in that way achieve some measure of freedom, and he could not very well succeed in a world where there was no meaningful relation—at least a logically possible one—between "ought" and "is."

Nevertheless, having over years pieced all this together in Dr. Morris's drape-drawn office, with the air conditioner lightly humming and dripping water on the other side of the wall in the white-hot sunshine (or with the radiators hissing, coughing, choking, gurgling and suspiring as if commenting on Norman's gray-winter-day monologues), he was now on the lookout against his own compulsive reactions. He knew that he perceived any threat to this conceptual structure as a threat to his psychic structure. When anyone doubted him— his abilities, his judgments—his initial response was to feel rejected. Knowing this and knowing why, he reminded himself that Hacking's wife could be mistaken. Then he remembered afresh—each time it smarted, like sand on a scratch— that Gus had not been one hundred percent satisfied, or else she would never have attacked his work—or his sexual performance. Then he remembered that only that morning— the day before, five minutes ago—she had said she loved him, and said it so unambiguously that she must at least think she meant it, and he did his best, watching her fill Tweetie's water bowl or iron her white blouses, to understand why she had gone back to that son of a bitch. He even found himself watching with a degree of fascination, like watching a foreign language film without subtitles—the cinematography was beautiful, the action incomprehensible. How could she seem so little disturbed? Didn't she care about him at all? Didn't she know how he was suffering? He adopted a tone of sarcasm; this served to keep his own emotions at bay as well as Gus's, and while it pained him to see her flinch at his voice, it also gratified him. A little.

34

It was a sad time, a gloomy stretch in which the days seemed to disappear like snowballs hurled into a river, becoming water and rushing downstream. The light from the favorite lamp took on a bluish tinge against the Persian rug; the ceiling bulb burned out. Even Tweetie seemed lackluster, and Gus had to let him perch on her finger while she stroked his breast with her other hand to perk him up. Only Gus seemed to switch on, like a light, as the nights fell earlier, but that was an illusion—her mood was as blue as the blue in the rug or the quilt, not golden like her hair. Norman's mood was one of crescendoing panic, augmented by frustration. Was this all there was to marriage? To life? He wished more and more that some action would present itself to him as a possibility—anything.

They didn't do much about Christmas, not being entirely clear about which tradition they were supposed to be following. They had no family to celebrate the season with in any case. They had dinner across the hall with Tom and Cyril one rainy evening, but the night before Christmas, there was nobody stirring—not even, Gus remarked guiltily, a mouse.

She and Norman were lying side by side, dressed, on top of the dark red and blue quilted comforter. The radiator hissed; the landlord evidently had the seasonal spirit. A Brandenburg Concerto was spinning on the Garrard turntable, and the joyful noise of the music underscored the restraint with which Gus and Norman approached each other. Gus was tracing Norman's face with her fingers and hoping he would make love to her. She didn't dare ask him, feeling that if he really wanted to make love to her, he wouldn't make her ask him. She wondered what the other woman did in bed that was so splendid. Could Gus learn to do it? Or was making love like playing an instrument? Technique could be acquired, but all the technique in the world wouldn't do you any good if you didn't have the gift of music in your soul. Could she be sexually tone-deaf? Then what was this hemidemisemiquaver she heard in her heartbeat?

Norman felt her fingers on his face, light as snowflakes. She dissembled magnificently, he had to give her that. He listened to the felicitous notes in the background, a dance of sound as full of light as Gus's hair on his cheek, the miraculous balance between rule and abandonment, and he felt as though he was crying internally, tears dropping on his heart, his spleen. What was she trying to do to him?

"Merry Christmas," she said. "I love you."

He turned his face away, and her fingers fell on his mouth. He kissed them in spite of himself.

"Why don't you say it?" she asked.

"Merry Christmas," he said.

"That's not—"

Before she could say what she meant—because he knew perfectly well what she meant—he said, "I should say Chanukah." He smiled, stretching his arms over his head. "You can think of me as your Chanukah *gelt*. How about that?"

"Norman—"

"That's what my parents used to call Rita when she was a kid. Mitzi told me. You remember I told you about Mitzi? She brought me up. Rita was so much older I hardly even knew her. She smelled of hair straightener. She wanted to be a golden Gentile girl, like you. I wonder if she remembers that now, wiping the Manischewitz stains from the transparent plastic slipcovers in Far Rockaway? The thing is, she was born at Chanukah. Rita Gold. Now she's Rita Fishbein. I still don't know her, not really. It's like having an aunt for a sister."

"I don't want to talk about your family, Norman," she said flatly. "I haven't even met your family."

Unfortunately, she couldn't tell him she felt uneasy talking about his family partly because she owed his mother a letter. Esther's letter was still in the Thayer, where Gus had remembered, too late, leaving it, and Gus was afraid of seeing Richard again, under the circumstances (suppose she succumbed?). She felt guilty about not even sending season's greetings to Esther. But how could any young bride play the role of daughter-in-law, if she weren't first approved as a wife? It would be a farce!

Defensively, she continued, "They don't want to meet me, remember? I doubt very much if Rita and her husband are lying on their bed on Christmas Eve talking about me."

"It's not her fault, it's the system. Her husband should be grateful to you. Because of you, he'll pick up an extra half-million, eventually."

"Do you love me, Norman?"

"Sure," he said. "Why not?" He lit a cigarette.

"You smoke too much."

"It doesn't matter," he said. "I don't play the flute."

"You can play the flutist."

"Can I?"

"You've seemed very—I don't know how to say it," she said. "Distant. Lately. Have I done something wrong?"

"Do you think you've done something wrong?"

She waved the smoke away from her face. "No," she said, "of course not. But I think you think that I have. Otherwise, I don't know why you would be so distant. Maybe I've done something wrong without realizing it. If you'll tell me what it is, I'll try to correct it. Whatever it is."

"People are what they are," Norman said. "You can't go around asking them to be something else."

"You don't believe that for one minute, Norman. I've heard you say time and again that if you just know enough about a situation, you can manipulate it to your own ends. If you know what goes on in your own mind, really know, you can change it. You can change your mind intelligently. Please, Norman, I'm only trying to find out what you want from me. If you don't like the way I am, I can change!"

"Don't be silly, Gus. Nobody's asking you to change." This conformable Gus disturbed him deeply—he preferred the Gus who conducted her life as if she were a member of some artistic aristocracy unbound by housewifely convention to one who pledged servilely to revamp her whole spiritual constellation for him. In any case, what good was it when people changed because you asked them to? They had to do it on their own, or it didn't mean anything. Norman considered saying "I don't want you to change," but ended up saying again, "Nobody's asking you to change."

"But something's bothering you, isn't it?"

"I'm preoccupied, that's all."

With whom? she wanted to ask.

"With my work," he said.

She didn't say anything.

"My derivative work." He smiled again, but his eyes were unyielding, mocking, flat. They let in light without admitting any new impressions—he wasn't going to be fooled into seeing anything in a new light. He knew how he must look to Gus because he happened, rolling over, to catch a glimpse of himself in the mirror on the nightstand. His eyebrows almost met in a single line above the extravagantly expressive eyes, and hurt and confusion were inscribed on his face for everyone to see. Self-pity kicked him in the stomach, leaving him stunned. Self-pity was supposed to be pleasurable, one of the forbidden delights which everyone was always running around furtively indulging in, but Norman felt only a sudden searing pain, like having his heart branded with an R for Reject. "God," he said, still staring at the mirror, "I'd like to fuck you through the floor."

"Promises, promises," she said.

35

HE WAS LYING on the bed, on his side, looking at her bare back. She was lying on her side, looking at the frosty triptych, ghostly gold and silver from the street lamp. The room was silent.

"Gus," he said, trying not to let his amusement show in his voice, "you should see what I've done."

"What haven't you done?"

"I've torn a mole halfway off your back. It's half on and half off. I've been meaning to trim my nails."

"*What* have you done?" She sat up and twisted around, trying to see her back.

"Here," he said. He held the mirror up for her. "You see it?" He was grinning.

"I don't see what's so funny."

"I'm sorry," he said, straightening his face out, "it isn't. You'll have to get it removed. It doesn't hurt. I had several moles removed from my neck when I was a teen-ager. You can't keep it like that."

"Can't you just pull it all the way off?"

"I wouldn't dare. I know a doctor. I'll call him tomorrow."

"Norman"—she slid into his arms, resting her head in the crook of his elbow—"are you through being angry?"

"Shhh," he said, kissing her on the nose. "Merry Christmas." He fell asleep still dressed.

36

THE DOCTOR insisted on operating in a hospital, although no anesthetic was required. His reason was that as an in-patient Augusta could collect insurance; if he treated her in his office, he wouldn't have the heart to charge them, because he knew Norman was still in school. The mole had to come off. Gus didn't feel she could refuse to enter the hospital, since that would then be tantamount to asking the doctor to do it for nothing. Unfortunately, the only day the doctor could schedule her was February the first. She had to check in on the afternoon of the day before—and that was her first wedding anniversary. She didn't tell the doctor—how could she, with all this good will floating around (toward everybody except the insurance company)? But who wanted to spend the first wedding anniversary in a hospital? She joked about it with Norman, not wanting to make him feel any worse about it than he already did—he was blaming himself—but after she had had her blood pressure checked, her temperature taken, her finger pricked, and her urine whisked away in a paper cup, and she was tucked into bed, her rings removed and signed for and replaced with an ID bracelet, she realized it would be the first night she had spent away from Norman since they had gotten married. Did this mean anything? Was it significant? She wanted to ask someone, but all the nurse's aides spoke only Spanish.

A different doctor, young, sallow, and callow, came in to ask her some questions. He looked at her nails. "Why do you bite this one?" he asked, tapping the tip of her ring finger, now ringless.

"Because I harbor unresolved resentment against my gender," she said, tired of being treated as the slave of her subconscious. "What are you going to do about it?"

"What would you like for me to do about it? Let's see that mole."

She showed it to him.

"How did it happen?"

"My husband did it."

"You're kidding! How come?"

"It just happened. We were— And while we were— And then afterward— I explained all this once, isn't it written down somewhere?"

"You mean your husband gouged this mole out while he was screwing you?"

"Look, doctor, I don't think you've got a very good bedside manner!"

"Maybe not," he said, "but it sure beats your husband's."

"Speaking of the devil," Gus said, looking up.

Norman was standing in the doorway. "You all right, Gus?" he asked.

"She's fine," the young doctor said, slapping him on the back and winking. Instinct told Norman to throw a punch at the guy, but by now, the Voice of Experience was making itself heard also, saying, Forget it. So he winked back at the doctor and waited until he'd left the room before going up to the bed. Gus saw the wink and it made her feel helpless, relegated to a walk-on role. All the world's a stage, and all the women merely bit-players. She used to get the same feeling back in high school, the feeling of being talked about by the boys rather than talked with. You went through life never knowing for sure what they were saying.

"Are you going to be all right?" Norman asked again. "You're not lonely, or anything?"

"I feel ridiculous being in here when I'm not sick."

"They're going to make me leave in a minute."

"Are you going home?"

"Where else?"

Elsewhere.

"I might give Phil a ring," he said. "I'll be here as soon as it's over in the morning." He seemed, to Gus, oddly exhilarated, as if he had to restrain himself from smiling. His gleaming, dark, lavishly abundant, tight curls seemed to bristle, like a cat's back in a thunderstorm.

"I'll be thinking about you," she said, forlornly.

"On the other hand," he said, "if Phil is out, I might look up an old friend."

After he left, she wondered if he had used the phrase *old friend* on purpose. Did he mean *old friend* as in *old friend,* or did he mean *old friend* as in "your *old friend,* Richard"? And was it significant? Again, she wanted to ask someone, but no other English-speaking personnel came into the room the rest of the day. She tried to look on this operation as a free trip to Puerto Rico.

37

SHE'S HAVING this mole removed," Norman said. "It seemed like a good opportunity." He was seated on the Empire sofa in Birdie's apartment, leaning forward earnestly with his hands clasped between his knees. "You must think I'm crazy," he said, "barging in on you like this. I've got to talk with somebody."

"I don't think you're crazy. Truly I don't." But she did think he might be just the tiniest, fractional bit mad. He had Sidney's knack for dramatizing everything, which as a person of known dramatic flair she personally appreciated, but his eyes were different. They weren't like his father's eyes, and they weren't like Richard's eyes either. They were very attractive eyes though, she thought, moving her chair closer to him until their knees bumped. "You have very interesting eyes," she said. "Like a person in a book. I would say they are devastating. Yes," she said, peering into them, "they are quite definitely very devastating eyes. Have you ever tried to hypnotize anybody with them?"

"No," he said. He reconsidered. "In a way," he said.

"I thought so. You're the Svengali type."

"Nobody ever said that before."

"They probably weren't as perceptive as I am."

"That's why I decided to call you. I could have called Phil, but it's something you don't want to talk about to someone you grew up with. Phil thought I was a jerk for getting married anyway."

"Your friend Phil is not married?"

"He goes with a girl named Dinky."

"Dinky!" Birdie said. "I know a Dinky. Or rather, I know her mother. What does she do?"

"She's a model."

"That's the one," Birdie said. "Her mother is always bragging on her. Is she pop-eyed?"

"A little," Norman admitted.

"It must be her. Ledbetter. The mother thinks she's really hot stuff for raising her kid up to be legitimate, but she couldn't have done it by herself. Her John paid the school bills and the orthodontist. I could have had a John who would keep me like that, but I prefer to be independent. If I weren't independent, how would I know that what I feel for Sidney is genuine? I think," Birdie said, frowning, "being independent is just about the most important thing in the world. Sometimes. Other times, it doesn't seem so important. Do you find that your opinions change like that? Mine seem to shift with the wind, like clouds." She giggled. "Not really," she said.

"Well, then you can understand why I would be reluctant to discuss my wife with Phil. For one thing, he might start to compare her with Dinky Ledbetter."

"Oh, if he does that, you can just tell him that she isn't strictly legit. She only models part of the time. I know, because her mother told me. Not that I think there's anything wrong in that. As Mrs. Ledbetter told me—she is known in the trade as Mrs. Bedletter, by the way—you trick 'em, you don't treat 'em. Though speaking for myself, I prefer to lay down for pleasure."

"Lie down."

"Now?"

He flushed. "What I was trying to say, Miss Mickle—"

"Birdie."

"—Birdie, is that one of the things I never realized marriage does is, it isolates you from everybody. I've heard women complain about this, of course, but shit, Birdie, I don't have anyone to talk to either. The only people a man could have a discussion of this type and quality with are the same people you *can't* have it with after you're married, namely, women. I know that Bunny Van Den Nieuwenhutzen, for example, even if I could locate her, doesn't want to discuss my wife."

"You'd be surprised what women will listen to from a man."

"But only if they think there's something in it for them, right? So women are out, and Phil is out, and it's sure as hell not possible to talk about these things in a seminar or a poker game. I don't know any tribal elders or fellow warriors. If this is the nuclear family, I think I'm going to explode. I feel so *lonely,* Birdie. I can't even talk to my mother, since she seems to be in league with Gus. And obviously this is not something I can discuss with my father. Boy, wouldn't he just love it if I told him what was going on!" Norman thought for a second about what was going on, while Birdie watched distress and anger chasing each other across his face. "My father has a mole that I always thought he should have removed," he said, "talking about moles."

"Don't worry about your father's mole," Birdie said. "Or his sinuses. But you can worry about his prostate."

"What's wrong with his prostate?"

"Nobody knows. He won't go to a doctor."

"That's ridiculous," Norman said. "Who ever heard of a member of the Gold family refusing to see a doctor?"

Birdie shrugged. "The only member of the Gold family I know is Sidney's," she said. "He says it would be a waste of money."

"Money," Norman said with disgust. "That's all my father thinks about."

"Are you still blackmailing him?"

"I wouldn't dream of stopping."

"I thought a lot about how you explained what you were doing, Norman. It's so deep. I really admire deep men. They're so . . . deep."

"I think it would kill him if I quit. I see him every week, this way. If I quit blackmailing him, he'd have to stick to the standard he set for himself. Or rather, the standard that he thinks religion, politics, and tradition have set for him; i.e., to act as if I don't exist. It is a hell of a hard standard for a father to live up to. Emotionally lethal. Why do people insist on doing these things to themselves? I can guess, but frankly, Birdie, I don't feel like trying. Not now."

"You poor boy. You look so miserable."

"It stands to reason," he said, glumly. "I feel miserable."

"I'll do anything I can to help," Birdie said, meaning it fervently, "anything at all. However," she added, "you haven't told me what the problem is."

"My wife is having an affair."

"But you just got married! I know, because I remember that Sidney wept all day long. Right here. He was sitting in the very spot in which you are now sitting, Norman! Isn't that amazing?"

"I don't know what to do, Birdie. I just don't know what the fuck to do!"

"I don't understand how this could have happened in so short a space of time, Norman."

"Neither do I. If we had been married for years, okay, I suppose it would be predictable. There would be ways of dealing with it. Maybe I would have had some peccadilloes too. But Christ, am I supposed to storm out of the apartment? It's my apartment. Do I kick her out into the street? The bastard's married, she would have no place to go. It's a one-room apartment. How do we live in it if we talk about this sensibly and openly, the way they do in Swedish films? I wouldn't be able to look her in the eye. I assure you, Birdie," he said, glowering, "I am not Scandinavian!"

"No, no," she said quickly, "I can see that." She was still trying to figure out how this had happened. "I remember you were having a fight with her the first time I called."

"We'd have to sleep side by side at night while one of us looked for another place in the day. Besides, I love her. Meanwhile I am having trouble thinking. These images of wholesale slaughter keep interfering with my mental processes. You should try writing a dissertation sometime while another man is shagging your wife. It isn't easy," he said.

"I'm sure it isn't," Birdie said, soothingly.

"Anyway," he went on, "I'm hardly irrational. I thought about killing the guy but all that would do is create who-knows-how-many fatherless children. His wife would undoubtedly seek revenge. She's the one who told me this was going on, and I know for a fact that she is the revenge-seeking type."

"You mean you know who he is?"

"Hell, yes. His name is Richard Hacking."

38

Birdie jumped up from her chair. She was wearing a white feather boa—Sidney had bought it to replace the fox—and one tail of it swung loose, dangling in front of Norman's face. He tugged on it and she leaned down, those things, those bowls of mellow Jell-O, quivering at the tip of his nose. They were double trouble, like a Popsicle. It was all he could do not to start licking them, like sugar cubes. But Birdie was whispering frantically. "You have to leave now, Norman. You have to!"

"What's wrong?" he asked. He was happy in this warm, low-lit, amniotic room with the semi-classical music in the background.

"Oh," she said, "oh. Go, Norman, please. Scram. I have to make a telephone call. I have to see somebody."

"My father?"

"That's right," she said. "Sidney. I forgot I have to see Sidney. Norman!" she called, showing him out the door.

He turned back to look at her, asking the question with his eyebrows.

Her face was as white as one of Gus's blouses, except in the crevices where her nose joined her face, where the powder had caked and turned a light orange-frosting color. And except for the purple beauty spot and her eyeshadow. "Nothing," she said, giving Norman a wild look, "nothing. Just—

Oh, Norman, if misery loves company, I am your boon companion!" Then she shut the door and he was left standing there, staring dumbly at the painted wood with its one-way peephole.

39

Richard said he had to go to Boston before he could come to Madison Avenue. Waiting for him to answer her summons, Birdie polished her shoes. She read half a dozen novels. She embarked on a new regimen of diet and exercise. Women who let themselves go learned that men would let them go too, Birdie always said. When Richard rang her doorbell a couple of weeks later, she was wearing a purple sweatband with a bow around her hair and a purple leotard and she was sweating from her workout. Richard gazed at her raptly. "What are you staring at?" she demanded.

"I was admiring the way you sweat. You seem to do it all over." The damp leotard clung to her body like Saran Wrap. Her boobs and backside seemed to be wrestling for right-of-way.

"You took a long time getting here! I've been worrying and worrying!"

He took off his coat and settled in. "I couldn't come before, or believe me, I would have, Birdie. Not only did I have to go to Boston, but my wife suspects something. I feel her eyes on me all the time. In fact, just the other day I realized for the first time that her eyes are the color of seaweed. It is staggering how you can live with someone for years and not even notice these elementary facts. Of course, part of the problem is that while I see her eyes every day, I very seldom get to look at seaweed. It is one of the many professional liabilities in being a conductor. Your world is bounded by hotels and concert halls. You have really been an eye-opener for me, Birdie. What have you got to drink?"

"Here," she said, handing him a Scotch-and-water. "I'm out of ice. I used it all up drinking Hawaiian Punch. Exercise makes me thirsty."

"I can see why," he said, lovingly. "I get hot just looking at you."

"Don't be stupid, Richard."

"No. Actually, it's quite cold outside. Blustery, even." He leaned back on one of the Désirée pillows.

"I have something very important to ask you, Richard."

"I told you I would get you a dance engagement. It takes time, Birdie." He said this without having any intention of furthering her career. What could he possibly do, anyway? But it was not as if he were lying—he wouldn't sink so low. He was sure she didn't really mean for him to *do* anything: women just found it reassuring when a man made promises. It meant they had some claim on the man's future, that they entered into his thoughts about what he intended to do as well as what he had done the night before. That's all. Richard was beginning to feel that he understood women pretty well—well enough to make them happy, at least. He liked making women happy. When they were happy, he was happy. He could relax. He could drift off in their arms, thinking about fishing off the coast of Florida. He had been to Florida only once, but he thought of it as the place he would like to pass on to when he died. There were no sound engineers in Florida. There were no symphony patrons, no cocktail parties for the radically chic. Leonard Bernstein did not live in Florida. Oh, Richard remembered the smell of fish on the floor of the boat, the sun drying the water that splashed on the deck, leaving salt that he had to wash from the soles of his feet at night. He even remembered seaweed.

"It's not about that," Birdie said. She blurted it out: "Are you cheating on your wife?"

"Of course I am," he said. "With you."

"Not counting me," she said. "I don't count."

"I think Elaine would disagree with you about that. So would I. You count for a lot in both our eyes," he said, a great ache in his heart.

"You are not with me, Richard," she said, sternly. "Now you must listen carefully. This is very important." Sometimes it seemed to her that Richard was very dim. He certainly was not as smart as Sidney. "Your wife thinks that you are having an affair with Gus Gold."

"Who told you that? Birdie! You haven't been talking to my wife, have you?"

"It doesn't matter who told me. Richard, are you going around with her? I can understand if you are. After all, you are not the only man in my life. But I told you about Sidney, and you kept this girl a secret from me. That's not right, Richard!"

"Birdie, I'm not seeing Gus Gold. What you heard is old news. I told you she was a friend of mine. I *used* to see Gussie, before she got married to this creep what's-his-name. Norman."

"Norman is not a creep."

"Did he tell you this?"

"He heard it from your wife."

"She must think that's who I'm seeing now. That means she doesn't know about you, Birdie." Richard was feeling better and better.

"But if it isn't true, you have to tell Norman! You can't let him go on thinking his wife is having an affair with you."

"I don't mind."

"Richard!" she said. "I mind."

"Okay, but I can't tell Elaine. If I did, she'd try to find out who I *am* seeing who would know that she was mistaken about who I'm seeing."

"You could tell Norman."

"Like hell I could. I refuse to get involved with Norman. After all, he married the girl I *was* seeing. When I wasn't looking."

"Well, I can't tell Norman. He'll wonder how I know who it is you're having an affair with. He thinks I'm exclusively his father's mistress." She stopped, as if she'd stumbled onto something. "That's true, you know. Maybe you don't know. Honest, these young men think in very old-fashioned terms. Mistress, for example. They don't really know how to appreciate a woman who likes to be independent. I tried to explain this to Norman, but I am not sure he understood. I thought Norman was very attractive, eyes-wise, but I don't believe he would ever understand my deepest desires the way his father does," she added, thoughtfully. "I'll call your wife."

"You'll what! Over my dead body," he said.

"Don't worry, Richard. I won't tell her who I am. I'll remain totally anonymous." She gave a little shiver, and to Richard's eyes, the purple leotard seemed to vibrate, like a violin string. "Isn't it exciting?" she asked.

"I don't know, Birdie, do you really think this is the thing to do?"

"The only other alternative is for you to tell Norman's wife that her husband thinks you are seeing her. I don't see how that would help her, though. She would have to deny it to Norman, and what husband would believe his wife if she suddenly announced out of a clear blue sky that she was not sleeping with someone?"

"I see your point."

"It's settled, then. I'll call Elaine. Don't worry, it'll be all right. Gee, Richard, I am really glad you aren't seeing Norman's wife. I thought I was sort of special to you."

"You are, Birdie, you really are."

"If Norman's wife told him she heard this from you, she'd be in even a worse mess unless she could explain that you got it from me, and that brings us back to one of the places we were before. Why, if Norman thought I was cheating on Sidney, which is how he would view it, being very idealistic, he might even think he had no grounds for blackmailing his father anymore, and Sidney would hate that! No more weekly redemption! It's better this way."

"Poor little Gussie. I don't think she should have got married. She's a lovely girl, Birdie, very talented. However, she is not built the way you are. There is built, and then there is built," he explained, appreciatively.

"I have always thought," Birdie said, "that it must be very difficult to be married and have a career at the same time. Even for a man."

"It is," Richard said, gratefully.

"You're probably worn out yourself. Why don't you lean back and I'll massage your temples?" She adjusted the pillow behind his head. "Sidney loves it when I do it for him. He says you can't get a real massage anymore."

"He's right," Richard said, leaning back and closing his eyes. Birdie stood behind him, rubbing his temples. After a while she leaned over and kissed him. It gave her a most peculiar but interesting sensation, an upside-down sensation such as she used to get when she was a child hanging from a Jungle gym. Richard had his nose in her cleavage. Neither of them heard the key turning in the lock.

40

O<small>H,</small> S<small>IDNEY,</small> I'm sorry! I didn't mean for you to find out like this."

"Relax, Birdie," he said. "I may be old but I'm not an old fool."

"Nobody knows that better than I do, Sidney," Birdie said. "I would have told you myself." She waved a hand at Richard. "At the right time."

"It's okay, Birdie." He turned to Richard. "Sidney Gold," he said.

"Richard Hacking." They shook hands.

"That's nice," Birdie said. "I love to see men being manly together. It's so . . . manly. You want a drink, Sidney?"

"I'll take some of your Hawaiian Punch," he said. "Lately I just don't seem to have the heart for booze. The stomach, but not the heart. Ah, Birdie, Birdie. What age does to a man."

"I'll leave if you like," Richard said. "I should be going anyway." He had risen from the sofa and was straightening his tie.

"Why?" Sidney asked, taking his place on the sofa. "You're in too big a rush to say hello to a friend of Miss Birdie Mickle's?"

"But I thought—" And furthermore, he had said hello.

"I know what you thought. I haven't lived all these years for nothing. I don't know what you do for a living, but you are the criminal type, that's for sure. I can tell it from looking at you. It's okay by me. I don't care what you do so long as you treat Birdie nice and don't get sent to me for sentencing."

Richard was rather pleased by this and sat down in the Louis Quatorze chair. "Do you really think I have the physiognomy of a criminal?" he said.

"It always shows." It was plain to Sidney that the man was a harmless dunce, but it never hurt to flatter people. If they were experts in graft you flattered them by talking about their church contributions. If they were naive, you flattered them by suggesting they were experts in graft. Nobody got to be a judge of any kind without being a judge of character. Or without being a flatterer.

Birdie was taking off Sidney's shoes and massaging his feet. He looked down and saw the pert purple bow on top of her head.

"That can wait, Birdie," he said. "You must be tired from giving Mr. Hacking his massage. Rest."

"I knew you two would like each other. It was inevitable, because I like you both. I *love* you both." Birdie was beaming.

"We love you," Richard said, feeling safe so long as he could speak in the plural.

"Richard's going to help me with my career, Sidney. He's going to get me a dance engagement. It'll be very classical."

"I'm not really a criminal," Richard said, seriously. "I'm a conductor."

"Same difference," Sidney snorted. "How much do they give you for telling the players to do what they had to know how to do anyway or they wouldn't be in the orchestra in the first place?"

"I see what you mean," Richard said, ever agreeable. "There is something extortionary about it."

"Sidney is a great teaser," Birdie said. "Aren't you, Sidney?"

"Who's teasing? Mr. Hacking, I'll tell you how come I'm such an expert on orchestras. You should meet my son the musicologist."

Birdie gasped and tried to shake her head at Richard but he didn't see her.

"I don't think so," Richard said. "I know his wife."

"You know his wife and not him? What does this mean, Mr. Hacking, you shtupped his wife? Why else would you not know her husband my son?"

"You're jumping to conclusions, Sidney," Birdie said, desperately.

"So? It's not so big a jump."

"I'm professionally acquainted with her. Sir," Richard added, trying to give his statement weight.

"Oh well, what's it to me? Nothing. Because I disinherited my son when he married your professional acquaintance. I suppose you think I was wrong, Mr. Hacking."

"I never really thought about it, sir," Richard said.

Sidney was squatting on the Empire sofa, legs spread, arms crossed, like a toad on a toadstool. His white fringe was thinning.

"A man's gotta do what a man's gotta do," Birdie said, rhapsodic. She would have hitched her thumbs under her belt but it was impossible to mime John Wayne in a leotard. For one thing, she had no belt. She ducked out of the room for a minute and returned wearing a crotch-length wraparound purple skirt which didn't quite cover what she thought of as her derrière. The effect was to make her look like a feather duster.

"Birdie tells me," Sid said, looking at her legs and free associating, "that you are giving her a leg up."

"Yes sir, so to speak, sir," Richard said.

"Stop calling me sir."

"Yes sir. I mean, Your Honor, sir. Yes, Your Honor."

"Young people," Sid said.

It was the first time Richard had been called a young person in approximately ten years, and this, coupled with Sidney's earlier observation, gave him a peculiarly exciting feeling, a kind of existential titillation, as if he was on the edge of developing new and perverse inclinations—heights of degradation. The podium was merely a beginning; next, the world, in all its convoluted richness.

However, Sidney didn't stop here; he had merely paused, as if to state the subject of his speech: "You're all authority-ridden," he said, and at once, Richard felt himself wilting. "Either you're rebelling against authority or you're sucking up to it. When I was your age I was running arms to Palestine. Why don't you do something with your life?"

"Build a country, you mean?"

"So what's better to do?"

"I don't feel as young as you think I am."

"It's immaterial," Sid said. "Take it from me, you're young. Birdie's young. Birdie's practically a baby, but she has a good mind. Don't let appearances fool you. A man who lets appearances fool him is a fool, and also generally a young fool in my experience. Appearances can be deceiving."

"That's very true," Richard said.

"I can see you're nobody's fool, Mr. Hacking. So you'll understand what I'm saying when I say you take good care of Birdie and see that she gets the break her career needs, and then when you need a little help behind the scenes, why, you come to me and we'll see what we can do."

"Birdie said you were going to be on the Supreme Court."

"It's not so definite as that, but could be, could be. If Amato goes in, Leibowitz goes in, and if Leibowitz goes in, yours truly will not exactly be standing out in the cold because I once did Leibowitz a favor or two, such as I am now suggesting you'll do for me if you know what's smart."

"Actually, sir, I don't see how you could ever do anything for me. I'm not planning to test the Constitution."

"Richard is very mild and dreamy," Birdie said. "If you don't mind my saying so, Richard."

"Birdie's right," Richard said. "Frankly, aggression scares the hell out of me. My wife is all the aggressiveness I can handle."

"Let me say it another way then. If you don't come through for Birdie, I personally will arrange that your wife finds an outlet for her aggression, and I don't mean tennis. I may have neglected to mention that I have one or two small arms left over from when Israel won its statehood."

"I get your meaning, sir, yes sir, I would say your point is very well put. I'll do my best by Birdie."

"Swell," Sidney said, glaring at him.

41

As AGREED, Birdie called Elaine and told her that Richard was not sleeping with Gus. She made the call from her apartment on Madison Avenue. She had a French telephone and next to it a small neat pad of white paper with a golden magnetic ballpoint pen, with which she and Richard left messages for each other, as it wasn't always easy to coordinate their public and private performances. She dressed in negligee and peignoir for the call, feeling that it was an occasion of sorts. On the other hand, Birdie found almost everything an occasion of sorts. "So you see," she said to Richard's wife, "you just must tell Norman."

"Who are you?" Elaine said. "How do you know all this?"

"My name is—" Birdie said, catching herself. "It doesn't matter. I'm a friend. I'm a real disinterested party. I just think it's only fair to Norman that someone should let him know that his wife is not cheating on him. A very well informed source told me that she's very sweet."

"Sweet, my eye. Who are you?"

"I told you, a friend. Don't you believe me?"

"Not much. I think if you're telling the truth, it must mean that Richard is sleeping with you."

"But somebody has to tell Norman! Will you do it?"

"Why don't you do it, if you're so eager for him to know it?"

"I don't want him to know who I am!"

"Who are you?"

"If I tell you, will you promise not to tell Norman?"

"Look, do you want me to tell Norman or not tell Norman?"

"I just want you to tell him his wife's not sleeping with Richard—"

"Richard! So you are sleeping with Richard!"

"—and don't tell him you heard it from me."

"I'll do this," Elaine said, "but only on one condition. You tell me your name."

"I knew you would do it," Birdie said, burbling. "I knew you had a big heart. My name is Birdie." She giggled. "You didn't say I had to tell you both my names."

42

But Elaine changed her mind, although it was several weeks before anything so definite as that took place. At first, she simply put off telephoning Norman while she fixed herself a vodka gimlet. Then she decided to drink her vodka gimlet while sitting in the polished living room with the framed mirror and bouquets, now tulips. Then she fixed herself another one. All this time she pondered Birdie's message. The children were asleep. Richard was at a rehearsal. Purportedly. Presumably, he would not have been with this woman, Birdie, when she made the call. Richard did have rehearsals to attend. Indeed, it seemed to Elaine that ever since she could remember, Richard had been at a rehearsal and the children had been at home, awake or asleep. What was left, besides vodka gimlets? Sometimes, when Elaine asked herself this question, it was a rhetorical question; but sometimes she put it to herself with a painful sense of existential emergency. Whether the former or the latter depended largely on how many vodka gimlets she had put away.

She could recite to herself how it had been before the children came, but she could not really remember it. The events in those early days—she tended to think of them as having occurred somewhere around the start of the century—no longer carried with them the stamp of personal validation that emotion lends to life, like a visa in a passport. She could look at herself in the photographs on the wall over the bar, fresh-faced, manicured and level-gazed, with a beguiling inkstain on her cheek, and she felt only a formal recognition, no inner link to that girl who went to Wellesley and spent all her spare time making prints in the lithograph workshop.

If she drank enough vodka gimlets, she grew sorry for the girl in the photographs. Enormous waves of pity would roll in on her unforeseen like an offshore squall, washing over and choking her, but it was not *self*-pity because she could no longer feel that she and the girl in the photographs were one and the same. Elaine Hacking was not Lainy O'Hara, voted Perkiest and Most Forward-Looking in her dorm. It was Elaine Hacking, not Lainy O'Hara, who had a husband who slept with other women and left her to take care of his children and his laundry.

If the world only knew what it was like, being the wife of a conductor. From the outside, it looked like a profile in *The New Yorker,* or a layout in *Town and Country,* but what the captions didn't tell you was that you had to devote all your time to protecting your husband from other women. And of course Richard required that protection, demanded it, even if he would say he didn't. Richard would fall to pieces if she ever said the hell with it and turned him loose in that mob ... It must be the baton. It had to be the baton. They took one look at him up there on the podium, wielding that little stick, and they went berserk. Somebody should have warned her, when she was still Lainy O'Hara and lived on coffee and doughnuts, art and ambition, generating ideas for masterpieces even in her dreams at night, just what being a conductor's wife entailed. She had seen herself as Alma Mahler. It had all looked so beautiful, from the outside, an age ago. She had not been oblivious to that dumb baton herself.

Now Richard was sleeping with a woman named Birdie. Really, that was going too far. Did Gustav sleep with a woman named Birdie? Why should she, Lainy O'Hara herself, do anything this woman asked, much less what she was asking? Did Elaine Hacking née Lainy O'Hara owe anything at all to a woman who was very likely trying to steal her husband from her? And how had this woman heard what Elaine had thought, anyway? Had Norman Gold told his wife, and his wife told Richard? But if the woman was telling the truth and Richard was not having an affair with Augusta, then when would Augusta have told him that Norman thought, because Elaine had told him so, that she and Richard were having an affair? The more Elaine drank, the more complicated the situation appeared.

It was so complicated that Elaine took several weeks to mull it over. From her point of view, there was no urgency about the situation. Most of this time she was absorbed in other tasks as well, fixing fresh orange juice for the boys in the morning and tucking them in at night and in between trying to socialize them without de-socializing herself beyond reclamation. Another thing that none of her professors at

Wellesley had warned her of was that being the mother of sons meant learning everything you ever wanted to know about sex and also everything you didn't want to know. She was doing her best to help them grow up with the minimal number of hang-ups, but it wasn't easy, not when their father's attention kept wandering. From the time he was an infant, almost, Jeremy had been taught by Richard that whenever he wanted to do what Elaine, in spite of Dr. Spock, could only think of as indulge himself, he should simply say so and excuse himself from the room. Now she had an eight-year-old son who indulged himself while watching Batman on the twelve-inch portable in the room he shared with his brother. She could deal with this, a son with a Penguin fetish, but what was driving her up the wall was that whenever he vanished into the room to indulge himself, he locked his younger brother out. In fact, Elaine sometimes suspected that Jeremy used Richard's modern notions of child-raising as a cover, and what he was really doing was watching Batman.

Jeremy's younger brother, Jeff, was a sturdy, pugnacious, round-faced five-year-old with a tucked-in chin, close-spaced eyes, and an Aldo Ray voice. God only knew what he was going to be when he grew up. In jail, probably. He had an incipient gruffness that Elaine loved—she could look into his crossing eyes and see a boxer, a jockey, or a boss of big crime. When she was an old lady and Richard was too weak to lift his baton anymore, at least there would be someone to take care of her. Elaine nurtured a special affection for her baby boy, the little tough one. When Jeremy locked the door against him, Jeff went at it with such vigor that Elaine was convinced it would one day cave in. Nevertheless, Jeremy refused to open it until he was ready to, which generally meant after the show was over. And then Jeff would hit Jeremy. It might seem that the simplest solution would have been to fix the door so it wouldn't lock, but Richard refused to allow this. He said that children needed their privacy quite as much as adults did. Elaine pointed out that Jeremy was enjoying his privacy at the expense of his younger brother. Richard said Jeffrey would simply have to learn that in this world you had to make concessions. It was plain to see where Richard's sympathies lay, but it was not clear to Elaine whether Richard sided with Jeremy because he favored self-indulgence, privacy, or Batman.

Introduction to Marriage and the Family 101 had never warned her that she would spend the best years of her life shouting. For years she had been shouting. It seemed to her that life since Wellesley had been one long scream—at the kids, at Richard. Not hysterical screaming, mind you; merely motherly screaming. Elaine toyed with the idea of someday starting to scream and never stopping, but she had not gone to Wellesley for nothing. She knew how to keep her hysteria well under control. No, this was beneficent screaming and shouting, dutifully undertaken for others' sake, not her own. Admonitions delivered in a normal tone of voice went unheeded. If you wanted them to put their rubbers on, to take their vitamins, to remember a meeting, to do their homework, to refrain from falling into bed with the latest dolly bird, it was necessary to scream. Frequently over the din of music. Elaine's most treasured moments were those she could spend in silence, with the boys asleep and the phonograph off. She drank her vodka gimlets and sank into a restful contemplation of the sound of one hand clapping.

What Richard dreaded, she loved.

She drank her vodka gimlets and the fluffy snowflakes turned thin and gray, and then the thin gray falling snow turned to a sharp, stinging needlelike rain stitching a veil in front of her eyes as she walked home from Gristede's in raincoat and rainhat.

She drank her vodka gimlets and the bitter wind off the river changed direction, bringing spring breezes light as muslin, the sort of spring peculiar to Manhattan, promising fame and fortune in the fullness of summer. If you were under thirty-five. She shopped for mandalas and ming trees, after-dinner liqueurs and roach clips. (She didn't do grass herself, preferring vodka gimlets, nor did Richard, preferring Scotch, but that year it was the in-thing among patrons of the symphony; Elaine used the clips to hold place cards for her table settings.) She shopped for tennis shoes for the boys for when they went to the Hamptons for the summer, a one-piece suit for herself to hide the gallstone scar, thong sandals for herself and for Richard, and tickets to *Hair*. She wore a navy blue shift and tied her hair back with a matching piece of yarn, in what, when she went to school, had been called a horse's tail: it didn't ride high on the back of the head like a pony tail. The heat from the sidewalk seemed to slide up her stockingless legs like a not-unwelcome hand. The do-nothing clouds lazed in the blue sky, elegant, diaphanous, and disinclined to stir, like guests at a Roman banquet. The sun glinted off shop windows and the braided epaulets of doormen, and she developed an itchy rash directly under the face of her watch and had to give up wearing it, so that she lost all track of time. Nevertheless, though she was only barely conscious of herself thinking and of time passing, one day she realized that over a period of time she had arrived at a conclusion: it had hung on the edge of her consciousness like a nest on a branch. If it was true that Augusta Gold was not sleeping with Richard, she could not have told Richard what Norman had heard from her, Elaine; therefore, this woman Birdie must have heard it from Norman. *Therefore* Norman was acquainted with the same woman who was seducing Richard from the more important things in his, Richard's, life. THEREFORE Norman was no friend of hers. That explained why he had been so noncommittal in the bar on Amsterdam.

That was how the book had wound up in Elaine's apartment: from Norman Gold to Birdie Whoever to Richard. Did they know yet that they were sharing the same woman? God. Talk about a bird in the hand being worth two. The more she considered this, the more convinced Elaine became that Norman Gold had thought it was pathetic of her to tell him about Richard; she could remember distinctly the look in his eyes when they were sitting in the booth. He had been burned up to hear that his wife was running around on him, all right, but he had never once questioned Richard's right to run around. Why was it when a man was jealous of a woman it was high tragedy, but when a woman was jealous of a man it was low comedy?

That night, Elaine fixed herself a drink *before* she put the boys to bed. Several drinks. When Jeremy and Jeff had restored their toys to the toy chest and climbed into bed—twin beds, with a lamp with an anchor painted on the base and ships' helms printed on the shade on the nightstand between them, and a stack of comic books on the open lower shelf of the nightstand—she crouched on the scatter rug between them and told them a bedtime story.

It was a story about a woman who was forced to scream at her two sons and her husband so many times that one day she lost her voice. She had to look all over the world for it. The Queen of Sheba couldn't find it for her. The King of Siam didn't know where it was. Oh, she searched everywhere. Finally, after many years during which she grew old and shriveled, she found it perched in a mulberry tree in a remote and mountainous part of China, singing like a nightingale. *Come home,* the woman—by now she was "Mommy"—wanted to say, to the beautiful voice, *please come home*—but she couldn't. She had no voice to say it with. So the woman spent the rest of her days as mute as a silkworm, trailing her hand in the limpid lightshot pure green pool beside the very tree in which her former voice sang its heart out, ever after.

The boys were too terrified to say anything. Elaine turned the light out and went back to the living room. Richard was at a rehearsal. He said. She sat on the couch, examining her profile in the mirror, mirror, on the wall, and after a while, screwing up her eyes and dialing very slowly because the numbers had a tendency to blur, becoming reminiscent of one of Jeremy's New Math problems, she telephoned Augusta Gold. If Norman answered, she would hang up.

43

Gus ANSWERED. Except for Tweetie, she was alone in the apartment. The telephone rang while she was in the middle of drying her hair with a towel. "Gus Gold speaking," she said. By now she was used to thinking of herself as Gus Gold.

"This is Elaine Hacking."

"Elaine?"

"We know each other, I believe, by sight."

"I didn't realize you knew me."

"I make a point of knowing who Richard's girl friends are."

"I'm not one of Richard's girl friends."

"You were."

Gus was trying to wrap the towel around her head with one hand while holding the receiver with the other. She managed to do this, but then she couldn't hold the receiver to her muffled ear. She tried to work one ear free from the towel, and the whole towel came down again. "Mrs. Hacking, why did you call me?" In a temper with the towel, she added, "It's a little late to play the aggrieved wife, isn't it?"

"For me, maybe. Not for you."

Gus froze. It was warm in the apartment, the one room beginning to take in what Norman called its summer boarder, Stifling Heat, but Gus felt as if someone had stabbed her through the heart with an icicle. "What do you mean?" she asked, knowing she was asking only for the details, not the sense.

"Your husband is—" But suddenly Elaine felt ashamed of all the ways of saying it, and reaching for something gentler said, "Your husband is having it off with another woman."

"Having it off?" Gus had never heard the expression before.

"With another woman," Elaine said.

"You?"

"Me?" Elaine shrieked, with pleasure. It had never occurred to her that Augusta Gold might think her husband would cheat on her with *her*. "That's rich. What makes you think I would even be *willing* to sleep with your husband? He's too short. Besides, this may come as a surprise to you"—Elaine actually said "comes sprise you"—"but some women leave other women's husbands alone. They let them get on with the more important things in life."

"More important things?"

"There are more important things in life than sex. Nightingales, for instance."

"I don't understand what nightingales have to do with anything."

"You do want to know how I happen to know that your husband is being unfaithful, don't you?"

"Yes," Gus said, faintly.

"A little Birdie told me."

44

Gus sat for a long time on the big bed, staring at the door—long enough for her hair to dry, waving softly—and she had made up her mind to confront Norman as soon as he walked in. There was no way she could have known that when he walked in he would be covered with blood.

It was all over his face and hands, as if he had taken a bath in it. Gus found herself saying, "Oh God, Norman, are you all right? Are you all right?" over and over, and later, after she had washed off the blood and discovered that the cut was not so bad as it had seemed, she didn't know how to work her way back to the words she had originally intended to say. It would be too huge a leap from loving concern to anger— she couldn't bridge that gap with a single sentence.

Norman had a jagged gash across his forehead, and though the bleeding had stopped, it looked nasty enough. She dabbed it with rubbing alcohol and Norman jumped. "It stings," he said.

"It's supposed to." However, she dabbed him a little longer than was strictly necessary. It wouldn't hurt him to feel a little pain. "You probably should see a doctor," she said, "to be safe."

Norman was in an exultant mood. "You should have heard me, Gus, it was something. God, it was really something!"

"What was?"

"Those idiots want a revolution, let's give them a revolution. Listen, Gus—"

"I'm listening."

"—you could turn all those radicals upside down and you

wouldn't be able to shake loose a single idea. There isn't one real idea in the whole bunch. Hell, I really wish you had been there, Gus!" And he suddenly realized again how very, very fond of her he was, how pleased he felt when he knew he had acquitted himself well in the world's eyes for her sake.

"What happened?"

"They took over Low Library. They're calling it a Liberated Area. *Be free to join us,* they said. They put up a sign saying that. So I decided, Right, I'm free, and besides I need to use the library. I had to cross a picket line."

"Oh no!"

"Oh yes." Norman tucked her hair behind her ears and ran his finger along her chin before he went on. "This pea-brained revolutionary with an infantile desire for instant gratification raises a clenched fist over my head and calls me a scab. Can you believe it? I assured him he was no flower child himself."

"You might have been killed, Norman!"

"I know," Norman said, with immense satisfaction. "I went into the library but it was impossible to work in there. Too noisy. Mark Rudd and his baby thugs were trashing Kirk's office. I left, but somebody caught me with a piece of glass as I was coming down the steps."

"I love you, Norman," Gus said, wearily. "Don't do that again, please."

"You smell good," he said. "Are you wearing perfume?"

"It's the shampoo. I washed my hair."

"Come here."

She moved closer to him on the big bed.

"Marx was not too bright to begin with," Norman said, "but sometimes I feel sorry for him. He's been unluckier in his ideological descendants than just about anybody."

"Maybe you could write a dissertation about that."

"Too bad he can't disinherit them. Do you know," Norman asked, "that Lenin said listening to Beethoven made him want to pat the composer's head but that he couldn't afford such sentiments? He said it was his duty to *crack* the heads of people like Beethoven."

Gus laughed. "The devil probably thinks it's his *duty* to destroy goodness."

"The devil? The *devil*? Sometimes I wonder about you, Gus."

"I can't see Beethoven allowing his head to be either patted or cracked, especially by Lenin."

"I'm going to tell you something," Norman said, changing his tone.

"About Beethoven?" Gus asked. But she was alarmed.

"I miss you."

It was the phrase Gus had heard so often from Richard, but when Norman said it, he didn't give it the same spendthrift sense Richard had given it, a kind of throwaway lightheartedness. When Norman said the words, every one of them seemed hard earned. "That's a funny thing to say," she said, shyly. Timidly.

"I'm married to you," he said, "but I miss you. You're never around."

"I'm around," Gus said. "You're the one who's always out." She tried to make a joke. "Getting wounded by the New Left and the Old Right. Or just . . . out. It seems to me that you work late at the library an awful lot."

Norman looked away, testing his forehead with his fingers as an excuse not to look at her. He couldn't explain at this point that the weekly late nights were dinners with his father. She might even think he was—what? Betraying her. Collaborating with his father. He knew how the mind could work, turning things around. She might understand that he had been his father's son for longer than she had been his wife and that he was only trying to do the best thing for everybody concerned, and she might not. It was better not to bring everything out into the open; things in the open took on a new, distorting emphasis. "It isn't just me," he said. "You're busy all the time."

How had it happened that he was accusing her, instead of the other way around? "I have to practice. Don't touch it, Norman, it'll get infected."

"How is it going?"

"Dieter's finished his piece. The one I'm going to use for the last number."

"I've been meaning to speak with you about this, Gus. Isn't it risky to put it last? Suppose it's no good."

"But it's brilliant. Even Julie Baker agrees. I'll be giving the première of something really special. Between Dieter and me," she said, forcing herself to smile, "I don't see how we can miss. I'm scared to death."

"I know," he said. "I'll bring a claque."

"I love you," she said.

"You said that already," he said, full of himself. "But if it makes you feel better, you can say it again." He pulled her down with him, and when their mouths met, Norman felt invincible, and Gus felt less inclined to bring up the phone call. It was not as if she hadn't already suspected what Elaine had told her.

45

IT WAS TRUE that Gus was busy. All her energies were concentrated on one endeavor—the approaching debut. If she had not been involved with that—learning her program, keeping up with her regular lessons, providing her manager with material for brochures, programs, and posters, and so forth—she might have thought more fully and precisely about the turn her marriage had taken, but as it was, she felt she had no solid grounds for complaint. Married men did, after all, sleep with other women; her sexual experience had been limited, but it encompassed at least this much knowledge, since she had been a woman with whom a married man had slept. She worried about the lack of money but did not know of any other young couple who didn't. She regretted the loss of her independent social life, but that was what marriage was all about, wasn't it? She owed allegiance to Norman, and this meant that her role in society was to express that loyalty always, meeting other people, or writing to them, as Norman's wife. She had her programs printed up with *Augusta Gold* and felt a kind of creeping guilt, subtle and pervasive as kudzu in North Carolina, as if she had betrayed her parents' ambitions, but it was as Norman's wife that she was making her debut, and it was as her husband that he was paying for it.

Gus did not consider herself unhappy or even discontent. There was, she admitted to herself, an air of malaise that seemed to hang in the apartment, but perhaps that was because living in one room was growing tedious. Tweetie trilled his brilliant, golden notes, like little balloons filled with helium, and sent them floating over the room, and he swung on his swing until he was dizzy. Sometimes he practiced with Gus—she blew her notes and he blew his. It made Gus laugh. But Tom and Cyril were her only frequent visitors. She had no time to entertain, nor the money nor the room nor the equipment nor the skill with which to do it, and if she was disinclined, Norman was even more so: he was living in his research these days, and she had to respect that, knowing for herself the unbeatable exhilaration hard work of any kind can bring.

So nothing was really wrong, and yet it seemed to her that something was very wrong. When she tried to talk with Norman about it, he became impatient. If she suggested to him that she felt somehow spiritually constricted, he reacted as if she had attacked him critically, whereas she meant—or thought she meant; she had learned from him to doubt her own motives—merely that marriage had removed an element of surprise from the future; the future was correspondingly emptier and the present heavier. There was a feeling of overfullness about her married days, a sense of time as a thick syrup. While playing the flute helped her to lose track of time, when circumstance recalled her to the present she lamented the loss of the myriad possibilities which once had quickened each day unfolding from sunrise. She could hardly blame Norman for this; she believed that Norman must feel the same way, since it seemed to be the price you paid for the benefits of marriage, and it seemed sensible to her to assume also that an open admission and sharing of the problem would itself alleviate it, but every time she broached it, Norman grew irritable. He said she was suffering from personal grandiosity.

As nearly as she could follow him, what he had said was that she was now, with the debut looming before her, for the first time facing the real possibility of failure and on an even darker level the limitations of her ego's ability to feed the id, and not being able to handle this new awareness of powerlessness, an awareness which her parents had conspired to keep from her so that she was reaching it later than other women but which was rooted in her having been born a woman, she mistakenly attributed this novel, acidic taste of powerlessness in her mouth to marriage—and to him for marrying her. He spoke so eloquently, collapsing Flatbush and Freud in a dialect which she found endlessly fascinating, that she began to rely on his explications of her moods for entertainment: they lifted the weight of present time from her shoulders. In fact, she suspected Norman was satisfying precisely that personal grandiosity he accused her of. It was like watching herself on a wide screen. The only trouble was, she was relegated to the role of audience; the Gus in Norman's speeches was only an image, a flat projection thin as light. Sometimes it seemed to her that her entire inner life was being directed by Norman, and while she had all the freedom she needed to conduct her outer life how she wished, she had no *moral* freedom at all: every motive or intent was subject to Norman's evaluation. This *did* make her feel powerless, downright helpless, unsure of herself on even the most insignificant level.

She'd go to the neighborhood housewares store and stand for minutes at a counter, unable to choose between two dishtowels, as if empires might crash if she selected red when she should have taken blue, or blue when she should have chosen red. She ironed her hair, trying to achieve the swinging sixties look, but gave it up when it wasn't successful; her hair still waved and tumbled, wings over temples, with a completely un-cool sunniness. She found herself gazing at Norman with an even more obsessive longing than she had experienced before they were married, mesmerized by his hot, hurt eyes, entranced by his graceful attacking tones, as if he boxed with his voice the way other men box with their hands; she was in love with the way he held his cigarette, dropped his pants to tuck his shirt in his jeans, shaved, combed his Afro with a dog comb, wrote in the margins of his books (mispunctuating), in love with the forward plunge of his walk, the way his boots smelled when she took them off, his Burberry, his dominance. As she became dependent on him for her view of herself, she became increasingly grateful for his presence in her life, and anxious about losing it.

But the more dependent she became on him, the more distance he placed between them.

The dark eyes cooled. Now she saw less anger in them and

more mockery, as if, observing her so much more dispassionately than she could observe herself, he saw that her limitations, relative to her personal grandiosity, were contemptible, ludicrous, and this left her no choice but to depend on him even more deeply, recognizing through him that her inadequacies were so unlovably blatant. She could not name any other reason for the hardening of the light in his eye.

Gus's natural cheerfulness colored her life golden, the way for some people gray gloom infects their every perception, slanting it; Gus's basic disposition slanted everything she felt or thought in the direction of optimism, but these daily frictions, downers, were there, intensifying. Still, she thought that to old friends (in any sense) she would appear pretty much the way she had always been, and when Richard Hacking, running into her one May morning at McGinnis and Marx, asked her what was wrong, she didn't know what he meant. "Nothing's wrong," she said, genuinely surprised.

"You can't fool me, Gussie. It's been almost a year since we saw each other, but I remember you perfectly."

Richard had been searching for a score by Dallapiccola, when he saw Gussie riffling through Rampal's latest transcriptions. That special, flutelike ambiance of hers was unmistakable even from the back, her hair like an aureole, like the focal point in an Old Master. He had not thought about Gussie since the night Birdie had mentioned her, but as soon as he had seen her here, head bent over the open drawer of sheet music, he felt that he missed her supremely.

"Richard," she said, pleased and amused, "did anyone ever tell you that you are really dopey?"

"Elaine," he said.

"Speaking of Elaine—"

"Do we have to?"

"No," she said, biting her upper lip. "I guess not."

"There. You bit your upper lip."

"What's wrong with that?"

"Nothing. But you never used to do it when you were my girl. You only bit your nail."

"Something is wrong," she said.

"I knew it." And he did—he could sense it in the hesitancy with which she framed her words. The fact that he had made a correct deduction elated him; he propelled her by the elbow to the side of the store, propping her against a filing cabinet as if she needed support. Women frequently did need support, in Richard's experience, and he thought Gussie looked a little green in the face. "You're not pregnant, are you?"

"No, Richard. Why do you keep asking me that?"

"It happens to women. Look at Elaine."

"I thought you didn't want to talk about her. How are the kids?"

"Oh well, you know kids. They fight all the time. I try to keep everybody happy, but it's not easy."

"I know," Gus said, starting, to her own horror, to cry. She blinked and sniffled, turning her back to the other customers in the store. "Norman's not happy either."

"Not happy?" Richard asked, wondering what that meant, exactly, in this context. Norman was not one of the people he had tried to make happy.

"It's like you said, Richard. It's not easy. I've tried. At least, I think I have. Norman says I have conflicting desires."

"Doesn't everybody? Mine conflict all over the place."

"That's all right for you, but your wife isn't having an affair."

"No," he said, "I don't think so. I couldn't be sure, though. She goes shopping all the time." He thought of something that gave him pleasure: "For Elaine, the three B's are Bendel's, Bergdorf Goodman, and Bloomingdale's."

"Norman is."

"What?"

"Norman is having an affair." There; it was out. "Richard," she said, starting to cry again, "he hardly waited until we were married!" A man behind the counter looked over at her. She ducked her head. "I was right."

"That's strange," Richard said. "Norman thought you were having an affair with me."

"You mean from before. But he doesn't even know who you are! He knows your name is Richard and that you're a conductor, but that's all."

"I mean from not very long ago. He thought we were still, you know."

"He didn't!"

"Don't worry, it's all straightened out now."

"But you don't know Norman! Who told you this?"

"Birdie Mickle."

"Birdie?"

"Someone I know."

"Oh my God," she said, "you mean Birdie is a name?"

"You think that's questionable, you should hear her stage name."

"And she told you that Norman thought you and I were having an affair? I know he heard me talking with you on the phone once, but that was before we were married."

"I told you, he knows better now."

"Richard, this Birdie—she's the woman he's sleeping with."

"Birdie?" he said. "Not likely."

"Yes, she is," Gus said. "I know because—"

"Because how?"

"Never mind. I know. Besides, how could she be privy to what Norman thought if she didn't know him? It tallies, Richard."

"With what?"

"Everything."

He was flabbergasted. "Do you mean to tell me that your

husband is humping—excuse me, sleeping with—Birdie Mickle?"

They looked at each other, stricken. "Why, Richard? Why, why?"

He shoved his hands in his pockets and looked glumly down at her nose, shiny from weeping. "Search me," he said. "I would never have suspected it."

46

RICHARD DID what seemed to him the only gentlemanly thing to do, under the circumstances—he called Birdie and asked her why she had not told him she was doing a father-and-son number. "You didn't tell me you were climbing into bed with Norman Gold," he said, aggrieved. In fact, formulating his feelings out loud seemed to aggravate them, and he began to feel sexually gypped, intentionally made a fool of as well as deceived. He couldn't believe she had been lying the first time he met her; but it was almost worse to think this had begun after their meeting. "I'm not a prude, Birdie, really I'm not, but I don't like the idea of sleeping with someone who's sleeping with someone who is married and sleeping with the girl I used to sleep with. You can see my point."

"But I'm not, Richard! Norman is just a friend."

"That's what people always say. *We're just friends.* God, Birdie, I wouldn't mind if it was anybody else, but I'm beginning to feel like the person I'm really in bed with is this Norman Gold."

"Oh, Richard!" Birdie said. "Oh, oh!"

"No," he said, "that's how it stacks up. You can save your

oh's for Hollywood, along with the *We're just friends* stuff. I am going to call it quits. Gussie is a good girl, and I can't continue with our arrangement knowing what I now do about her husband's involvement. I'll miss you, Birdie. You have the most beautiful boobs of anyone I've ever known. You have a luxurious body, Birdie. I really appreciate having known you. I will always remember you with profound affection and lust."

"But Richard—" she said.

Richard hung up. He felt he had acquitted himself rather well, but this didn't begin to compensate for the sudden sense of loss that smacked him right in the back of his knees. He really felt quite weak, and had to sit down.

47

Birdie called Sidney.

"The son of a bitch!" Sidney said. "Where did he come up with this cockeyed notion?"

"It's not true, Sidney." Birdie was crying.

"Okay, okay. The fool has his wires crossed. Somehow somebody thinks I'm my son instead of myself. I have been taken for worse, I guess, though on second thought maybe not. Birdie, don't cry, please. For me, your Sidney." When she cried, he felt like the father of all the world.

"All right, Sidney," she said. "I'll try not to."

"Now listen, Birdie. I want you to think carefully. Have you got any idea how Hacking could have come up with this idea that is fit only for burlesque, and not even that now that the great names are gone?"

"None," Birdie said, beginning to sulk. She had not expected him to interrogate her.

"You know what I think, Birdie, I think Hacking's mind is a mystery. Not even he knows what's going on in it. Sherlock Holmes couldn't solve the secret of this man's reasoning process. It's *too* elementary."

"Well," Birdie said, "actually—" But what could she tell him? If she explained that she had met Norman, she would have to say why. But that wouldn't be fair to Norman. It would be like squealing on him, to tell his father that Norman was distraught because he thought his wife was having an affair, especially after his father had warned him not to marry the girl. That would put Norman in an A-1 untenable position, and furthermore, you did not get to be a star stripper without learning that you did not talk about one man behind his back to another. Sidney might feel he would have to stop allowing his son to blackmail him, and their relationship would be on the rocks for good. Birdie couldn't do it. Anyway, she had only seen Norman once, and how could Richard construe this out of that, about which he did not even know, presumably? Birdie, sucking at the end of her golden magnetic ballpoint as if it were a lollipop, decided that what Sidney didn't know wouldn't hurt him, and it certainly was true that she had never slept with his son.

Sidney caught the delay in her voice, the train of her thought switching tracks. What did this mean? "What is it, Birdie?"

"It's just that I'm very upset, Sidney. Richard says he won't see me anymore and I naturally have inferred that he does not intend to fix me up like he said. Oh, Sidney, I had my heart set on it! You know how much class means to me!"

"I know, Birdie. Class means a lot to you."

"It truly does, Sidney. And the thing about Richard is, he's very classical. I didn't expect this concert to change my life, but I certainly have been hoping that I would at least have an opportunity to strut my stuff in style, for once. A girl goes through her whole life asking only for one little break, an opportunity to show what she can do before she's too old to do it, and then something like this happens. Sidney, from my point of view, this is a tragic misunderstanding. You can see that, can't you?"

"Here's what I want you to do, Birdie. You dry your tears first of all. Then I want you to fix yourself a tall glass of Hawaiian Punch and you take a long hot bubble bath and drink the punch while you're relaxing in the bath and letting this whole *schmeer* float away. There is nothing like being cold inside and hot outside at the same time for refreshment. This I learned from Esther. Meanwhile, I will myself straighten out this schmuck. You'll get your chance to dance."

"You are so good to me, Sidney. I was ready to kill myself."

"Now you listen to me, Birdie," Sidney said, sternly. "Suicide is not a live option."

"I know it isn't, Sidney. Deep inside, I know it. And besides, death is a waste of time, isn't it? So I rejected this alternative in the dark night of my soul, which you are the everlasting twin of, you know that, don't you, Sidney? I know how hard it would be on you in addition to being not so delightful for me, if I did myself in."

"Thank God," Sidney said. "I don't know what I would do without you."

"All the same, Sidney, I remember my father, and sometimes I feel like I'm filling up with tears. You've heard of the water table? I have a tear table, and I think it's flooding. I feel, Sidney, like a bottle of sadness. Sometimes I think you could take the cap off this bottle and pour out all the misery in the world. Not that I'm not basically the fun-loving type, as you well know, Sidney, but when I remember my father, this is how I feel. Poor Mama never had a chance."

"Was he mean to you, Birdie?"

"Only when he'd been drinking. The rest of the time he was just dried up. He was like a desert, Sidney. He had a heart that if you planted a flower in it, it would die in a day from lack of emotional irrigation."

"You shouldn't think this kind of thing, Birdie. You want to think positive, that is the way to get ahead in this world."

"I know, Sidney. It was just being thought to be a bad girl that put me down in the dumps. My father always thought I was a bad girl. Now here I am forty years old, nudging forty-two, in fact, and I am still being thought of as a bad girl. When I'm eighty, I'll still be considered a bad girl."

"Not by me, Birdie. When you're eighty, I'll look at you and say to myself, There is one of the finest old ladies that ever crossed my path!"

"Oh, Sidney," Birdie said, crying again. "When I'm eighty, you'll be dead!"

48

It was a thought that was often in Sidney's mind these days, a presence as unignorable as a fly in a closed room. Sidney chased it around once or twice, but then he decided to live with it. What choice did he have? The worst thing was, he couldn't forget how he felt. And how did he feel, you should perhaps want to know? Rotten, that was how he felt. His whole life, all the backbreaking work he put into it, had come down to this one thing, an overwhelming desire to take a leak. As soon as he did, this desire visited him yet again, more demanding than any woman. A woman he could tell to get lost. His body he could not say this to. "Age is a terrible thing," he told Jocelyn, in the middle of dictation. "No," he said, "that's not part of the letter. It's a philosophical observation I just thought I would throw out."

"It's very profound," she said. Alas, she didn't say it with Birdie's adorable straightforwardness. There was something accommodating in her tone.

Sidney sighed, his down-through-the-ages-since-the-Temple-was-sacked sigh. He couldn't blame Jocelyn for what life had done to her. In all probability, deviousness was the essence of being a good secretary. Still, he would have welcomed some response from her. It was not every day that a boss said to his secretary that age was a terrible thing, he was sure of that.

"That's enough for today, Jocelyn. I have a dinner engagement. I'll lock up."

It was his night to see Norman. For months they had been meeting at the same place. "They make chicken livers here like nobody's business," Sidney had told his son, with finesse, but being secretly much relieved when Norman agreed.

Jocelyn waved and left, a pink-covered tail disappearing out the door, iridescent like the moon of a baboon in heat, which is something he knew about from his days as an adolescent reading the *National Geographic*. He did not know why Jocelyn chose to wear pink all the time. There was bound to be a better color for her somewhere in the spectrum.

He locked his files and closed the door. How many hours he had lived in this office, and before that, other, mingier offices! You work, he thought; you love, you hope, you sweat, and it comes to this—the need to pee. It was not fitting, it was inelegant. Man was made of earth and water, mud. His dreams were air. But law, ah, law—and here Sidney's chest swelled—law was fire. It warmed the hearts of men and gave them a light to see by. Before the heavens and the earth existed, there was the Torah, and it was black fire scripted on white fire. So maybe he, Sidney Wallechinsky Gold, was a man that looked like a toad, and maybe his prostate was a pain in the ass and maybe in a figurative sense the earth was already up to his ankles, that they would bury him in, but his mind was like a coal glowing in the grate, and nobody but nobody could put one over on him. This went even for his beloved Birdie.

The summer air was muzzy; no doubt it was thermally inverted. It reminded him of so many days in his life that he couldn't bear to think of them all—the years, the string of events that tied him to his first days on earth. He couldn't be mad at Birdie for being nostalgic. It was the climate of the times. The population of the nation was jumping off into the future like lemmings into the sea (also from *National Geographic*), but here and there, there were people like him and Birdie and who knows, in his own way Norman, who felt a deeper impulse, something tugging, a compulsion to turn around and go back against the blind-to-thought onrush. He felt a kind of gentle yearning for the sepia-toned past in which much was still possible that now was out of reach forever, fallen down behind the cold cliffs, a future like death.

Yearning. In his squat body with its wide waist and baggy trousers, Sidney felt a sadness settling on him, an unseen layer like pollen on a rose. It was not happiness he ached for so much as a lack of harassment, a peaceful afternoon with no school and no errands to run, when he could curl up on the parlor floor and read the comics. Where were the Katzenjammer kids now? Where was the waggletailed, white-haired, black-nosed puppy in Mr. Zweifel's shop on Delancey Street, that for two weeks he begged his mother for until one day he went to see it and it was gone, poof, like magic, and nothing ever made up for it? Was there a kennel in Gehenna where the angels watched over the souls of animals who have died to this present earth, this infinitesimal speck of greenness budding with hope, watered with sorrow, with Birdie's tears? There should be a heavenly home for puppies with black noses and for old dogs with sharp but increasingly rheumy eyes, a place where everyone could meet again, the people and their pets, spending the long nights of eternity in utter languishment naming for one another the events that had most mattered in the days when they were full of division and torment, and why, and saying how those events appeared in the cool light of eternity's radiant visage.

49

N ORMAN WAS in the restaurant already. Sidney saw him drawing invisible pictures on the tablecloth with a spoon.

It cheered Sidney hugely, to see his son at the table. And yet he was not sure it should. He had not forgotten Birdie's evasiveness. He didn't object if she had secrets from him — a woman without secrets was like a woman without her own checking account, defenseless in a voracious world (Sidney believed that all women should be independent, except his wife, whom it was his appointed duty to protect) — but for a father and a son to share the same bed would be incestuous, and in addition, he could not very well threaten to shoot off Hacking's nuts with an M4, which was very nearly employed in the *aliyah,* the return to the promised land which is where the sun is like honey and the air is as sweet as bread, and every place that the sole of the foot treads upon has been given by God, without he should know if Birdie was telling the truth or not.

"So," Sidney said, waving the *maitre d'* away and easing

himself into the chair without, as he termed all such offers of help, outside interference, "you're here."

"It would seem so." It saddened Norman to see his father beginning to fail. The soft voice was even softer. How old was he now?

"Don't be a wiseguy. Ever since you were a baby, you were backtalking."

"As I recall it, I was too obedient for my own good."

"To your mother and me, it looked different."

"How is Mother?"

"How do you think? She has a son she never sees, who is dead to her because he had no respect for the traditions of his family."

"Yeah, well," Norman said, thinking of the letter she had written to Gus, "it could be that with this as with everything else you are living in the past. Someday you should ask Mother how she really feels."

"Me? In the past? Ha. Speaking of somedays, someday you should find out what goes on in an average day in the life of your old father the fossil. I am up to my neck in political intrigue. In the future, I may be ruling on the Constitution of the United States of America, to your enlightenment and benefaction. Past!" Sidney snorted, all the more furious for having just been thinking of it. "You're the one that lives in the past, Norman, with your theories of history as refracted through the prism of musical development. Has anyone informed you what Beethoven is doing these days?"

"Beethoven?"

"Decomposing."

Norman stared disgustedly as his father laughed at length, slyly, his shoulders heaving.

"You are really something," Norman said.

"If you want to top me, you're going to have to get up earlier."

Norman vaguely remembered having said something like that to himself about Gus once, but he couldn't remember in connection with what.

"Did you order?" Sidney asked.

"Chicken livers," Norman said. "For you too, I took the liberty. Since when did you order different? Here it comes."

"They make chicken livers like nobody's business," Sidney said.

"You said."

"Hearing me repeat myself is one of the little nuisances you have to put up with if you want to go on collecting your fifty smackers a week." Sidney fished the money from his wallet and waited while Norman slipped it into his. Then he tucked his napkin into his collar, and not until his mouth was full, as if having a mouth full of food might ameliorate the effect of what he was about to imply, said, "You know Birdie Mickle?"

Norman's hand paused in midair. He brought it down and said, steadily, "Sure. I scorched her fox in your office."

"Okay, Norman, so there will be no beating about the bush I am going to ask you this in the baldest possible terms, without any nuances under which a person might take cover if he was so inclined. Consider that you are in court, because it comes to the same thing. Perjure yourself and you'll wish you were not Norman Gold, son of Sidney. Believe me."

"What is this, a threat? Are you threatening me? What a thing for a father to do to his son! Christ! I come to dinner—"

"Here is the question, Norman. I am warning you that it is coming so you can give your undivided attention to it. The question is, Are you pecking in Birdie Mickle's nest?"

"Am I what?"

"I do not think I need to repeat myself this time. Miss Chicken Delight is not chicken liver."

"What an idea! What a crummy idea! Jesus, Pop. Do you

think I would do such a thing? What am I, a heel?"

"You take a little money from your old man, maybe you also snitch a little snatch."

"That is not the same thing. That is not the same thing at all. It is one of the points about which I take issue with Freud."

"You didn't answer my question."

"Then listen. You want an answer, you'll get an answer. Here is the answer. I am warning you in advance that it's coming so you can be on the lookout for it."

"Sarcasm ill becomes you, Norman."

"I'm only thinking of you. Who knows, if somebody doesn't tell you a fact is in the vicinity, you may never realize it's there. It could go right by you."

"Enough, Norman."

"No."

"No what?"

"No, I am not poking your girl friend."

"You don't have to put it like that."

"You were refined?"

"This is Birdie Mickle we're discussing, not some insignificant streetwalker, which is what most of your longhaired loose female persons are, from your generation. Birdie has heart, soul, a mind. By the way, eat."

"I'm not hungry. I have other things on my mind now than food, thanks to you. What I want to know is, what made you think it was necessary to ask such a question."

"Fine, I'll tell you the person whereof whom the idea originated. He knows your wife."

Norman felt sick.

"His name is Hacking. Richard Hacking."

"How do you happen to know Hacking?"

"Met him at Birdie's."

"I don't believe it."

"What's to believe?"

"How would Birdie Mickle and Richard Hacking know each other?"

"I don't know. Why shouldn't they know each other?" Norman frowned.

"Oh ho," Sidney said. "I see. By the dawn's early light no less. The big liberal with a heart that bleeds at the merest mention of discrimination is perplexed at this crossing of social lines. He wonders what a fancy schmanzy classical conductor sees in a Forty-second Street stripper."

"Don't be an ass. I know what he sees in her. I saw them myself."

"Rude! Rude! How come you never learned from your mother the fine manners she's got?"

"I thought Birdie was your private piece."

"Birdie doesn't belong to anyone but herself. The more I listen to you, Norman, the more I believe you are fundamentally reactionary."

"You don't have to wave the knife at me. You're evading, Pop. You think I don't know when you're evading the issue? It was the way to stay D.A.—when you're threatened, attack."

"Norman, Norman. If you only knew how far off the track you are."

Sidney was bluffing, but he was damned if he'd admit to his son that his relationship with Birdie was at this point not entirely what it appeared to be. His son at thirty was still too young to have learned from personal experience that a woman could be a sweetheart one day, a mistress the next, and virtually a daughter the day after that, so to speak. True, even on this long third day of their relationship Sidney did not feel about Birdie as if she were Rita, exactly. But Sidney was a true sophisticate, not one of those tricked out in medallions and Man-Tan, and as such, he knew that every thing has a season, every purpose a time, and so forth, and what else was sophistication, but realizing this?

But why should he break his neck educating his son in the ways of the world, when sooner or later the world would do that? Let the boy find these things out for himself. On reflection, for one thing, Sidney did not want the son to know that the father wasn't getting it up so much these days. Not that he couldn't, and sometimes it rose all by itself, impromptu, a little bit of secret life under the desk in his office, but he had just lost interest in using what was there. After all, at seventy-two, he could not imagine that there was any mystery about what would follow when he heaved his spreading hulk onto some woman's bed. As for pleasure, what could match that of the imagination, besides friendship and work? And rest. He felt increasingly a desire to put his head on a pillow in the middle of the day and sleep until something happened, something that he had not already experienced.

These feelings he could convey to Birdie, but not to Norman, who would no doubt decide that his father was once and for all over the hill, when in fact, so far as Sidney was concerned, the culmination of his career was yet to come. If he tried to explain to Norman what he really felt for Birdie, it would stain it—it would be like pissing on the most precious part of their relationship. But a brain is not a chamberpot, and as much as he longed to urinate, he would die before he would do such a thing to the twin of his soul. So he said to Norman, "Can't you conceive that Birdie just might happen to know a man who knows your wife, without there has to be more to it than that? Birdie is very musical. Maybe they talk music." In a way, Sidney thought, it was only fair to Birdie to let Norman think her relationship with Hacking was platonic. If Norman thought she was sleeping with both of them, he might conclude that she was a whore. Birdie was always annoyed with men who jumped to conclusions. This way Norman might get it backwards, but the score came out the same.

Norman had been eating slowly, and thinking his own thoughts. He doubted seriously that Hacking and Birdie Mickle discussed music. If Hacking wasn't balling her, he was getting something else off her. And then he realized what it must be.

"Now I get it," he said, choking. "Oh boy, now I really get it. It is clear as fucking crystal. God, God, God."

"What on earth are you yammering about? You should see yourself in a mirror, believe me. You look like your blood is boiling. And they talk about hot-blooded—I'll bet your blood is two hundred twelve degrees Fahrenheit. Drink some water."

"I don't want any water."

"What did I say? I said maybe Birdie and Hacking discuss music. Is there anything in that to be so upset about?"

"I'm not upset. I choked."

"On a chicken liver? How is it possible to choke on something this slithery?"

"It takes talent, obviously," Norman said, drinking a glass of water.

"I'm glad to see you follow my advice sometimes," Sidney said. "A son who is too big to take his father's advice is too small to give it."

"If you don't mind, Pop, I think I'll split. I want to make a phone call."

Sidney was surprised and let down, but he tried not to show it. "Now that you mention it," he said, "I have to make a call also. Isn't modern life something, Norman! I keep trying to magnify your awareness of the miracles we live among. Telephones, for example. Where would we be without them, I'd like to know? And refrigeration by dry ice, also modern transportation, computers, and snoop ships. Though this *Pueblo* thing, now there is a real can of worms."

"I'm going, Pop. I'll see you next week."

"Sure," Sidney said, but as he watched his son walk to the door of the restaurant and out, he felt deep sadness settling on him once more. This time it was not an envelope, like a second skin. It was internal. It invaded his mouth and nostrils and ears, packing his lungs and gut like pressurized air, a feeling of fullness and tightness. Heartburn, Sidney said to himself; but it was more like heartache. He picked up the check. The restaurant was still fairly empty—it was too early for the main trade—and the waiters were whispering among themselves, as if they were spectators at a play and the diners were the show. What did they think of the props? The vinegar bottle at Sidney's elbow was sticky and the leftover rice on Norman's plate had a jaundiced tinge under the ceiling fixture.

When Sidney tried to reach Hacking by telephone, to inform him that he had a screw loose and that if he didn't come through for Birdie, he, Sidney, would personally break his balls or at least arrange for somebody to carry out that minor task, the line was busy.

It was busy because Norman was trying to reach Elaine at the same time.

What Norman had figured out, sitting at the dinner table with his father, was that her husband and his wife could not conduct their assignations in deep space. They had to have somewhere to meet. Obviously, they met at Birdie Mickle's place. Why else had she ushered him out so precipitously the night he was there?

50

A MACHINE answered. It had Elaine Hacking's voice. "We will be out of town for the summer," it said. "If your message is urgent, please ring Mr. Hacking's manager at ———." A number followed. "Otherwise, your call will be returned after Labor Day. Please leave your name, number, and message at the sound of the beep. Beep."

So much for his father's celebration of the miracles of modern gadgetry. Norman was in no position to leave his name, much less a message. He could not discuss his matter of urgency with Richard Hacking's manager. There was nothing he could do but wait.

It was summer now, warmer than last year's. Norman sacrificed an inch of height and exchanged his boots for desert shoes. He and Gus both slept naked with the windows open and the curtains up. If that made the perverts happy, Norman was glad somebody was happy. All over New York, you could look in people's windows and get an eyeful of flesh. It was too hot to be sexy. Even the perverts appeared to have lost interest.

It was too hot to sleep well even naked. Tweetie-Pie spent half his time in his bath, or lounging beside it like a movie mogul with dark glasses and cold drink. When he swung, sunlight danced on his wings and breast and head and back. When he sang, it was as if he owned the world. He was certainly master of his cage. At night, he slept in its comfortable darkness while Gus and Norman lay on that shelf of semi-consciousness poised between sleeping and waking, draped in dreaming.

In the morning, Norman rose groggily and turned on the

television . . . Shaving with TV Accompaniment. The accompanist was supposed to remain neatly in the background, and at first Norman didn't register what the reporter was saying. Robert Kennedy? California? The reporter continued to speak into his microphone, but some time passed before Norman could assimilate the meaning of the statement. By then, Gus had wakened and was sitting cross-legged on the bed. "Here," Norman said, throwing her his shirt, "put this on." She did, but she still didn't say anything.

There were some Grape-Nuts in the cabinet in the kitchen and Gus fixed two bowls and they tried to eat in silence, but it wasn't possible to eat Grape-Nuts in silence. The crunching seemed obscene to both of them. Norman would crunch, and it echoed in the room like gunshot. Gus would crunch, and it echoed like an answering volley.

Finally, feeling the need for saying something, Gus said, "They ought to hand out some guidelines for people like us. A kind of Emily Post to the etiquette of assassination. I don't know how to react anymore."

"You don't *know*! Jesus Christ, how do you feel?"

"I feel the same way you do. That's not what I meant. It's just that—" She hesitated. Norman's face looked like the victim of his feelings; it seemed to be collapsing under the weight of anger, panic, grief and more grief; it was being overcome by anguish. She wanted to reach out and touch it.

"Tell that goddamn canary to shut up," he said.

"Don't take it out on Tweetie. It's not his fault."

"I know whose fault it was. The fault of an Arab."

"You can't blame all the Arabs, Norman. It's an isolated instance of a crazy man."

"It was a crazy *Arab,* and it's hardly an isolated instance."

"You mean his brother?"

"And King."

"King wasn't killed by an Arab. Neither was Jack Kennedy."

"You wouldn't understand."

"Because I'm Gentile?"

"And Southern."

Gus carried the dishes back out to the kitchen and dumped them into the sink. "You're being unfair," she said, returning. "I'm sorry about Bobby, I know how you felt about him. I felt the same way."

"You may have felt similar. You could not feel the same thing I felt." Norman knew he was being unfair, but he couldn't stop—he had to rail at someone, and Sirhan Sirhan was not available. It felt to Norman almost as if he had been programmed to say these things, and there was no way he could not say them. Input X resulted in Output Y. What Norman wished he could have conveyed to Gus was that this compulsion was as painful for him as it was bewildering to her.

"You think nobody else knows what it's like to be the underdog," she said. "You forget that the South was defeated. You forget the carpetbaggers and Reconstruction." As she conjured up these bygones, she realized she herself had not remembered them since high school. "There were years of some of the ugliest and dirtiest fighting in history, followed by years and *years* of hypocritical self-serving righteous moralizing on the part of the North. If you think the North was fighting for high ideals, you don't know as much history as you think you do. And if you think the South lost because it was morally inferior and deserved to, you don't know the first thing about military strategy!"

"What do you know about it?"

Gus couldn't answer. She knew nothing about it. She had no idea where these words had come from; they had simply materialized out of nowhere in answer to his, but as she said them, she realized they were a protest against being lectured to by him as well as by the North. Instantly, she shut up.

Norman caught it—the self-realization and the clamping

down on it. "What I want you to tell me, Gus, is how come you're acting like Scarlett O'Hara? You know perfectly well that it was a damn good thing the South *didn't* win. Where would we be if you had? Lester Maddox could be eating turtle soup in the White House."

"I don't know why you're so angry with me."

"I'm not angry with you," he said. "It just happens to be a lousy stinking morning!"

"Don't shout at me!"

"I'll shout as much as I feel like it and right now I feel like it!"

"Tom and Cyril will hear you. You'll wake them up."

"Somebody should wake them up," Norman said. "Somebody should wake them up and inform them that in the middle of the night a fucking Arab madman blew the brains out of the only hope this country had!"

"From what you told me," Gus said, "the country still has your father to look forward to."

51

AFTER the quarrel wore off, dissipating into the general heat and noise of a New York summer, this particular summer being overlaid by a heightened sensitivity of national proportions, a harplike quivering of highstrung nerves, a shimmering of the spirit as it stretched like a transparent but luminous trampoline across the land from sea to shining sea, Gus and Norman felt closer than ever. They *were* closer, sitting side by side on the dark red and blue comforter. The television, which had always been there as background, source of late movies, afternoon talk shows, and falsified body counts, became the instrument of their mutuality, became the way they communicated with each other. Even Tweetie felt neglected, and sometimes squawked off-key. In fact, for the rest of the summer, Gus and Norman lived in front of the television set. In the daytime, Gus practiced and Norman worked on his dissertation, but in the evenings and on into night, they watched the country fall apart on an eighteen-inch screen.

It drew them together, the sense of being besieged. They felt that they agreed on a number of important things and that this agreement differentiated them from many of the people they saw on television, in the streets, or at other people's apartments. Dinky Ledbetter, whom Gus had seen only once or twice since their wedding "reception" at Max's Kansas City, called to ask if she could stash some acid at their place until Phil got back from L.A., where he was meeting with a sales rep, and could pick it up, and Gus said no almost automatically, knowing that Norman would have said no. "Hey," Dinky said, "I didn't mean to offend you. I didn't know you were straight. Straight like a strait."

Looking at the blank wall over the desk, Gus had a clear image of Dinky's delicately bulging eyeballs and wet lips. She must be high now, Gus thought. "It's all right," Gus said. "I didn't realize it either."

But hanging up, Gus whispered to Tweetie that it was really Norman who was the straight one. Norman wouldn't tolerate drugs on the premises. He had tried grass once at blood-brother Phil's instigation and flipped out for about five hours. "It was the most horrible time of my life," Norman reported—and that was grass, not acid. Phil said it was an extreme reaction and the problem was Norman's love of rationality and fear of not being in control. Norman said that was a lot of shit. Either way, it was of no concern to Gus. She wouldn't have objected to holding the stuff for Dinky, but she wouldn't touch it herself. Gus had never smoked. Anything. It was hell on your lungs and a flutist could get away with it only if he was somebody like Kincaid, a man and a man with a large chest. Even Kincaid had confined his smoking to the summers, when he wasn't giving concerts and was swimming daily. He quit every fall.

On the whole, then, Gus and Norman were aligned with the counterculture in some respects, and with the establishment in others, and because of this they belonged to the very large class of people in the industrialized world, East and West, who do not belong to any of the traditionally defined classes and who therefore have no institutions or organized methods for making their feelings and opinions known even to one another, much less to the other classes. They were not, properly speaking, bourgeoisie, since they employed no one and had no capital, nor as yet qualified academicians; they were members neither of the ruling class nor the working class. They were not part of the Silent Majority or the People, because these groups always had very vocal spokesmen who quite frequently said things Norman and Augusta disagreed with. Gus and Norman were, in fact, part of a large and much neglected class, the *silent* silent majority, that group of people for whom the only reasonable political platform is one which can encompass all the many ambivalences of any honest person's attitudes to life, and who therefore have no merit in the eyes of political philosophers and no theory. The only party that ever attempts to speak for them is the multipartisan party, Music.

In August, Gus and Norman watched the Democratic convention. This time it was at night that the world reversed itself in front of their eyes, turned upside down and left them feeling they had fallen off. They felt weightless, unreal, as though they had lost all link to any specific time and place and would merely float forever through a universe of whirling events.

Gus scrunched her knees up to her chin and wrapped her arms around them, nibbling on her fingernail.

"Fucking Fascists," Norman said. He put his arm around Gus and she leaned her head on his shoulder.

He kissed her hair, the black-and-white images from the television screen flickering over it. "Hush," he said, calming her. "Things have to get better someday."

52

IT WAS September. Sidney called Richard and told him that if he knew what was good for him he would deliver the goods to Birdie. Richard found his hands shaking and his heart leaping, two things not easily accomplished at once. Birdie was not sleeping with Gussie's husband! He could restake his claim, as it were!

"You set up that dance recital for her," Sidney said, "or everything you don't know about an M4, you are going to learn from looking into the barrel. Do I make myself clear?" Sidney had no intention of doing anything even semiserious, but he figured Hacking was just unversed enough in the ways of the real world to fancy that the loss of his life would make a difference to it. All conductors had egos as big as kettledrums. The man would enjoy thinking somebody was after his tail. Besides, Sidney was still furious, when he thought how miserable Hacking had made Birdie by doing exactly what she so often said men did, jumping to conclusions.

"This is the best news I've had all day, Mr. Gold," Richard said. "For my wife as well. You may not understand this, Mr. Gold, but my wife is really unhappy when I'm not cheating on her. It's been a long, hot summer."

"Personally, Hacking, I could care less what makes your

wife happy. My concern is for Birdie. Does your wife know you and Birdie got a thing going?"

"Well, not precisely."

"What, pray tell, is imprecisely?"

But at this point, Richard began to realize that he didn't have to tell Sidney Gold his life story. "Look here," he said, "I don't have to tell you my life story."

"By which I give infinite thanks, believe me."

Richard felt wounded. "It's not an uninteresting life story," he said. "But I've only just turned forty. You of all people will appreciate that I have a lot of time to go yet." Remembering his father's heart attack, he looked around for wood to knock on. "With any luck, I could have an extremely lengthy life story."

"Not if you don't get Birdie that concert date she wants, you won't. Just try not coming through for her, and we'll see how deliriously cheerful your wife is when I tell her what you've been up to. My guess is, she'll be most interested in my guns. I hung on to some shells too."

53

NORMAN DID NOT CALL Richard Hacking in September. He decided to wait. After all, there had been a summer. A summer for everybody in the northern hemisphere. To Norman, it had been a summer like the *then* clause in an *if-then* statement: if 1967, then a subsequent season of unraveling, riots fizzling into streetfights, aims into their contraries. Something about the way things had turned out satisfied Norman arcanely—not the way they had developed, but that it was the way he had foreseen. But why shouldn't this satisfy him? Noah would have felt like a fool, boarding his ark, if the sun had kept shining.

It seemed to Norman that there was no need to borrow trouble—it would come sooner or later anyway. Meanwhile, who knew what difference this summer of television might not have made to everyone? Gus was practicing—or said she was practicing. Norman found it difficult to believe that so much work could go into a two-hour debut, but he was willing to believe it was necessary. What did he know from flutes? If playing the flute on stage was such a complicated business, maybe Gus had given up her extracurricular pastime. Norman watched her polishing her flute with the soft rag, ironing her white blouses, washing dishes, and he knew he loved her very much, though perhaps not as much as he had when he married her. And as he thought about it, he began to feel that perhaps he did not love her even as much as he was currently under the impression that he did, that how he felt and how he told himself he felt were not necessarily in this instance more than in any other the same thing.

That there was no pain associated with this realization embarrassed him; he felt somehow ashamed before his conscience, but of course, this was ludicrous, since his conscience was only an internalized value structure, and, he should ask himself, internalized from what or whom? Modes of thought (or non-thought) which were excusable when you were five, say, were absurd, even comic, when you had hit thirty and were well aware that your old man was not only not God but was an old lech . . . because that was undeniably what he was, however much sympathy he might feel for his father's itch.

Norman now saw that one by one he had been letting go the lines of emotive affect that linked him to Augusta, and that, furthermore, many of the lines had operated as connectives only on a superficial level, surface to surface. The need to remove himself from the pain that Gus's infidelity threatened him with had made it impossible to feel pain now. And some pain would have been proper, he thought—until he convinced himself that in feeling such a need he was only giving in to a certain set of social expectations—namely, that failing to love someone (your father) was punishable (by castration)—and he was on a guilt trip that would get him nowhere. This, at any rate, is how it looked to Norman. What he was totally unprepared for and failed to analyze was the effect the Onassis marriage had on him.

Jackie Kennedy married Aristotle Onassis on the island of Skorpios on October 20, 1968, three days after Augusta's birthday, and unwittingly plunged Norman into fresh and angry gloom. So much for the memory of the Kennedy brothers. Bobby had not been dead six months. That Jackie had not been married to Bobby didn't mitigate the main fact: women's sexual loyalties were as easily shifted by chance as the fumes from an exhaust pipe by the wind off the Hudson.

Although Norman sensed that he was being unreasonable, this only added to his general irritability. He did not actually say to himself that Jackie Kennedy had no right to marry Aristotle Onassis, but the fact of the wedding put him on edge all the same, he felt in general annoyed with the state of the world, and one afternoon, on a whim, in a condition of generalized, unfocused, metaphysically pervasive disgust, when Gus was supposed to be in a practice room at Juilliard, he retrieved the Beethoven book from under the pile of socks in his chest drawer and dialed Birdie Mickle's number. If she answered, he would hang up. At most, he would find something inane and innocuous to say. But she didn't answer.

Norman knew his own father's voice, and this wasn't it any more than it was Birdie's. He took a chance. "Hacking?" he asked.

"Yes?" Richard said.

Norman slammed the receiver in its cradle. It was an old

New York trick, and it had worked. His hunch, because he now discovered that he had had a hunch, was right. Practice room! For what Gus was blowing, she didn't need a perfect embouchure.

54

HURTING TERRIBLY, feeling as if his heart were a piece of glass that splintered in his lungs every time he drew a breath, and at the same time experiencing that state of being existentially pacified, of being proved right, that the world's political deterioration had produced in him during the summer, Norman made another call, the one he had tried to make back at the summer's beginning. This time he succeeded.

He told Elaine Hacking the whole story—that her husband and his wife were meeting at Birdie Mickle's place on Madison Avenue and that Birdie was a stripper. He waited for her to say something, but she let the pause lengthen until he began to be uncomfortable. He supposed she needed time to come to grips with the concreteness of the information.

Elaine had forgotten all about Norman, but now she remembered everything in an instant. Everything. She could not very well tell him, half a year too late, that his wife was not in fact sleeping with her husband. What the hell, maybe Augusta Gold was sleeping with someone else. Like Richard. She said, "You called her Birdie?"

"That's right."

"I've heard that name before," she said. "This is very interesting. Do you know the telephone number?"

He gave it to her. "The last name is Mickle," he said.

"M-i-c-k-l-e. She could be a friend of his and he borrows her apartment. Or else he rents it for a fee. It's done. It's cheaper than hotels or leasing one yourself."

"You sound very calm. Do you plan to do anything?"

"Do?" he said. "What's to do? Gus is just my wife. I don't own her."

"No," she said, "but you wouldn't have called me if you didn't want something done."

"Mrs. Hacking, don't take this as a comment on your own person, but the truth is I think your husband is a reprehensible mother of the first water and if you want to murder him when he comes home, don't let me stand in your way. Did you have a nice summer?"

"Yes, thank you," she said, thinking that she wouldn't wait until Richard got home.

55

It was clear to Elaine that Norman, like all men, had an ego that prevented him from seeing the truth wherever it downgraded his self-image. Evidently, he had figured out that Richard knew this Birdie Mickle—which was probably not hard to deduce, since Richard was so incompetent at deception that he left telltale signs wherever he went, an adulterer's spoor—but he couldn't believe that the woman he was cheating on his wife with, could be cheating on him with another man. Where did Norman Gold get off, calling her husband names? Richard had his faults, but he was no hypocrite. Elaine was glad she had told Augusta about Norman's affair. If Augusta hadn't said anything to Norman about it, she was either saving it for when it would be most advantageous to let him know she knew, or she had a reason for being glad he was occupied elsewhere.

That night, Elaine roused Jeffrey from deep slumber—in sleep, he was still a baby, his breath hot and earnest and his face flushed—and brought him out to the living room in his Dr. Dentons while she dialed the number Norman had given her. It was after midnight, and Jeff immediately started to fall asleep again, his wandering eyes pinwheeling in his round face. He didn't know why his mother had waked him up and brought him out here. Where was Jeremy? Then Jeff remembered—Jeremy was staying overnight with one of the boys in his class.

Jeff was still in kindergarten. He had to wait one more year before he could go to school, but if Jeremy could do the work, Jeff wasn't worried. It must be easy work. In Jeff's opinion, Jeremy was not very bright. Was his mother calling Jeremy now? Was something wrong with Jeremy? Jeff sat up, wide awake. Suppose something had happened to his brother? He began to cry.

56

"RICHARD!" Birdie gasped, thrusting the receiver at him. "It's your wife!"

"I'm not here!"

"I heard that," Elaine said, her voice materializing like a genie through the receiver into the airy space between Birdie and Richard. Birdie thought it was creepy.

"Hello," Richard said, taking the receiver. "How are you?"

"How am I!"

"Good grief, Elaine, I'm just trying to make pleasant conversation."

"How can you even think of such a thing?"

"But why did you call, if you didn't want to talk? You make it sound like conversing is a sin."

"Don't talk to me about sin!"

"I'm glad to hear you say that, Elaine. Now, the way I look at it, there are two possibilities. We can make pleasant conversation or we can make unpleasant conversation. I have spent the entire evening giving the clarinet hell, and I really don't feel like shouting anymore. He was flat."

"I'll flatten you, Richard."

"How did you find out where I was?"

"It wasn't easy."

"I know," Richard said, proudly. "This time I really kept you guessing, didn't I!"

"Richard, all my adult life you've been doing this to me, but now the time has come. This time you're not going to get away with it. I know all about your Birdie Mickle. I know where she lives."

"Where she lives? Who told you that? Who gave you this number? Oh no," Richard said, thinking of Sid, "he told you! I didn't think he meant it!"

"He meant it," Elaine said, thinking of Norman, "and what's more, he said he would be glad to see you dead."

"Did he say that?"

"More or less."

"Uh," Richard said. "That's not how you feel, is it?"

"I've been doing a lot of thinking lately about how I feel. Richard," Elaine said, looking at the photograph over the bar, "I keep remembering the girl I used to be. Lainy O'Hara. I was so bright, Richard! You remember, don't you? I didn't know I was going to devote my life to shouting. You're the one who made me do that."

"I didn't mean to make you do that, Elaine. I don't mind if you quit shouting."

"You're missing the point, as usual. The point is all that lost promise, down the hatch. It's gone for good, Richard."

She said this as if Lost Promise were a dear departed one, and Richard felt he should wait a decent interval before speaking again. In the silence, he heard sobbing. "Are you crying, Elaine?" he asked. She had probably been drinking.

"That's your son," she said. "In case you've forgotten, you have two."

"What's he doing up at this hour? What's going on, Elaine?"

"I'll tell you what's going on. What's going on is that you're going to start keeping your promises. No more lost promise, Richard. You"—she meant people in general—"can't go through life not fulfilling the basic contracts." She was speaking existentially, after the manner of Camus, but to Richard's ears, sensitized by Sidney, it sounded more like Al Capone. "From here on out," she said, "we're all going to keep all our promises."

"I'm always willing to do whatever you say, Elaine," Richard said. "You know that." But he was surprised that she was so eager for him to fulfill his promise to Birdie. Sid must have told her the whole story. God, she must really hate him if she was willing to conspire with Sid Gold and resort to violence to keep him. "Why is the kid crying?" he asked.

"He wants to tell you himself," Elaine said. "Don't you, darling?" she asked, putting Jeff on the phone.

"Daddy?"

"Jeremy?"

"I'm Jeff, Daddy," Jeff said, gravelly. "I hit Jeremy. He's not dead, is he?"

"Ask Daddy why isn't *he* at home," Elaine said to Jeff.

"Why aren't you here?" Jeff said. "Mommy wants to know."

"Because you keep hitting Jeremy," Richard said.

"He won't let me watch Batman."

"That's no reason to hit him."

"It's all your fault, Richard," Elaine said, speaking into the other side of the receiver. "You told Jeremy he was entitled to his privacy. Frankly, I don't see why a person should be allowed privacy if he's not going to make good use of it."

"What do you want him to do? He's only eight, Elaine!"

"I'm five," Jeff said, claiming the receiver again.

"You shouldn't beat up your big brother. If anything, he should be beating you up," Richard said.

"He can't. He doesn't know how to. I box like Cassius Clay, Daddy. When I grow up, I'm going to be the greatest."

"If you were ever here," Elaine said, "you'd see what a wonderful boxer your son is."

"I don't need children who box. Elaine, why couldn't we have had a couple of pacifists? If they were old enough, our sons would be Green Berets. Have you checked Jeff's nightstand for scalps lately? He probably hides them under the mattress."

Jeff started to cry again.

"Now see what you've done," Elaine said. "He only wanted to ask you to come home."

"Jeff," Richard said. "Listen to me, Jeff. Are you listening?" Jeff sniffled. "You're not crying anymore, are you? Now listen to me, Jeff. Daddy's very tired. You have to forgive Daddy. Daddy thinks he needs a good long rest in Florida, but first he has to take care of some promises he made. Maybe next spring we'll all go to Florida, would you like that?"

"Can we leave Jeremy at home?" Jeff asked, brightening.

"We'll see," Richard said, sighing.

"There," Elaine said. "That's just like you, isn't it? Equivocating. I am warning you, Richard. This time you had better come through for all of us. If you don't, there's no telling what could happen. You are forewarned, all right?"

She had divorce in mind, but he thought she meant murder. He didn't think she was capable of pulling the trigger, but you never knew. Ninety-five percent of all violent acts in the United States were perpetrated by people who knew their victims. Husbands and wives killed each other all the time. Look at the fruit of Elaine's womb. Jeff was a natural-born killer if ever there was one. Would Sid Gold really go this far just to give Birdie what she wanted?

"Forewarned," Richard said, softly, to himself, as he put the receiver down. "Birdie, how powerful is Sidney Gold?"

"Sidney? Why, he's extremely powerful. If he gets on the Supreme Court he'll be one of the most powerful men in the United States of America. Being a classical musician, you probably don't know that you have to *be* one of the most powerful men in the United States if you want to *get* to be one of the most powerful men in the United States. I should know, because this is Sidney's area of expertise."

"Did he really run arms to Israel?"

"Certainly," Birdie said, with pride. "Sidney is a secret partner in a munitions firm!"

"Oh my God," Richard said. "Why didn't you tell me this before?"

"Well," Birdie said, "it's a secret."

"Birdie, I'm going to get you that engagement you wanted. You can tell Mr. Gold that."

"Oh, Richard," Birdie said. "Oh, Richard, oh, Richard!" She knew better than to ask him what his wife had wanted or how she had tracked him here. The time to ask questions was when things were going wrong, not when they were going right. She clapped her hands and said some more, "Oh, Richard, Richard!"

"Well," Richard said, "that's enough, now." But it was nice to see her so excited. It was why he had agreed to this in the first place, wasn't it? The trouble was, he had no more idea now than he had had then of how to set up an inter-pretative dance concert for a strip-tease artist.

"When will it be, Richard?"

"Very soon," he said. "Next month." Recklessly, he added, feeling that at this point he might as well go the limit to keep absolutely everybody happy, "On my word of honor!"

57

THE VISITOR who rang the downstairs buzzer said via the intercom that he was a friend of Norman's, so Gus pressed the buzzer to open the downstairs door. When she opened the door to the apartment, she saw the bellhop. She shut it again, in a panic.

"Wait!" he said. "It's okay! I do know Norman."

She opened the door again.

"I came on business," he said, looking at her. He was re-membering what she looked like without any clothes on.

She could see her diminished image in both of his blue eyes. She was wearing jeans and an army shirt, but he made her feel as though she were dressed in skin and sunlight and nothing else. He was about sixteen, maybe seventeen, and he looked like something out of a Zeffirelli movie. "What do you mean?" she asked. "What kind of business? My husband will be back soon. He just went out for cigarettes." Norman was at Columbia and might not be back for hours.

"Then I'll wait. It's him I want to talk to."

"You'd better tell me what this is about," she said, re-gretting her lie. "Sometimes it takes longer than you expect to buy a pack of cigarettes."

"Are you expecting it to take a long time?"

She chewed on her fingernail. If he jumped her, she could scream for Tom and Cyril, but they wouldn't be much good in a situation like this. "What do you want to see my husband about?"

"You shouldn't do that," he said, "it's a bad habit."

"Nobody asked for your advice."

"Shit," he said, "you haven't even asked for my name."

"I know who you are."

"My name is Mario."

"Why do you want to see my husband, Mario?"

"It's between him and me. I got something for him."

"He'll kill you if he finds you here."

"No, he won't. We got that all worked out a long time ago."

"What did you get worked out? I don't understand. When did you see my husband?"

Mario looked around the room—the canary, the desk, the television, the bed. Gus became alarmed as his glance hovered over the bed. He was young, but he wasn't too young.

Mario saw the fear on her face and it embarrassed him. In spite of his manner of practiced cool, he had not often been alone in a room with a double bed with a beautiful blonde whom he had seen in the altogether on her wedding night, and he felt that the whole thing was rather a lot to ask him to process right off the bat. She was really a looker. The way Mario had it sized up, there were two kinds of girls in the world, and the kind that this one was, was the kind that when she looked at you, you ought to be ashamed of what you were thinking, even if you had not been thinking it. Mario found that he felt deeply protective of her.

"Your husband lent me some money," he explained. "Well, actually, he didn't think it was a loan. He was under the impression that he was being blackmailed. Isn't that far out? My mother gave him that impression. She says she finds it an effective way of doing business."

"He lent you money?"

"That's what I said, isn't it?" The fact that he had been struck by a desire to do anything for Mrs. Gold that she might ask meant to Mario that he had better come on superlatively nonchalant. It was always fatal to let a broad know she was calling the shots.

"I think you're talking crazy," Gus said, narrowing her long eyes. "You're on speed, or something."

"I never touch the stuff," Mario said, offended. "It wrecks your looks, and I'm going to be an actor."

Gus thought he was certainly beautiful enough to be an actor. If he were ten years older, she'd be swooning over him. But he was just a tough-talking kid. "Why did my husband get the impression that you were blackmailing him?" she asked. She tried to make her voice sound older, upper-hand-ish, but it gave way on the word "blackmailing."

"Uh, well, you see," Mario said, pulling out a knife to clean his nails, "we told him that his old man might not like it if the papers knew his son was going around kicking the daylights out of minors. *Italian* minors. That kind of thing is very bad for race relations. As my mother said, it would be even worse for a Jewish father who needs Italian help if he wants to sit on the Supreme Court. My mother has a lot of inside information. Besides, it hurt like hell," Mario added, whining slightly in spite of himself. "Man, it felt like ten tons of pillowcases fell on my head. My mother thought that was hilarious, but let me tell you, ten tons of anything is still ten tons."

"My husband beat you up for a very understandable reason. I wish you'd put that thing away."

"Don't sweat it," Mario said, meaning to put her at ease. In fact, the way these words rolled off his tongue, as if he frequently said them while dangling motorcycle chains in front of terrified teeny-boppers, upset her more. "I'm not dangerous," he said. "Why do you keep saying *my husband*? I know he's your husband. Are you afraid I might try something?" Why did girls always think a guy had evil motives? Fuck and goddamn.

"He'll be back any minute," Gus said, desperately.

"Yeah," Mario said, "I'll wait."

"You could go, if you want to. I'll give him a message."

"Not a message. Two thousand dollars."

Gus abruptly forgot she was supposed to be afraid. She couldn't believe what she'd heard. "What?" she asked.

"Yeah. It's the amount my mother took him for."

"Norman doesn't have two thousand dollars!"

"He does now," Mario said. "Here it is." He pulled two thousand dollars out of his hip pocket and put it on the desk.

Gus sucked air, sharply. "Where could he get that kind of money?"

"From his old man. I told you."

"Norman doesn't have anything to do with his father. His father disowned him for marrying me."

Mario shrugged. "Anyway," he said, "he got it."

Birdie!

Gus fingered the money. She had never seen so much at once. "Tell me, Mario," she said, beginning to feel less tense, "why are you bringing it back?"

"It's not exactly the same bread," Mario said. "It's a repayment."

"But why? You could have just disappeared."

He looked at her closely, his eyes suddenly flashing, the lashes fluttering like a young girl's. "We don't need to steal from anybody. I keep telling my mother, but she won't listen. My father wouldn't do such a thing, if he were alive! I keep telling my mother, it is not a thing a man would do! But she's just a woman, what does she know?"

"But where did you get the money to pay it back? You can't earn very much bellhopping."

"Panhandling."

"Begging?"

"Panhandling. Like you stand on a street at a subway entrance, St. Mark's for instance, that's a hot spot, and people give you bread. It's as simple as that."

"But that's taking money from people. It's just like taking it from Norman."

"Don't be stupid," he said, "it's not the same thing at all. The first way is stealing, the second way, you're just letting people do what they want to do. Norman didn't want to fork over two grand, but those squares who come in for hip weekends, they're dying to buy back their consciences. They think I'm a runaway. So it makes them feel better to think they are not letting down the youth of the nation. I'm performing a public service. I'm like a safety valve which lets the country blow off steam and keeps it from blowing up. Somebody that don't think about this kind of thing in depth, he might think I was ripping people off, but as I see it, I am practically sacrificing myself so they don't have to torment themselves with questions like, Where did we let our kids down? What did we do wrong? Why was I thinking only about money instead of my darling baby? My mother is not the only person who reads the books in our apartment, but the way I look at it, she comes to some pretty flaky conclusions. What I'm giving you here is only the larger view, naturally."

"What's the smaller view?"

"The smaller view is that these idiot couples from Long Island come in to the East Village for weekends to look us over like we were monkeys in a zoo or something, and the girls want to impress the guys with how frigging compassionate they are, so they say, Oh look, Lance, or Bruce, or whatever the schmuck's name is, give him some money, I'll bet he's starving. And the guys, they want to impress the girls, so they throw their small change at us. Can I help it if people are stupid?"

"Would you like a Coke?"

"Sure," he said, sitting on the desk. He put the knife away. "You are a real knockout. Even with your clothes on."

"Thanks," she said. She handed him a can of Coke from the icebox. "Does your mother know you're here?"

"I told her I was flicking out. You know, at the movies. How is the marriage going?"

"The marriage?"

"With Norman. I'm interested. After all, I was in on it from the beginning. Does he make you happy?"

"Sure," Gus said, looking at the floor.

"I don't believe it," Mario said. "He's a real creep."

"He is not!"

"Well, he has a kind of brooding intensity, I'll give him that. Like Humphrey Bogart in *Casablanca*. I figure my style is more of a romantic thing. Did you ever think of going into the movies? With your face, you could be a Tuesday Weld type. Easy. Or Candice Bergen, only smaller-looking."

"Thanks," she said, "but no thanks. I'm a flutist."

"No kidding! Like Herbie Mann?"

"Same instrument," she said. "I'm making my debut in a couple of weeks. You can come, if you want."

"Why not?" he said. "It could be a gas." Actually, he was pleased and flattered, but it would not be cool to go overboard with gratitude.

Gus gave him a ticket—she had dozens, along with the throwaways which her manager had printed and which for days she'd been littering the city with. "Here," she said. Then, while she half wished she could keep on talking with Mario—it was like having a younger brother, something she'd always missed—she said, "You better go now, though. I lied about Norman. He won't be back for ages."

"He shouldn't leave you alone so much," Mario said. "In

the city, you can never tell who's going to show up when you're alone in your apartment." He crushed the empty Coke can with one hand and went to the door, but at the last minute he turned around and said to her, convinced that he was speaking the innermost feelings of his heart for the first time in his life, "You are a really out-of-sight chick, Mrs. Gold. I mean that. Really fine!"

"Thanks," she said, again, startled. *"Ciao!"*

58

CREEP, Gus was thinking, as she looked at the money on the desk. Two thousand dollars. Next to it was a book . . . a book on Beethoven. The Thayer. Gus turned it over in her hands, wondering how it had got there. Wasn't this the book she had lent to Richard? Norman did not know Richard. Then she remembered: Richard knew Birdie Mickle. Again! The weight of all this evidence heaped on Gus was finally too much, and she felt that she had to tell someone everything. She had to get it off her chest before she tried to play the flute in public. But to whom could she talk? She didn't want to tell her mother; her mother wouldn't say it, but she would remember that she had warned Gus not to get married in the first place. Gus didn't have any friends separate from Norman anymore. She couldn't talk to Richard, who knew Birdie. Philip Fleischman was Norman's friend, and Dinky was Phil's. She couldn't talk to Tom and Cyril about Norman behind his back—they were Norman's neighbors and had been even before she moved in, even though they hadn't known each other then. So far as Gus could see, there was only one person left.

59

Esther Gold, wife of Sidney and mother of Norman (also the ritually clean Rita), had all her married life worked hard not to be like the Jewish wives and mothers in all the books. Where they mixed in, she kept herself apart. Why should her life be the butt of a running joke? She was not without a quality of self-reflectiveness and inner grace, not abundant but utterly trustworthy, all the stronger for having been wrested from circumstance rather than freely bestowed. The circumstance was Sid, or, more specifically, Sid's money.

Often she said to herself, If only Sid had been content to become a CPA! A Grade Twelve with the IRS! A little auditor with a big company! Instead he had to make a fortune and become a big shot, leaving her alone in the rambling Victorian house with gingerbread trimming and solid oak banisters on Ocean Parkway, unfit for mahjong and miserable at fund-raising dinners. She fulfilled her role to the best of her ability, wore mink in July and turned her children over to Mitzi, but her heart was as fragile as a flower vase in which the immortal Rose of Longing stands, and she had to carry it carefully to keep it from tipping over and breaking into a thousand uncollectable pieces. Her hair was blued and she wore upswept plastic eyeglass frames with rhinestone clusters, in this way accenting her soft green irises and giving the illusion of what is known in the women's magazines as youthful maturity, but her heart was like a candy store where no children ever came to buy.

Once, when Sid was still D.A., burglars had broken into the house, stealing all her diamonds, and who did Brooklyn's Finest suspect but herself, Esther Gold! It was Sid who had called in the police. He noticed that she wasn't wearing them to a party when in his opinion she ought to have been wearing them, and she had to confess they were missing. First, to Sid's surprise, the police pointed their collective finger at her. "This is ridiculous," she told them, "why would I steal from myself?" "Insurance," they said. "They weren't insured," she said. "What, not insured?" "You heard," she said. "So," they said, "this is very deep. A D.A. who doesn't insure his wife's jewelry must have an ulterior motive." "No motive," she said, as they began to frisk her son. (Norman was nine that year.) "He forgot. It's my fault. I never put it on his list." "His list?" "I have to make a list for him of things to do each day." They demanded to see a sample list. They had it in for Sid because he was D.A. and out to make a name exposing corruption in the police force, graft and bribes. However, her lists were no clue, and in the end they had to give up. They never recovered the diamonds.

This was because Esther had donated the diamonds anonymously to a certain organization in Israel devoted to desert reclamation. It required some doing, but she had learned a lot from Sid about how to smuggle in the days when he was running arms. She would have liked to send her mink as well, but it was too bulky to ship easily and in any case Sidney expected her to wear it constantly to political functions, and she didn't want to endanger his career. She was much happier without the diamonds, although now she sometimes wished she had them back, for Norman's and his wife's sake. Rita, her daughter, she didn't need to worry about. Rita's husband could buy Levittown and have money left over, but how could Norman and his young wife live, with Sid cutting off his own son, like cutting off his schnozz to spite his face, and Norman being, she had to admit it to herself even if she was his mother, about as worldly as her own father, who, he should rest in peace, thought a man's birthright and duty was to sit in the attic reading the Talmud all day while his wife worked her tail off to keep him from starving in his piety.

When Augusta stopped writing to her, Esther wanted to telephone, but she had learned from years of being Sid's wife to behave with enough dignity for herself *and* Sid. Inside, she felt undignifiedly hurt. It seemed to her that all her life all she had ever wanted was to do just the things everybody caricatured. She had an almost biological urge to cook chicken soup. She had almost irresistible impulses to take people's temperatures or give them enemas. She thought wistfully of how it would feel if only once, coming home from a hard day's shopping at Abraham and Straus, she could say, "My feet are killing me," in a loud, dramatic voice, and then add, "I know, I know, to be a wife and mother, it means that you sacrifice your life at the hands of your feet, but who understands this? Another wife and mother, maybe, but children? Your husband? God forbid they should deign to understand!" She never did or said any of these things. She was the daughter of a rabbi and as soon as they were married, Sid, out of pride in his catch and respect for her background, had put her on a pedestal. She was not supposed to think about sex. (Did he think Rita and Norman were virgin births?) She was supposed to be refined and sponsor modern art. Esther thought modern art was sick. It had no life. She had a great hunger to love people, but she was sixty-two years old and shy.

60

When Gus finally did telephone her, Esther was overjoyed. Distressed, but overjoyed. "What's wrong?" Esther asked, on the alert. "I can tell, something's wrong," she said, her heart singing. "For months I haven't heard so much as hello from you or Norman. This is not a good omen!"

"I know," Gus said. "I was too ashamed to write. It's because Norman is having an affair."

"He's not! My son? An affair? My God, who with?"

"A woman named Birdie. Birdie Mickle."

"This I find very hard to accept, Augusta. From the photograph you sent of you and Norman, I can see that you are very pretty. Why would Norman pass that up for somebody named Birdie? As Paul Newman says about his lovely wife Joanne Woodward in the magazine I read under the hair dryer last week, Why go out for hamburger when you can have steak at home?"

"I guess I don't make him happy," Gus said. "But he must make *her* happy. She gives him money."

"No!"

"Two thousand dollars," she said.

This was, if Esther had thought about it, the last thing she had ever expected to hear anyone say about her son the scholar. "You're dreaming," Esther said. "I know my son. I love my son, but he is not worth two thousand dollars, if you'll pardon my split lip for saying so."

"What am I going to do, Esther?"

"I don't know, this is terrible," she said, still delighted that Augusta was consulting her. "It's because Mitzi spoiled him when he was little. But maybe you've got it wrong. Maybe there are mitigating circumstances. I believe there must be such circumstances, Augusta."

"Esther, I'm staring at two thousand dollars. This boy, Mario, just brought it back. Norman gave it to him so he wouldn't tell the newspapers about what happened on our wedding night. Esther, Norman got this money from Birdie Mickle! There's no other answer!"

"What happened on your wedding night?"

"Nothing."

"Nothing?"

"I mean, nothing of any importance."

"Nothing of any importance! Augusta, tell me. Don't be afraid to speak frankly. Have I got a fairy for a son?"

"No," Gus said. "He sleeps with this woman. He sleeps with me. I don't know if it stops there. For all I know, he sleeps with the entire student body of Barnard."

"You mean my son is a nymphomaniac? I thought that only happened to women."

"Men can have something called satyriasis, but I don't think that's the trouble with Norman. I think that may be when you can't get it down."

"My God," Esther said, "I never heard such things. Sidney never— Go on."

"That's all there is to it. Norman's having an affair. I don't know why. I think the trouble must just be me. She gives him money, because she likes him, I guess. I think I'm going to cry."

"Augusta, you must not cry in the crunch."

"Okay," she said, "but what do I do?"

"You got two thousand dollars in front of you, is that what you said?"

"Yes."

"Spend."

"What? Esther, I can't do that!"

"Why not? Does Norman know you have this money? Did he ever expect to see it again? What would he use it for if you gave it to him? Would he give it back to this other woman, when you can barely make ends meet and have to cook in a kitchen full of cockroaches?"

"I don't cook very often."

"My God," Esther said. "Why didn't you tell me you're starving?"

"We have hotdogs. Also creamed herring, Grape-Nuts, root beer, Coca-Cola, and eggnog."

"Alcoholic?"

"No," Gus said.

"That's good, but my God."

"It's awful, isn't it? Sometimes I think Norman never really loved me. He married me just to strike a blow at his father."

"If so, I'm the one it hit. My own son, my own husband, not speaking to each other. It's unnatural. I told Sid again and again, It's unnatural, but he said his constituency expected it. Sid has devoted all his life to his constituency. I can't ask him to turn his back on it now. He's not a bad man, Augusta. He has his reasons."

"I guess Norman does too, but I can't figure out what they are. I think maybe I don't please him. You know."

"In bed? What *did* happen on your wedding night?"

"He beat up somebody, that's all."

"In your room, he beat up somebody? My God," she said, "what is the world coming to! Three in a room, my God!"

61

THE FOLLOWING TUESDAY Richard Nixon was elected President of the United States. Sidney swallowed so much Alka-Seltzer he began to feel he might effervesce internally, but nothing helped. "Ruin, ruin, ruin," he moaned, listening to the returns on the radio in Birdie's apartment on Madison Avenue. She blew on his white fringe, but even that didn't help. "Tragic, tragic," he kept saying, under his breath. In a single night of disaster, it was sunk, lost, gone, wiped out and smashed all to hell—his dream.

He waited—what was the rush?—until his regular weekly

dinner with Norman to tell him that there was no longer any *quid pro quo* for continuing with the blackmail.

"I realize that," Norman said.

"I'm sorry," Sid said.

"It's not your fault," Norman said.

"If only we'd won! It was a sure thing, almost. Amato, Leibowitz, and Sidney Wallechinsky Gold. If Bobby Kennedy—"

"Yeah, I know. It must be hard on Leibowitz."

"And Amato."

"Well, Pop, I guess we won't be seeing each other anymore. This is good-bye, as they say. *Sayonara,* and so forth."

"What will you do now?"

"I don't know. I had been planning, if you had won, to hit you up for another two thou at one blow. Gus's concert is coming up and there's still the hall to pay for. You wouldn't want to pay for it even in your present mood, by any chance?"

"It's not a question of mood, Norman. It's a matter of principle. You should never have married a *shiksa.*"

"What's done is done," Norman said.

"What's done is that you are disinherited. I can't change that."

"Sure you could. Anyway, I'm only asking for two thousand. The other four hundred and ninety-eight you can keep."

"No," Sidney said, taking a fifty from his wallet. "Here's this week's, never say I welched on a deal, but that's the last of it. How can I back down now? I don't even want to back down. For the pleasure of your company I was glad to pay you fifty bucks a week when there was a legitimate business reason, namely blackmail, but I cannot support a girl that I don't think even my own son has the right to be supporting."

"If it helps you to feel better morally, I don't support her very well." Norman put the money into his wallet.

"You could get a job."

"I have thought about it," Norman said, "but it gives me the cold shivers. Being at somebody else's beck and call. After all, it's not so long until the dissertation is done."

"Well," Sidney said, "I can't say I blame you. I've always taken pride in being able to say my son the scholar. You take after your mother's father. You smoke too much, though. You should switch to cigars. Try one of these."

"Not bad," Norman said, leaning across the plates of abandoned chicken livers to reach his father's match.

"Cuba," Sidney said. "Havana."

"Havana?"

"My old connections still come through for me now and then."

"There's nothing like a good cigar," Norman said, as a way of telling his father that he loved him.

"No," Sidney agreed. "Nothing."

62

I HAVE TO TALK with you about something."

Norman was addressing Augusta in their apartment on West Eighty-eighth Street. It was a gray day outside; the sky looked soft, like a down quilt. It looked as if, were you to poke it in one place, it would bunch up in another. There might be snowfeathers instead of snowflakes. Norman felt as if he had a boa constrictor wrapped around his chest.

Gus thought he wanted to tell her about Birdie. "I'm on my way out," she said.

"This is important," he said. "I'm afraid it's going to make you unhappy."

"Then don't tell me," she said.

"I have to. It affects what you're doing right now."

She was getting ready to go up to Juilliard to use the practice room.

"I don't have the money for your hall. You'll have to cancel the concert."

Gus didn't say anything.

"Jesus Christ, Gus, say something." He was hating himself. "I'm sorry! I thought I was going to have the money, but I don't."

"It doesn't matter," she said. "I already paid for the hall."

"You did what?"

"Paid for the hall."

"But where did you get the money?" he said, despairing.

"Where do you think!" she shouted, and slammed the door behind her as she left.

63

Norman sat down at the desk, blindly. He had to feel his way into the chair. It took several minutes before the red in front of his eyes dissolved and he could focus on objects. He felt not only angry, so angry that he believed he would never recover from it, but forsaken, as if, because he did not have two thousand dollars, he was no use to anyone. He lacked the wherewithal to run around providing concert halls for flutists. He was minus managers and money. As for Hacking— What could Norman do about him (that wasn't illegal)? It would be fatal to himself, if not to Hacking, to let jealousy take control of him. And as he thought this, releasing slowly, word by thought word, the possibility of beating the fucking shit out of the bastard, Norman felt a deep desire, so deep that it seemed to spring from the wellsource of his being. It was a desire to lay his head in his mother's lap.

He turned over the books and papers on the desk until he found the Beethoven book. Then he held it upside down by its spine, letting the pages part, rustling like a fan. There it was—the letter from his mother to Gus, hitting the desk with a gentle whack that reverberated in Norman's blood-filled head like the entire percussion section of an orchestra. There must be some sort of statute of limitations on letters, a point after which you could open a letter addressed to somebody else without being tried and condemned by the omnipresent judge who held court at the back of your brain to death by unerring lightning bolt. It was, after all, *his* mother, not Gus's.

The glue had dried up anyway, and the flap came open almost of its own accord when he prised it up.

What did he think he would find? A check for two thousand dollars? An incriminating document? He hoped, most of all, that there might be some clue to how Gus felt about him, but he had taught her, too well, not to reveal their lives on paper to anyone else. But his mother must have sensed that she was not getting the full story from Gus. "Anytime you feel like a chat," she had written, "you just let me know. I can come into the city. Sid doesn't need to know."

Norman felt obscurely cheated not to have found anything more exciting going on between his mother and his wife. Had they ever met, or had the lost letter prevented them from ever getting together for their koffee klatch? On the days when he was secretly eating dinner with his father, was his wife secretly eating dinner with his mother? For a moment, Norman's spirits climbed: maybe Gus had gotten money from his mother, just as he had gotten it from his father. Then they dipped and sank again: his father had never permitted his mother to have her own checking account. She had no money to speak of.

He let the letter drift back down to the table, but then he picked it up again. "Sometimes it does a person good to talk things over," his mother had written.

It did; it did. And if she was willing to listen to his wife, wouldn't she listen to him? The story would be the same whichever of them told it to her, and maybe she could help. God knows, he needed help. But the mere possibility that his mother might be able to provide it filled him with such glad anticipation that he was out the door and on his way to Brooklyn before he had altogether made up his mind to go there.

64

E<small>AT</small>," Esther said. "For once in your life you've come to me for advice, so for once I'm giving it. Eat." She had cooked him a steak and a side dish of buttered spaghetti, just the way Mitzi used to. "I know how you kids live on thin air, and to tell the truth, Norman, it worries me. I lie awake at night wondering what can I do, but I know I'm not supposed to mix in. Who wants a nosy mother-in-law? Sid says, They don't exist, your son and his *shiksa* wife, they're nogoodniks; and I say, Okay, Sid, whatever you say. Because all my life I've said, Okay, Sid, whatever you say. Only, at night I have dreams. My son, who my husband says is effectively speaking dead, comes back to haunt me. And he's as thin as a skeleton. No flesh on his bones. How can I sleep? Would you sleep if you were a mother and your son who is alive and well and living on West Eighty-eighth Street is practically starving already, and you shouldn't lift a finger to help?"

"No," Norman said.

"So I'm complaining. Did I ever once complain in all the years you were growing up? No. I sponsored modern art. I wore mink and for what. So Sid could use up his whole life working to get on the Supreme Court and break his heart in his old age by failing. Now I'm complaining. For once in my life I'm complaining, Norman, because it's not right that a mother should have to imagine that her son is dead, and also I'm giving advice. Eat."

"It's not half bad," Norman said, eating. "In fact, it's better than Mitzi used to make. I never knew you could cook."

"I wasn't allowed. Your father said Mitzi should cook, that's what Mitzi was for."

Finished, Norman pushed the plate away, lit a cigarette and blew several smoke rings. They rose toward the Tiffany chandelier hanging from the ceiling. In this room he had eaten many of the meals of his life. On such facts, Norman thought, feeling stuffed and mellow, the world turns. He remembered how he used to eat upstairs and then again down here and then tear out to Loew's with Phil Fleischman. Who knew Phil was going to grow up to be a hip ad-man? Who knew he himself would end up learned, lonely, married, and visiting his mother on the sly?

Esther waited. Behind the winged frames, her pale green eyes watered. It was almost two years since she had seen her son, and now here he was, blowing smoke rings over the leftover spaghetti. Her heart was full.

Norman felt suddenly bashful. On a full stomach, it no longer seemed so reasonable to tell your mother that your wife had found another man more satisfactory than your mother's son. It was not something he really wanted anybody to know. But then when his mother said, "Go ahead, unburden yourself, I'm your *mother*," Norman found himself talking in an unexpected access of freedom, as if he were jettisoning months of hurt, anxiety, and anger like useless cargo overboard, and as he talked, he began to feel wonderfully light. Ah, Dr. Morris, Dr. Morris! If Norman had only known in the years since elapsed what he discovered now, under the Tiffany chandelier, he might never have lain for so many darkened hours on the leather couch in your air-conditioned, centrally heated womb room! For what he discovered now was that talking to his mother made him feel exactly the way he had felt talking to you, his analyst, mentor, parental-substitute, and way-out-of-high-school-and-the-army. Relieved.

It was like emptying himself of the heavy emotions, the ones that weigh a person down and prevent him from exercising successfully that backstroke of the soul, breaststroke of the heart, which propel said person through the deep and turbulent, the capable-of-causing-to-drown elements of life, and the lighter he became, the higher he floated, until once again he was on top. Norman preferred being on top and considered this a normal enough preference, if a sexually loaded one, and indeed, when he felt he was on top, he became a kinder person, more expansive and receptive to other people's feelings and generous with his own. Right now, for example, he was becoming aware that his mother had been quite prolongedly silent. "That's it," he said, coming to a halt. "Hacking gave Gus the money for the hall and she took it from him."

Esther said, "Augusta never wrote me about anyone named Hacking. Richard, you said? She never mentioned a Richard either."

"Well, she wouldn't, would she? Considering."

"I want to be very sure of something," Esther said. "You said they meet at this woman's apartment, Birdie something?"

"Birdie Mickle."

"How did you find that out?"

"I heard it from"—he couldn't say his father—"someone who knows her."

"This someone," Esther said. "It could be a confused person."

"Why do you think that? There's no question in my mind."

"I'm just suggesting that maybe there should be."

"I don't see why."

"Norman, I want you to do me a favor. Don't go off the deep end."

"What the hell does that mean?"

"Norman," Esther said, thinking hard, "I don't believe Augusta would do what you are saying. What's more, I have reason to think that there is some element of confusion here. I can't quite put my finger on it, but something is, if you'll excuse the expression, screwed up."

"I never heard you use an expression like that."

"Before you weren't such a big boy. I know all about satyriasis too."

"Why would you know about something like that?" Was his father even more active than Norman realized? Christ, he must be a horny old bastard!

"Never mind, I know. My God, I think I know too much. Now tell me something else, Norman. This Birdie. Did you ever have anything to do with her?"

"What do you mean?" he asked, stalling.

"Did you ever, you know. Hanky-panky."

"Don't be silly."

"I'm a silly old lady."

"No."

"Okay, that's all I wanted to know."

Norman relaxed again. "What do you think I should do?"

"What do you think?" she said. "What I said. Eat. Have dessert. Don't go off the deep end. And don't blame Augusta for something she hasn't done."

"Don't tell me you think she's not acting like a prostitute. Not your average streetwalker, I'll admit. Two thousand dollars is a rather steep price. But what else do you call it?"

"A boy gave this money to her. His name is Mario."

"Mario?"

"You beat him up."

"Oh Jesus. Mario."

"On your wedding night. Three in a room, my own son! My God."

"He was the bellhop."

"The bellhop! My God!"

"I had to give him the money or he would have caused trouble for Pop. Political trouble."

"So where did you get it, the money?"

"You know where money comes from," Norman said, mumbling. "It's just sort of there, wherever it is."

"I don't understand, Norman."

"I can't explain. Maybe Mario's mother could."

"Did you get it from this Birdie Mickle?"

"I told you," Norman said, "there was no fucking hanky-panky, as you call it!"

"Don't tell me," Esther said. "Go home and tell your wife, who is dying from heartache already. My God. She thinks you're having an affair with Birdie Mickle. Also while you're at it, wash out your mouth."

65

WHEN Norman got home, he found Gus cleaning Tweetie's cage. "There," she was saying, "all nice and clean. You did not tee a puddytat. Now you can sit on your swing and sing. Twing and ting." She didn't hear Norman entering, and when she turned around and saw him, she jumped.

"You scared me," she said.

"I did not sleep with Birdie Mickle," Norman said.

Gus went into the bathroom and washed her hands. When she came back out, she said, "What makes you think I thought you did?"

"I went to see my mother."

"She told you to say that so I wouldn't feel bad."

"I'm saying it because it's true."

"I don't believe you."

"Why the hell would you? You've been too busy getting laid by that conductor friend of yours."

"I have not!"

"Why else would you think I was having an affair? People get suspicious of other people when they're doing something suspicious. It's a basic principle." Norman looked at his wife's face, a face which, if he had been a thousand ships, would have launched him, a face which seemed to him a miracle, as beautiful as a Bach chorale, honey hair tipped with electric fireshine from the round white lamp with the Chinese coolie shade, and he waited for her to convince him that it was not a basic principle.

"What about you, then?" she said. "Doesn't it apply to you? How else could you get such a ridiculous idea about me!"

His glance fell from her face to her hand. "Where's your ring? The pearl?"

"Oh God, I must have left it in the bathroom." She ran back to the bathroom. "I can't find it, Norman!" she called. Her eyes were blurred with tears, which made looking difficult, and she felt panicky, as if this was a portent.

Norman found the ring as soon as he went to look; it had fallen from the sink into one of the cracks between the peeling tile and the floor. "It's all right," he said, handing it to her.

Gus put it on at once, soothed, but Norman went back out to the other room and sat down heavily on the dark red and blue bed. He was still wearing his Burberry. He was thinking that women didn't lose their engagement rings without wanting to. It was another basic principle.

66

CONCEIVABLY, Esther thought, there were four thousand dollars involved. It would explain the confusion, but it seemed unlikely. Augusta must have paid for the hall with the two thousand dollars that Mario had returned, and Norman must have gotten that two thousand dollars originally from Birdie Mickle. When he said there was no hanky-panky between them, he had blushed sinfully. Esther knew her son, even if Mitzi had raised him.

But why did he think Augusta was being unfaithful? That piece of news he had got also from Birdie Mickle. If nothing else, the answer, at least, lay with her. What's more, she was listed in the Manhattan directory: B. Mickle. Getting into her coat, scarf, and galoshes, shutting up the house, Esther saw the situation as an opportunity that could never knock again if she didn't hearken to it now. She had a purpose finally, and nobody could accuse her of being a busybody or a nosy mother-in-law. She was only trying to help.

The snow had begun to fall, in lazy, sweeping blowings, but by the time she got out of the subway station on the Upper East Side, the wind had changed, and the flakes were smaller, whirling radially. It was dark now. The street lamps were on, and the Christmas decorations glowed in the shop windows, and the headlights cast dancing yellow images on the icing asphalt and the gutter, like little yellow figures, seasonal shoppers made of light. The real people were all shadows, dark coats that bumped insubstantial shoulders and swore at each other, or laughed insanely. A familiar and chilling sense of loneliness enveloped Esther as she walked through the crowd.

She always felt left out at Christmas time. She knew this was not an admirable feeling and would never admit it to anyone else, but all the same, no matter how many Chanukah presents she received, all her life she had felt as though Santa Claus and his reindeer stopped at everybody's house except hers. In a way, she was still listening for the sound of hooves on the rooftop, the jingle of bells, sled runners scraping against the wood shingles. Santa never came. A good thing, too, Esther told herself. How could she explain to her dead father, a rabbi and a son of a rabbi and a son of a son of a rabbi, that the fat man stuck in the chimney was a saint already, and not a neighbor up to no good?

She picked her way carefully through the slush and shoppers, wheezing a little from excitement and exertion. When she reached Miss Mickle's building, she had a bad moment, but the doorman didn't even bother to ask for identification. It was the holiday spirit, and besides, why pester a sixty-two-year-old lady who said she was a friend of Miss Mickle's mother? "No," she said, "don't ring. It's a surprise." He directed her to the elevator.

At the door to the apartment, she stopped to get her breath before she knocked.

Birdie peeked through the peephole. An old lady. UNICEF? She opened the door.

"You don't know me," Esther said. "I'm Esther Gold."

Birdie couldn't think what to say. She had never— It was so— Nobody had warned— "Oh," Birdie said, "oh, oh! You can't come in."

"What do you mean, I can't come in? I'm here, aren't I? We have somebody in common, don't we? If that's not an introduction, I don't know what is."

"I didn't mean to be rude," Birdie said.

"So ask me in."

Birdie chewed her lower lip and then said, "Okay." She didn't see what else she could do. Sidney's wife must have known everything anyway, or why would she be here? "If you're sure you want me to," she said, leading Mrs. Gold inside.

Esther followed, stamping the snow off her galoshes in the hall. At first, she didn't see Sid; she was tangled in her wool scarf, which she was taking off and using to wipe her glasses with. Sid didn't see her because he was seated on the Empire sofa, head bent, hands clasped between his knees. When he looked up and saw her, he didn't say anything. She said, softly, "Sid."

"Esther," he said, in his high, fading voice like the whistle of a train headed out of town. "I don't feel so good, Esther," he said. "I think I'd like to go home now."

67

M<small>Y</small> G<small>OD</small>," Esther said, "look at you." The flesh seemed to have come unstuck from his bones. It was still there, loose rolls of it; but about those overlapping flesh-folds there was an aura of unreality, of insubstantiality, like ghosts multiplying a television image. The essential man was scrunched up at the center, a tiny beam, a soul in a sack of living-and-dying light. Why did she not notice this at home on Ocean Parkway? It became clear only here, in alien surroundings. The place looked to Esther like a scene from *Pillow Talk.* What did her Sid know from satin and velvet and so forth? He was a kid from Delancey Street who worked hard all his life for mixed motives his children, her children, were too innocent to grasp. They needed straight lines. A straight line, Sid was not. All right, then, if this was where it had led him, who was she to bitch about it? She knew a little something about how a person travels from infancy to senior citizenship herself, and it was not such a simple thing, getting there. Now Sid—he would be trading in his judge's black robe for a white heavenly robe. What would he do if there was a heaven and everybody in it was already perfect and there was no one to lay down the law to? He would be lost. Esther wanted to cry. "I didn't realize," she said. "You don't notice how people change when they're at home, but here—"

"It's not like you think, Mrs. Gold," Birdie said. "Sidney is the twin of my soul but that's as far as we go, usually." Birdie was feeling very bad; this woman was not at all the way she imagined her: she was vague- and sad-looking, shapeless and kind-eyed; she looked like a mother. Because Birdie had never been a mother, she was easily touched by mothers and somewhat in awe of them, although the reason she had not been one herself was that she had never wanted to be one. Birdie remembered her own mother with an affection that caused her to choke up whenever she thought about her.

"I thought you knew my son," Esther said, "not Sid."

"Oh," Birdie said, "I know Norman too."

"My God."

"But that's not like you think either!" Birdie said, frantic not to be thought ill of by someone who was, like her own mother, a mother. "Why are people always jumping to conclusions about me? Even other women do it."

"It could be your bustline," Esther said, trying to help.

"Listen," Birdie said, "I think you should make Sidney see a doctor."

"Doctors, schmoctors," Sidney said. "What do they know, besides to overcharge? This is some coincidence, Esther," he added.

"To tell the truth, Sidney, I didn't expect to find you here."

"What brings you?" he asked.

"Her," she said, pointing at Birdie.

"She's a good girl, Esther. She didn't mean any harm."

"Then what I'd like to know is, why does our son, who is supposed to be dead legally speaking but whom I saw this afternoon so take that Sid, why he thinks his wife is using your place, Miss Mickle, to meet illicitly for immoral purposes with someone named Richard Hacking. And why does our daughter-in-law, which she is no matter what you say Sid so don't say it, why she thinks Norman is having an affair with Miss Mickle herself."

Birdie gasped. Unpremeditatedly.

"Now one thing is plain to me," Esther said. "If they were both right, they would have run into each other sooner or later. In this room."

"I never even met Norman's wife," Birdie said. "I only met Norman once. I *told* Elaine to tell Norman that his wife was not having an affair with Richard. I am. Was."

"Elaine? Who is Elaine?"

"Richard's wife."

"Then if you weren't paying Norman for his services, excuse me but it's what Augusta thought, who gave Norman the two thousand dollars that he gave to Mario which Mario returned to Augusta so she could pay for her Town Hall concert with the result that Norman thinks Richard gave it to her?"

"I did," Sidney said.

68

IT MAY BE, in fact it almost surely was although the unconscious is not to be treated too familiarly but with a certain respect, that one reason Sidney had never divorced Esther was that in the back of his mind he knew this moment would come; and while Esther would not have wished for it, she felt as if her natural talents at last had found a mode of expression. They turned to each other almost with an air of elation, though it was muted by Sidney's dark side, the profound pessimism that always underlay his manic temporizing, and by Esther's unsureness, the habit of self-doubt that came from years of living in a social world foreign to her inner temperament, altering her personality to fit the world when it was the garment of world that was too large, cut unsuitably, like her mink coat. Nevertheless, it was as if Sidney and Esther discovered in their old age the reason they had married each other forty-two years before, in 1926, on a day when it seemed to Esther the whole line of her forefathers must have been ranged invisibly along the walls, smiling behind their invisible beards, and the sun had been shining and the trash-cans gleamed as if they were made of silver and flashed like diamonds and even what the horses left in the streets gleamed like ebony, and in the distance a radio played "All Alone by the Telephone," and later Sidney kept trying to talk to her father about the Scopes trial, which the day was the anniversary of although it was also their wedding day; and this discovery was a cause of jubilation, however modified it might be for the sake of appropriateness and to the eyes of outsiders. In fact, the only visible sign of it was a heightened flush in Esther's age-soft cheeks, a sharpened modesty in her pale green eyes as if she were newly aware of her husband's affection for her; and in Sidney, the yearning in his glance as he pushed himself up from the sofa and the Désirée pillows in Birdie's apartment and clasped Esther's hand in his. For if Birdie was the twin of his soul, what Sidney needed now was someone to minister to the needs of his body, needs that Birdie could not yet fully understand, and, Sidney felt, ought not, because she was only forty-one or -two, and although Birdie was beginning to think that was old, she was, so far as Sidney was concerned, only a baby yet—too young to be told the facts of death. After all, she had not even gone through menopause yet. And Sidney remembered Esther's hot flashes and erratic depressions with an immediate welling of sentiment. He had fought McCarthyism by day, contending with Esther's change of life at night, and while both had left him frazzled in 1953, the absurdity of the relation now endeared Esther to him tremendously, as if it were a wholly new event and not one which he had just relived in retrospect in the space of a few seconds.

After they had left, Birdie tidied up the apartment and then she fixed herself a stiff drink of Hawaiian Punch. She was still jealous of Esther, even if she was a sweet old lady. It was the way they had left, Sidney not even turning around to look back, Esther taking Sidney by the elbow like a Girl

Scout. Arm in arm, as if they had come that way—not to Birdie's apartment but into the world, two people united by society and time, which, it seemed to Birdie, were clearly a stronger cincture, nexus and bond than even the deepest spiritual comradeship. She blew her nose and went to bed, curling up between the satin sheets the way she used to when she was a child, except that because of her chest she couldn't draw her knees up very high. And because of this, which seemed to her the bitterest fact of all, Birdie began to cry again, just a little. After a while, she fell asleep.

69

SOME DAYS LATER Norman telephoned Birdie's apartment, hoping to reach his father.

Norman did not know that his father was now and for as long as remained to him safely back in the house on Ocean Parkway. Why had Esther failed to tell Norman this? For one thing, she figured he and Augusta at least now knew that neither was breaking the marriage vows with anyone else. For another, her first concern was with Sid. For *another,* she couldn't help being just a little bit hurt that for nearly two years her husband and her son had been seeing each other behind her back, when she was supposed to be trying to believe that her son's was a name not to be mentioned among the living and the decent.

There was a fourth but not final reason. (The final reason was that Esther was planning on having a big reunion at the holiday season, very ecumenical so nobody should feel left out, with everyone coming together and being a family again. It would be her triumph, the moment of her *raison d'être* realized, compensation for all those years of not mixing in.)

Number Four was that if Esther told Norman how she went to Birdie's apartment and brought Sid home, Sid would be mortified. It was not good to embarrass a father in front of his son, this much she knew from being a wife and mother. Better to let Norman think Sid was still seeing that woman!

Which is what Norman thought, and why he telephoned Birdie's apartment, hoping to reach his father. He had tried the office, and Jocelyn said he wasn't in. Birdie wasn't in either.

Richard Hacking was.

This time Norman didn't hang up. "Hacking," he said.

"I believe you have the advantage of me, sir," Richard said, chortling into the telephone. It was a line he had always wanted to use.

"This is Gold," Norman said. "Norman Gold. You know my wife, I believe."

Richard came to a full stop, braking with a kind of internal screech. "Uh, yes," he said. Had Sidney sicked Gussie's husband on him too? Oh fuck, he thought; oh bloody fuck. What was he going to *do*? He hadn't been able to find out the first thing about how to give Birdie what she wanted. Who did they think he was? He was only a conductor, for crying out loud! A lousy, dumb, well-meaning conductor! Did Seiji Ozawa get into fixes like this? Did Georg Solti find himself having to set up interpretative dance concerts for platinum blondes? Of course, it was the sort of thing Zubin might know something about. Richard wondered if he should give Zubin a ring in California but he wasn't sure what time it would be there now.

"Relax," Norman said, in his most mellifluously sarcastic voice, the one he reserved for times of high stress, when he wished to remove himself from the immediate situation without being seen to turn tail. It was a voice that said: I feel such contempt for you that I cannot even be bothered to express the contempt I feel. He had melded this voice from elements of fear, self-loathing, ambition, and narcissistic play, the usual adolescent mix, but with his special intensity, it had come together rather effectively, and Richard, at any rate, was devastated. When Norman said, "Relax," Richard was ecstatically adrenalinized, intoxicated by tension, thrilled and transported. He nearly went through the roof.

"What's up?" Richard asked. "Is anything wrong? Birdie isn't here." Then another thought jolted him. "You haven't been talking with my wife again, have you?"

"I'm trying to get a message to my father." Norman couldn't call his mother with the message without giving away the fact that he had been seeing his father without her knowledge. "As you know, my father and Birdie are" — Norman paused delicately — "friends."

"He's not here either," Richard said.

"You hang around in Birdie's apartment because you like the view from the window?"

"The view from the window? I don't know," Richard said, puzzled, "I'm not sure which window you mean. The living room looks out on a fire escape."

"For Christ's sake," Norman said, "what do I want to know about the view from the living room for? Are you really as dense as you would appear to be?"

"You don't have to be offensive. I mean, fuck it. Why do I have to hang on and listen to you being offensive? You asked about the view!"

"I asked what you were doing there."

"Nothing," Richard said, "I'm doing nothing. If it's any of your business, I'm trying to decide between killing myself and going fishing." He was collecting certain items to take back home, now that he had been found out and was dedicating himself to Elaine again—his electric razor and Fabergé.

"Where do you go fishing in Manhattan?"

"Talk about being dense! Not here—in Florida! Oh, no. Oh," he moaned, foreseeing possible dire consequences of a Mafian nature, "wait a minute. Do me a favor, huh? Don't tell your father I said that. I wouldn't want Mr. Gold to think I was thinking of skipping town."

"This may come as a shock to you, Hacking," Norman said, "but I couldn't care less what you do. I don't see why my father should care one whit more than I do. Do you suppose you could manage to take a message?"

Richard reached for the memo pad and little gold-plated ballpoint beside the French telephone. "Go ahead," he said.

"Okay, this is it: my wife's concert is at Town Hall on Friday night. That's so he should know that she's giving it with his money, ironically for him, and he's welcome to come if he can bring himself to stop acting like a medieval ass. I trust Gus has already invited you, against my better judgment, you understand. Incidentally, it might amuse you to know that for a while I thought it was your money that was paying for this."

As Norman spoke, Richard wrote carefully, printing in block letters: CONCERT. TOWN HALL. FRIDAY. MEDIEVAL ASS. BALAAM'S? "What do you mean, my money? Of course I'll be there. In spite of your gratuitous insults. Gussie is an old and dear friend," Richard added, filling with righteousness. "I knew her first, you forget that. And what do you mean, my money? I never *paid* anybody, the way you're insinuating. Except my wife, if that counts. Elaine shops a lot." Richard thought, and then went on: "I never *took* any money either. *I* don't go around blackmailing *my* father." But he wanted to be fair. "Of course, my father is dead. He died when he was only fifty-two. The old ticker. I am not a nervous wreck without foundation, but I expect to be a very relaxed and unflappable fifty-three."

"Have it your way," Norman said, "but it wasn't blackmail. It was atonement money. Your type always thinks atonement comes cheap. It probably never occurred to you that you have to ransom your soul if you plan to live even as long as your old man." Warming to his subject, Norman remembered the mallet called Life. "It's not just heart attacks that you have to watch out for. There is also plague, the black death of the soul. Retribution by a vengeful Jehovah. Fragmentation and alienation, spiritual separation." And in a fit of inspiration, Norman asked, "Do you know how Lully died?"

"Lully? I don't think so," Richard said. This reference to a seventeenth-century conductor, it seemed to Richard, was not exactly relevant.

"It seems that during a rehearsal Lully dropped his baton on his foot. Not long afterward he died of gangrene of the big toe."

"No kidding!" Richard said, impressed.

"Yeah," Norman said, in his best threatening tone. "So watch out."

70

Richard wasted no time getting out of Birdie's apartment after Norman's call. With his wife and his mistress's ex–Big Daddy and his ex–girl friend's husband, or, to put it another way, the son of his ex–girl friend's father-in-law, or, to put it another way, the husband of the daughter-in-law of his current girl friend's ex-lover, or, to put it another way . . . At any rate, Richard figured more people were gunning for him than was healthful for a conductor in his hyperstrung condition, and he felt the time had come to get the hell out.

He would call Birdie later, and he would go to Gussie's debut recital—Richard always did the gentlemanly thing—but he was damned if he was going to sit around and let a lot of megalomaniac Tammany Hall types and culture vultures take potshots at him with rusty bullets. Richard was not that big a fool.

He was gone by the time Birdie came home. Birdie reflected bleakly how day by day her much-loved apartment was becoming emptier. It was a process of divestment of persons. First Sidney; now Richard. So soon? She knew he planned to go, but not so soon. Even the Fabergé was gone from the bathroom cabinet.

Birdie changed from her outdoor winter clothes into lace the color of new snow on a sill, stopping at the dressing table to check her face in the three-way mirror. Under the makeup, her cheeks were red from the winter wind; the tip of her nose glowed daintily, like an extremely feminine version of Rudolph's. She touched up her powder and returned to the living room. Everywhere, she thought, looking around—Désirée pillows. But what good were Désirée pillows to her now? Then she found the note on the memo pad.

CONCERT. Concert! Oh, she thought: Oh, oh! She thought how sweet and clever it was of Richard to leave it there for her, the way they had traded so many other notes; he really was a romantic something. TOWN HALL. Town Hall! That showed you it did make a difference when you had a classy contact like Richard: this would be the highlight of her career, the culmination, the top spot from which she could retire gracefully, knowing she had made it not only out of the chorus line into neon, but out of neon into the world of real art. Town Hall was the perfect place—close enough to Times Square to bring in the old crowd from The Joint, far enough away to take on the aura of classicalism and professional seriousness she was aiming for. She should have known Richard would do the right thing; he was a *conductor,* after all. Birdie thought about calling him and thanking him but then she decided to wait until after the concert; thanks would embarrass him, he being basically shy like Sidney and herself. Furthermore, she fully intended to blow his mind with the exceptional beauty and versatility of her audacious performance.

"Audacious" was Birdie's favorite word of late; Sidney had said she was audacious. Poor Sidney! Birdie wished him well and hoped that his thing was not giving him too much trouble.

For Birdie wished all the men in her life well, and assumed they wished well to her—making that assumption was exactly how she had always coped with her very deep doubt about men's intentions toward her. If some part of her said, concerning anything a man did: Whoa, this should be thought about, another part of her knew that that was absolutely precisely what should not be thought about. Was this note for her? But Richard adored her! He would not leave her in the lurch! *Of course* the note was for her.

She looked again at the note. FRIDAY. No time specified—that must mean ten o'clock. Ten o'clock was when every performance Birdie had ever given had begun. MEDI-EVAL ASS. Some sort of association; maybe they ran Town Hall. It had a medieval look about it. BALAAM'S? Birdie couldn't quite figure out what that meant, though she thought she might have come across the word in *Time* magazine once. Richard's mind tended to drift anyway.

FRIDAY . . . That didn't leave her a whole lot of time. She'd better get her act together pronto. She put Mantovani on the phonograph, to get herself into a good semi-classical mood. Mood was everything, when it came to interpretative dancing. Then when she was in a mood to rehearse, she used the snow-white telephone to call her accompanist, Jock.

71

THERE WAS a hush in the city only a few selected folk were
sensible of; for them, the city was holding its breath. The
subway whizzed along its tracks, but silently. The automobiles hauled their passengers from street to street, but made
no sound doing it. Planes took off and landed, trucks picked
up and delivered, motorcycles did the dance of the weaver's
shuttle through the loom of traffic, doors opened and
slammed, dogs barked, people shouted hysterically at one
another, and not one of these sounds violated the hush,
which had a texture like that of a rose petal . . . as swiftly
rippable as fabric unrolled from a bolt but, while it held, so
smooth and simultaneously so various it was like a topo-
graphical map of the emotions, showing ups and downs in
different colors, a hush in which even a heartbeat was an
event felt rather than heard. It was a hush of anticipation. It
was the kind of silence only great music is capable of,
holding all voices tacit in a Grand Pause before the final
prestissimo.

72

A COLD, CLEAR December night.
Gus caught a cab on Broadway for Town Hall. She
flagged it down with Tweetie-Pie, who was coming along in
his cloth-draped cage for good luck. Her hands were full.

She carried Tweetie's cage by the brass circlet at the top with one hand, and in the other she had her flute case and her music.

Every star in the sky was as bright as if it had just been polished with a soft rag and a squirt of Pledge. Bits of mica mixed in the sidewalk pavement glittered like rhinestones in the frosty starlight. There are nights when all things blur into one another, outlines dissolve and what seemed to be one thing turns out to have been another; this was a night when all the edges were ice-sharp; Gus felt as though her mind could encompass the universe at a glance, pinpointing every item of interest in it, including her own position. She was wearing a long black skirt and a white Edwardian blouse with a high neck, long sleeves, and drapery over the bodice, and she had to hitch up her skirt as she climbed into the cab. On the collar of her blouse she wore a cameo brooch that her mother had given her, since her parents couldn't be present. Her thick honey-rich hair was swept up off her neck. She would have felt like a princess on her way to a gala concert, if she had not been going to give the concert. As it was, she felt, climbing into the cab, as though she were mounting the scaffold. Her mouth was ominously dry.

All day she had chewed her fingernail nonstop, until Norman asked her if nibbling cuticle could wreck her embouchure. She was thankful he was not with her now; she didn't want him backstage with her while she warmed up. Norman would arrive later with Tom and Cyril, and Dieter, who was nearly as nervous as she was. Dieter was bringing the synthesizer—a Synthi, he called it—for his piece; he was to wait backstage, in the wing opposite Gus, until time to join her on stage.

The way Gus dreamed her debut, the first half would go wonderfully. Norman would come backstage during the intermission to report that the Critic, the Critic with a capital C, was smiling. Bravo for Bach *et al.* Gus would have lost all her nerves by now; she'd be eager for the second half of the concert to begin, and when it did, she would sail through the Schubert. Then she would knock 'em dead with Dieter's piece.

First, however, before any of this could begin, she had to meet with the pianist, and she wanted to get to the hall early and alone.

At the hall she played arpeggios and set up her gear, conferred with her pianist and fretted once again over the fingering in Dieter's piece. As the time approached, she suddenly became strangely sleepy; she felt altogether drowsy and couldn't stop yawning. The pianist said it was a natural reaction. "Nerves," he said. The explanation was comforting but she wondered how she was going to play if she didn't wake up.

Somehow it happened—the people came, the lights dimmed, the moment arrived, all without her doing anything to start it or being able to do anything to stop it. From the spyhole in the curtain she could see Norman and Tom and Cyril in the front row. The Critic, the one with a capital C! Then, a row back, Richard. And Elaine, who had no doubt come to keep an eye on Richard. And two little boys who must be Jeremy and Jeff. And farther back, some of the kids from Juilliard. (Julie Baker was on tour: she had a student's typical luck there.) Some of Norman's colleagues. His blood-brother from Flatbush, Phil Fleischman, and Phil's girl, Dinky. Gus saw Mario take a seat in the back. It wasn't bad for a flute debut—about fifty or sixty, and the most important one was the Critic with a capital C. There was only one problem: How was she going to walk out there?

In the first moment of facing an audience, there is a sense of having stumbled into the wrong room; this is not your usual place, this is not where you are accustomed to be. Only a minor part of the world is a stage, and you are used to standing on the part that is not the boards. You feel disoriented—there has been a mistake; you, foolish person, are dreaming with your eyes open. Perhaps if you close your eyes, this confusion will be as good as gone, and space and time will reassert their normal roles. Gus felt as though she moved on stage through a cloud of utter stillness, an invisible mist that muffled her mind's perception of sound and distance—in short, a fog.

She raised her flute.

Her mind awoke.

As soon as she began to play, the sleepiness wore off and she became more alert than she had ever been in her whole life. This alertness was of a twinned nature. On one level, she was thinking only about what she had just gotten through, what she was playing right then and what was coming up that might be difficult to handle, and this level occupied all of her conscious mind; but there was another level too, not subterranean or subordinate or subconscious, but in a sense superior, a mind above the mind she consciously exercised. It was as if she had been dreaming for years—she realized at once that the past two years had lapsed in a kind of waking dream. She had been active, studying, practicing, walking, talking, but all of it had been only a preparation for this conclusion, for this wide-opening of all her intelligence to the one experience that counted, sound. Structured sound. All her life had been bent to the one task of negotiating musical notes as finely as possible, and to do that now was to redeem herself from all that was flat and static in her soul, was to recover herself from the alternative life of death-in-life, that world which appeared to be moving with such purposeful swiftness but which was getting nowhere and was in reality as still and lifeless as a computer. The mind undelivered from its death-dealing hostages by the power of love was not a ghost in a machine but a machine in a ghost, a figure with only a flickering semblance to the human shaping of sense and spirit that was what touched the heart and left you full of exquisite, nearly unbearable longing in the middle of the night when you dreamed, wakefully, of life at its highest pitch, its fullest expression.

Gus felt now as though each note she played was a drop of rain in the parched regions of the inmost world where humans are reluctant to go, being diffident and unbrave; and she felt as though each note was a star like the stars in the sky she had seen while standing on Broadway, and out of her flute, as she played, stars fell, tumbling onto the stage, red and white and blue and yellow stars, according to the keys she pressed. She was knee-deep in imaginary stars.

This was love, this lifting of the eyelids to sound, and for feeling this and for being this she would be ransomed forever from the black giddiness of despair, the silent falling down endless steep corridors without walls or exits. She would walk through the earth in a glory of concentration and everything she touched would sparkle, transfigured by her wakefulness into light-pulses of activity, of calling and welcoming, of showing forth and being glad. Every brook would be an arpeggio. Every tree would be a symphony, a choir with alto doves and soprano wrens and a coloratura nightingale. Every note played with perfect intonation would reverberate even to the time after time, when nothing else lasted, and shed a white light like the ash from a dying coal, a radiance that no future could eradicate because it existed not in the realm of the touchable but in the spirit, where what has been goes on forever by definition, by the purest and most irrefutable of definitions. For Augusta had made music so much a part of herself that it had become something outside herself—an outself, a laser-like projection of the spirit in a continuous curved line, a trajectory alphic and omegic, and this process is always a kind of prayer, a rendering of the self to the wholly other. It is like building a kingdom and throwing the doors to it wide open.

73

It was ten to ten. Birdie breezed past the guard at the stage door. The guard didn't know what on earth a platinum blonde in a raincoat with a record tucked under her arm was doing entering Town Hall with a man in a raincoat and a phonograph tucked under his arm, but he was not about to ask. The fellow in the raincoat looked like the "after" half of a Charles Atlas ad, and the guard was looking forward to a peaceful retirement with the New Year. Night after night, for most of the nights of his life, this guard had sat next to this door, and nothing extraordinary had ever happened; if it was about to happen now, he fully intended to ignore it. The raincoats puzzled him, though. It wasn't raining.

In the wings, Birdie threw her raincoat off. She was wearing the costume she'd worked on for months, waiting for this night to materialize. It was a show-stopper. Newly freed, her tailfeathers sprang to admirable dimensions. Nonetheless, Birdie did not go in for garishness à la Ziegfeld, and she kept the rest of her costume classically simple — nearly nonexistent, that is, since the point was to display the evocative flow of movement, if not the flow of evocative movement. When you had a soul as artistically bright as a Klieg light, you did not need to signal the fact tackily. This was not a strip show, after all; this was art. *Not* high art; Birdie didn't fool herself about that, but it was darn serious semi-classical art, and she was going to give her one shot at it all she had. Reluctantly she comprehended that someone else was already on stage and that despite her frenzied last-minute rush she would have to wait for whoever it was to end. She took deep breaths, trying to relax; she fluffed her feathers, getting set. Her transparent heels were four inches high. Her G-string was sewn of iridescent sequins, and her tittie tips, as Richard had fondly referred to them, were pasties in the shape of baby chicks, matching the beauty spot that adorned her chin. Birdie considered it vital that everyone on this most special of special occasions should identify her with her signature. It had taken her two hours to make up her face, coating each lash on the lower lid four times individually with beads of mascara and drawing new lashes with a pencil, gluing two strips of false lashes to each upper baby-blue lid; and now her violet eyes, which shuttered and opened with a doll-like click whenever she blinked her weighted lids, gazed curiously at the cloth-covered cage near the stage entrance. She whisked the cover off, and, whether it was because the luster from her platinum wig was so brilliant, like the sun rising over his swing bar, or because he heard Gus's playing on stage and took that as a cue to do his bit, Tweetie-Pie began to sing. In clear, loud notes he trilled, like a piccolo counterpointing Gus's flute. "Oh," Birdie said, clapping her hands, "isn't he cute!" She held the cage up by the ring at the top to get a closer look at the canary inside.

It was the first mistake.

On stage, with a kind of horror—she lacked the leisure to experience true horror, being called on by circumstance to continue performing rather than feeling free to let horror be done to her as at a movie, say, or around a campfire—Gus heard Tweetie-Pie take up the part he had practiced with her at home. Maybe they couldn't hear it in the audience? They might think there was a bird in the chimney. Did Town Hall have a chimney?

"Record's ready," Jock said to Birdie, backstage. He too had taken off his raincoat, and had set up the player. The turntable spun the record around, but the needle still lay on its armrest.

Jock had also donned the upper half of his costume, a rubber bald-head mask with a rooster's comb on top. (The bottom half was a red bikini.) Jock was by nature taciturn; he tried to stay out of things—everything, life—as much as possible. Vaguely, he was aware of feeling like an idiot in this get-up, but a gig was a gig, and besides, he had long ago quit arguing with Birdie about anything.

"You want me to start it?" he asked.

"I don't know," Birdie said, sneaking a look at the girl playing the flute out front. "I didn't realize I was going to have to share the bill. Who do you suppose she is? Is she any good?"

"Highbrow," Jock said. "You know the type."

Birdie set the cage down at her feet and put both hands akimbo on her waist. For a moment, she and Jock listened to the music from out front. There was no tune she could fathom, no melody; the girl was accompanied by a piano and a series of strange noises emanating from a mysterious collection of boxes stage right; a young man seemed to be turning dials on the boxes. "I told you this would be the real thing," Birdie said. Then she added, troubled, "I thought it was set for ten o'clock. Who ever heard of starting before then?"

Jock grunted. "Crowd's right on time, anyway," he said, and jerked his head in the direction of the auditorium.

Half a dozen regulars from The Joint burst into the auditorium. Birdie gave them the high-sign from around the side-drop. She was on the side behind Gus, and Gus didn't see her, but Gus did see the pianist half-rise from his bench, as if he were poised for takeoff at Cape Kennedy, his bench a launchpad, and then sit down again, still playing, and Gus could not imagine what might be happening behind her back that disconcerted, as it were, the pianist so, but if he could continue to play uninterruptedly, so should she, even though the rattled page-turner, a student, turned the page too soon, forcing the pianist to skip a bar, and Gus had to jump to keep up with him. She hoped nobody would know, and turned her eyes to the audience to see if anyone did. What she saw was a bunch of drunks waving beer cans.

She could not, through the spotlights and lowered house lights, see their faces clearly; but she saw their sidewinding motion *en masse,* their snakelike meander down the aisle stageward, and the glint of beer cans raised high, raised high like their voices. "Hey, Birdie, didja think we forgot?" called one of the men, as, at the same time, he flattened an usher who sought to halt his progress. The human snake snapped into half a dozen pieces, each piece grabbing a seat in the center, right, or left section. Oddly enough, separated, they sank one by one into a deep silence, perplexed, perhaps, by the girl on the stage, and what had been about to become a disaster was for the moment forestalled. Gus continued to play.

"Just how the hell long *is* that broad going to play," Jock said. It was not a question, leading or otherwise. He wanted to get the thing over with. He leaned down to move the birdcage away from the record player, but suddenly Tweetie began to flap his wings, crazily, squawking at Jock's red comb. Tweetie-Pie seldom squawked; he was far too *bel canto* for that. There may have been, in Tweetie's little mind, some intent to protect his place in the pecking order. Be that as it was or wasn't, Jock was certainly startled. He stood up sharply, and bumped, with his knee, the corner of the record player, fatally jarring the needle from its rest position. The record began to play.

On stage, Gus heard music—other music. Not from her flute, not from the piano, not even from the Synthi, which, under Dieter's direction, was doing its electronic thing quite respectably, oscillators, filters, reverb units, and assorted gizmos working together in perfect discord. No, other music. It was Ravel's *Bolero.*

There could not be, in all of so-called classical music, a piece more precisely diametrically opposed to Gus's intelligence and talent (unless maybe it was Debussy); and it was as appropriate to what she was playing just then as a James Bond soundtrack to a movie by Ingmar Bergman.

Gus was not alone in realizing this. By now, Birdie understood, to her shame and sorrow, that she had gotten something badly wrong. Frantically, she lunged for the phonograph—and tripped over Tweetie-Pie's cage. The cage door swung open and Tweetie-Pie flew out. The record kept on playing. Tweetie-Pie sang, exalted.

Still singing, as if he knew this was the high point of his career too, Tweetie-Pie fluttered onto the stage, circling once around Gus, and perched on the half-raised piano lid. Someone in the audience clapped.

Gus had, she thought—thinking at what seemed to her to be top speed, reaching a conclusion so quickly that the very velocity of it surely was an act of daughterly disloyalty, an act in direct defiance of the reserve and deliberation which had characterized her mother's upbringing of her—a choice: she could play or not play. She kept on playing. What hope would ever again attend her world if she did *not* play? It was not as though she and Tweetie had never played together, and his voice blended into Dieter's piece not unmelodiously.

Worse things had happened on stage. Actresses lost their half-slips on opening night. Actors flubbed their lines. Prompters fell asleep in the cue box. A canary might be an idiosyncratic touch; *Bolero* might go unheard, or be unrecognizable, in the audience . . . It was Gus's last attempt to carry things off the way they were meant to go. She was playing steadily, even now unflustered, when a strange apparition in four-inch plastic heels, Marie Antoinette coiffure, and tail-feathers pitched forward from behind her, teetered, arms outstretched as if reaching for Tweetie, and tipped headfirst into the piano. There was a thud. Immediately the piano's music stopped, as Birdie's sprawl damped the strings.

And then Gus saw something else. Norman.

Just prior to Birdie's appearance onstage, Norman had risen to his feet, thinking desperately that there must be some way he could entice Tweetie-Pie offstage, but now he remained standing, in dazed disbelief.

Sit, Gus thought, doing her best to telepath her desire to Norman. Once upon a time, he had been so attuned to her consciousness that he could hear her words before she spoke them.

It didn't work now. Instead of Norman's sitting, Richard arose.

Richard was behind Norman in the center section; when Birdie went down, he went up, seesawing instinctively as they had done in other surroundings, and Norman turned around to see what was happening, and he and Richard found themselves facing each other for the first time. The crowd from The Joint was applauding. "Down in front," somebody yelled. "What an entrance! Hey, Birdie, what an entrance!" somebody else shouted. Birdie was stuck in the piano.

Elaine was tugging at Richard's sleeve, looking all around her wildly. "Will you for God's sake sit down?" she hissed.

Indeed, the pianist, in an attempt to cover up this inexplicable event, had gotten up from his bench and leaned under the lid, as if the composer's score had noted: play inside here.

The usher who had been hit reappeared with the guard. The guard took in the scene, listened to the flute, the canary, the synthesizer, the hollering and stomping, and the resonant aftermath of Birdie's mighty plunge into the piano, the pianist playing inside the piano, and said, "Hippies." He was a Johnny Cash fan.

The page-turner fled.

Augusta played.

Birdie's plumage quivered.

Dieter tried not to cry.

Elaine continued to tug at her husband's shirt.

"You must be Gussie's husband," Richard said to Norman.

"I take it you're Hacking."

Just then Norman became aware of a mini-commotion somewhere around his waist. He glanced down and saw Tom, grave Tom, pulling at his belt. "It's too late," Norman said, dismayed to find, the moment he said this, the merest taste of gratification on his quick tongue; but more, he felt sad for Gus, painfully sad. It made him angry. "A doctor couldn't save this show."

"An actor might," Tom said quietly, and headed for the stage steps.

"Oh dear," Cyril was saying, "oh dear."

Norman turned his attention back to Richard. "Did anyone ever tell you, Hacking," Norman said, "that you are put together very loosely?"

"Why are you always insulting me?" Richard asked. "What did I ever do to you?"

"How dare you insult my husband," Elaine said, looking up at Norman.

"It doesn't take much courage," Norman said.

"Oh dear," Cyril said, wringing his hands, "oh dear, oh dear."

But Birdie was still stuck in the piano.

And Jock looked out at her and saw those tailfeathers quivering, and he felt such huge pity surging in him, a perfect wave of pity like an ocean wave a surfer would spend his life haunting beaches for, that he was damned if he was going to switch off the record and put an end to what Birdie had worked so hard to get, a single chance. A somersault into a piano was a misfortune, but what the fuck, the Joint crowd clearly loved it. If they knew what was good for them,

Jock thought, they better love it. Stripped to comb and strap, Jock strode onto the stage. Now, originally Birdie was going to dance around him, interpretatively, while he struck various poses of an aesthetic nature, and crowed. When Jock pulled Birdie out of the piano, he noticed that her eyes were red; not all the blue eyeshadow in the world could hide that. Fiercely, on her behalf, he turned to face the audience. "Cock-a-doodle-doo!" he crowed—and crowed and crowed again. He reckoned in addition that he ought to get paid no matter what.

It seemed to Gus—oh, God, it seemed to Gus as if no nightmare she could ever have conceived was so insanely orchestrated in such ornithological detail as this. There were pockets of activity, busy on-off flashes of noise and light scattered throughout the darkened auditorium. People were bobbing up and down everywhere, semi-shadowy shapes elongating and then shrinking back into nowhere. Norman and Richard were shouting at each other. Birdie—for plainly this was the one and only Birdie Mickle, this platinum creature blinking her painted eyes and checking out, realigning, her pasties (Gus did not know what Birdie looked like, but there couldn't be too many women named Susan who wore baby chicks on their breasts)—Birdie was leaning against the piano like a chanteuse, which Gus ardently prayed she was not. Mr. Universe was monotonously crowing, "Cock-a-doodle-doo," as if something of importance was rising. (Gus ardently prayed it was not.) Tweetie-Pie was zipping around overhead, from stage to balcony and back again, like a miniature fighter plane, bombing all targets indiscriminately, touching down from time to time on the piano lid as if it were a carrier ship. Ravel was gaining ground on the Synthi. The kids from Juilliard were laughing hysterically—at her, Gus thought. She looked at their faces and saw shock, incredulity, delight, and that relief no one can hide completely when a rival wipes out. And now Tom had come on stage, and instead of taking all these peculiar people *off,* he had begun to declaim Shakespeare. Shakespeare?

> *Hark, hark! I hear*
> *The strain of strutting chanticleer*
> *Cry, "Cock-a-diddle-dow."*

Tom winked at her. She began to see what he was doing.

In the meantime, Birdie was right-side-up but feeling as though someone had turned the world upside-down. She felt very much as though her feathers had been ruffled. The pianist was glaring at her.

"Oh," she said, "oh, oh," and backed away into the piano, accidentally knocking the support stick out, and causing the piano lid to crash shut. On her tail.

"I've got to get her off," Norman said, tearing up the side steps to the stage. Whether he meant Birdie or Gus was not immediately clear to Richard, or even to himself.

"Wait a minute," Richard called. "There's an explanation—"

Richard followed Norman.

"What explanation?" Norman asked.

So Norman was standing there, talking with Richard, on stage, and Gus considered simply walking off stage, but what good would that do at this point? It was too late to try to pretend she didn't know what was going on: she might as well pretend she *did* know what was going on. Tweetie-Pie was singing like mad from the fly loft, where he had flown when the lid of the piano came down, a loud little ball of airborne yellow fluff; Birdie was dancing in a way that seemed to Gus very weird, with elaborate gestures and solemn expressions, to judge from what she could see out of the corner of her eye—but at least she was no chanteuse; and Tom was reciting Shakespeare nonstop. Gus took all these as cues and together they said: *Ad lib.*

She had read about a topless cellist—why not a topless flutist?

She put down her flute, took off her brooch, blouse, and brassière. Norman did not notice. She picked up her flute.

The audience whistled. Birdie was miffed.

Norman and Richard had resumed their argument.

"The explanation," Richard was saying, "must be that Birdie must have gotten the message you left with me. I told her I was going to get her a dance engagement. Incidentally, I thought you knew that. Why else did you say that about Lully?"

"Let me get something straight. Do you mean you really never were making it with my wife?"

"Not as long as she's been your wife."

"Well," Norman said, suddenly angry, "why the hell not?"

"Don't get offended, Norman," Richard said, hastily. "It's not that I'm not turned on by your wife. Obviously I was. Gus is a lovely girl, God knows. But look at that," he said, turning around and pointing first at Gus and then at Birdie, both more or less bare-breasted. "There is class, and then there is something which is definitely not class but has a value of its own which unfortunately Birdie doesn't recognize and which is very hard to come by in the world of classical music, which is, I'm sorry to have to agree with Birdie about this, all class." Richard thought highly of his ability to talk his way out of a dangerous situation. He stopped for breath—and had an afterthought. "Unless you go for divas," he said, "and they tend not to have Birdie's accommodating nature."

Then Norman looked at Gus's shining breasts, so infinitely vulnerable, sweet, pure and sad, and a dark cloud of the most unbearable despair rolled in on his heart, as if it might rain there forever. He felt he had lost her—if not to Richard, then to some part of herself that would rather be bold before all the world than merely happy with him; and he felt he could not handle this, not then, not there, and god-dammit to hell anyway, and—and— "You've been humping Birdie?" he asked.

"Of course," Richard said.

"Why, you bastard," Norman said, and he hauled off and socked him, "take that. For my father."

Richard landed on the floor. Looking up, he said, hurt, though more by the fact than the effect, "But your father knew! That's why he said I had to come through with the engagement for Birdie!"

The Joint crowd was counting. "Ten, nine, eight, seven..." Richard sat up.

Elaine, mobilized by Norman's left hook, had raced on stage and was now kneeling beside her husband. "Poor Richard," she crooned, "poor Richard." With her arms around him, she looked up. "Would you like to hit him again?" she asked Norman. "It's all right with me."

. But it was not all right with a certain guest in the audience: Mario.

Mario, furious at what Norman was doing to Gus's big moment—stealing it—had also found his way to the stage, running down the aisle from the rear and leaping over the footlights. "You're crazy," he said to Norman, "man, are you crazy! What's wrong with you, always slugging people?" Every time Mario met this fink, he was taking a swing at somebody. Well, he, Mario, was older, wiser, and most germanely, bigger now, and enough was enough. "Are you coming off peaceably, or do I have to drag you out of here?" (He thought he might make Italian Westerns someday.) However, all the time he was delivering this ultimatum, Mario kept his eyes averted from Gus, feeling that he had no right to look at her naked in public. When he had seen her on her honeymoon night, it had been in private.

"You," Norman said. "What is this?" And he landed an upper right on Mario's jaw.

(Mario had grown but he was irremediably the fine-boned Renaissance beauty–filled living Davidic sculpture he had been since childhood.)

"What the hell is going on?" Jock said, sending Norman to the floor with a single punch.

"It's a madman!" Elaine screamed, getting her first good look at Jock. She grabbed him around one leg, holding him either so he couldn't hit Norman again or because it was the most magnificent male leg she had ever seen, she wasn't sure which.

Birdie went over and pulled Elaine's hair. "You leave him alone," she cried, "that's my accompanist!" Birdie felt the least she could do was come to Jock's defense, after he had helped her out of the piano; and she felt terrible for having got him into this, and she felt Fate had been unkind to her, making her such a dizzy dame that she thought she had a dance concert to give when she didn't, and she hated herself for being dumb. She yanked Elaine's hair all the harder.

Norman, Richard, and Mario were rubbing their respective jaws.

The Joint crowd was cheering for Birdie. The Juilliard kids were rooting for Elaine. The guard gave the usher five bucks to keep his mouth shut and left. In the fifth row center, Phil and Dinky stirred, as if after long hibernation.

"Look," Phil said to Dinky, as the situation began belatedly to make itself known to him (he was stoned). Until now, Phil had been listening to the music with his eyes closed. As he surveyed the scene, his plump face took on an expression of, for want of a word, mingle-ment: there was a flush of fellow-feeling, the lost pathos of Ocean Parkway, the pride of being needed again as in the old days, irony at the counter-culture's being called to the rescue of straight culture, but in his present spaced-out condition, no single one of these registered so prominently on his features as did the confusion of them all.

Dinky said, slowly, moistening her red-glossed lips, "We'd better go help him, hadn't we, Philip?" And she led Phil by the hand to the stage.

"Hello, Norman," Phil said.

"Dinky Ledbetter!" Birdie exclaimed. "I'd know you anywhere. I know your mother."

"Shhh," Dinky said, putting a finger to her lips and shaking her head. This seemed, at the time, to Dinky, the most sensual act she had ever performed, and she prolonged it. And prolonged it. "They call me Kinky Dinky," she whispered, mostly to herself.

"You should be ashamed of yourself." Beneath her own spectacular bosom, which no one had ever thought of as functional, Birdie became aware of a swelling maternal impulse, a burst of emotion impromptu but by no means superficial. "Your mother says you never even visit her." Perhaps too, Birdie was relieved to find someone besides herself who deserved scolding. "Don't you know there's chic inside like there's chic outside? You probably forgot everything she taught you."

"That's not true," Dinky said. "And I can prove it." She began to take off her clothes ... extremely languidly, because she had smoked enough hash before coming here to slow all the clocks in the universe by about twenty-five hours and in her mind there was no urgency—she had twenty-five hours to go before it would even be now.

"Not bad, huh?" Phil said, watching Dinky.

She was wearing a black lace bra.

"A little exophthalmic for my taste," Richard said.

"So who asked you?" Phil said, forgetting that he had. "I don't know who you think you are, but I'll tell you something. I don't even know who you *are,* but I'll tell you something. That girl and I are making a fortune off the sexual revolution. So think about that, all right? Just think about that." Phil felt just exceedingly angry, and this annoyed him because anger interfered with the smooth cosmic flow of God-beamed energy sluicing through his veins and flushing the Atman-soul with its regenerative fluids.

Then Richard saw Mario take out his penknife—did Mario plan to stab Norman? did he plan to clean his nails? Mario had not made up his mind—and that, unlike Phil's speech or Norman's insults, Richard did understand. "Oh my God," Richard said, "it's you. *You're* the one."

"One what?"

"Sidney Gold sent you to take care of me, didn't he? I should have known. You look Italian."

Instantly, Mario jerked the penknife up; the tip of the blade was against Richard's handsome throat.

Gus kept playing; Tweetie kept singing; Tom kept reciting; the Synthi, although Dieter had retreated to the white back wall and stood there, soundlessly sobbing, went on and on—

But for everyone else, that knife was the focal point of the stage, the Chekhovian moment of inescapable realization, when the gun hung on the wall in Act One goes off at the end of Act Four. Unreasonable though it seemed to him, Norman, watching Mario hold the knife to Richard's throat, felt a certain cold point midway in his own chest that was like a frozen light, fire like ice, an ice-cold point of incandescent glow like the tiny bulb in a refrigerator.

Swift as a magician, Mario turned the blade flat against Richard's throat, indenting the flesh with the lightest, most graceful touch, a flick that refrained from becoming a nick. "I am Italian," he said. "You better watch what you say, mister."

"I knew it, I knew you were Italian."

"Big deal," Mario said to Norman. "He knows I'm Italian. This guy could go far with a brain like that."

"It's the blue eyes that are misleading, but so you're a blue-eyed Italian. Well, you're not going to get away with it,"

Richard said. "Your boss may be powerful politically but he's not the only one who is. I have friends. Isaac, Yehudi— they can get to people at the top. You just better tell Sidney Gold to lay off me." Never in his life had Richard been so just plain sore.

People began to relax. This was not *The Sea Gull.*

Even the confusion had begun to dissipate, as it became clear both on stage and off that nothing more untoward could happen, having already happened; and the audience continued to shout and laugh, but by now, they were entertaining themselves.

"I doubt seriously if my father ever had to lean on you very hard," Norman said.

"A dead conductor," Richard said, "is not likely to be overlooked in this day and age. In Lully's time, maybe."

"Don't worry," Jock said to Richard. "If the kid tries anything, I'll take care of him."

"And while we're on the subject," Richard continued, as if simply being on stage had supplied him with his usual concert-performance rush of confidence, control, and calm, "how dumb do you think I am? It wasn't a baton, it was a tactus rod, and he didn't drop it, he smashed his foot beating time with it."

"Same difference," Norman said. "Who the hell is this?" He indicated Jock.

"My accompanist," Birdie said. "Jock the—"

"I get it," Norman said, "I get it."

"Yeah," Jock said. "Well, that's fine. Only tell this lady here to let go of my pecker, will you?"

Elaine still had her arm wrapped around Jock's leg. Blushing, she backed off, backing into her two children, who had come to save their father from Mario. Jeffrey didn't know what Jock meant; however, Jeremy, having had the benefit of Richard's advanced notions of child-rearing, did, and in response he bit Jock on the leg. The other leg.

Jeff was not deflected from his main purpose. He kicked Mario on the ankle. "Daddy," he yelled, "don't let him hurt you!"

"Don't worry, Jeffrey, it's all right."

Mario dropped the penknife and grabbed his ankle.

"You're not going to let them do anything to you, are you?" Jeff asked. He looked as though he might cry.

"Of course not," Richard said.

Jeffrey smiled, worn out and serene, as if a great problem which had been keeping him awake since birth were at long last solved, and rubbed his close-spaced eyes, climbing contentedly into his father's lap. "I knew it all the time," he said, in that wacky voice of his. "When you were gone all that time, it was because they wouldn't *let* you come home."

Richard patted his son on the shoulder.

Dinky crouched down beside Phil and said, pointedly, "Isn't that touching? Father and son."

Before Phil could formulate a reply, Jock said, "Ouch!" as Jeremy's small teeth sank deep enough into that large leg to make an impression.

"Jeremy," Elaine said, astounded, "you've come to your mother's aid! Jeremy, that's just . . . that's just . . . grand!" She felt quite warm inside, looking at her elder son.

There was, going on, a quieting down, inch by inch, of the stage.

"Oh dear," Cyril said, "oh dear."

His voice carried clearly. He was on stage.

He was on stage, at the Synthi, saying "oh dear" and turning dials, switches, and knobs, fiddling, so to speak, with the sequencer, in total confusion attempting to determine which dials controlled the length and pitch of which notes, because Dieter had, as stated, retired against the wall, his head in his hands, and Cyril wished, as Tom had, to help. What Cyril was coming up with bore no relation to Dieter's piece, although, of course, Dieter was one of the very few people in the world who could say this with certainty.

But by this time, the insanity from the stage had moved on, like a storm cloud, and had advanced into the audience. The noise out there was thunderous. The Joint crowd were on their feet, whistling, and yelling at Gus, "Take it off! Take it off!"

"She's getting my applause," Birdie said, sadly. Yet, deep down, Birdie knew that she had gotten Gus's applause, and she felt awful.

Jock said, "The record's over." He was rubbing his leg.

Mario was rubbing his—Mario's—ankle.

Birdie's chin started to tremble.

"Don't cry," Richard said.

"Let her cry," Elaine said. "I hope she cries till she drowns."

Norman remembered his father's using an expression like that about his mother. He had gone to his father's office to tell him that he was getting married. "If you marry this person," Sidney had said, "you are herewith disinherited. I will make it official. I would make it religious, but that would ruin your mother. She would die of tears. I don't want your mother should drown." How long ago was that?

Birdie thought it was not a nice thing to say, but she didn't feel like fighting about it.

Silence was overtaking the stage.

The Synthi slowed, then stopped, a long note falling off to the edge of the universe like a quasar, descending with distance, until it seemed to touch on silence and drop stunned, like a bee hitting a glass pane, into the place where sound goes when it isn't heard anymore, the forest at the end of time.

"Take it *all* off!" the crowd chanted.

"I wonder which one of us they mean," Dinky said, lazily.

Tweetie fluttered down to Gus's flute and perched on the low B key, still chirping. The tailjoint—the flute's—dipped. Gus gave up. She set the handmade silver flute, with its gold mouthpiece and added key, down, and picked up her blouse.

All at once, Cyril jumped back from the Synthi, landing in a sitting position in a tangle of wires, and the overheated, hardworking, huffing-and-puffing, plugged-in and plugging-away little modular system went up in a ball of smoke, like a devoted robot whose electronic brain had been stretched beyond capacity, whose mechanical heart had taken a beating beyond endurance, and with a single poignant last lost cry, collapsed. It was a coda to make men, women, and androids weep.

When the smoke cleared, the Critic with a capital C was gone.

Swearing to himself that never again would he play except as a soloist, the pianist walked off and rang down the curtain. Nobody took any bows.

The curtain separated the cast—if they could be said to be a cast—from the audience. Its heavy folds, as if laden with the history of God knew how many other final acts, comforted the people on stage; it was as if they were wrapped in it against the cold winds of disapproval—or even the warm winds of acclaim.

They could hear clapping out front, shouts and calls of bravo, encore, and more! more! and, from the Joint crowd, less! less!, but it was as if, slumped in silence on the hidden side of the stage, behind the lowered curtain, Gus and Norman, Birdie and Jock, Richard and Elaine, Jeff and Jeremy, Phil and Dinky, Mario and the pianist, and the two dapper dwarves and now Dieter had formed a tableau, a tacitly agreed-upon outward pose while all but one inwardly wondered what to do next, now, or ever. Alone among them all, Tom reviewed the night's events as they might have appeared to the critic: the canary and the chick—the bird and the "bird" — dancers, actors, musicians, the audience participating. He peeked through the part in the curtain, and thought to himself, secretly amused, *The aisle is full of noises.* He let the curtain close again.

Such silence possessed the stage as if everyone upon it had been a puppet without a puppeteer, a dummy without a ventriloquist, a spirit, ravishing, awesome or laughable, *sans* sorcerer, or a doll without a little girl to make it walk and talk, and in the final miraculous toyland stillness, as if in a world where all clocks were cuckoo clocks and no time ever brushed with its hands of change golden hair to gray, one serious, measured voice was heard, Tom's, speaking, as if he lived inside them, Caliban's simultaneously achingly accepting and marveling lines:

> *Be not afeard. The isle is full of noises,*
> *Sounds and sweet airs, that give delight and hurt not.*
> *Sometimes a thousand twangling instruments*
> *Will hum about mine ears, and sometime voices*
> *That, if I then had wak'd after long sleep,*
> *Will make me sleep again; and then, in dreaming,*
> *The clouds methought would open and show riches*
> *Ready to drop upon me, that, when I wak'd,*
> *I cried to dream again.*

Only Tweetie-Pie hopped around, preening, but he was so sleepy that finally he flew to Augusta's bare shoulder, and slept.

74

Gus DREADED even to look at the papers but Norman insisted that he and she and Dieter should stay up for them. The pianist had disappeared. Tom and Cyril had tactfully withdrawn to their own apartment across the hall. Norman and Gus and Dieter sat around in the one-room apartment on West Eighty-eighth with the television buzzing in the background and Tweetie snoozing in his cage, once again safely draped.

"Do you suppose he'll ever speak again?" Norman asked, nodding in Dieter's direction.

"I don't know," Gus said. "He never said much to begin with."

The room was cold—the landlord believed nobody had a right to heat after midnight. Gus was wearing one of Norman's cardigans over her Edwardian blouse and black skirt, with the sleeves rolled up. Norman had on a corduroy jacket. Dieter had wrapped himself in the dark red and blue quilted comforter.

"I'm going to scramble some eggs," Gus announced.

"You don't know how," Norman said.

"I'll figure it out," Gus said, and went into the kitchen. When she turned on the light, several hundred cockroaches skittered for their hiding places. "You know something," she said, pensively, "I wish we hadn't drowned the mouse."

Norman said, "You didn't have to take off your top. It was indecent."

She said, "I should have turned my back to the audience so everybody could see what you did to my mole."

Norman said, "At least it would have been decent."

When the eggs were done, nobody could eat them. They were a pale cream color, like paste. "I'll go get the papers," Norman volunteered. Gus said again that it was a waste of time, ludicrous, but Norman said she didn't understand New York. "Sometimes, Gus," he said, "your background really shows. It's too bad, but it's a fact." He ducked out, grinning, before she could throw anything at him.

When he returned, she opened the paper to the music section. "I can't believe he even reviewed it," she said. "Here, you read it." She thrust the paper at Norman and he read:

An extraordinary event occurred in Town Hall last night: the debut of a brilliantly gifted young flutist, Augusta Gold. Executing the more conventional pieces flawlessly, with a masterful fusion of technique and expressiveness, she nevertheless came into her own in the première of the last piece, a purposefully chaotic "happening" illustrative of the musical mood of the radical avant-garde, a wickedly humorous demolition of all that is safe and accepted in our unadventurous academies, which seem to suffer from a kind of cultural lag. Surely we cannot have too much of this high-spirited—dare we say rambunctious?—Miss Gold, who pursued her playing of Dieter Schuyler's theater piece, aptly titled "The Solarbird Suite: Alternative Energy Music," with what this critic of an (alas) older generation can only respectfully recognize as great "cool."

Accompanied by piano (frequently played inside), canary, synthesizer (timed to self-destruct, in a witty allusion to Tinguely's kinetic assemblage), a pair of dwarves (one of whom astutely parodied Joseph Papp's Shakespeare-in-the-Park productions, of which we have heard overmuch these days), male and female dancers impersonating striptease artists in a dead-accurate two-pronged satire of high art (Fokine) and low ("Hair"), and audience participation of the sort so well known to us from The Living Theater, which provided a running commentary of a psychodramatic character and perhaps inadvertent phenomenological depth *as well as defining a broad new area of musical gesture through deploying said sound sources in the total sound field of the auditorium, Miss Gold triumphed in a performance of multidimensional import whilst never losing the sense of phrasing that sustained the work as a whole. If one may say so without detracting from the otherwise altogether exceptional debut of a remarkably promising new talent, the final low B was to this utterly charmed critic's ears listing dangerously.*

"You did it!" Norman said, tossing the paper into the air.
"I did it!" Gus shouted.
Dieter was inconsolable.

75

THAT WAS the end, more or less. Norman and Gus stayed together a little longer, but not long enough for Esther to have her reunion. The marriage had ended with the concert. It seemed to them both now that they had only been waiting for the concert to take place, before they ended the marriage. Shortly before Christmas, Norman said to Gus, "I want a divorce." She was expecting it, but she felt abused anyway.

Norman was smoking a cigarette, lying on the bed. He had been waiting for her to ask for the divorce, but time was going by and still she hadn't asked.

"I was hoping you might decide to stick it out," she said. "We could give it another try." She had been lining Tweetie's cage with clean newspaper; now she turned around slowly to face Norman. She dreaded seeing his dark eyes full of fire, his uncombable hair, the way his eyebrows tapered at the ends. She didn't know how she was going to detach herself from these specifics, the particular living definition of "Norman" that she had learned with her fingertips and mouth and legs. But of course it had to be done. She could see that. All the same, she felt as if her heart were a phonograph record, and he had snapped it in half across his knee.

"I thought about it," Norman said, "but what is there to stick out? Gus, something never quite took. Some connection was never made. All the wires crossed but ours." He delivered these words nonchalantly, but inside he was aching, his heart was weeping. He happened to see the rings on her finger, the wedding band and the engagement ring, and he felt as if he were the base Indian, throwing a pearl away richer than all his tribe. His wife stood there next to the canary in the cage, drenched in cold winter light, her chin lifted slightly against the pain and humiliation, the upper lip sexy as hell and her hair in flight from her temples, and he didn't want to go. But he also wanted to go—a lot.

The lawyer (Norman got a name from his father) drew up a separation agreement, and on a Sunday afternoon Norman and Augusta walked to a pharmacist on Broadway. The pharmacist was also a notary. He notarized their signatures on the agreement and Norman and Gus were officially dissolved, more or less. It would be two years before the divorce was final. Gus bought a tube of toothpaste and a box of Kleenex—a small one—for crying.

Norman found an apartment on 105th so Gus could stay in the place on Eighty-eighth until she was ready to leave. She was going to Germany. It was something she had always wanted to do—to study with Karlheinz Zöller. Dieter gave her some names and thought she might get a post-Webern music group going and make enough to get by, that way; her folks would do what they could to help. She shipped the leaves to Chapel Hill, along with the favorite lamp, and packed her white blouses, and Norman's apartment wound up looking almost exactly as it had before she had ever moved in.

Norman, seventeen blocks north of this activity, felt as though his head was splitting into a thousand pieces with the centrifugal force of the whirl; it would fly off in all directions at once, fragmented. He tried to get hold of Bunny Van Den Nieuwenhutzen, but she had apparently left town. He didn't even try D. D. Jones. He felt that he had had enough of artistic women for a while.

They had to get the news around. Norman had told his family. After the separation agreement was signed, Gus called her mother in Chapel Hill to tell her to expect the box of leaves. She didn't know exactly how to say what she wanted to say. Finally, she said, "You remember that you said you and Dad would get us a wedding present when we decided what we needed?" Her mother said yes. "Well," Gus said, "we won't be needing it."

Part Two

LUNCH

76

THE HEADLINE said: MASSACRE AT MUNICH. It sharpened the edge of Norman's anxiety.

Gus had been back in New York for three days. She had telephoned Norman—the phone was still listed in her name—and said she would like to have lunch with him. She said there was a reason. A special reason.

Norman met her in a bar-cum-restaurant on Broadway, planning to walk up to Columbia afterward. It was a warm day, brightly lit by the September sun, and he stood for a moment just inside the doorway, while his eyes adjusted to the darkened room. Then he saw her, already seated.

Her beauty took him by surprise; in nearly four years, he had forgotten what she looked like, but now it came back to him, and he realized that although she had been beautiful then, she was more so now. There was a new elegance in the way she held herself, sophistication in the way she looked at him. The golden light that had always surrounded her had taken on a darker hue; she was still the possessor of cool brilliance, but now it was mixed with a warmer, throbbing tone, a jet of rare mystery, a steadily glowing flame at the center of her aura. She was wearing a khaki midi skirt, pulled tight, as he saw when she twisted in her chair, across the pelvis, a tight pale yellow tee shirt, and some kind of shoes—wedgies, he thought they were called—with straps that wound up her calves like ballet shoes. Her hair was down, but at the front, from the center part, she had braided a thin yellow ribbon through a single long pencil-thin plait.

As Norman considered all this, sitting down across from her at a small square table laid with large red napkins, he noticed her hands. "You've stopped biting that nail," he said. He also noticed that there was no ring on the finger.

Gus was wondering if Norman had noticed that nobody had supplanted him. "Do you remember the delicatessen we went to the day we bought the engagement ring?" she asked.

"*That* son of a bitch. You picked a great country to go to."

"It was a good place to get started. After what happened here," Gus said, "it seemed sensible to grab the review and run."

"So what brings you back?" Norman asked this question with enormous casualness, but suddenly a part of him was hoping for an answer with the status of revelation, one that would turn a key and set free everything he sometimes felt must be locked in his heart, and hers. "Something must bring you back."

"The same thing that took me to Europe. My work."

"You've been playing with a modern music group, you said."

"Tomorrow Music. We tour. Turkey, Bulgaria, Greece, Tunisia. The State Department sponsors us. I was able to work in a few lessons with Zöller in Berlin," she added.

"You still haven't told me why you're here." He meant *here.*

"I have a couple of solo engagements. Richard—do you remember Richard? He's the conductor for one of them."

"How could I forget Richard," Norman said. "Is the dodo a forgotten creature?" He waved the waitress over. "What do you want to eat?"

"Cheeseburger." She smoothed the folded edge of the napkin with her finger. "And a Bloody Mary."

He ordered two cheeseburgers, French fries, a Bloody

Mary for her and a root beer for himself. The restaurant was crowded, and the waitress had to do a contortionist's act to slip between tables, but Gus's and Norman's table was next to a partition, giving them a small pool of quiet in the larger swirl of chattering voices and clattering dishes.

As Norman handed the menu back to the waitress, Gus stole a look at him and inwardly named what was bothering her: it was the absence of heat in his eyes. If it was possible for eyes to look silenced, that was how his eyes looked to her. He must be thirty-four now. Was this dying of the eyes inevitable with time, this fatal disconnection from some inner source of creativity inescapable, this power failure universal? His profile, when he turned his head toward the waitress, was still startlingly heavy on his slight body. There was a masculine thickness about the thrust of his head into space, the strong neck, that she still found, she now realized, with a shock like a bolt of electricity being sent to her heart, immensely attractive. But the dead eyes put her off.

"Did you finish your degree?" she asked. "You said you had to go up to Columbia after we eat—"

"Where else would I steal books? But yes, I teach in Philadelphia three days a week."

"I'm glad you're doing well."

"I'm surprised you think I am. After all, it's derivative, what I do."

"Are you still angry about that?"

"I was hurt, Gus. You were too wrapped up in yourself to realize it. Who knows, if you had respected my work more—"

"Don't you even remember the context? I didn't call your work derivative out of a clear blue sky." She felt an almost painful urgency, an awareness that what didn't get said now might never get said, might lie dormant forever in the dimension of silence, larval words, chrysalid thoughts awaiting the metamorphosis of sound. She leaned forward over the little table. "Don't you *remember* why I called your work derivative? You explained the ground level significance of my claim all right. You said I was getting back at you because you wouldn't go down on me."

The waitress set the food in front of them.

Norman glanced furtively around the restaurant. "Lower your voice, Gus. People can hear."

"Let them. Maybe they have nothing better to do."

"Then get it right. It's not true that I wouldn't go down on you. I did."

"Once."

"It's not my thing," he said, helplessly. "You could at least allow me my inhibitions."

"If you'll remember," she said, bridling, "I did."

"You've changed." He hit the bottom of the ketchup bottle with the heel of his palm. Once upon a time, even Gus's vocabulary of euphemisms had been limited. He had also observed that there was now a feathery edging of down above the sexy upper lip, the most feminine of moustaches.

"I'll tell you something," she said, "if you won't laugh. I used to be frightened of you. When you were angry with me, I used to get scared of what you might do."

He laughed.

"You hit Mario," she said. "*And* Richard. *And* you ripped the mole off my back. There were times when I thought you wanted to kill me."

"That's projection for you. I mean, when you get right down to it, you're not without your violent streak. You remember when you made me drown the mouse?"

"Norman! I didn't make you drown it."

"Sure you did. You forced me to get rid of it. It made me sick, seeing that mouse swim for its life in the john. Like a fetus, for Christ's sake."

"Like a what? Just what are you accusing me of? I've never even been pregnant!"

"It's not a question of reality. It's a question of meaning. It made me sick, that's all."

"I didn't know that."

"I know," he said. "I know you didn't know. That was part of the trouble. I guess," he said, sighing in the way his father used to, as if from a range of comprehension that encompassed all of human history, "we married precipitously."

"We divorced even more precipitously."

"I had to get out. If you knew how unhappy I was—"

"Is that an explanation or an accusation?"

"Both," he said.

"You're making me feel miserable. I didn't come to lunch to be made to feel miserable," she said.

"You might like to know that it looked to me as though you couldn't have cared less about our marriage. Jesus Christ, Gus, you never even bothered to cook dinner! For two years I was starving!"

"Why didn't you say so?" she asked, stricken. "How was I supposed to know that? You said you wanted a wife with a career of her own! I thought I was just doing what you wanted me to do."

Norman was trying to find a way of telling Gus, without hurting her, that her always wanting to do what he wanted her to do had been her most egregious error. It wasn't merely that such compliance charged him with the responsibility for all consequences; it went still deeper than that—and that alone was deep enough for trouble. But the ghastliest thing had been that he'd felt guilty for not always knowing even what he wanted. From her, from himself, from anybody. Goddammit, he did not know everything, even about what went on in his own head, and he'd gotten tired, tired, tired of having to act as though he did.

"Gus," he said, gently, "I thought I wanted something that I didn't really want. All I ever really wanted was"—he held back for a fraction of a second—"a wife who would *pay attention* to me. Isn't that what marriage is, *agreeing to pay attention to each other*?" He had thought about this for four years. "What I really want is a wife who'll care enough about me to make me the center of her life. If Gloria Steinem doesn't like it, she can eat shit. I'm certainly not going to marry her."

"Who's Gloria Steinem?" Gus asked.

"I forget you've been out of the country for four years," Norman said. "And boy, what old Dr. Morris would have to say about why you picked Germany!"

"I think you married me to get back at your father and dumped me to revenge yourself on Hitler."

Norman, chewing on his cheeseburger, choked. Damn, he had missed her sassiness! "It's true I did once take out the daughter of a former SS officer. Phil and I both did. The same girl. Same date, for that matter."

"Did he ever marry Dinky?"

"Dinky? He traded her in on a new model several light-years ago. The new one is named Dawn."

"Was I right about why you're gloomy? Is it this morning's news?"

"There's certainly nothing non-gloomy-making in a pogrom."

"Maybe Israel should give back the land it took in 1967."

"Took! You mean reclaimed, don't you?"

"There's wrong on both sides. Take Deir Yassin, for example. That was a massacre too."

"What do you know about Deir Yassin?"

Gus felt her courage unraveling, like a slipknot coming undone. "I read about it once," she said.

"So what's your solution? Surrender? May I remind you that we have tried that once or twice in the course of some two thousand years?"

Gus put down the rest of her cheeseburger and concentrated on her drink. "If just once somebody would give something back to somebody . . ." She fixed him with her narrow eyes. "It would be an action even more redolent of grace than redemption. Why does there have to be a price tag on everything? I've spent four years thinking about this." Norman jumped. "Even Christ's body is a price tag. Suppose God just came down to the world and said, Here, here are your dead. All of them, renewed and living. Take them back—they're all yours. Or suppose Israel said, Here's the West Bank and the Gaza Strip and the Golan Heights—we would like to have them but we managed before and we can go on managing without them. Even though they were ours yesterday, they are yours today because we give them to you. Suppose, Norman, just suppose you said to me, Here are all the grievances I have stored up against you. I don't need to hang onto them any longer and I won't make you pay for them. You can take them. Throw them out the window. Dance on them. I don't care, they're no good to me anymore."

"If they were no good to me anymore, I wouldn't be giving you anything of value. And what kind of gift is that? It's not worth anything unless it's worth something. That should be obvious."

"I was just talking," Gus said. "Don't mind me, I'm just a musician."

"Oh Jesus, don't start sulking." He had resolutely stuck to the abstraction of argument, because if he had replied to what seemed to him to be the sense of self-congratulation motivating her speech, she would have thought he was attacking her. And he didn't want to attack her, although he felt as though she had deliberately, pyromaniacally, struck a match and set fire to his brain.

"I'm not sulking," she said. But she realized she was; only it didn't have anything to do with politics. It was because she had caught him thinking, at one point, I was smart to marry that; and then at another point, he had thought, And I was even smarter to divorce it. She had seen these two thoughts blink into being and settle into the back of his mind, as clearly as if she had been inside his mind.

"Too bad my father never heard you on redemption," Norman said.

"How is your father?"

"Dead," Norman said. "He died a couple of years ago. Cancer of the prostate."

"I'm sorry."

"You don't have to be."

"I know I don't *have* to be. I am, though. I'm sorry for Esther."

"She's okay. She still lives in Brooklyn."

"Do you realize I never actually met Esther? Did your father re-inherit you?"

"I guess you could say so," Norman said. "The money went to my mother first. She'll divide it between Rita and me. Talk about irony. It's entirely possible that by then there won't be any money left for her to pass on. My mother tends to give away whatever's available."

"She was nice," Gus said. "What about Birdie? I miss Tweetie-Pie." Birdie had adopted Tweetie when Gus went to Germany.

"Birdie's at City College, majoring in sociology. She says she's going to be a marriage counselor."

"Maybe we should have seen one," Gus said, sharply.

"I think we could have done with a little less counseling."

"What I never understood, Norman, was why you decided to quit precisely when things were getting better for us. Both of us had discovered that the other was more trustworthy than we believed. We both discovered that we were not humiliating each other. I loved you and you loved me, and boom, as soon as we figured that out, you called it off."

"By the time we found it out, I *wasn't* in love with you anymore. And all you cared about was success."

"Not success," Gus said, "music."

"Success," Norman said. "Your mother too—she wanted that marriage to end."

At this, Gus almost whooped, except that she was appalled at the same time as she was amazed. She wanted desperately to say something about *his* family—it was *his* family that had tried to stop their marriage from the beginning. It was his father who had treated her as if she were dirt, and who had made her feel that she was stealing his son from him. It was his family who had discriminated against hers, and because of his father, her father, whose whole life had been devoted to preserving life on paper, felt for the first time an urge to destruction that, Gus knew, was still there: he would have welcomed at the very least the chance to knock Sidney Gold flat on his back. Well, Norman's father was now on his back for eternity, sleeping in a pine box with death for a pillow and earth for a blanket.

"I know what you're thinking," Norman said.

Norman was thinking that his family had at least had reasons for behaving as they did, and that they had tried to come to terms with the situation, no matter how they bungled it. "Your family couldn't even be bothered to come up for your concert. Why? Because they wrote you off as a serious flutist the minute you married me. You think I didn't see that? I was the monster who converted their daughter—not to a different religious persuasion but to the most diabolical thing of all."

"What?" Gus asked, hanging on his words in spite of herself. How she loved his voice! She had forgotten the way it rose and fell, switching from Brooklynese to Academe as if from the Lydian to the Mixolydian mode and back again. His eyes had begun to burn again, rekindled.

"Dailiness," he said. "The ordinary everyday breakfast-lunch-and-dinner life that most women, and most men for that matter, lead. That wasn't good enough for their daughter."

"You're crazy, Norman. They didn't come up for the debut because my mother's nerves couldn't have stood it. Besides, they couldn't have stayed in our one room with the roach-infested kitchen, and hotels are expensive."

"Anyway, they didn't need to worry. You couldn't be content living with me"—Norman felt his throat tightening the way it sometimes did and was disgusted with himself; he drank his root beer to open it up—"and you were bound to leave sooner or later. You used me, Gus. You were going to get that debut one way or another. That's what you married me for." He could tell by the way Gus had bowed her head that he had told her something about herself that she would rather not have acknowledged but couldn't deny. For a moment, he wanted to reach out and touch the top of her head, the single bright beribboned braid, but he didn't. "And it's also why you were ready to divorce me."

"Do you really think I wanted a divorce?"

"I really think you needed it."

"What about you?"

"What about me?"

"You're the one who asked for the divorce," she said. "Do you plan to get married again?"

"Yes."

"You have somebody in mind?" She was sure her heart sounded like the percussion section of the New York Philharmonic.

"No," he said.

"Why don't you ask about me?" she suggested.

"Why?" he said. "What good would it do?"

"We *lived* together, Norman!"

"That was in the past," Norman said.

"And you don't think the past can ever be brought back? Not ever?"

"You're talking about redemption again," Norman said. "Maybe I'm more Jewish than I ever knew. Maybe my father was right. I don't understand why anybody wants anything the price for which is a life. Any life."

"You pay with your life anyway. If you can get life back for life given—"

"But you don't," Norman said. "My father hasn't risen out of his grave lately. I doubt seriously if he's going to rise and shine in Forest Lawn tomorrow. If we hand over the West Bank to the Palestinian Liberation Movement, do you think we're going to get anything in return? Peace and brotherly love? As for buying the past back, listen, Gus: Give us a little while longer and there won't be anything *but* the past."

"I forgot you're a historian," Gus said.

"A derivative historian."

"Cunnilingualphobic."

"I told you, I accepted all the blame for that."

"You didn't have to make me hate myself."

"I didn't do that, Gus."

"Well, I could see your point. I thought about what it must be like from your point of view and it made me want to throw up."

"You have to worry only if you don't want to go down on *men.* Although Kate Millett might disagree with me about that."

"Who's Kate Millett?"

"Forget it."

"You're wrong about one thing, anyway. The past *can* be redeemed. Through art."

"I remember you told that moron in the delicatessen something like that. You also said that art's touch was as cold as an unused crematorium."

"I don't really believe that. Not about music anyway. Music isn't a museum. Art isn't somebody's name."

"I'm relieved to hear you say it. It's a hell of a way to keep warm at night." He felt unaccountably jealous.

"But it does do that," Gus said, "believe it or not, it does. And it brings back all the time in the world. It liberates the past from the future."

"I could tell you something my father once told me about Beethoven, but I won't."

Gus wanted to say: If there's something you don't want to tell me, don't try to intimidate me by telling me you're not going to tell me, but she let it pass.

Norman saw the quick flare and fade-out of anxiety in Gus's face, realized she had magnified his comment, and started to explain, but let *it* pass.

"Besides," Gus said, "what makes you think I like living alone?"

"We both know that marriage is not an answer to problems."

"Maybe not, but it cured you of your fear of the dark."

All through the lunch, Gus had been lively, conscientiously vivacious, talking skillfully with her hands, smiling, joking. It was important to her that Norman should not think that she had ever felt defeated by him. This was not purely a matter of pride. If he thought that she looked irrecoverably damaged, emotionally, he would feel guilty; and Gus considered that her only chance of emotional survival lay in sending him away free of guilt. If he felt guilty, she would have to walk around knowing that it was on her account—and the whole point of this lunch, to her, was that she should acquit herself of the last debt she owed him.

"Maybe it depends on the particular problems," Gus said. "Richard and Elaine Hacking are still together."

"Well, hell," Norman said, laughing. "Of course they are. It stands to reason. They're very careful to go looking for exactly the problems that marriage can answer. Neither one of them would know what to do with a real problem."

"I wanted to ask Richard if he still sees Birdie."

"Who knows?" Norman said. "Birdie is the most liberated broad I ever met. Personally, I find her terrifying. A man could get lost in that cleavage and never find his way out again. Years could go by. He could grow old wandering in the wilderness between those boobs. There's manna, and then there's glut."

Gus giggled. "What about Jock?"

"Jock's in a flick on Times Square that makes *Deep Throat* look like *Shallow Tonsils.*"

"Everything's changed," Gus said, sadly. "Even Juilliard isn't where it was. Do you realize that if it was all starting right now, we wouldn't even meet each other? We'd be walking down different blocks forever."

"But here we are," Norman said, looking at her intently, "meeting." He still didn't know why.

"It *is* a kind of redemption. A starting over."

"Is it? Everything's changed. You just said so."

Gus sucked the ice in the bottom of the glass, not looking at him. "What about the apartment?" she asked. "Is that the same?"

"Never changes," Norman said. "The cockroaches are still there. The tile is still peeling. The room still gets cold in the middle of the day and the middle of the night and most of the time in between. It's a bargain now—rents have gone sky-high."

"Are Tom and Cyril still across the hall?"

"Mario moved in with them."

"Mario!"

"Why not? He wanted to be an actor. He went to Actors Studio and now Tom coaches him. That's the excuse, anyway. I guess Mario needed a father. Cyril likes having Mario around for protection. You wouldn't think muggers would pick on dwarves, but this can be a crummy city. Not that I would ever live anywhere else."

"Mario," Gus said. "Well, that brings me to why I asked you to lunch. I guess the time has come to do it and be done with everything. I have something that's yours."

The last time a woman had said this to Norman, Elaine Hacking had brought out the Beethoven book. For a second, he expected to see Thayer on the table now.

Gus extracted an envelope from her bag and set it on the table by his plate.

"What is it?"

"Two thousand dollars."

"Two thousand dollars!"

"Shhh," she said, "keep your voice down."

"You don't owe me two thousand dollars," Norman said.

"Yes I do."

"I won't take it."

"Dammit, I saved it just in order to give it back to you. It's not for your sake. It's for mine. I want to be able to tell myself that I paid for my own debut."

"Shit," Norman said. "In any case, the money was originally my father's. Believe me, unless Castro sells cigars in Gehenna, he's got no use for it now."

"Then give it to Esther."

"What for? She doesn't want it. She hates the million bucks she's already got."

"Your sister, then."

"She's rich, remember? Not even counting her share of the inheritance. Besides, her husband wouldn't let her touch money from a *shiksa*. You don't know how it is. She has to take a ritual bath if she sneezes. If she took this money, she'd probably have to spend the rest of her life underwater."

"What about Birdie?"

"No sir," Norman said, "not on your life. Birdie won't

take cash anyway. It would be treating her like a whore. She only takes fox furs and dance recitals and junk, and it's impossible to give a present and then run. The trouble with presents is that it *is* the meaning that counts."

"I don't care who you give it to," Gus said. "Give it to Mario!"

"But he's the person who gave it to you in the first place."

"Then give it to the waitress!" Gus shouted. "I'm going to pay the check." She picked up the check and walked to the cash register with it.

"I'll do that," Norman said.

"I invited you."

Norman looked back at the white envelope lying on the table. "The waitress is going to be getting one hell of a tip," he said. "She wasn't all that good."

Gus shrugged. "It's up to you. I don't care about it." She turned around and held out her hand. "Good-bye," she said.

Norman shook her hand, feeling rather peculiar about it. Did one shake one's ex-wife's hand? But before he could think what to say, how to summarize his attitude, she was gone, a yellow-and-khaki beauty, a primary source for a painting by Vermeer or God knew who in this present age, angelically golden and less than saintly, cheerfully, energetically bound to the world's wishes, a part of his life disappearing out the door. He ran back to the table and closed his fingers on the envelope seconds before the waitress, leaning over backwards with her tray, reached it. "Sorry," he said, smiling ruefully at her, "my companion forgot this." He folded it into his wallet and then rushed out the door. She was nowhere to be seen. No—wait, there she was.

He watched her walking away, downtown, and suddenly, unpremeditatedly, he went after her feeling as if his heart was in his mouth and a cheeseburger in his chest, and tapped her on the shoulder. She wheeled around. "It's only me," he said. "Not somebody trying to goose you." He thought his heart might give out on the spot, quit beating and grow as cold as cold meat.

"What do you want?" she asked.

He looked at the unbowed upper lip, the downy shadow in the crevice above it, the long eyes that matched her hair, the well-mannered nose and vulnerable cheek, and the hint of a line at the side of her mouth, the barest suggestion of strain under the eyes, that showed she was on her way to losing something, youth, that no one would ever be able to buy back for her, and he said, "I had an idea."

She smiled. "I never knew you to be without one."

"I thought maybe I could buy you a concert at Town Hall. Why not?" he asked. This time he did flick her braid, tossing it back over the gilt-edged temple. "It just so happens that I have two thousand dollars in my pocket, and no one to spend it on. I might as well spend it on you."

Gus looked at Norman's eager, anxious, blood-dark face, the heavy head pitched forward at her the way he always stood and walked, the eyes with their history of hurt and anger and humor and hypnotic intensity, and almost, for the sake of a sheerly aesthetic satisfaction, she said yes, but then she smiled instead, shook her head no, dropped her eyes, and turned away.

Norman watched her go. At first he was furious. What right had she to act as though she was rejecting him? He turned around and started to walk uptown toward Columbia.

It was a warm day but there was an edge to the air, a delicate hardening of the light that meant fall was on the way, that peculiar season in which hindsight and hope are so dolefully and stimulatingly joined, when the stars come out and promise everything and the ground turns as stubborn as ice, promising nothing.

Sunshine scintillated on the sides of buildings and lay deep on the tops of automobiles. Luggage racks glittered in the noonlight like jungle gyms. The street was crowded; people were back from summer vacations. Norman walked past a jewelry store, its folding gate pulled back for business; a shoe store; a newsstand; a grocery store; a hardware store, with a sign saying GUARANTEED LOCKS: IF ONE DOESN'T WORK, ANOTHER ONE WILL; a store selling trusses and orthopedic shoes, corsets and backbraces; a store selling lingerie; and then the whole thing started over again, with another gated jewelry store. He passed a pizza parlor, the one in which he had met with Mario and Mario's mother. He remembered what Mario's mother had told him, and, thinking of the money in his billfold, decided she was right: there was always more where it came from in the first place. Where else *could* it come from? Money not only didn't grow on trees, it didn't spring spontaneously into being like hydrogen atoms in outer space. But what Mario's mother had neglected to say was that it was worthless. More of nothing was still nothing.

But as Norman walked, musing on marriage, money, music and redemption, the exhilaration of the city preparing for autumn began to seep into his own spirit, and he thought: Besides the money in his wallet, he had obtained something else from this lunch. He had successfully managed to let Gus think that he was not entirely content to be without her.

He had been worried about this, getting ready to go to lunch. If he looked too pleased with himself, she would go away feeling like a failure, and if she felt that about herself, Augusta being a girl for whom nonfailure meant being like a star, a center and a light-giver, he would have to carry for the rest of his life the knowledge that he was responsible for it. But he had not darkened her or her life. She had not gone away feeling like a failure. She had gone away wondering at the dampened fire in his gaze and the tremor of longing in his voice, and if it had cost him something in pride, he had gained from it—he knew that he had been willing to come through for Gus no matter how foolish it made him look, and that meant his conscience had no claims on him. He had acquitted himself like a gentleman . . . no easy accomplishment for a boy from Flatbush, and if Shulamith Firestone didn't like it, Shulamith Firestone could go screw herself.

And now as he walked, Norman began to feel positively good. It was a beautiful day, a day for stretching your legs and winking at girls, and the warm air with its coolish edge filled his lungs; he tasted the tang of autumn on his tongue and his body seemed to fill with anticipation like a balloon until he felt so light and lighthearted that he thought he might begin to ascend, like Christ.

And now as he walked, Norman began to think that for a *luftmensch* with his head in the clouds he didn't do half bad. He felt a huge surge of mental energy, as if the air was filled with philosophical power, a kind of metaphysical kilowattage, that he inhaled. Oh yes, oh Jesus yes, it would all come clear, the bulbs were flashing, the lights were coming on, and it seemed to him that his heart twitched almost galvanically with a certain long-known but never-wearied or -superseded excitement, the excitement that comes with having, at the last dangerous instant, escaped. It was a sensation that tingled delicately on his nerves, causing them to vibrate like the strings of a violin, the merest memory trace from some experience he couldn't quite call up to consciousness—a kind of secure happiness, like being in a candy store.

Norman began to whistle. By the time he reached Columbia, he felt terrific.

$\mathcal{V}$OICES OF THE $\mathcal{S}$OUTH

Louis D. Rubin, Jr., *The Golden Weather*
Evelyn Scott, *The Wave*
Lee Smith, *The Last Day the Dogbushes Bloomed*
Elizabeth Spencer, *The Salt Line*
Elizabeth Spencer, *The Voice at the Back Door*
Max Steele, *Debby*
Allen Tate, *The Fathers*
Peter Taylor, *The Widows of Thornton*
Robert Penn Warren, *Band of Angels*
Robert Penn Warren, *Brother to Dragons*
Walter White, *Flight*
Joan Williams, *The Morning and the Evening*
Joan Williams, *The Wintering*